Lucifer Just Wanted To Pet Kittens

The Oceanview Trilogy: Book Two

Lucifer Just Wanted To Pet Kittens

Published by Red Crown Publishing

Cover Design by Preying Mantis Designs

Grim Reaper character inspired by www.clipartlord.com used with permission.

ISBN 13: 978-0-9909010-3-7
1st Edition
Printed in the USA

this is for Tera as much as ever,
as now
as always

and to my daughter, Lily...
...who is too young to read it

Oh, little town of Oceanview
Is now a pile of rubble
A demon army fucked it up
And caused a lot of trouble
So God came down to be their guide
And nearly all the townsfolk died
But, if you think this story's done
It's barely getting started
A bigger threat is yet to come
Moves us to these realms uncharted

CHAPTER 1

Gracie Monroe was born a woman of faith. She was baptized by her pastor at just four days old and attended church twice a week for eighty-five years without fail. Neither a tickle in her throat, sweat on her brow, nor the threat of intemperate weather could keep her away from God's house. Even the births of her children posed no barrier between Gracie and her Lord and Savior. The older she became, the more she opened her heart to God and the Holy Spirit, and the more she opened her heart, the more she devoted herself to her beliefs. Her kindness and generosity were without equal.

Every waking moment consisted of God. As a child, she attended a Christian academy, and on the weekends, she went to Sunday school. Her friends and family shared her love of the Lord, and not a day passed without his name mentioned in discussion or praise.

From her first moments of speech, a routine was established that never changed. Each morning before breakfast, her hands were clasped together in appreciation for the opportunity to start a new day fresh. At lunch, she thanked her Heavenly Father for her good fortunes, and at dinner, she expressed her gratitude for the bounty spread out before her. As the sun disappeared behind the mountains and the day ended, she thanked Him for the minutia of the previous twenty-four hours, for the smiles and the warmth, and the potential to do it all over again the next day.

When her parents passed away, her faith offered comfort, and when she found herself with cause for celebration, she counted her blessings. Her God was by her side each step of the way.

Gracie met her husband, James, in her senior year of high school, and they consummated their relationship two days after their wedding night. She bore him five beautiful children, who, in turn, gave her seventeen beautiful grandchildren. Her hand was never raised in anger or her words to cause harm, and for sixty-seven years, she honored her wedding vows with the same dedication and devotion she offered the Lord. Her eyes never wandered, and her heart stayed true. Even to her last minutes, she loved her husband with every ounce of her being. Gracie loved her family as much as she loved God, and she was a Christian in the truest sense of the word.

However, even a life spent in flawless servitude was insufficient to prevent the end. The one thing her faith could not grant was immortality. Her final moments arrived, and she found herself in a hospital bed surrounded by her family and friends. The fruits of a pure and full life stood before her. Loving her in the past, cherishing her in the present, and preparing to remember her long after the physical form was gone.

Her breathing became slow and labored, and James held her hand tighter than ever before. As the remaining seconds counted down, his mind raced with a million things to say. To recall days gone by, of shared laughter and memories. A reminder of the glorious times they shared together.

A vicious stroke three days prior cruelly erased much of her humanity. She could no longer speak or move her mouth, and her brain barely functioned. James stared at her face, desperate to take in every wrinkle, every contour, until it was etched in his mind. He gazed upon her as though seeing her for the first time. While time took its expected toll on her skin, she was as beautiful as the day they met. He knew his time was short, and he would never again look into her eyes. His safe place, his heart, and his home was leaving.

James desperately fought back the urge to cry as he watched his love slowly slipping away. He needed to stay strong, just for a while longer. A single tear rolled down Gracie's cheek and James reached over to gently wipe it away, caressing her skin. It was time to say goodbye.

As the glimmer in her eyes began to fade, he lost the fight and started to weep. He was not ready to lose her. He needed more time, time he could not bargain for or demand. James was at the mercy of entities far more powerful than he.

Connor, their eldest son, placed a hand on his dad's shoulder and gently squeezed it as if trying to transfer the pain. James reached up and acknowledged the gesture, never taking his eyes off his dying wife.

Gracie held just three more breaths left in her lungs.

James knew they were on borrowed time, and she was ready to go. He leaned over and kissed her tenderly on the forehead.

Two more breaths.

"Safe travels, my sweet, sweet angel. Thank you for every second of every day. I'll see you again."

One last breath.

"I love you."

And with those final three words, her mortal journey was complete. A perfect end to a perfect life.

The bright light came and went, but Gracie kept her eyes closed tight. Excitement coursed through her body like a child on Christmas morning receiving a surprise gift. Knowing she was moments away from seeing the Kingdom of Angels, the anticipation turned her stomach in knots. All her life, she had waited for this moment. Never at the expense of the present, but deep down at her core, she wanted nothing more than to gaze upon her God.

"That's a pretty dress," said an unfamiliar female voice.

Gracie slowly opened her eyes to find herself standing in a dark hallway, and towards the end of what appeared to be an awfully long line of people. An unidentified man stood in front of her, obviously not the source of the voice. She turned to see an equally mysterious younger woman in line behind her. "Thank you." She looked down to see which dress the women referenced. The last thing she remembered wearing was her nightie and was pleasantly surprised to see her favorite blue flowered dress. One she could not squeeze into for many years. "My husband always liked this dress," she recalled with a sad smile.

"Is he here?" asked the woman.

"No, not yet. Soon, I hope." Gracie paused at the weight of her reply. "No, that didn't sound right. What I meant was—"

The woman gently touched Gracie's arm. "I know what you meant. We all want to be with our loved ones. My David was taken from me last December."

"I'm so sorry, sweetie. Were you married long?"

"No, we weren't married. He moved to Arizona ten years ago, and we split up. I never got over him. I don't think he ever got over me. I heard he died in a car accident, but I never got closure."

"Maybe he's here waiting for you, and you can get your happy ever after?" offered Gracie.

"Doubtful," said the woman.

"No?" asked Gracie. "Was he a different religion?"

The kind woman shook her head with faint sadness. "Atheist."

Gracie looked genuinely distressed at this news. "Oh, no. I'm so sorry. Maybe he saw the light before he died. It happens more often than you'd think."

"Probably not. David was a stubborn fool. It was his biggest flaw. Well, that and the whole not believing in God thing." She noticed Gracie looking around the dark hallway. "I'm Karen, by the way."

"Gracie. Gracie Monroe. Like the president."

"Excited?"

Gracie frowned slightly. "Yes, but a bit confused. If I were to be perfectly honest."

Karen raised an eyebrow in surprise. "Confused? What's wrong?"

"Something doesn't feel right."

"What do you mean?" asked Karen.

Gracie looked around her and gestured to the hallway. "I mean, all this. It's a lot darker than I expected. I thought there would be grand sweeping halls with angels and harps. All I see is a dark wall with candles every twenty feet or so."

Karen smiled. "Have you ever been to Disneyland when it's so crowded, they have to let people out through the back area behind Fantasyland and Main Street?"

Gracie shook her head in the negative.

"It's weird. You know you're in Disneyland, but all you see is behind the scenes. It's just the trash cans and broken props. It looks nothing like the public side of the park. This is just the same thing. We're just behind the scenes before we get to Sleeping Beauty's castle. Maybe the original hallway is being redecorated or something."

Gracie smiled at the comforting thought. Karen was probably right.

"You're just excited to meet the big guy. I understand. I got this way when I met Harrison Ford a few years back. I was at once excited and terrified. It's perfectly normal. He's someone you've fantasized about meeting most of your life. Of course you're excited. You've painted this picture in your mind of what Heaven looks like. Don't let this hallway dishearten you. This is your moment."

Gracie was visibly nervous. "But this is God. I've waited for this since I was born."

"So, enjoy it then."

The man standing in front finally spoke. "I feel it too."

Gracie turned to face him. "What do you mean?"

"This." He glanced around the corridor. "It's all wrong."

Karen laughed. "Oh, he's just winding you up."

The man shrugged. "Whatever. But this isn't Heaven."

Gracie laughed uncomfortably. "Of course it is. Why would it be anywhere else but Heaven?"

"You don't smell that?"

Gracie sniffed the air. "I smell burnt matches."

"That's sulfur."

"Yes. From matches. There are candles everywhere." Gracie was not having any of his ridiculous arguments. Something did feel off to her, but not for a moment did she contemplate being anywhere other than Heaven. The very idea was preposterous. "I've been a devout Christian my entire life. I've dedicated myself to God and his teachings. I haven't missed a day of church in eighty-five years. As Karen said, we're just backstage. Everything will be fine."

"I wouldn't be so sure about that," said the miserable line dweller. "None of this feels right."

"You're not funny," said Gracie. "Please don't ruin the moment. This is a big deal for me."

"I'm not trying to be funny. Something is wrong. I know it, you know it, the nun standing behind you knows it."

Gracie turned to see a lady standing a few bodies away step out of line.

The woman wore a black and white habit, and a string of rosary beads hung around her neck. All the trimmings of a traditional nun. She smiled at Gracie with warmth. "My child, if I'm in the wrong place, there's something much bigger going on."

Gracie looked at Karen and started to laugh. The mood began to lighten up, and Gracie relaxed. She knew the situation was making her hypersensitive.

The nun smiled again. "I'm quite sure we are in the exact place we need to be, my child. Appearances can sometimes be deceiving."

"See," said Karen. "Disneyland. There's nothing to worry about."

"Thank you, sister." Gracie sighed nervously. She knew she was on edge, but Karen was right, she was just anxious. Seeing the nun in the same line eased her fears. While she expected Heaven to be slightly more gilded, if a long dark hallway was, in fact, the way in, it seemed a small price to pay for an afterlife of peace and tranquility.

The line started to move again, and Gracie could see a set of large double doors in the distance. She could feel the excitement knotting her stomach again and passed the remaining hour laughing and joking with Karen and the delightful nun. Soon, she was at the front of the line, and the jaded man ahead of her disappeared behind the doors.

"Are you ready?" asked Karen.

Gracie nodded, her eyes fixed on the entrance. She wrung her hands nervously as it started to swing open.

"Knock em' dead, kiddo," said Karen.

"I hope you're reunited with David," said Gracie as she inhaled and stepped through the dark entrance.

She found herself in a small room, barely the size of her guest bedroom. Another set of doors barred her way, causing her to clench her teeth together. The anticipation was almost unbearable. The urge to swing the doors open and charge in threatened to overwhelm her. She raised her hands to give the handles an encouraging push.

"Name?" demanded a disembodied voice.

"Excuse me?" asked Gracie as she pulled her hands away from the door.

She turned to see a disheveled man standing in the corner clutching a clipboard to his chest.

"What's your name?" he asked again.

"Gracie Monroe."

"Gracie Lily Monroe?"

"No, Gracie Anne."

The man lowered his clipboard and looked over a list clamped down on the front of it. He flipped a page and continued to read. Then a third, and soon after, a fourth. "Nope."

Before she could respond, he pressed an intercom button on the wall. "Scooter, we got another one."

"Send her in," a crackling voice responded.

"Another what?" asked Gracie. Something was definitely wrong.

"In you go." The man pointed to the doors.

"Another what?" she pleaded again as the man shooed her away and returned to his list.

Gracie stepped over the threshold as the door slammed shut behind her.

The seemingly endless room spread out in front of her exploded with a deluge of strobe lights and electronic bass. A tsunami of manufactured and cigarette-made smoke slammed into her, filling her lungs. She coughed loudly, trying to take in the events of the room. Her critical gaze locked on a table less than ten feet away, where a half-naked stripper was snorting a line of coke from the cleavage of an equally topless woman sitting in her lap. Not far behind the pair, a tangled mass of male and female limbs on a randomly placed bed enjoyed a rather vocal five-way. Gracie's eyes widened in horror at the debauchery unfolding around her, and she instinctively stepped back towards the door. Her mind tried to process what her eyes were seeing, uncertain they could withstand so much sin.

"Hey there, sugar tits," shouted a strange little man over the din of the music as he danced over to her. He wore a rainbow-colored tulle tutu and a t-shirt proudly claiming him to be 'Beelzebub's Bitch.' "What's your name, sexy mama?"

"Gracie," she stammered.

"Just Gracie? Like Madonna or Fergie?" he frowned as he mulled the name over in his head. "I dig it. It makes a statement without being overly pretentious. I don't believe we've had just a Gracie before. This is awesome. Welcome, just Gracie. We are delighted to have you."

Gracie continued to look around the room in horror as she ignored his greeting.

"The name's Mack, but people call me Scooter. But you, you can call me whatever you like, honey buns." He followed Gracie's gaze towards the orgy. "Looks fun, huh?

"Excuse me?" she stammered once again.

He nodded toward the group. "What they're up to. You want in? I'm sure they wouldn't mind."

Gracie failed to find a response. It did not look fun at all, and no, she most certainly did not want in.

Scooter shrugged his shoulders. "So, you're not on the list, huh?"

She struggled to hear him. "List? What list?" she shouted back.

"The list to get in, of course. You're not on it, silly pants."

Gracie frowned. Nothing was making any sense to her. "I don't understand."

"It's probably some administrative issue somewhere. It's not a biggie. We welcome everyone here, regardless of past indiscretions. Mostly." He gestured to the room. "As you can see, we're a lot more relaxed here than people give us credit for."

"Where am I?"

"I can tell you where you're not," he grinned as he started to vogue with a pair of neon glow sticks. "Voop, voop, voop," he said in synch with his stuttered movements.

The man's unorthodox presence made her skin crawl, and she could feel the pangs of outright panic beginning to claw their way in.

Another equally odd shirtless man donning a set of plastic devil horns and rhinestone nipple pasties, who may or may not have been under the effects of acid, sprinted by with a loud 'whoop.'

Tutu-man leaned closer to Gracie's ear. "I'm sure you have a lot of questions for me."

"Just one," said Gracie.

"Fire away, you pretty little thing."

"What part of Heaven is this? Are these the Mormons?"

"Heaven? Oh, fuck no. Let down your hair and slip off your giant panties. You're in Hell, Grandma. You're going to have the time of your life."

CHAPTER 2

The number seven holds significance for a variety of reasons. There are seven days in a week and seven magnificent justice-serving cowboys. Snow White had seven dwarves, and there are seven colors in the rainbow. Seven natural wonders are scattered across the globe, and unsurprisingly, the Bible is littered with references to seven. Seven sacred swords of scripture, seven seals, seven angels with seven trumpets, and seven bowls of God's wrath. Although most of his guests preferred the minestrone. God took his first-ever vacation on the seventh day. Even Ponticus jumped on the digit bandwagon with his seven deadly sins.

References to this magical numeric masterpiece can be found hidden under every rock. However, the most important value for seven has nothing to do with stunted polyamorous bearded oddballs or fourteenth-century monks with a crushing guilt complex. No, that accolade goes to the number of people who have laid eyes on God and lived to tell the tale. In the entire history of the Earth, and for the thousands of years that humans have believed in an almighty creator, only seven mortals have gazed upon Him and lived.

Unfortunately for these poor souls, this was not how things were supposed to be, and life was definitely for the worse because of it. They had collectively and unknowingly pulled on a small dangling piece of thread, and now the cheap argyle sweater of the Universe was starting to unravel. Humans were not allowed to look upon God, the Bible explicitly highlighted it in Exodus 33:20. '*And he said, Thou canst not see my face, for there shall no man see me, and live*'. Despite the appalling use of the English language, one could possibly take this to mean that God was either conceited or rather ugly. Why else would a god not want people to look at them? While it was true that God was a tad vain, he would not be considered ugly by any stretch. However, his physical appearance was moot, as that particular law extended far beyond the realms of a single god. Every bible or religious edict contained a version of the '*no looky*' rule. This directive came from the highest order in the Universe, the Council of Deities.

The Council of Deities was the supreme council of the Universe. It consisted of every type of god, deity, or prophet, real, made up, and imagined. Atheists and those on the fence were represented by neutral, but equally essential members, such as teachers and scientists. They made sure everything functioned correctly, and nothing happened without its direction or approval. It appeared the fate of the Universe was dependent on one giant committee, and this committee spelled it out clearly. Looking at flowers was good. Looking at a deity was bad.

The survivors of deity exposure became known as the Oceanview Seven. A ragtag bunch of misfits from a small insignificant town on the northern end of Arizona who found themselves in the middle of a pissing match between God and Death. A contest that killed five-thousand, seven-hundred, and thirty-nine people and left a once-peaceful town in ruins, just so Death could prove a point after having his daily routine thrown into chaos by God's incompetence.

These seven heroes were the first humans to look upon the face of God and not suffer an agonizing and fiery death. Mostly because God wore sunglasses, and the UV protection blocked his life-ending gaze. The fame garnered from seeing God did not earn the Oceanview Seven a merchandise line, and likewise the Lifetime Channel did not release a made-for-television movie starring Dean Cain and Tori Spelling. In fact, they were just regular plain old people to anyone they ran into on the streets, and there was no one with whom they could share their tale of adventure. Who would believe them? Publicly going on record saying that God came down to help fight an army of bloodthirsty zombie-demons that Death accidentally unleashed would be enough to find even the sanest person locked away in the looney bin. Most people would have an issue believing that Jiggles, the town's strip club, operated with a daycare. Accepting a holy interaction was nigh on impossible. So, the group kept their secret buried. Each one carried the heavy burden of knowing that thousands of people died, and nothing was ever going to be done about it. It was as though the Universe had all at once targeted them and then tossed them aside.

♦♦♦♦

At the epicenter of the crisis was Oceanview, a quirky yet peaceful town of five thousand, seven hundred and forty-six. Back in the days before it became ground-zero for a heavenly royal-rumble, it resembled any other town. There were coffee shops and libraries; there was a butcher, and a restaurant or two. The locals would eat shitty pizza at Pilano's, and drink their sorrows away while playing pool at Jacob's neighborhood tavern. The town's founder was an obnoxious prick called Jason Reynolds, who reveled in his peasants kissing his pompous and self-righteous ass. Each year they celebrated his existence with a three-day-long ego-boosting festival called Forefather's Day and sang the town's anthem that highlighted all the things Reynolds never achieved while developing Oceanview.

The citizens loved their small but utterly dysfunctional town. Well, at least they did until God got involved and completely fucked it up by inadvertently unleashing an army of flesh-eating zombie-demons on the unsuspecting population. Mr. Pilano was decapitated by a trash can lid, and Hank, the owner of Jacob's, was eaten alive by his pompous British neighbor. The strippers at Jiggles were dragged screaming from their poles and torn to pieces in front of a room full of dollar-danglers. After that, they chowed down on the children at the day care. Nothing in the town would ever be the same, especially those who wanted pizza, boobs, and beer for breakfast.

On the day when Jason Reynolds finally questioned himself on whether he should continue his life-long mission to be an absolute prick, he was trapped and violently torn apart by zombie-demons in the comfort of his panic room. Sadly, there were no other survivors on his staff to report on his heroic deed, so no one ever updated the Oceanview theme song to reflect his final bloody ending. An ending where he did, in fact achieve something worth remembering.

God making an appearance to fight an army of zombie-demons was not the only strange thing to happen to Oceanview. The oddities surrounding the town continued long after the handful of survivors fled its borders. It was not strange enough that ninety-nine-point-eight percent of the population disappeared without a trace, but not a single county, state, or federal official came to inspect the town, and a case was never opened to investigate the missing people. Oceanview was never declared a disaster zone, and the rubble was left to gather dust and weeds. Directions disappeared from freeway signs and old-fashioned paper maps, and Google maps ceased to acknowledge its presence. It was as though the town never existed. Yet, with a surprising lack of evidence or supporting paperwork, each survivor received an insurance check allowing them to leave the remains of the town and start fresh elsewhere. Equally curious was the fact that none of the survivors even filed with their respective insurance companies. Acts of God were generally a loophole for the policy providers to avoid making payments. And if God coming down from Heaven and destroying the town was not considered an act of God, well, then nothing would. But, paid out they were, and each was able to leave. Maybe God had twirled his finger and worked some celestial magic after all.

♦♦♦♦

After the dust settled in Oceanview, the handful of survivors decided to pack up and leave. There was nothing left to save or stay for. The town was lost. No one from the utility company came to turn the electricity back on. High-speed internet quickly became no-speed internet, and with fresh supplies running thin, there was nothing left to do but flee.

Reverend Ellis was the last resident to remain in the town. He knew his duty was to his flock, but deep down, he also knew none of them would ever return. Ellis stayed in the church because, most of all, he sought answers. He spent his days combing through the Holy Bible, reading, rereading, and analyzing psalm after psalm, convinced that somewhere within its pages it held the key to his countless unanswered questions.

Not long after meeting God, his world started to fall apart. God was nothing like he expected. He was brash, arrogant, and rude. Ellis could not quite put his finger on what disappointed him so deeply. He set up his own mental version of how God was supposed to be, and his lord failed to live up to it. The real God felt different. He felt flawed. He felt human. And that was the last thing Ellis wanted him to be.

Ellis spiritually prepared himself for the second coming since he could first read the Bible. When it finally arrived, when he was face to face with his Heavenly father, they spent the time arguing about his son's race and the criteria for getting into Heaven. He knew he would never get another opportunity like that again and kicked himself for freezing and asking inane questions. Apparently, deity anxiety was a real thing.

The whole zombie-demons coming back from the dead thing fitted into the description of the Apocalypse. But God most certainly did not. The Bible repeatedly spoke of the second coming. Jesus would return, and the fury of the Heavens would rain down upon the Earth. Instead, God showed up with a flip chart and a flimsy argument for stopping the Apocalypse. The poor reverend became so disheartened, he was unsure if the Bible held any answers at all. Maybe his standards were simply set too high, and he needed to temper them to something more reasonable. Much like the anticipation for The Phantom Menace or Chinese Democracy.

He made supply runs once a month for food and firewood, but spent most of his days cold and alone. Cam Harris was the last of the seven other survivors to leave the town and said her goodbye's five months earlier. Neither Cam nor the others returned to check in on him, despite pledging to do so. He used the time to reacquaint himself with the holy scriptures, but even that started to get dull. Ellis paid particular attention to the Old Testament sections, as God performed most of his human-targeted rage in that era. As he flicked through page after page, stories of God coming to Earth and acting like an asshole never appeared. Anytime God went into douchebag mode, he did it from the comforts of Heaven. Ellis read, reread, and read again, but all answers evaded him. Everything he thought he knew had changed.

He looked up from his book as the candles beside the pulpit flickered erratically, as though a heavy breeze drifted through the knave. For six months, he stayed in his church studying, trying to make sense of the events that unfolded.

"Hello?" he asked. "Is anyone there?" The candles flickered again, and the pages of his Bible fluttered as the breeze passed over it. He looked down to see the book open on Exodus 33:20. Ellis frowned and closed the book. It would seem the Universe was having a joke at his expense. He stepped down off the riser.

"Hello?" he shouted again as he walked to the front of the church. He entered the lobby and saw the front door was still closed. He pulled on the handle to find it locked.

A large shadow fell across him, and Ellis froze. Knowing the church was locked from the inside, he was certain who just appeared behind him, and he smiled. God had returned and he could finally get the answers that eluded him. He would not waste the opportunity a second time. Ellis closed his eyes and relaxed. "You've come back. I've been waiting for you."

"You are Seven," said a deep, menacing voice.

Ellis' eyes snapped open. It was not the voice of God. "Excuse me?" Ellis slowly turned around to see a dark-shrouded figure standing before him. Its eyes glowed red from beneath its hood.

"You are Seven," the mysterious visitor whispered again.

Ellis furrowed his brow and looked at the stranger. "Seven? I don't understand. Who are you?"

"I am the Caretaker, and you will gaze upon my form and face the inevitable."

"I'm guessing you're not here to turn the cable back on, are you?" Ellis laughed weakly in a feeble attempt to hide his fear.

The shape leaned in closer to Ellis. "I carry a message."

Ellis was unable to see a face among the shadow and took an uncomfortable step back. "A message?"

The shadow nodded. "You have touched, and you have seen. These senses must be purged for the celestial realms to become whole once again."

"You mean God, don't you?"

"You have seen what must not be seen. The Seven must be cleansed for their indiscretions."

Ellis took a cautious step back. "It wasn't our fault. We didn't ask for his help, he just showed up. If anything, he made it worse because we lost five thousand, seven hundred and thirty-nine of our brothers and sisters. They were good souls. Innocent souls, who did not deserve their fate."

"Your protests are worthless, mortal. You cannot change what has transgressed. Do not resist me."

"I will go peacefully if my time in this world is at an end." Ellis stepped back to a small table beside the door. "But, before I go, I have one last thing to say." He reached behind him, and his hand found an ornate, jewel-encrusted, metal cross. He swept it up and pointed it at the creature. "This is a holy house. A house of God. And it's time for you to leave."

The Caretaker moved forward as Ellis stumbled into the table.

Fear began to spread across Ellis's face, but he continued to hold the talisman before him. "Begone foul beast not of this earth. The power of Christ compels you."

The shadow laughed a deep maddening laugh. "Fool, you think these worthless trinkets can stop me?" It swiped at the cross and sent it flying across the room. It crashed onto the floor with a loud clang.

Ellis's eyes widened as he looked down at his empty and stinging hand. "I am so sorry," he stammered.

The shadow clenched its fists and advanced on the terrified man. "Seven. You saw nothing. You know nothing. You will be purged."

It lowered its hood to reveal a creature drawn from the most terrifying of nightmares. Six razor-sharp teeth protruded from its upper mouth, and five more below. Behind them, a forked yellow tongue danced in its mouth. Its skin black and leathery and devoid of life or beauty. It raised a finger before Ellis' face, and a red bolt of light arced from its tip and burned into Ellis' eyes.

Ellis screamed and spasmed as a waft of smoke drifted up from his eye sockets. The Caretaker lowered his hand and Ellis disappeared with a loud electrical crack.

The number six holds significance for a variety of reasons.

♦♦♦♦

"Shit." Dan Wallace looked up at the flashing blue and red lights reflecting in his rearview mirror, as he cursed under his breath. Wanting to appear responsible, he steered his car over to the side of the road and turned off the engine. He placed his hands on the steering wheel as he watched the cop car pull over behind him.

"Hide your fucking beer, Ryan," he said to the teenage boy in the seat next to him.

The boy obliged and slowly placed the open bottle down beside him and out of view.

Dan watched as the police car's driver-side door opened, and an officer stepped out. He only received his driver's license the day before and was approximately thirty seconds away from being arrested for felony speeding. He looked into his side mirror as the officer closed his car door.

"Can you smell it on my breath?" asked Ryan.

"Huh?" said Dan as he focused on the officer.

"The beer. Can you smell it on my breath?"

"I don't know."

Ryan exhaled a long breath into his friend's face. "Well?"

"Yeah, dude. You stink. If he smells that, he'll think I've been drinking too."

"You have been drinking."

"Shit," said Dan. "I need some gum."

Ryan fumbled in his pockets as Dan watched the officer walk towards him.

"Hurry, dude," mumbled Dan as his heart rate started to increase. "He's getting closer. Give me the fucking gum."

"Got it," said Ryan as he pulled a stick from his pocket and handed it over to his friend. "It's my last piece."

"I need it more than you do." Dan quickly unwrapped the green stick and popped the gum into his mouth as the cop reached the door. He dutifully lowered the window to see Officer Lee Adams leaning down to look at him. "Officer," he said politely.

Lee nodded. "Good evening, sunshine. You're in a bit of a rush, aren't you?"

Dan lowered his eyes in shame. "Was I? Sorry, Officer, I didn't know. We were just coming home from Bible studies."

"Uh, huh," said Lee, unimpressed with the blatant lie. A line he heard many times before. "License and registration, please."

Dan handed his paperwork to Lee and flashed a toothy grin as he enthusiastically chewed on his gun.

Lee glanced over the license. "You do realize this license is less than twenty-four hours old, right?"

The young man slowly nodded. "Yeah, I passed my test yesterday and wanted to celebrate with Jesus."

"Uh, huh," said Lee again, not even remotely buying the kid's bullshit. "This isn't getting you off to a very good start. A mile or two over the limit and I could have forgiven you. Maybe even ten. You were doing ninety-two in a thirty-five. That's fifty-seven over the limit if math is a struggle for you."

"I had no idea," said Dan in mock surprise.

"Right," said Lee. "Do you know what that is considered?"

"Speeding?"

"Felony speeding. Do you know what a felony is?"

"Bad?" The kid kept his head down.

"Very. This goes far beyond a ticket. You will lose this license before the ink has dried on it, but that is the least of your problems. Have you seen the inside of a jail cell before?"

The boy shook his head.

"You do realize felony speeding puts you in front of a judge, right?"

The poor boy looked to be on the verge of tears.

"And that comes with some hefty fines. Do you have ten grand kicking around doing nothing?"

The distraught boy shook his head again.

"You've put me in an awkward position, kid. I know you've probably worked hard for this license so you can get your freedom, and I can respect that, but I can't let you drive on my streets doing that kind of speed. It's dangerous and someone could get hurt. You could kill yourself or someone else. Or me. And I just want to make sure we're all able to go home at the end of the day."

"I'm sorry, Officer."

"Wait here." Lee turned and headed back to his vehicle with the boy's documents.

Dan raised the window as he spied on Lee in his side mirror.

"We're fucked," said Ryan softly but urgently to his friend.

Dan held his hand up. "Shh. Relax, dude, I've got this."

Back at his squad car, Lee picked up a clipboard from his passenger seat and started to write out the kid's ticket. He held no intention of carting the kid off to jail, he just wanted the opportunity to scare him straight. The juvenile idiot would have to get a ticket, there was no way around that, but a jail cell seemed harsh. Were it the kid's second or third offense, that would have been an entirely different story. Half of the role of a police officer was to provide an education to possibly help deter future bad behavior. He hoped that by going easy on the kid, it would pay off later and make him a safer and more responsible driver. Although the smell of beer on the breath of the passenger would need to be addressed separately.

He finished writing the ticket and walked back over to the car. The window lowered again as he approached the door.

Lee smiled as he passed the clipboard over for the boy to sign. "Okay, kid. I'm cutting you a break this time. You still get a ticket, but it won't be a felony."

The boy grabbed the ticket and read over the citation. "Now what do I do?"

"You sign it, pass it back to me and say thank you Officer Adams for not ruining my life."

Dan stared at Lee as he passed the clipboard back to him. "Yeah. I don't think I'm going to do that."

Lee raised an eyebrow. "Excuse me?"

"You do know I can report you for writing a fraudulent ticket, right?"

"Excuse me?" Lee said a second time with considerably more emphasis and surprise.

Dan's posture suddenly improved as he gained confidence. "You admitted to me that I was driving fifty-seven over the limit, but you're writing me a ticket for eleven over. That's deliberately falsifying a legal document." The boy's position changed from prey to predator in a blink. "So, you are going to either let me go, or you're going to have to stand in front of a judge and tell them why you're falsifying evidence." He flashed his phone at Lee. "I've got the whole thing recorded, sunshine."

Ryan chuckled as Dan gained the upper hand. "Snap, bro," he said as he high-fived Dan in celebration.

"Really?" asked Lee.

A broad smug grin spread across Dan's face as he gained the upper hand. "Yep. Now give me my license back, piggy, and let me be on my way. I've got better shit to do." He turned to his friend as he continued to gloat. Without making eye contact with Lee, he reached out for his license, but Lee pulled his hand away.

"Not yet."

"Whatever." Dan reached for the key in the ignition.

Lee rested his arm on the side mirror and leaned in closer to Dan. "See, I was trying to do the nice thing and make your life a little bit easier. You're young and dumb as a box of rocks. But you're still young, and we all make mistakes as kids. God knows I did." He paused. "I wanted this to be a learning opportunity for you. You know how it goes. You commit a felony, then I put the fear of God into you, you sweat a bit, and then I give you a smaller punishment. Enough to teach you a lesson, but not enough to ruin your life. You learn something and hopefully, become a smarter driver."

The arrogant boy rolled his eyes and waved his phone at Lee again. "Evidence."

"If you pull off now, you're driving without a license, and I promise you, I will cart your ass off to jail regardless of what you have on your phone. Sure, you can use your phone as evidence. The fact is, you were still speeding. But the bigger issue is you blackmailed a police officer and would be driving without a license." He taps the body camera at his chest. "Got the whole thing recorded."

The boy gulped as he slipped back into prey mode.

"Are we clear?"

"Yes, sir."

"There, that's better. Wait here."

Dan lowered his eyes in his recently acquired respect, not quite as cock-sure as he was a minute prior.

"That cop's a pussy," said Ryan as he slugged Dan on the arm. "He ain't gonna do anything. You've got him by his bitch balls."

"Shut up, man," replied Dan through clenched teeth. "He's going to fucking hear you."

Lee stopped and turned back to the car. He learned in the window to look at Ryan. "And you're underage and sitting with an open bottle of alcohol next to you. I can smell beer on your breath from here, son. I'll deal with you next."

Ryan's gulped and he made the wise choice to stay silent as Lee returned to his vehicle.

After finding his home in ruins from the Oceanview disaster, Lee packed up the few items he could salvage and headed to Flagstaff to join their police force. While life was a bit more fast-paced than the one he was used to, there were undoubtedly some perks to being in a bigger town. For one, he got his gun back, and while he missed his small town, Lee finally felt like a real cop again. He grew complacent living in Oceanview and relished being able to go out into the field and do actual police work. He took a demotion from sheriff as no equivalent positions were open, but he was happy, nonetheless. Lee was back in his element again and enjoying his choice of career.

Although Flagstaff was a significantly larger than Oceanview, it was still a relatively peaceful town. Most of the crime came from the university students zipping around town in their hybrid, millennial, hipster cars. He fielded the occasional theft call, but it was usually petty and manageable issues for the most part.

Lee reached his car as a dark shadow fell across him. Lee sighed. "Kid, I told you to wait in the damned car. You're not making this any easier on yourself. Go back to your vehicle, and I'll be right with you."

The voice that responded was not that of a seventeen-year-old boy. "You are Six."

Lee turned around. "What?"

A large, hooded shadow stood in front of him. "You are Six." It moved closer to Lee. "I am the Caretaker, and you will gaze upon my form."

Lee immediately went into cop mode. He took a step back and assumed a defensive stance as his hand instinctively moved to his holster. Unlike his later years in Oceanview, it now held a fully loaded weapon. "You need to get out of my face and back down, right now." He pulled his gun and aimed it at the shape.

The stranger inhaled a sharp breath and reached out towards Lee. Lee fired once, and the bullet penetrated the Caretaker's forehead and disappeared. The wound immediately healed, and the Caretaker wagged a condescending finger at Lee.

"What the fuck?" shouted Lee. He inhaled and focused his aim on the creature's chest as it moved in on him. He fired again, and the second bullet disappeared.

Lee fired off two more shots before the creature grabbed him by the throat. Lee placed the barrel of his gun against the creature's head and fired. "Die, you demon fuck."

"Number Six. You have seen the unseeable."

Lee dropped his gun as he clawed at the hand grasping his throat.

The shape raised its right hand, and red lightning crackled between its fingers. "You must be purged," it said as it raised its glowing hand to Lee's eyes.

Lee screamed and disappeared in a flash.

And then there were five.

CHAPTER 3

The early morning sun slowly peeked through a pair of tacky pink unicorn-print curtains as the first fingers of light crawled across Warren Hart's face. Despite the sun's abrasive demands, he was not ready to get up and face the world. He pulled the pillow over his head and remained still, hoping for the talons of slumber tried to claw back into his skull.

He felt the familiar tingle of the beginnings of sleep as a woman's arm fell across his shoulder, and its owner leaned in and kissed him on the neck.

"Good morning, sweetheart," she said.

Warren groaned in contentment as he slowly moved the pillow from his face, and a large, content smile erupted. Sleep could wait. His morning was looking to get off to a good start. "Good morning, Ash."

The limb promptly pulled away and Warren's eyes snapped open. "Shit," he muttered under his breath. He realized his faux pas immediately and clenched his teeth as he waited for the fallout. The arm in question was not attached to his former girlfriend, Ashley. However, it did belong to his new girlfriend Kim, who snapped upright in bed, her face flushed purple with rage.

"Ash?" she asked. Her voice seconds from exploding.

"What?" asked Warren with mock innocence.

"You just called me Ash."

Warren held up his hands to try and defuse the situation. "Are you sure?"

"YOU CALLED ME ASH!" Kim screamed as small droplets of rage

saliva splashed onto Warren's face.

"I'm sorry, babe, I didn't mean it. I was just dreaming."

"Oh, because dreaming about your whore-ex is so much better?"

"Ash is not a whore." Warren was not making the best of his situation, and his choice of words helped his defense little.

Kim's face continued to redden as fury ripped through her. "Stop standing up for her, Warren. She's your fucking ex. I'm supposed to be your girlfriend, and you're apparently still dreaming about her. Care to explain yourself?"

"I was just saying she's not a whore. I wasn't standing up for her. I was correcting you. Big difference."

"If you miss her so much, why don't you go back to her?"

Warren scrambled for the right words to defuse the situation. "Kim, she broke up with me months ago. There's no way she would take me back now."

Those were not it.

Kim jumped out of bed and scooped up Warren's clothes from the floor. "Get out," she screamed as she launched them at Warren. "Get out, you fucking asshole."

Warren rolled out of bed as the pile of clothes smacked him in the face. He stumbled back towards the bedroom door, trying to avoid dropping his balled-up socks. "But—"

Kim pointed to the front door as she corralled Warren down the hallway. "Get out."

"Can I at least put my clothes on before you throw me outside? It's a bit breez—"

"GET OUT," she ordered again.

Warren opened the front door and stepped outside. He turned to face Kim. "Can I call you?"

Slam.

Warren frowned as he stared at the closed door, as naked as the day he was born. "Okay then."

He sighed at the current circumstances. It was way too early in the morning to be dealing with such crushing rejection. For him to be able to suitably process the events that just transpired, acquiring coffee needed to be the first order of business. He was mildly disappointed as Kim was a stunner to look at, but now that Ash's name resurfaced, he found himself thinking about her again. An event that occurred all too often, despite having dated non-stop since he last saw her in Oceanview.

Warren rummaged through the small stack of clothes in his arms as he prepared to start getting dressed. "You forgot my boxer shorts," he whined softly.

A light gasp grabbed his attention, and he turned to his left to see Mrs. Kramer, Kim's elderly neighbor standing at her front door staring at him, clutching a garden trowel tightly to her chest, her mouth open wide.

Warren raised a hand and politely waved to her, dropping a sock in the process. "Good morning!" he said cheerfully. "A bit brisk this morning."

Mrs. Kramer remained silent as she slowly raised a hand and waved back at the naked man, uncertain where to focus her eyes. Her trowel slowly slipped out of her hands and crashed to the ground with a loud *clang*. The noise snapped her attention back, and she frantically fumbled for the front door handle. She pushed the door open and disappeared inside.

Warren crouched down to pick up his fallen sock. He sighed a second time as a dark shadow fell over him. "Listen, my day really isn't starting off so good. I really don't have time—"

A pair of arms wrapped tightly about his waist and his world turned black.

"What the fuck, man, get off me. I'm naked," shouted Warren as he struggled and kicked out in vain against the firm grip. "Don't touch my junk, you pervert." He tried to break free of the grasp, but the arms around him were too strong.

A bright red light flashed, and Warren disappeared.

Four.

♦♦♦♦

Greg Hart, Warren's older brother, stared at his cell phone as he moved colorful blocks of candy around on a digital background. For five hours, he sat on a bench and watched his fiancé, Amber McKenzie, try on almost every wedding dress at the bridal store, and he was starting to get bored. Although he would never make such a confession publicly. While he appreciated her enthusiasm for their upcoming nuptials, the dresses were starting to look the same, and he struggled to maintain the same levels of excitement he was able to show four hours prior.

"Shouldn't you be paying attention to me?" asked Amber as she twirled in front of the mirror. The large white wedding dress billowed around her as she spun in circles like a Disney princess at a glamorous ball.

Greg continued to play his game. "You look fantastic."

"I don't like it."

Greg looked up at his bride-to-be. "What's wrong with this one?" he asked, his voice tinged with mild frustration. "It looks as good as the last fifteen you've tried on.

"It lacks oomph," she said as she stopped spinning and the dress settled down around her feet.

"Oomph? You damn near took off when you turned around. That is the oomphiest dress you've tried on yet. I don't think it's possible for a dress to have any more oomph. This is what the forty-eighth one?"

"The twenty-second. Being snarky isn't going to speed this up any, so I'd suggest getting back on board and helping me pick one."

Greg smiled. "You've looked stunning in every dress you've put on. Can we just decide on one and go home?"

"This is important to me, Greg. It must be perfect. I don't want to be standing at the alter worrying that I wasn't looking perfect."

"This dress is perfect."

"It's perfect-ish, but I know there is a more perfect one out there. So, we keep looking until I find it."

Greg frowned. "I thought we agreed you wouldn't go all bridezilla on me?"

"This isn't bridezilla. I just want to be in the perfect dress for when I marry the perfect man." She batted her eyelashes in an exaggerated and flirtatious manner.

Greg smiled again. "Flattery has bought you an extra thirty minutes. Nice save."

"Oh, there's plenty more where that came from. I can buy all the time I need." She smiled as she stepped back into the changing room and wriggled her way out of the dress. "Besides, if I was going to go all bridezilla on you, I would be sending back your tux."

"What's wrong with my tux? I like my tux."

"It has pinstripes. I want to stand next to a groom, not a nineteen-twenties gangster."

Greg pouted. "It's a bit late to be telling me that now."

Amber poked her head out of the changing room and smiled at the playful ribbing. "I'm just teasing you. I think you look quite dapper in it." She disappeared back behind the door. "Speaking of, we still need to get the tux fitting set up for Warren," she shouted over the changing room door. "Have you spoken to him yet about it yet?"

"Yeah, he asked if he could come in jeans."

"And you told him?"

"That I didn't care, I just want him there."

The door fully opened, and Amber's concerned face peeked around the side, a judgmental eyebrow raised. "What?"

It was Greg's turn to smile. "I told him no, and if he doesn't schedule an appointment, I'll write his best man speech for him, and he'll have to read it."

Amber mock-scowled at Greg as the door closed. "Good. I'd hate to file the wedding license and divorce paperwork the same day." Inside the changing room, she struggled to climb out of the dress.

"He asked if he has to pay for it," said Greg from outside.

"Of course he asked that. You told him we have it covered, right?"

"Yeah. It's the only way I'm going to get him into one."

"I can't believe you're letting him write the best man speech. You know he's going to embarrass the shit out of you, right?"

Greg did not respond.

"Greg?"

Silence.

Amber pulled the last of her clothes on and pushed the dressing room door open. "Did you tell him we—" She paused and looked around the room.

Greg was gone. Only his phone remained on the bench.

"Greg?" There was nowhere else in the room he could have hidden.

She looked up as a shadow fell over her.

"You're not funny. Why didn't you answer me?" The dark shape moved towards her, and the world turned black.

Two.

The naked man pouring cereal into a bowl in Cam's kitchen naturally had a name, but she could not remember it, or be bothered to ask him for a recap. It mattered little. She took all she needed from him the previous night. The nameless guest was digging through her fridge for milk when she entered the kitchen, fully dressed. His disappointed face highlighted his surprise at her desire to put clothes on so early in the morning.

"Good morning, sweetheart," he said with the same charming smile she found mildly attractive the night before. "You're dressed already?"

"No, why?" asked Cam sarcastically as she walked over to the fridge and brushed past him.

He frowned at the obviously wrong answer. "I just thought we could continue what we were doing last night. I'm ready to go again if you know what I mean." He looked down at his flaccid penis as it began to stir at the thought of more action.

Cam's eyes followed his gaze down. "Nah, I'm good, thanks."

"Really? I thought last night was great." He paused nervously. "Didn't you?"

Cam shrugged as she sat down with a fruit smoothie and bagel. A stark difference to her old breakfast of donuts, potato chips, and beer in the days of Oceanview. "It was okay."

"Okay? I'd give it a nine out of ten."

"That's a bit optimistic, don't you think? I'd say a four, probably leaning heavily towards a three." She paused a moment as if genuinely giving the grading some thought. She wasn't. She just liked watching him squirm. "Yeah, definitely a two."

"A two? Really?"

"Yeah, you're right. Definitely a one. The constant exposition was really fucking annoying. '*Oh, I'm cumming, almost there*'. Jesus, next you'll want braille, judging by the way you were fumbling at my nipples. I knew what was going on. I didn't need a blow-by-blow account. '*Oh, I'm fucking you, I'm fucking you hard*'. Really? No, one says that, Barry."

"My name is Shane."

"Whatever. The same rules apply. I don't need a voice-over commentary. It's fucking weird. It ripped me right out of the fucking moment. You're not saying, '*oh my god, I'm getting fucking milk. Fuck me, I'm pouring it on my Count-fucking-Chocula fucking hard*' are you?" While her financial status improved, her penchant for cursing had not.

"You have Count Chocula?"

"No."

"Oh."

"Look, Barry—"

"Shane."

"Whatever. You're pretty to look at, but goddamn it, just stop talking."

"No one has raised complaints before, and believe me, I have a lot of satisfied customers." Shane smiled with an aura of overconfidence. "Women love riding the Shane-Train. Choo, choo!" He mimicked pulling his imaginary horn.

"Maybe they should raise their standards a bit."

"Excuse me?"

Cam looked down at her watch. "Okay, cupcake, it's time for the Shane-train to leave the station. I have to go to work."

"I didn't think you worked on Sundays?"

"I don't. I just want you to leave."

"Huh?" asked Shane, now unable to mask his disappointment.

"You can go now."

"Excuse me?"

"Did I stutter? I said you can leave."

Shane frowned with mild confusion. "Yeah, I heard you. I'm just kinda surprised to hear that after the night we had."

"Yeah, we fucked, so what? Do you think we're married now or something?"

"No. I—"

"Then there's no commitment. We don't owe each other anything." She grabbed her keys off the counter. "You can see yourself out. And don't touch my shit, I have cameras" She pointed to a camera on top of the kitchen cabinets. "Choo-choo," she said as she mimicked pulling her own imaginary horn.

Cam was enjoying her newly found assertiveness and the shift in control that accompanied it. She was finally the one throwing people out of her bed and not the other way around. While she would not pass up true love if it happened to cross her path, she was no longer actively seeking it out. For the first time in her life, she was putting her needs first. She finally loved herself, and that was something she was unable to say in a long, long time. Before he passed, Donald showed her what true love meant, and then she knew that none of what she experienced was the real thing. No longer concerned if the one true love was just around the corner, she was going to have a lot of fun in the meantime.

Cam fumbled with her car keys as she stood by the driver's door. The door was stuck, and the windshield still wore a large crack from the zombie-demon who head-butted it in what felt like a lifetime ago.

In yet another momentous change of direction, she was finally smart with her money. The financial windfall from both the insurance company and Donald's generous donation made her richer than ever before. Instead of rushing out to buy a new car, she kept her old one. Instead of doubling her apartment's size, she moved to one that with the same space but used more efficiently. The most important thing she did with the money was to sign up for college. She no longer wanted to be the attractive dolt she assumed she was. Cam was in her third semester and, so far, maintained a 3.5 g.p.a. Her creative writing class was no longer the only A of her academic career. She could now add social studies, microeconomics, and intermediate calculus to her list of conquests. Things had finally turned around for her.

After a few moments of intense pulling, the door unstuck and opened with a loud agonized squeak. "Piece of shit," she muttered to herself as she tossed her purse onto the passenger seat. A large shadow fell across her. Cam's shoulder's slumped, and she exhaled a deep sigh. Apparently, she needed to be more assertive with her newfound friend.

"Listen, puppy dog. Go home. This is not your home. I appreciate you wanting to stay for a pre-engagement party, but I'm going to have to call a rain check."

Seconds later, her world went black.

And then there was one.

♦♦♦♦

Seven.

Seven.

Bell.

"Fuck."

Ashley McKenzie, sister of Amber and ex-girlfriend of Warren, was losing her patience with the money-gobbling slot machine. In less than three hours, she pumped in over eleven-hundred dollars and saw little return for her efforts. "Piece of fucking shit," she muttered as she fed the gambling device another five dollars and pressed the large orange '*play*' button.

Bell.

Bell.

Some random character that may have been a cat. Or a boot.

Ashley cursed under her breath as a shadow fell over her. She refused to look up from her digital money pit as she shoved another bill into the slot. Her quest to win more than a dollar or two from the damn machine crept closer to its depressing finale. The shadow moved in closer as she smashed the flashing orange button, and the three non-matching pictures stole another five dollars from her.

The shape hanging over her leaned in to look over her shoulder. "Aww, tough luck, beautiful," said a charismatic male voice.

"Get fucked," said Ashley, without looking up. She shoved another bill into the machine and slammed the button again.

Nothing.

"It looks like you need a change of luck. Can I buy you a drink?" the man standing behind her asked politely.

"Fuck off," said Ashley without looking up.

"I was just offering you a drink. There's no need to be rude."

Ashley refused to give a second of her attention to the man. "Do I have a sign on my back advertising my thirst?"

"No."

"Is there one saying I'm desperate?"

"No."

"Do you see I have two hands?" She held up her arms for emphasis.

"Yes."

"Did you not think that if I needed a fucking drink, I would flag down one of the roaming waitresses who cannot wait to pump me full of alcohol, so I spend even more money on their broken-ass, piece of crap machines?"

"I just wanted to offer you a drink."

"No, you asked if you could buy me a drink. In a casino where they give drinks away. For free." She pointed to a glass next to her. "One of which they have already just given me. For free."

"I was trying to be polite."

"And I'm trying to blow my potential future child's college fund. I've got a good rhythm going, so if you don't mind, please kindly fuck off."

The man would not take no for an answer. "How can you reject me? You haven't even looked at me."

Ashley turned to face the man. She did not expect to see someone quite as good-looking acting so desperate, but it changed nothing, and she held her composure. "When you say '*would you like a drink?*', what you're really asking me is '*would you like to fuck?*'. Is that about right?" She raised her eyebrows, waiting for his highly anticipated bullshit denial response to quickly follow.

The man squirmed. "I'm a little offended you think I'd be so forward with you. I wasn't asking that at all." He paused as his indignant mask fell. "Would you like to, though? You are really hot," he asked cheerfully, his voice laced with a combination of optimism and hope.

Ashley rolled her eyes at the handsome stranger's desperation and turned back to her game. "Fucking idiot."

"Excuse me?" asked the strange man. His ego bruised from the harsh rejection.

"Please leave me alone," said Ashley. "I'm really not interested at the moment."

"So, you might be later?"

"Fuck off," she repeated, her eyes never leaving the machine.

"You don't have to be so cold. I was only asking."

"And you don't have to be so desperate. Scoot along, you sad little panda." She rammed another five-dollar bill into the machine and pressed the play button.

Cherry.

Cherry.

She waited with bated breath as the last wheel revealed an identical cherry.

"Holy fuck," she yelped as a hundred dollars in tokens vomited from the machine. Maybe her fortunes were beginning to change after all. Were she even remotely superstitious, she would have wondered if her stalker was good luck. However, she was far too practical to consider mystical forces a valid option, and she crammed another five dollars into the gaping machine.

Lemon.

Lemon.

Orange.

Ashley sighed as she commenced her losing streak.

The women of Oceanview faced the world with a new strength than the ones they held before the events that tore their town apart. Dealing with a zombie outbreak tends to do that. Ashley was never a weak woman by any means, but she did things at her own pace. She knew that most women would have dumped Warren months before she finally got around to it. She did not feel trapped in the relationship. She just took her own sweet time to bring things to an end.

When she eventually pulled the trigger on something, she stuck to her guns. Warren begged and pleaded for her to take him back after the events in Oceanview. He was under the deluded impression that she would take him back as they both survived such a harrowing near-death experience. He pleaded for her forgiveness with flowers, crappy limerick poetry, and chocolates. One evening he showed up in her front yard and held his cell phone up over his head in a John Cusack 'Say Anything' pose.

Unfortunately, his playlist was on random and instead of playing their first date song 'Just No Way To Stop From Loving You' by Toby Jepson, he mistakenly played 'Ain't My Bitch' by Metallica. In his panic to change the song, he also gave Ashley a sample of 'Used To Love Her' and 'Back Off Bitch' by Guns N' Roses, and 'A Bitch IZ a Bitch' and 'One Less Bitch' by N.W.A. His concert of rejected love was mercifully canceled when the sprinklers turned on and chased him off, saving him from further embarrassment. But despite his proclamations of unrequited love, Ashley was having none of his reunion attempts, and they remained estranged.

She reached down and pulled the tokens from the tray below with a satisfied grin.

The shadow fell across her slot machine again, and her shoulders slumped. She turned to face the persistent lurker. "For fuck's sake, will—" Her world turned to black, and she was gone.

Zero.

The Oceanview Seven were no more.

CHAPTER 4

Tamara Sanders was twenty-two years old and on the cusp of building her modeling career around her stunning good looks. She was everything a world-famous supermodel should be, tall and slender with electric red locks that cascaded down her porcelain skin. A smile that could melt souls, and a pair of green '*come fuck me*' eyes. Many tried to listen to her eyes, and most failed. In fact, all failed. She was firmly in control of her destination and would not settle for just any scrub. Relatively unscathed by the modeling world, she was a daddy's girl who was kind to animals and fed the homeless. She was definitely the girl you would want to take home to meet your parents, but would most likely have to fight your father off with a stick. It was a shame she only possessed less than a minute left to live.

While seemingly perfect on paper, she was far from being free of vices. Her primary weakness revolved around her involvement with married men. She simply could not resist them. While she would never date more than one at a time, she kept a steady stream running through her revolving doors, and Adam, her latest conquest, was going to be in for one hell of an evening. Assuming his fucking wife didn't show up and ruin it again. She glanced up at the rearview mirror to check her lipstick and smacked her lips together with an exaggerated kiss.

The five-second distraction was enough to take her eyes off the road and drift into the opposite lane and barrel towards an eighteen-wheeler heading her way. The truck's loud air horn screamed as her attention snapped back to the road. She pulled hard on the steering wheel to avoid an imminent collision.

"Shit," she muttered as the car straightened up. Tamara continued to accelerate as the phone between her legs buzzed. She picked it up to see a new message from Adam. She tapped on his name, and a large, high-resolution picture of his erect penis popped open.

Tamara smiled. She held up the camera and mimicked licking the screen. She snapped a photo with her tongue hanging out and looked down to send him her enthusiastic response.

The second distraction held far more significant consequences than the first. Before Tamara realized she was drifting, the car smashed through the side barrier and careened over the edge of the mountain. Time froze, and the fall lasted an eternity. Tamara looked up at her mirror one last time, her eyes wide with terror. In two seconds, her face, windshield, and Adam's digital penis would become one, and her modeling career would be over. Her family would most certainly not be holding an open casket. What she didn't see in her rear mirror was a new passenger sitting in the back of the car.

The moment before impact, Death appeared in the seat behind her. He was happier than usual, and wore a slight smile on his face, despite the bloody scene unfolding in the seat before him. He'd seen this happen a thousand times and was desensitized to the whole gory situation. He did not care about her looks or her infidelity issues. She was just another name on a rather long list. Although, he was surprised she was scheduled to go down to Lucifer's office. Death smiled to himself. Lucifer would be pleased, he held a soft spot for redheads.

His smile was unrelated to the gore show. He was simply happy that things were going well and almost back to something that resembled normal. He was doing what he was best at. God was back in line, reapings were going as planned, and his quill was sharper than ever. In fact, he had not received a single incorrect reaping since the incident with Oceanview. Lucifer experienced a bit of a wobble shortly after, which involved exchanging some harsh words and God calling for his head, but things were back to being how they should, and Death was happy.

Death reached over and touched Tamara on the left shoulder. While adultery was generally frowned upon in the Kingdom of Angels, if it was a person's only flaw, it could be overlooked, and God would let you in. Unfortunately, she also retained a bit of a rap sheet for stealing credit cards, which earned her a one-way ticket to Lavaville. Also, she owned the attention span of a gnat, and this one particular flaw cost her dearly. The car slammed into the rocky ground below, and her beauty was instantly erased from existence. Death closed his eyes and disappeared from the smoking wreckage.

He reappeared on the sidewalk next to a towering skyscraper. He looked down at his list and grimaced. He pulled his stopwatch from his robe and clicked the pause button. A man appeared next to him, wide-eyed in terror, spread-eagled and three feet from hitting the ground. Death looked up. Four hundred feet above him, a window washer's deck hung down, one end detached from the cable. The deck's cleaning contents and hapless washer were ejected south at an exceedingly high rate of speed. The poor man was about to hit the ground. Hard. Death tapped him on the right shoulder. There were not many instances where he needed to freeze time, but shy of him jumping down with him, which he found rather unappealing, it was the only way he could catch the exact moment of death. However, it was better than dealing with a plane crash. He found them inconvenient and quite annoying.

With time frozen, he stepped aside before turning his attention back to his stopwatch. The unfortunate people standing by were about to get soaked with a bucket of soapy water and ten pints of fresh window-washer blood. Death clicked the watch, and time resumed. The man instantly hit the ground and erupted. The five screaming people standing beside the impact zone would be going home to a rather expensive dry-cleaning bill. Death waited for a second longer to watch the reaction and disappeared.

Seconds later, Death reappeared in the foyer of his office. "Good morning, Susan," he said in a sing-songy voice as he closed the front door behind him and dropped his scythe in the umbrella stand. "Did you know dick pics can kill?"

Susan didn't respond.

Death grimaced at his poor joke. "Sorry, that was inappropriate. Oh, but I did see the cutest puppy bobblehead this morning. You would have loved—"

A panicked look covered Susan's face. One that Death had seen before. It was a profoundly panicked look. Much time has passed, but it was one he recognized immediately. Something was terribly awry.

"Susan? What's wrong?" He paused as he tried to determine where the issue may lie. "Did I forget your birthday again?"

Susan shook her head.

"Are you supposed to be on vacation?"

She shook her head once again. "That's tomorrow. The temp will be here later this morning for training."

That was all Death could determine what could be wrong. "Then what is it, Susan?"

"It's the lists."

Death stopped dead in his tracks. "What?"

Ever since the cluster-fuck with Oceanview, the lists processed perfectly. Even the minor issue with Lucifer's list was quickly resolved once the missing 'inbox' label had been replaced on Death's inbox tray and the lists were placed in their correct locations. For six months, everything was peaceful and as it should be.

"The lists. We have a problem."

"What kind of problem? Did Gary screw up again?"

Susan shook her head.

"Did Lucifer?"

Susan rocked her head back and forth.

"Good. I really don't want to have to skip another reaping. We all know how that turned out. Turn one person into a demon, and the Universe loses its mind."

"It's worse."

Death frowned. "Worse? What could be more than what happened in Oceanview?"

Susan remained silent as she struggled to determine the best way to break the news to someone who hated receiving bad news.

Death was getting concerned. "Susan, what could be worse than what happened in Oceanview?"

"Oh, I think this qualifies."

"Show me the list. What's wrong with it?" He held his hand out expectantly.

Susan sat still. "That's just it, there isn't one. Gary never sent it."

"What?"

"He never sent the list over. I have nothing to scan and print out for you."

"Did we get Luc's list?"

Susan nodded and held it up, noticeably more substantial than usual. "Is there a chance no good people will die today?"

"Is anyone ever really good?" Death tried to joke, but Susan looked somber. "No, that's not likely, unless the entry requirements have been drastically overhauled. Have you called up there?"

Susan nodded again. "Fourteen times. All I get is a busy signal."

Death picked up Susan's phone and dialed. "Let me try." He was immediately greeted with a rapid series of beeps. He hung up and dialed again, only to hear the same annoying symphony of monotone chirps. He paused and looked at the phone. "Dammit."

"What's wrong?" asked Susan.

"It's not busy," said Death.

"Okay."

"It's disconnected."

Susan furrowed her brow. "How is that possible? That number has always worked. Has Gary moved to email?"

"It's possible, but highly doubtful. He hates changes in technology. We had a hard enough time convincing him to switch to phones. A change in procedure would take a formal notification, but this is Gary we're talking about here, so who knows. Have you checked your spam folder?"

Susan nodded in the affirmative. "Other than an email from Darren about water delivery rates going up unless we pay by the fifteenth, it's all empty."

Death sighed. "Of course they are. I thought we were grandfathered in on those rates."

Susan frowned at Death. He missed the point entirely. "Stay focused, please."

"I guess I know what I'm doing this morning. I swear, if he forgot to pay the phone bill, I'm going to be livid."

It appeared he needed to give Gary another visit. He was already over his quota for the year, and the thoughts of visiting the moron again irritated him. He let out a heavy, frustrated breath and flexed his fingers in an attempt to lower his rapidly rising blood pressure. "Susan, hold my calls. I'm going to Heaven, I'll be back in soon."

Death grabbed his scythe, pulled up his hood, and disappeared.

The way in and out of Heaven was a finicky beast. On a typical day, it was a one-way system that only saw people entering, for once people arrived, they never wanted to leave. There was no justifiable reason to provide residents an exit. However, as with all best-laid plans, it turned out that there were a couple of folks who needed the ability to come and go as they pleased, in particular, Death. Initially, he was able to bypass the inner workings of the check-in system and the annoying waiting room and teleport directly into the top-most floor of Heaven.

Six years before the events in Oceanview, God requested maintenance install an enchanted security filter to prevent Death from teleporting directly into Heaven, forcing him to line up with the newcomers. While God swore it was for the protection of the residents, Death was convinced it was done to make him have to beg Miley to buzz him in. Even more so when he found out that it only affected him and Lucifer. God assigned him a small closet in the outer hallway of Heaven's waiting room. He knew it was petty and childish and understood the limited access forced Death to deal with his front office receptionist, Miley, but it always brought a smile to his face when Death arrived at his desk flustered and irritated.

After leaving the waiting room, Death was then required to wait in the elevator lobby for one of ten elevators that may arrive. Whereas many Earthly buildings of substantial height reserved specific elevators for the higher up floors, these ten elevators covered all ninety-seven floors of Heaven. Upon arrival, the elevator would carry Death from the bottom of Heaven to the top and take him to the hallway outside of God's front reception area. Multiple work orders crossed God's desk to increase the number of cars, but he refused to sign them, and the only elevator that could travel through Heaven uninterrupted was his personal one.

Death reappeared in the small hallway closet and found himself alone and surrounded by darkness. He fumbled around for the light switch and flicked it on. He cursed under his breath as he turned towards the door and pushed it open. He stepped out into the corridor outside Heaven's waiting room. A long row of windows covered by vertical blinds ran the length of the room, blocking the contents from view. He looked around and furrowed his brow. The corridor was a lot quieter than usual. Typically, a lengthy line of bodies slowly filtered into the waiting room to be registered by the bright red-haired, makeup-caked receptionist from the seventh layer of Hades. Instead, he was the only person around.

Death stepped forward and pushed the double glass doors open, but they refused to budge. He tried again, this time exerting a bit more strength. Maybe the door just needed maintenance and was sticking, so he pushed harder. He was met with the same resistance. He leaned into the window and could see a sliver of the empty waiting room behind the blinds.

He knocked politely on the door. "Hello?" He waited for an answer, but the area was silent. "Hello?" he shouted louder. "It's Death. Can you let me in, please? The door seems to be stuck. I need to see Gary, it's rather important." He listened for a response, but none came. He slapped his hand against the door. "Hello?" he shouted again. "Is anyone here? Miley, where are you, you crotchety old hag?"

"She's gone home," said a voice from behind him.

Death turned around to see a frail old man pushing a mop and bucket standing before him. "Gone home? Why?"

The old man nodded. "Who are you?"

"Who do you think I am?" asked Death, his voice laced with irritation.

"Dunno. That's why I asked."

"How many show up in Heaven in a black robe carrying a six-foot scythe? I'm Death." He held up his scythe for emphasis.

"Oh, you mean like the Grim Reaper?"

Death sighed. "Yes, like the Grim Reaper, but I prefer to be called Death."

"Can I just call you Grim for short?"

"No."

"What do your friends call you?"

"Death."

"Do you have friends?"

"Yes, I have friends and they call me Death. Or better yet, you can just tell me why the door is locked and why I can't get in. Who is her replacement?"

"There isn't one. There's nobody at the front desk."

Death frowned. "Surely she has a backup for when she gets sick?"

"She's not sick. We never get sick in Heaven. It's quite nice, really. No colds, no allergies, no crapping yourself when you get stomach flu. I can't tell you how many times I've been grateful for that benefit."

"Okay, old man, that is way too much information," said Death as he cringed at the thought.

"I was just sharing some of the positives of Heaven."

Death ignored him. As far as he was concerned, there were no positives when Gary was involved. "So, then where is she? Heaven doesn't close for holidays."

"She's not here. Is there anything I can help you with?" the old man asked cheerfully. "I know all kinds of useful things."

"I'm trying to get in to see your boss."

"He's not here either."

"Well, where is he?"

"I don't know," said the janitor. "I can show you the library and artifacts room if you like. It's my favorite part of the tour."

"No, it's crucial I speak with him," said Death.

"I don't know where he is. We're closed, and he's left for the day."

Death stifled a laugh. "You're a funny little man, aren't you? Did Gary put you up to this?" He leaned back to the window. "You're hilarious, Gary. Let me in, I'm not amused."

The old man frowned. "Put me up to what? I'm just here to clean the floors while everyone is gone."

"What on earth are you talking about?"

"You didn't get the memo?" asked the old man.

"Memo? What memo? Look, can you just get to the point. I'm in a bit of a hurry."

"We're closed."

Death laughed at the apparent joke. "You're funny. Let me in, please."

"I'm not joking," said the janitor.

"What do you mean closed? Heaven can't be closed. You're twenty-four seven, three sixty-five. You can't be closed. You never close. You're like the holier-than-thou version of 7-11."

The old man stared at Death with genuine bewilderment and leaned on his mop. "I thought you were just feigning stupidity, but you really don't know, do you?"

Death was starting to lose his patience with the guessing games. "Everything was fine yesterday, and today, no lists, nothing."

The janitor sighed. It was time for a story. "They fired God, sonny. Heaven's been shut down. No one knew what to do, so Heaven is closed until we can get this all straightened out. Everyone goes to Hell now."

Death's eyes widened. He was unsure whether to panic or start laughing. "You're kidding?"

"Nope."

"How? What happened?"

"Now, this is all just rumors, so take it with a pinch of salt. Supposedly there was something called the Oceanview catastrophe. Have you heard of it?"

Death shook his head. "Never heard of it," he lied.

"Well, supposedly, thirty people in this town saw the face of God and tried to kill him, and they lived to tell the tale. They've spent the last six months telling anyone who would listen about God and Heaven."

Death frowned. That certainly was not how things went down. "Go on."

"There were witnesses in Oceanview. Well, supposedly, and this is where things get really interesting. There's this thing called The Committee of Supreme Deities. You have any idea who they are?"

"Nope." The lies were coming thick and fast. Death knew exactly to whom he referred.

"Well, the Committee is really upset. Apparently, they have this rule about no witnesses. I don't know much about it though, it's outside of my pay grade. I just hope the new owner lets me keep my job. It's not much, but I like it."

His words became background noise as Death stopped listening to the old man. He knew of the Council, naturally, but he never dealt with them face to face before. Life was simpler if he just did his job and stayed out of their way. He mulled over the information, and one particular comment stood out. "You said everyone is going to Hell now?"

The old man nodded. "It's the only place open to send them too."

"We can't send everyone to Hell," said Death. "That's not how the system works. Good up, bad down. Always has been, always will be."

"Not anymore."

Death paused. He ran the entire situation through his head and the ramifications that would almost certainly follow. Only one person came to mind. "Oh no. Lucifer is going to be furious." He nodded towards the door. "Have you seen anyone else around here?" he asked as he looked around for any other signs of life.

The janitor scratched his head as he gave the question some earnest consideration. After a moment, he shook his head. "No, just you. It's been really quiet."

"Are there any other doors around here I can try?"

"I have a janitor's entrance over there," said the old man as he pointed further down the corridor.

"Thanks." Death turned and walked away towards the second door.

"But I wouldn't go that way."

"Why not?" asked Death as he looked back over his shoulder.

"The hole?"

"What hole?" asked Death as he turned his head forward to see where he was going.

"The one you're about to step in," said the janitor as he pointed at eight-foot-wide hole in the middle of the floor

Death's eyes widened as his foot stopped an inch before he stepped into the abyss. "What on earth is that?" asked Death as he stepped back.

"It's a hole."

"I can see that. Why is there a giant hole in the middle of the floor and how come I only just noticed it?" He cautiously peeked over the edge to see a swirling maelstrom of white energy below them. Its end far from view.

"I don't know," said the janitor. "It opened up this morning. I didn't see it at first either. It seems to blend in until you're right on top of it. It's a bit of mystery, to be honest."

Death frowned as he strained his neck to see if he could locate the bottom. "It looks like a portal of some kind."

"I don't know much about that. I just do the mopping and occasionally pick gum from the bottom of the waiting room seats."

"Where does it go?"

"In the trash."

Death sighed. "Not the gum, the hole."

"Down."

Death rolled his eyes in frustration. "Well, of course it goes down, you silly man. But where does it down to?"

"I don't know that either. I threw a couple of things down it," said the janitor as he pushed his cart over to Death.

"You threw stuff down there?" asked Death.

"Of course I did. I wanted to see what happened."

"And?"

The old man shrugged. "I need a new mop." He frowned as he reminisced about his absent cleaning device. "I liked that mop."

Death sighed. "I mean, what happened when you threw it down there?"

"Nothing happened. It just disappeared." The janitor placed his hands on his cart handle and pushed it forward. "See?"

Death watched the cart idly roll towards the hole and disappear into the portal. "Why did you do that?" he asked.

"I thought you wanted to see what happened?" said the janitor matter-of-factly.

"I did, but I didn't want you to throw something else down there. You could hit somebody."

"That's not my fault, is it? They shouldn't be standing at the bottom of a strange hole." The janitor shoved his hand into his pocket and fished out his set of keys.

Death held his hands up. "Whoa! Could you stop throwing things in the portal?"

The janitor lowered his arm and looked at the keys in his hand. "Yeah, I probably need these anyway," he said as he stuffed them back into his pocket. "Want me to jump in?" he offered.

"No, I don't want you to jump in. I want to know why there's a giant portal outside of Heaven's lobby."

"We don't know that it's a portal," said the janitor.

"No? Well, what do you think it is then?" asked Death. "Because it looks like a portal to me.

"I don't really know. I've never seen a portal before."

Death sighed once again. "Well, I guess I'll just add this to the list of things that are broken because of Gary."

"Who?"

"Gary? Your boss."

"Oh, you mean God. We're not allowed to call him that. It's against the rule—"

"I don't care about your rules," snapped Death. "Are you going to let me in the lobby or not?"

"Not," said the stubborn, and rather annoying old man.

"Maybe there is someone inside who can help us. If you could let me, I can look around and get some answers."

The janitor shook his head and held up the bundle of keys he almost threw in the hole and jingled them in front of Death. "Not without these, you're not. The place is empty, and no one is getting through the front door without my approval."

"And the chances of you giving them to me are?"

The old man frowned. "Slim to none. I'm the custodian. It would be against my mandate to abuse my position."

"Would it help if I said please?"

"Maybe I mumbled. I said I am the janitor. I am the person who takes care of their assigned item in need of care. In this case, Heaven. What kind of employee would I be if I turned over my keys to the first person who asked for them?"

"I see," said Death.

"If you can come back with a warrant, I can let you in."

"A warrant?"

"Yes," said the old man matter-of-factly. "A piece of paper that gives you legal clearance to enter."

"I know what a warrant is. So where exactly does one obtain a warrant to open the doors to Heaven?"

"I don't know. I'm just a janitor. But without any formal documentation, this is as far as you're getting on my watch."

"I can just take your keys from you," said Death. "What is stopping me from doing that?"

"And I have no issues throwing them in the hole," said the janitor as he shrugged.

"That's a stupid solution. Then neither one of us can get back in," said Death.

"Then I get to go home early."

"You, sir, are the most useless person I have ever met," said Death. "I will be back."

"You'd better bring a warrant," said the janitor as he stuffed the keys back in his pocket. "Else you're wasting your time."

"Moron," muttered Death as he stepped back into his teleportation closet, pulled up his hood and disappeared.

CHAPTER 5

Death stood in front of his office and stared at the front door. He hesitated to push it open. He knew his routine was about to be turned hopelessly on its ass, and opening the door was likely to be the easiest thing he would do for the rest of the day.

He looked down at the bright and cheerful yellow daffodils growing by his front door and noticed a black slug slowly crawling across one of the leaves. Death watched its movement as it left a trail of clear mucus and random bite marks in its destructive wake.

"I think I'll call you Gary," said Death to the slug. "He ruins my life too."

He placed a finger on the slimy leaf-demon, and it promptly turned grey, shriveled up, and fell lifeless to the ground. He knew he was stalling, and abusing his powers was not the best way to pass his time. He inhaled deeply. He looked around at the rest of the flowers and miniature trees and sighed. His serenity garden was going to have to pull overtime today. While the events of Oceanview caused him a colossal pain in his ass, this was different. How could Heaven be closed? It did not make any sense. The gravity of the situation swarmed around his head. He failed to understand how millions upon millions of afterlife residents could simply disappear. This was a whole new realm of cluster-fuck, unlike anything he could ever imagine.

He pushed the door, and a nasally cackling voice slapped him hard in the face. The noise rang familiar, but Death was unable to pinpoint the source. He stepped inside, and the banshee howl stopped.

Death frowned to himself as he closed the door and dismissed the thought. "Well," he said out loud. "It looks like Gary really screwed up this time." Nine seconds later, he found himself face to face with the source of the ghastly noise. "Oh, fuck me," he said in one of his rare moments of cursing.

"You!" Miley turned around to glare at him as he entered the room. "This is your shit-box of an office?" She turned to face Susan. "I can't work for him. You never told me you worked for this miserable cock-goblin."

Death looked at Susan. "Are you kidding me? I can't work with this harpy."

Miley sneered at his retort. "You think I want to be stuck here with you for the next seven days?" you pale nutsack.

"Ten actually," corrected Susan. She turned to face Death. "Remember, you told me that if I didn't use them by the end of the year, I'd lose them?"

Death pointed at her. "That is not helping." He clenched his jaw as he weighed up his options. "Call the agency, Susan. There has to be someone else they can send us."

"There is no one else. This is who the temp agency sent over to me, so this is what we have to work with. There isn't exactly a large pool of qualified afterlife secretaries. And considering I'm not canceling my long overdue vacation for you or anyone else, your choices are limited. It's her or nothing."

Death pondered the situation a moment. He smiled a mischievous, wicked smile and reached inside of his robe. He pulled out a Blood Card and gently placed it on Miley's head.

"You dirty mother fu—" Miley disappeared, and the card tumbled to the seat.

Susan shook her head as she stared Death down. "You are so immature sometimes, you know that, right?"

Death smiled. "I know."

Five seconds later, Miley reappeared wearing a string of Mardi Gras beads around her neck and a pair of plastic devil horns perched on her head. She immediately ripped off the headband and threw them at Death.

He ducked as the plastic spikes whizzed past his head. Certain no other projectiles were coming, he stood up and reached towards her shoulder. "You have confetti on you. Let me get that for—"

Miley swatted his hand away. "You little bitch. You tried to take me out with a Blood Card? What in the actual ever-loving fuck?"

Death could not mask his smile. "It was worth a try."

Miley seethed with anger. "You sent me to Hell, you flaccid cock."

Death shrugged. "It seemed like a perfect match. Besides, Heaven's closed, isn't it? Where else was I supposed to send you?"

"Nice try, shit-stain. Blood Cards don't work on those already in the afterlife."

"As I said, it was worth a try."

She picked up the Blood Card from the floor and showed it to Death before tucking it into her wonky cleavage. "And I'm keeping this, and now you have to file paperwork for a missing Blood Card. That alone will take you a week to figure out. Longer, considering Susan will be on vacation, and I won't help you. I also assume you'll need me to help you use the computer, as you're probably technologically retarded."

Death smiled at the threat. "It was worth every second of it."

Susan could see things escalating further and held up her hands to settle the two combatants down. "Knock it off the both of you. I'm going on vacation, and you two will get along. You will keep this office running, and you will get to the bottom of what is going on with our lists." She turned to Miley. "I know I've just met you, but the same goes for you."

Death sighed. Susan was right. Unless he wanted to do the work himself, it was Miley or nothing, and with the events currently unraveling, he was going to need all the support he could muster.

Miley looked up at him. "You think I'm any happier about this arrangement? Well, guess what, fuck-noodle, I'm not. I hate you. I hate your gaunt, pasty face. Get some sun, for fuck's sake. You look like you have rickets. I take it you've seen what was left up there?"

"I have, and it's empty. What happened?"

"Fuck me if I know. I come into work this morning just like I did yesterday, and the day before that, expecting the waiting room to be full of clueless ass-lemmings who have no idea how the system works and expecting me to hold their sad little baby hands. Instead, there's a note on the door telling me I can either go home or come down here and take on some temp work. It was this or staying with my husband."

Death's eyes widened in mock shock. "Someone actually married you?"

Miley scowled at him. "Yes."

"What sorry excuse for a lottery did that poor soul lose to be forced to spend eternity with you?"

"I keep him perfectly happy. If you know what I mean?" She winked at Death and inserted her middle finger into her mouth and simulated enthusiastic fellatio.

Death's cheeks puffed as he dry-heaved at the visual display unraveling in front of him. "That is disgusting. If I wasn't already celibate, I would swear off sex for life."

Miley licked the end of her finger in a long, exaggerated sweep as she finished her torrid sex act. "You know you want this, don't you?"

Death ignored her question. "Your poor finger. Do you need to rinse it in bleach?"

Miley grinned at him. "So, what do you plan to do to fix things?

"Me? I don't see how any of this is my problem."

"How is this not your fault? You were the cause of all this last time."

Death sighed. "We're not going down this path again. Oceanview was all on your boss. I had nothing to do with it."

"That's not what Gary said."

"Yeah, well, Gary is a giant lying sack of dung." He noticed Susan's phone blinking. "Is someone on hold?"

Susan's eyes widened as she realized that there was, in fact, someone on hold. "Oh, I forgot. Yes, it's—"

Death reached out his hand. "Oh, for goodness sake, as if he wasn't going to be angry before."

Susan seemed surprised at the impromptu and predictive gesture, and slowly she passed the phone to him. "How did you know?"

"Hunch." He put the phone to his ear. "Good morning—"

"*WHAT. THE. FUCK. STEVE?*" Lucifer paused after each word for added dramatic emphasis.

Death cringed. "We've got a problem, Luc," he said in a remarkably calm tone.

"*No fucking shit we fucking do*," said Lucifer through the phone.

"No, I mean we have a huge problem."

"*Which part? The fact you kept me on hold for eleven minutes, and I know for a fact you ain't that fucking busy with other calls. Or that the population of Hell has doubled in the last six hours?*"

"The last part," said Death.

"*What the fuck is going on, Steve? I am not a happy man.*"

"Heaven is closed."

Susan's jaw dropped at the new revelation. "What?" she mouthed silently.

Death looked at her and shrugged. The cat was well and truly out of the bag now.

"*They're what*?" echoed Lucifer in a much louder voice.

"Heaven. They're closed. Apparently, the Council shut them down for violation of protocol seven."

"*Gary revealed himself to humans* ?" asked Lucifer.

Death nodded. "Yeah. He certainly did."

"*You mean physically or just his genitals*?"

"No," said Death with a slight smile. "All of him. He appeared in front of a group of humans and let them live."

"*What the fuck was he thinking*?" asked Lucifer.

"I have no idea, but he is off the grid, and Heaven has been cleaned out. There's no one there but a janitor."

"*So what about all of the people who have come my way*? *What am I supposed to do with them*?"

"I don't know. It looks like you're stuck with them until we can find a solution."

"*So, what about Gary*?" asked Lucifer. "H*as anyone seen him since he left*? *He should be around to help us fix this mess.*"

"No one knows. He's completely disappeared."

"*How did he do that*? *He's a fucking deity, they don't just disappear,*" said Lucifer.

"Well, he has."

"*I don't have enough room for all these people down here. We haven't finished building the extension. I'm going to need your support on this. Can you help me*?"

"I can send people to purgatory, but that only covers the freshly dead. There is nothing I can do with the people who are already in Heaven. They aren't part of my system anymore. The process doesn't allow me to."

Lucifer paused. "*You know, Steve, this is really fucking up my routine. I'm going to head up there to see what's going on.*"

"I tried that. I couldn't get in."

"*Well, you're not me, are you*? *Is the closet still working*?" asked Lucifer.

"Yes."

"*Good. Then meet me outside of the waiting room in five minutes.*"

Death sighed and hung up the phone.

Susan continued to stare at him in disbelief. "Closed?"

"Yes," said Death.

"Heaven is closed?" reiterated Susan for further clarity.

"Yes," said Death again.

"The kingdom in the sky where the well-behaved deceased have gone for thousands and thousands of years has shut down?"

Death was starting to lose his patience. "Yes, Susan. Heaven is shut down. There's no one there. No one is going to Heaven after they die."

Susan slowly nodded as she processed the information. "I'm still taking my vacation," she said indignantly.

CHAPTER 6

Consciousness slowly clawed its way back into Cam's head as she sat upright on an old wooden floor. As she cautiously opened her eyes, she was met with more darkness. She reached up to her face and felt a soft hood covering her. She pulled it up and tossed it on the floor, but the room remained in darkness. She held her breath and strained to listen, uncertain if she was alone.

Cam climbed to her feet and swung her arms out, trying to find something familiar, a table, a chair, a light switch. Anything to help her with establishing orientation. If she could find a wall, maybe she could find a door and escape, but her quick search turned up nothing. She stepped back and her leg bumped into a chair. It emitted a deep groan as it dragged along the wooden floor. She froze as her heart pounded aggressively behind her rib cage. The room remained silent, and she slowly regained her composure.

Cam reached into her jeans pockets for her cell phone, but her search came up empty. "Shit," she muttered to herself as she relaxed her eyes and tried to adjust to the darkness. She blinked rapidly, trying to get a feel for the room. Her skin started to scrawl as the possibility of blindness clawed its way into her mind.

A soft noise echoed from across the room, and she inhaled and froze. Another light scuffling followed, this time much closer. Cam pulled her arms close to her chest as her heart rate accelerated.

"Hello?" a female voice asked from the darkness.

Cam held her breath as she hesitated to answer.

"Hello?" the female voice called out again. "Is someone there?"

"Who is it?" asked Cam cautiously.

"Who are you?" asked the equally nervous voice. "Where am I?"

Cam frowned at the familiar voice. "Amber?"

"Cam?" said the voice as it raised an octave in relief. "Is that you?"

"Yeah," said Cam as she turned to face what she assumed to be Amber's general direction.

"I can't see," said Amber.

Cam exhaled in relief as she learned she was not the only one with vision issues. "Thank fuck for that."

"What?"

"Neither can I," said Cam.

"Are we blind?" asked Amber.

"I hope not. I think the room is just dark."

"Where are you?"

"Keep following my voice," said Cam. "Be careful, there's a chair around here somewhere. I just tripped over the fucking thing."

Amber cautiously shuffled over to Cam. After a moment of swinging her arms around and taking small half-steps, the two women brushed fingers and were reunited.

Cam opened her arms and pulled her friend in for a hug. "Are you okay?" she asked.

"Yeah," said Amber as she stepped back. "Where are we?"

Cam shook her head. "I don't know. I can't see shit. Do you have your phone with you?"

Amber patted down her jeans pockets. "Shit! No. I had it before I was brought here, but it's gone."

"Yeah. Same here. I don't know what happened."

"Don't you have a lighter?" asked Amber.

"No, I quit smoking a couple of months ago," said Cam.

"Good for you," said Amber with a smile Cam could not see.

"It seems I should have waited," said Cam with a smile. "My timing was always a little off."

"We're in trouble, aren't we?" said Amber with an air of anxiety.

"I don't know," said Cam. "One minute I'm standing at my car, and the next, I'm waking up in the dark with a bag over my head. I think someone grabbed me, but I'm not sure. What happened to you?"

"I was with Greg, trying on wedding dresses."

Cam's face lit up at the news. "It's finally happening then?"

Amber smiled. "In three months. Hopefully."

A scuffle echoed as a new visitor in the room gained consciousness. The two women fell silent, unsure if the new arrival was friendly or something more ominous.

"Hello?" a male voice called out.

Amber's eyes widened at the call. "Greg?" she squealed.

"Amber?" said Greg, his voice tinged with relief and surprise. "Where are you? I can't see anything. I think I'm blind."

"None of us can. We're over here," said Amber.

"Thank fuck for that." Greg extended his arms and shuffled over to the two women.

"Careful, there's a cha—"

Greg cut off Cam as he stumbled over the chair and fell to the floor with a loud crash. "Found it," he groaned.

"Are you okay?" asked Amber.

"Yeah," said Greg as he pushed the displaced chair aside and stood up. "Just a bruise." He reached out for Amber's shoulders. "Are you okay?"

"Yeah, but I'm not Amber," said Cam with an invisible grin.

"Cam?" asked Greg.

"Hey, Greg."

"How are you doing?" said Greg.

"Surviving."

Amber reached out for Greg's arm. "I'm here," she said as she touched him gently.

Greg pulled her close and wrapped his arms around her. "Are you okay?" he asked as he reached up for her face and kissed her.

Amber nodded. "I'm fine. I thought I'd lost you."

"Did they hurt you?" asked Greg.

"No. I'm fine. I'm just scared. Any chance you have your cell phone with you?"

"Yeah." Greg patted down his pockets. "Shit," he muttered. "I lost it. I had it in my hands before this."

"That seems to be a common theme today," said Cam.

"Is there anyone else here?" asked Greg.

"I think it's just us," said Cam. "Any idea what's going on?"

Greg shrugged his shoulders. "One minute I'm with Amber watching her try on dresses, the next we're here. You?"

"I was leaving my apartment," said Cam. "I got jumped walking to the car."

"I was in Vegas minding my own damn business," said a new female voice following another whoosh of air movement. "Some fucker grabbed me."

"Ash?" queried Amber as her sister's voice rang familiar. "Is that you?"

"Yep," said Ashley. "Where the fuck are we?"

"We don't know," her sister replied. "None of us can see."

"We?"

"Greg and Cam are here too."

"One sec," said Ashley. A moment later, a bright white light from her cell phone lit up the group. "Hey, guys."

The three of them held their hands to their faces as their eyes struggled to adjust to the new light source.

"Thanks for the warning, dude," said Cam as she squinted. Bright dots floated around the room as her vision slowly returned.

"Sorry," said Ashley as she lowered her phone and walked over to the group. She threw her arms around Amber and pulled her in for a hug. "Is everyone okay?" she asked.

"Yeah," said Amber. "We're just confused. No one knows where we are."

"Let's find a way out of here," said Ashley. She turned her phone and swept it around the room. "There must be a door or something." The beam of light stopped on a naked man sitting against the wall with a hood over his head. "What the fuck?"

Greg looked at the rest of the group and pointed at the naked stranger. "Who's that?" he mouthed.

Cam shrugged.

"Hello?" asked Ashley cautiously.

The stranger sputtered and coughed. His legs spasmed as he woke up, but he remained silent.

Cam and Amber looked at each other nervously. Greg held his hands across the group and gestured for them to stay still.

"Kim?" said the naked stranger as he looked around the room, his hood still over his face. "Is that you? I'm so sorry."

Greg frowned as he watched the man. "Warren?"

The body started to wriggle aggressively. "What the fuck? Where am I? I know you put out a hit on me, Kim. Get your goons away from me, man." He climbed to his feet and swung out his arms to strike someone. "I know you sent your brother after me. I'll kill every last one of you with my bare hands."

Greg stepped closer to the man. "Warren?" he said again.

"Who the fuck are you?" yelled the naked man as he took a poorly executed karate stance. "I'll kick your ass, you half-pint bitch."

"It's me, you idiot. Calm the fuck down." Greg reached over and pulled the hood from his brother's head.

Warren squinted as he looked at his brother. "Greg? Man, I was this close to snapping your neck."

Greg nodded as Warren started to mellow out. "Of course you were."

"Hey bro, how's it going?" said Warren gleefully. He dropped his sad combat pose as he opened his arms for a brotherly hug. "Come here you."

"No," said Greg. "You're naked."

"Any idea what's going on?" asked Warren as he lowered his arms.

"We're trying to figure that out," said Greg.

"Who else is with you?"

"Me, Amber, and Cam," said Ashley as she swept the light across the group.

"Hey, Ash. What's up?" Warren said with a polite and excited smile.

Ash smiled. "Not you, apparently."

Warren looked down at his limp penis. "It's cold. Give me a break."

"Why are you even naked?" asked Ashley.

"He was like that when I found him," said a new voice behind them.

The group cautiously turned to greet the next visitor as Ashley held up her phone.

Cam's eyes widened in surprise. "Holy fuck," she stammered. "David?"

David smiled. "In the flesh. Well, almost."

"What the shit?" Cam blinked and tilted her head, unsure if her eyes were deceiving her.

"Hello, Cam," he said with a grin.

She squealed and sprinted over to her former fellow Oceanview resident and drinking buddy, and wrapped her arms around his neck, "Oh my god, it is you." She held the hug a moment longer, paused, and suddenly pulled away with a raised suspicious eyebrow. "Wait, you died. I saw it happen."

"We all did," said Ashley. "What the hell?"

David smiled again. "I'm still dead."

"Oh," said Cam. Her face washed with disappointment. "I don't understand. I saw God take you. You were dead."

"He did, and I was," confirmed David.

"So, how have you come back?"

"I think the bigger question is why?" said Greg. "I don't think any of this is a coincidence."

"It isn't," agreed David. "I brought you all here."

"Any chance you have a light on you?" asked Cam.

"Of course," said David. He snapped his fingers, and eight lanterns around the room ignited. The group turned to evaluate their surroundings.

"Holy fuck. How the hell did you do that?" asked Cam. She was impressed with David 2.0.

"It's one of my new abilities," said David.

"Your new abilities. What are you?"

David smiled again. He was happy with Cam's warm response, but now was not the time to get them up to speed. "We have a lot to catch up on, but that's a conversation best saved for later."

"No," said Warren. "I think that's a conversation we can have now. Things are a little bit weird around here at the moment."

"Hey, Warren," said David with a smile. "How's it hanging?"

Ashley turned to face Warren. "You still haven't told us why you're the only one who is naked."

"I was standing around minding my own business when Captain Pervert over here came up behind me, wrapped his arms around my waist, and grabbed my junk."

"No one grabbed your junk, Warren," said David.

Warren turned to Ashley. "He did. With both hands." Warren placed his hands together to simulate grabbing an exaggerated, large penis, ten times the size of his own.

Ashley rolled her eyes. "Yeah, keep on dreaming, mini-man."

"That's harsh," said Warren. "And to think I was going to sacrifice myself to God for you."

"No, you weren't," Ashley quickly shot back at her ex. "As soon as you realized he was serious about killing you, you scrambled to get out of the way. I volunteered if I recall correctly."

"Aww, did you miss me?" said Warren with an ear-to-ear grin.

"Of course," said Ashley sweetly. "It hasn't been the same since we left Oceanview."

Warren's face lit up at the unexpected news. "Really?" His heart rate increased at the possibility of a reconciliation.

"No, fuck off. I'm doing perfectly fine without you. Dating you was the stupidest thing I've done, and I have a New Kids on The Block tramp-stamp."

Warren's rapid heartbeat returned to normal as his hopes were dashed. "Yeah? Well, I'm doing just fine on my own, too," said Warren defensively.

"Who's Kim then?" asked Ashley with a raised eyebrow.

Warren shrugged his shoulders. "She's my girlfriend. Well, ex-girlfriend now."

"Because she saw you naked?"

"Funny," said Warren as he rolled his eyes. "That's not why."

"Or did she catch you sleeping with Jill?"

Warren froze and visibly cringed at the mention of sleeping with Ashley's former best friend. He opened to mouth to speak, but in one of his few moments of self-awareness, he opted for silence.

"Yeah, I found out after we left Oceanview," said Ashley. "You know cheating is a one-way ticket to Hell, right? Thou shalt not commit adultery."

Warren remained silent. Anything he could add to the discussion was simply going to dig his hole deeper.

"So why did this one kick you out?"

"She didn't kick me out," said Warren.

"No? Then why are you naked and shouting out her name?"

Warren shrugged. "I accidentally called her Ashley when I woke up this morning."

"You did?" asked Ashley.

"Yeah," confessed Warren.

"Why?"

"Why? You're on my mind constantly, even when I'm sleeping. I can't help it. I never stopped loving you."

"That is so sweet." Ashley smiled.

"Really?"

"No. Put some clothes on. You're embarrassing yourself and giving me PTSD."

Warren frowned. "I had clothes, but David made me drop them. I swear he did this to me on purpose."

"I needed to get you out of there," said David. "I didn't have time for the formalities of getting you dressed before I saved your life. Again."

"I didn't ask you to do it either time," said Warren.

"But yet here we are," said David as the embers of their former feud started to glow.

"Why did we have bags on our heads?" asked Ashley.

"I needed to teleport you in and it's common to lose consciousness the first time," said David. "I couldn't risk you opening your eyes and looking into the light."

"Where are we exactly?" asked Cam.

"Somewhere safe," said David.

"Where?" pushed Cam. "We need some answers, David. You at least owe us that."

"You're safe, I promise. But I can't tell you where we are. It's too risky right now."

"We're at Jacob's," said Warren as though answering the most straightforward and obvious question in the world.

"What?" said Amber.

"Jacob's?" said Greg, confused as to how the group could have returned to their favorite bar. "As in Oceanview Jacob's?"

"Do you know of another Jacob's?" asked Warren. "Yes, Oceanview Jacob's."

"How do you know that?" asked Amber.

"We're in the basement. I've been locked in here a dozen times. I'd recognize this place anywhere.

"Why did Hank lock you in his basement?" asked Greg.

"Oh, he didn't know I was hiding down here. He thought the place was empty. I'd sneak down before closing time and hide in the corner behind some crates. He'd shut up and go home, and I'd have access to all this." He looked around to see the mostly empty room. "Well, it used to be stocked with beer and snacks."

Greg turned to face David. "Is he right?"

David sighed. "He is."

Warren's eyes lit up. "Sweet! Hank used to have a box of lost and found clothes."

Cam looked around behind her. Sure enough, a large cardboard box full of clothes rested in the corner. "Looks like that's it."

"Thank fuck," said Ashley, unimpressed with her ex's continued nakedness.

"Sweet," said Warren cheerfully. We wandered over to the box and started to dig through the contents.

Greg frowned at the unexpected news. "Why did you bring us back to Oceanview?" he asked David. "Don't get me wrong, man, it's good to see you again, but we fought our asses off to get out of here. Hell, you died before we left, and now you've dragged us back here against our will. None of this makes any sense."

Cam turned back to David. "So, what exactly are you keeping us safe from? What's going on?"

"Holy shit," interrupted Warren as he rummaged through the box. "This is my old Mötley Crüe shirt!" he said with an excited grin. "I lost this thing years ago." He pulled the shirt from the box and showed it to the group before dropping it over his head. "Still fits too!" He returned his attention to the box, singing to himself as he continued his search. "I'm the one they call Dr. Feelgood. I'm the one that makes you feel all right. "I'm the one they call Dr. Fe—"

"Please stop," said Ashley. She grimaced at the sight of Warren bending over the box, his naked ass proudly and unabashedly on display to the group. "Would it kill you to start with pants?"

Warren's eyes widened with delight. "Ooh, I wonder if he still has my pants," said Warren as he dove back into the box.

Ashley looked puzzled. "Why would he have your pa—"

"Found them," said Warren proudly as he hoisted a pair of jeans up in front of him. "There's no underwear in here, so I'll have to go commando, but beggars can't be choosers given the current situation," he said. He pulled his wardrobe prize up his legs, tugged on the zipper, and continued to dig through the box.

"David, safe from what?" Cam asked a second time.

"Yeah, now what?" asked Greg. "Did Heaven start another zombie-demon apocalypse?"

"No," said David.

"Thank God," said Amber. "I don't think I could stand to see another zombie-demon again."

"This is worse," said David. "Things have... escalated."

Greg sighed. "Of course they have. What is it this time?"

David bit his lip. "Uh, we don't know for certain what's going on yet. We received an alarm that a funnel opened in Oceanview." He noticed the confused looks on the group's faces. "A funnel is a direct portal between Heaven and Earth."

"Where did it open?" asked Greg.

"At the church."

"Why?" asked Amber. "What's so important about the church? Hell, I doubt it's even still standing after what happened with the zombie-demons."

"It's the exact location where you saw God," said David.

"Why is that relevant?" asked Greg.

David nodded. "Deity exposure creates a ripple in the Universe. Sort of like a red flashing warning light. There's an intergalactic rule that gods are not allowed to be seen by mortals."

"All gods?" asked Warren.

"Yes," said David.

"How many are there?" asked Warren, pressing the matter further.

"Millions," said David. "At a rough estimate, of course. I've only met one of them, and that was enough for me."

"That's a lot of followers to keep track of," said Warren. "You're telling us we're the first people in the entire Universe to meet a god?"

"No. To meet a god and live."

"I find that really hard to believe," added Greg. "So every person who has seen a god has died?"

"Yes," said David.

"Gods are kinda dicks then, aren't they?" said Warren with his usual tact and flair.

David smiled. "Yes, most of them are. My opinions on religion haven't changed despite being in Heaven. I think the whole concept is ridiculous."

"You're still an atheist, even though you live in Heaven?" asked Warren.

"Oh, I'm even more of an atheist than I was before."

"That doesn't make any sense at all," said Warren. "How can you not believe with all that you've seen?"

"Why didn't you just take us to the church?" interrupted Cam. "Why bring us here first?"

"We needed to scope the place out," said David. "I wanted you somewhere safe in case something went down. Now that I have you all together, the plan is to get you to the church and into the funnel."

Warren, newly decked out in a Captain Planet baseball cap and sneakers listened to David with intense interest. "Are you saying we're going to Heaven?" he asked.

"Once we reach the church, yes," said David. "That's where I'm taking you. It's the safest place right now."

"That's so fucking cool," said Warren. He turned to face Ashley. "Hey Ash, remember when you told me it was unlikely I'd ever make it to Heaven because I cheated on you? Well, you were wrong. It looks like I made it there after all."

"You're only going on a technicality. It doesn't count," said Ashley.

"Sure it does," said Warren as he turned his attention back to David. "Hey, will I get to see God again?"

"No. He's gone," said David.

"What?" asked Cam with more than a hint of concern in her voice. "Where is he?"

"I don't know what happened, but he's missing," said David.

"Oh, this just keeps getting better and better," said Greg. "Why am I having this nauseating sense of déjà vu?"

"Wait a second," said Amber, interrupting her fiancé. "There were seven of us that survived Oceanview."

"Yeah," agreed Cam. "Where's Lee and Reverend Ellis? Why aren't they here? They saw God too."

David inhaled as he prepared himself to give the news he hesitated to share.

"Ellis is dead. We haven't found Lee yet."

CHAPTER 7

Few things in life were as absolute as Lucifer's good looks. Most people who made his acquaintance referred to him as Heaven's most beautiful angel, and for those fortunate enough to lay eyes on the Dark Prince it was easy to see why. Everything about him was just simply perfect.

At six foot two, he was tall but not awkward tall. His shoulders were broad, but not sack-the-quarterback broad. His posture was commanding, but not intimidating or threatening. He was toned, but not vein-popping steroid abuse bulk. When it came to clothing, his choices were impeccable. His custom-tailored suit was form-fitting, but not tight. The black shirt beneath the jacket was professionally pressed, and the design of his tie varied based on his mood. His black gloves fitted his hands as though they were a second skin. Both cheeks held a perfectly round dimple. Small enough to be cute, but not big enough to be derpy. And this overall package presented why God detested him so much. The man was flawless, and God oozed with jealousy.

However, despite his numerous positive qualities, the one area he struggled with was patience, and any time he needed to deal with God, he found himself possessing surprisingly little of it. His phone call with Death forced him to return to the kingdom in the sky and he was most displeased with the current status of things. Even more so having to use Heaven's annoyingly small transit closet. After a moment of struggling with an aggressive mop, he stepped into the hallway to greet Death.

"Where's your scythe?" asked Lucifer, aware that Death was not carrying his usual accessory.

"I left it at the office," said Death. "It's a bit cumbersome for non-reaping activities." Since Death's previous visit, the door handles were bounded by a heavy chain and padlock. "That wasn't there before," he said.

Lucifer pulled on the metal bindings. "Someone isn't fucking around," he said as he dropped the chain and stepped back. "This door isn't budging." He turned to Death. "I don't suppose you have a pair of bolt cutters underneath that flowing robe of yours, do you?"

Death patted himself down as though he was looking. "No, I can't say that I do."

"That's a shame. They'd have come in handy."

"Why would I have a pair of bolt cutters under my robe?"

"It lets you become invisible and teleport anywhere on Earth. I thought it might be bigger on the inside. You know, like a magician's hat or a TARDIS or something."

"No, it's not bigger on the inside. Can't you do Jedi things like Gary?" asked Death.

"Not anymore. The dick stripped me of my powers when he kicked me out of Heaven. Outside of Hell, I'm pretty much powerless until he decides to give them back to me. He likes to watch me suffer. And people believe I'm the one who likes to torture folk"

"Powerless? Really?" asked Death, not believing a word of Lucifer's claim.

"Well, mostly," said Lucifer with a sly grin. "I still have one or two tricks up my sleeve, but I can't give away all of my secrets, can I?"

"Can you teleport?"

"No. I can't even fucking teleport down to Earth without this stupid fucking ring." He held up his hand to show his ring. "And the damn thing stopped working."

Death raised an eyebrow. "When?"

Lucifer shrugged. "No idea. I tried using it before I came here and it wouldn't work. The regular teleporter works, so I was at least able to get here. But I can't get to Earth. Do you think this is all related?"

"I don't know," said Death. "We need to find another way in here."

Lucifer glanced around, hoping to see an alternative option. "We could just smash the glass," he suggested.

"We're not at the vandalizing stage just yet," said Death. "Even if we can get past this lock, we're not getting out of the lobby. It's key-carded."

"Shit. Maybe we—" Lucifer paused and cocked his head. "You hear that?"

"What?"

"Someone's whistling."

"It's probably the janitor?" offered Death.

"Janitor?"

"Yes, he was here when I stopped by earlier. He wasn't exactly what I'd call useful."

"He'd probably have keys on him, though. I'm sure if I ask nicely, he's let us in."

"He does, but he wouldn't give them to me when I asked."

"Did you ask nicely?"

"Of course I did," said Death.

"Maybe you just needed to be a bit more assertive then," said Lucifer with a smile. "Everybody has a price if you ask in the right way."

The distant whistling continued to get closer.

"I have an idea. Closet," said Lucifer as he pushed Death towards the nearby janitor's storage room. He pushed the door open, and the two men disappeared inside.

Lucifer closed the door to barely a sliver so he could see out into the hallway.

"How is hiding in a closet being assertive?" whispered Death. "It feels a bit passive to me."

Lucifer held up a finger to his lips to silence Death. "Don't worry, I have a plan. Shh, he's coming," he whispered as the old man came into view.

"What are you doing?" asked Death in an equally hushed tone.

"Getting the keys. We'll jump him when he walks by."

"Ambushing an old man is not being assertive, it's assault," countered Death.

"It's all a matter of perspective."

Death was not convinced that mauling the elderly was the best course of action. "We can't attack an old man," he said.

"Do you see another entrance anywhere around here?"

Death shook his head, but the lack of further options did not mean Lucifer was right.

"Then we jump the old bastard and take his keys," said Lucifer, exerting little effort to find an option that did not involve physical contact. "It's simple."

"You can't attack senior citizens. Especially ones in Heaven."

Lucifer shrugged. "Why not?"

"It's not proper."

"Oh, come on. I'm Lucifer, being a dick comes with the title. It's expected of me. It's a perk of the job."

Death sighed. He was not okay with the plan, but having failed to offer something different, he resigned himself to Lucifer's idea. "Fine. Just try not to be too rough."

Lucifer held up his hand to silence Death. "Okay, here he comes."

The janitor slowly pushed the mop past the door. Lucifer jumped out and jostled the old man toward the opposite wall, pinning his right arm behind his back.

"Ow," the janitor cried. "Stop it, you're hurting my arm."

"Listen, old man, I'm going to ask you a question, and you're going to answer with a yes," ordered Lucifer.

"Yes," said the janitor.

"I haven't asked you yet."

"Sorry. Ask me anything. Just don't hurt me."

"I want your I.D. badge and keys."

"That's it?" asked the janitor.

"Yes."

"Take them," said the old man as he dug his free hand into his pockets and pulled out a bundle of keys.

"Really?"

The janitor nodded as Lucifer released his grip. He reached down and unclipped the badge from his belt and handed it over. "You didn't have to hurt me. All you needed to do was ask, and I would have given it to you," he said as he rubbed his sore shoulder.

"You would?" asked Death.

"Of course I would. I'm a janitor, they don't pay me enough to be security. I don't care who comes in here."

Death stepped forward, an eyebrow raised in suspicion. "Excuse me? Earlier you told me you wouldn't let anyone in on your watch. You said I needed to come back with a warrant."

"You didn't threaten me with bodily harm." He nodded towards Lucifer. "He did. That's as good as a warrant."

"What?" said Death.

The janitor shrugged his shoulders.

"And that's why nice guys always finish last," said Lucifer as he inserted the key into the lock and removed the chains. He then swiped his ID card through the reader. He turned to face Death and smiled. "Like I said, you need to be more assertive. We really need to work on that."

"I've done quite well without it," Death mumbled under his breath.

The door clicked, and Lucifer pushed the doors open to reveal the stark white waiting room. "Oh god, it's —" he fumbled for the right words. "It's so shiny and sanctimonious." He looked around the room, taking in the rows of seats and the customer service window. "Man, this has changed since I was last here. I don't even recognize the place."

"How long has it been?" asked Death.

"Three, four thousand years? I lost count." Lucifer stopped and looked around. "I try not to think about this place too much. It gives me indigestion."

"You should meet the receptionist sometime," said Death as he walked towards the window Miley used to occupy. "She's a delightful woman. You'd love her."

"You mean Miley?"

"Oh, you know her?" said Death. "I thought she was hired after you left."

"I know of her. Do you know how many people have gone to Heaven, arrived at her window, spent thirty seconds talking to her, said fuck it, turned, walked out, and came down to me?"

"She is my temp."

"As in temp secretary?"

"Yep."

Lucifer laughed loudly at the news as he stopped at the door marked private next to her customer service window. "How did that happen?"

"Susan is on vacation for the next ten days, so the agency sent me a temp."

Lucifer laughed as he held the I.D. badge up to the scanner next to the door. "Well, that makes sense why you're so calm about all this." The door beeped, and Lucifer pulled it open. "After you," he gestured towards the opening.

"It's a good distraction from the office," said Death as he passed through the door.

"You know you're going to have to go back at some point, right?" said Lucifer.

"Thanks for reminding me. I'm hoping this drags out for a bit so I can stay out in the field. With no lists coming in, I have no reason to go back.

Besides, everyone is going down to Hell anyway." Death smirked from beneath his hood.

"You're funny," said Lucifer. "Hey, can I come back with you when you go back to your office? I want to meet her."

"If I said no, would that stop you?"

"Nope," said Lucifer.

"Well, then you just answered that question for yourself then, didn't you?"

Lucifer grinned as he headed towards an elevator bank at the end of the hallway. "So, where do you think we should start?"

"Let's go straight to the top. I think we should visit Gary's office. Maybe there's a paper trail we can follow?"

"Sounds like a plan," said Lucifer as he pushed the call elevator button nearest to him. "I wouldn't mind stopping off on a few floors to see if anyone is left. Surely someone is still here."

"That's not a bad idea," agreed Death as they waited for the elevator to arrive. "I just want to know why I keep getting dragged into this nonsense?"

Lucifer shrugged. "I guess we form a symbiont circle. None of us can exist without the other. Me, you, Gary. We're one big happy, dysfunctional family."

"That's a horrible thought," said Death. "I can always go back to being a farmer and live quite happily off the land."

"You don't have to be so cold all the time. You know you love me," Lucifer replied with a grin.

"I like you marginally more than Gary."

"While that bar is set really low, I'll take it as a compliment."

Death smiled. Truth be told, he did rather enjoy Lucifer's company, and he was one of the few people in the Universe he could be himself when around him. However, he would never openly admit such a confession to his companion.

The elevator door opened with a cheerful *ping,* and the two men stepped inside.

Lucifer once again gestured before him and pointed towards the opening. "After you," he said politely. For someone dubbed The Prince of Darkness, his manners were impeccable.

Death stepped inside and turned to face the bank of floor numbers as Lucifer followed him inside. "Where to?" he asked.

"No idea," said Lucifer. "I haven't been here since the renovations.

It's been a couple thousand years, I doubt I'll recognize the place. You've been here recently, what do you think?"

"I've only ever gone to his office on ninety-seven. I couldn't tell you what's on the other floors."

"Well, then let's go on an adventure," said Lucifer as he pressed the number ten button.

"Your idea of an adventure is really warped, you know that?"

"What can I say, I'm a glass is half-full of whiskey kinda guy."

"You? The eternal optimist?" laughed Death.

"Guilty as charged," said Lucifer.

The doors closed, and the elevator started to ascend.

"This is exciting," said Lucifer with a grin. "It's like playing pious Russian roulette."

"Exciting is not exactly the word I'd use," said Death as he watched the numbers above the door increase.

"Oh, you know you love coming up here." Lucifer smiled to himself as the doors opened to reveal an empty lobby. "How could you not? It's always so much fun."

Behind the receptionist's desk, a brightly painted mural adorned the wall. It contained pictures of obnoxiously happy families, and Jesus holding various babies, and the word *'Watchtower'* emblazoned across the wall.

"Nope," said Lucifer as his smile faded and he quickly stepped back into the elevator. "Let's try a different one. I'm not staying here."

"Wait," said Death as he jammed a foot in the door to stop it from closing. "They have a floor chart by the desk." The doors reopened, and Death stepped out.

"No way—" Lucifer protested as he rolled his eyes and reluctantly followed Death back out into the lobby. "Dammit, Steve. I hate these people."

Death stopped at the sign. "Okay, Baptists are eight floors above us. Catholics nine about that. Lutherans and Protestants, thirteen above that. Oh, this one looks fun. Born Again's twenty-four above that. Would you like to go up there? I know how much you love those guys."

Lucifer threw Death a '*really*' look. It was unnecessary to voice his disgust.

Death smiled to himself and continued to read the signed. "Mormons are on sixty-five. Miscellaneous and non-denominational Christians are on seventy-one. Do any of these sound appealing?"

"Can I be honest?" asked Lucifer.

"No. Pick one."

Lucifer sighed with resignation. "Fine. Let's visit the Baptists. Maybe they have a Bundt cake or something hiding up there. My blood sugar is getting low, and I'm feeling snacky. And man, do those fuckers like their potlucks."

Death turned and walked back to the elevator. "Sixty-four it is then." He smiled as he pressed the button for the eighteenth floor.

"Wait, did you say sixty-four?"

CHAPTER 8

"What?" said Cam in disbelief as David briefed the group on the fates of Lee and Reverend Ellis. "What happened to them?"

David bit his lip and looked down. He never enjoyed delivering unwelcome news, especially news that involved death. "Once the funnel opened in Oceanview, we immediately came to find you. I went to the church, but there was no sign of Ellis. All I found were some strange scorch marks on the altar. I searched the area and outside the church but found nothing. Fearing the worst, I went to look for the rest of you."

"You found us so fast. How did you know where we were?" asked Greg. "We'd all moved away from Oceanview."

"Uh—" started David.

"Yeah, that's a really good question," agreed Warren.

"David?" asked Cam.

"You've been tracking us," said Ashley bluntly. She was not asking.

David cringed. "We've been keeping an eye on you from Heaven, but we've never used it until now. We never needed to. It was for your own safety."

"Gross," said Ashley, visibly disgusted at the confession.

"As soon as we got word of the funnel opening, we came for you."

"We?" asked Amber. "Who's we?"

"I have an emergency response team working with me. Finding all of you was our highest priority." An intercom device on David's wrist chirped. He pressed a flashing red button as he raised his hand. "Yeah?"

"*It's Muriel,*" an out-of-breath female voice stated from the miniature wrist-com speaker.

"Did you find Lee?" asked David.

"Who's Muriel?" whispered Warren.

David swatted at the air to silence Warren. "Shhh!" He turned his attention back to his wrist-com.

"*We found his car, but there's no sign of him,*" said Muriel.

"Shit," David cursed under his breath.

"Who's Muriel?" asked Warren again. "Is she your girlfriend?"

David lowered his wrist-com. "She's my lookout at the church. Now shut up and let me talk."

"*David*?" asked Muriel.

"Yeah, I'm here," said David.

"*Nathaniel is at Lee's car, but it's empty. There's carbon scorch marks on the driver's side door. It's the same thing you found with Ellis.*"

David exhaled a weighted sigh. "Fuck," he muttered to himself.

The group looked at each other in panic at the news that another survivor likely perished. David inhaled as he processed the news.

"*You know what this is, David,*" Muriel continued over the wrist-com.

David hesitated to respond as the rest of the group stared at him for either guidance or comfort.

"*David*?" asked Muriel. "*Are you there*?"

"Yeah, I'm still here," said David.

"*You heard me, right*?" asked Muriel.

"I did," confessed David.

"*We need to move fast,*" said Muriel. "*It's going to be looking for you.*"

"Understood." David flicked off the wrist-com and looked up at the group.

Warren crossed his arms in frustration. "What did she mean when she said you know what this is?"

David puffed his cheeks and sighed. "We've got a problem."

"We kinda figured that out already," said Cam. "What kind of problem are we talking about here? And don't bullshit us, David."

David sighed again. "I was hoping I was wrong, but we're pretty certain the Council has sent a Caretaker after you."

"The Council? You mean that pompous group of intergalactic douchebags Gary was talking about back at the church?" asked Warren with his typical level of tact.

"Yes, those guys," replied David. "You're all living witnesses to a deity, and it violates a significant number of protocols. So, they called in a

Caretaker to clean things up."

"A Caretaker? Really?" asked Warren. "Is that the best name they could come up with? He sounds like an old man with a bucket and mop or something."

David shook his head. He knew the group was running on borrowed time. "The Caretaker is no laughing matter, Warren. It's a nasty piece of work. Look, can I explain to you this later? We need to get you all to safety before it finds us."

"No," said Amber, breaking her silence. "If you're telling us that this Council personally sent something down to Earth to kill us, I think we deserve to know what's coming."

The rest of the group muttered their various levels of agreement.

"No, not personally," said David. "This is an automated standard procedure when there is a protocol violation. I doubt there's any one person on the council who would authorize this. It's not personal, I assure you."

"It certainly feels personal," said Cam.

"Don't get me wrong, I'm not standing up for the Council, but I honestly doubt it even realizes this has happened. You're not exactly the center of the Universe. Caretakers are employed across all of space to clean up deity messes."

"Well, that makes me feel so much better," said Warren. "We're being eradicated as a footnote. It's a fucking hit, no matter how fancy you dress up the words."

Greg bit his lip and shook his head. "I'm about to get married. Amber is pregnant. I'm trying to build a new life for myself. We all are."

"Wait, you're pregnant?" asked Warren.

Amber smiled and nodded. "We are."

"Greg's pregnant too?" grinned Warren, his excitement quite apparent on his face. "I'm going to be an uncle." His smile spread from ear to ear. "If it's a boy, are you going to name him after me?"

"No," said Greg. "Who'd want to be friends with a boy called fuck-nugget?"

"Middle name?" asked Warren, ignoring the dig.

"Walter," said Greg.

Warren's eyes widened. "What? Are you shitting me? You'd name your kid after the man who tried to eat you?"

"No, we would name him after Amber and Ashley's dad."

"That's what I said. He tried to fucking eat you, Greg, or did you forget about that?"

"Really?" asked Greg, unsure why his brother failed to remember there was a human there before Walter turned into a flesh-eating monster. "He wasn't always a zombie-demon."

"Remember when he tried to shoot us when we went to rescue the girls? I'm pretty damn sure he was human then."

"Warren, just let it go." Greg had indeed forgotten about Walter shooting at them a few days before succumbing to his bite. "It's important to Amber. Therefore, it's important me."

Cam was pleased with the joyous news, but there were more pressing issues at hand that still needed to be addressed. "Why are they coming for us now?" she asked. "That was over six months ago. What changed? We haven't done anything. None of us have said a word about what happened. We left as soon as we could, and we never looked back. We've never even so much as set foot back in Oceanview."

"It needed to go through a committee first," said David. "They had to approve the motion, then they escalated it to the approval committee, and they have to make a resolution before a motion could go to the floor. It's an arduous process."

"Wait," said Greg. "You just said they most likely didn't even know this has happened, then you say it went through a committee for approval."

"It was on the consent agenda, and nobody ever reads the fine print. They just blanket vote on a dozen or so smaller items. I doubt the item was even heard in its entirety."

"So, everything is decided on by a committee then. I guess not much changes after death, does it?" griped Warren. "That's depressing as all fuck. First, I find out I can go to Heaven as long as I go to church at least once, and now you're telling me Heaven is run like one big committee. Is it too late to change my mind and go to Hell?"

Ashley laughed. "You're acting as though you weren't going there to begin with."

"What's that supposed to mean?" asked Warren.

"You were cheating on me, dude. I think that's a one-way ticket to the man downstairs. Speaking of which, I wonder how soon it will be before he shows up and really makes this a party."

Greg tired of the fighting in the group. "Can we focus on the problem, please?" He looked back at David. "What does a Caretaker do?" he asked. "Is it a bounty hunter? Hitman?"

"It's a demon," said David solemnly.

"Pfft," puffed Warren. "Do you know how many zombie-demons Greg and I have killed?"

"Yeah, I was there, Warren," said David. "I killed a few too."

"Then you know we are zombie-demon ass-kicking machines."

"It's not a zombie-demon. This is different. You've never faced something like this before."

"Have you?" asked Cam.

David shook his head. "No. Which is why I have a team. I don't know what we're up against."

"Oh, great," said Warren. "You have a team. I feel safer already."

David raised his wrist-com to his mouth. "Okay, bring them in."

The air next to David started to flicker. Moments later, four people materialized beside him. The Oceanview Five looked at each other in bewilderment at the new arrivals.

Cam frowned at the group of guests standing in front of them. "This is getting weirder by the minute," she said. "Who are these guys?"

David stepped forward and held his arms out. "These are Guardian Angels. Until we can get you to the funnel, you've each been assigned one to protect you. Heaven has a contingency protocol if something like this happened."

"A protocol? Has this ever happened before?" asked Cam.

David shook his head. "No. You are the first."

"But you had a plan ready?" asked Cam.

"Heaven has plans for all kinds of doomsday scenarios," said David.

"How many scenarios?" asked Warren.

"Lots," said David.

"Two lots? Ten lots? That's pretty generic," said Warren.

"Eight-hundred and sixty-three million, three hundred and seventy-two thousand, one-hundred and five," said David. "Give or take a few."

"There's that many ways to destroy the Earth?"

"The Universe is a dangerous place, Warren," said David. "There are threats that Earth minds can't even begin to comprehend."

"So, what are you expecting to happen?" asked Ashley.

"We don't know," admitted David.

Ashley continued to press the issue. "So, there is a chance that this completely fails, and we all die?"

"Yes, that is a possibility. Unlikely, but anything is a possibility. We need to get you to the church before the Caretaker finds you," said David.

"Why does Heaven care if we're get snuffed?" asked Greg. "We're just seven people."

"Five," corrected Warren.

"Dude, way too soon," said Greg, taken aback at his brother's casual attitude to the likely demise of their two absent friends.

"Because once the Caretaker is successful in killing you, it will then target everyone you've been in contact with since Oceanview," said David. "Friends, family, coworkers. It won't stop until every loose end has been terminated."

"What's to stop it from just killing them now?" asked Greg.

"It doesn't know who they are," said David. "It reads your mind when it kills you. While you're alive your friends are safe. Which is why we need to hurry."

"Won't it just follow us to Heaven?" asked Greg.

"No, it can't use the funnel." David beckoned to his right, and a tall man with short jet-black hair stepped forward. "This is Antonio. Greg, he has been assigned to you."

David beckoned again, and a thin, good-looking woman of average height with similarly black hair stepped up. Warren's eyes lit up in the hopes she would be assigned to him.

"Amber, this is Celestial."

Celestial smiled and offered her hand to Amber. "Celest for short."

Warren's smile faded.

"This is Donovan," he said as a second good-looking black-haired man took his place in front of David. "Cam, he's yours."

Cam smiled and rubbed her hands together with exaggerated glee. "Lovely. I'll take him."

Donovan blushed as he lowered his eyes and stepped over to Cam. David looked at the last woman standing beside him. "Augustine, you're with Ashley."

Warren looked around as it quickly became apparent that this was the last stranger to enter the room. "What about me?" he asked. "Who's my Guardian A—" He knew the answer the moment the words passed his lips. "Oh, come on. That's not fair."

David smiled. "Sorry, Warren. You're stuck with me."

"Augustine is gorgeous. She could escort me to Heaven anytime. Why can't I have one of the real Guardian Angels?"

"I am a real Guardian Angel," said David.

"You're a Guardian Angel now?" asked Cam.

"Surprise," said David. "I bet you didn't see that plot twist coming."

Warren frowned in a combination of confusion and mild disgust. "You can't be a Guardian Angel, you're a godless heathen. You're an atheist. You can't serve on behalf of Heaven. We've gone over this before."

David shrugged. "Yeah, well, I'm in Heaven, and you're not, so I must have done something right." He hesitated. "Or wrong."

Warren was not having any of David's arguments. "You only got in on a technicality."

"Yes, and in Gary's eyes, that is enough."

Warren's jaw dropped, incredulous at the latest revelation. "You're allowed to call him Gary?"

"No, of course not," said David. "He hates that. But I never said I followed all the rules. I'm not even allowed to drink gin up there as all hard alcohol is supposedly banned, so I need to have at least a little fun."

"It's bullshit," said Warren. "This is seriously ruining Heaven for me."

"I don't want to be here, but there's not a lot I can do about it. Look, we can sit here arguing about the merits of why I'm here, but I'm here, and I'm your only chance of surviving this."

"This is some grade-A bullshit," griped Warren again.

"It's only bullshit if you get me killed," said David. "We're going to be escorting you to the church. We'll use the funnel and get you to Heaven, because right now, it's the safest place you can be."

"Won't the Caretaker just chase us up there?" asked Greg.

David shook his head. "The Caretaker can't use the funnel. It's forbidden. If we can reach it, we can keep you safe until we figure all this out."

"Why are we running?" asked Greg. "We can survive this. We've fought off zombie-demons before, surely we can fight this Caretaker? There's ten of us. We have the numbers."

"It's far too powerful," said David. "This thing is fast, strong, and relentless. It will kill you."

"Even with the Guardian Angels?" asked Cam.

"We're not immortal, Cam," said David.

"Why can't one of you teleport ahead, check to see if the Caretaker is there, and if he isn't, come back and get us?" asked Amber

"Anytime we teleport, it sends a ripple through the funnel. It'll sense it and head right back there. Our best chance is on foot."

"What if we promise to keep quiet and not tell anyone?" suggested Amber. "Besides, who would believe us? We'd sound like ranting lunatics."

"The protocol assumes you would tell a friend, who then tells a friend, and before you know it, the entire world knows."

"We're being judged on something we didn't ask to see, and on things we have never said? That hardly seems fair," said Ashley.

"I never said it was fair. They are just tying up loose ends," said David.

"Six months later," said Ashley. "This is really sloppy."

"I also never said they were efficient," added David.

"I'm glad our lives are considered loose ends," said Warren, a hint of anger in his voice. "You know what, fuck this nonsense, I'm leaving." He turned and headed to the stairs.

"Warren?" What are you doing?" asked Greg. "Get your ass back over here."

"Come on, man. This whole thing stinks. We keep getting told how small and insignificant we are, but then we're expected to believe that this Council has decided to terminate us. Which is it? This seems like a lot of effort to silence people who don't matter. And you know what? If there is something coming after us, I'm not running away to Heaven and hiding."

"Really?" said Greg.

"Yeah."

"You used to hide when we played dodge ball. Now you want to go out and hunt demons?"

"I didn't run from the zombie-demons and I'm not running now. It beats sitting here scratching our collective nutsacks."

"You can't leave," said David. "We have to keep you safe."

Warren turned to face David. "I'm not sitting here in a basement waiting for some demon to come and snuff me out like some sniveling coward. If I'm going to die, then I'm going to do it on my terms, not some biblical douchebag's."

"Get your ass back in here and quit being a martyr, Warren," said Greg. "We're leaving this place together, and we'll arrive in Heaven together. You don't get a say in it."

Warren rolled his eye and closed the door. "Fine."

"*David*?" asked Muriel's voice from his wrist-com. "*Are you ready*? *We really need to get moving*."

"We're ready," said David into his communicator. He turned to the group. "Donovan, we're going out the back door and up into the street."

Donovan nodded as he cautiously opened the door and looked out into the street. "We're all clear," he said.

"Shouldn't we wait until night?" asked Warren? "It's broad daylight out there. It'll see us the second we break cover."

"No," said David. "Caretakers have night vision. We'd be at a huge disadvantage at night."

"And we're not now?" asked Cam.

"It has an edge no matter what time we go. This evens the playing field a little bit more. Right now, we stand as much chance seeing it as it does seeing us. The faster you can run, the faster we can get you to safety," said David. "My angels know what to do to get you to the church."

"So, what does a Guardian Angel do exactly?" asked Warren.

"We protect you," said Donovan.

"From what?"

"Environmental threats, danger, but mostly from yourself."

Warren pointed to his chest. "Even me?"

"Especially you," said David with a smile.

"What's this thing armed with?" asked Greg.

"Knives, a sword, possibly a crossbow," said David.

"Possibly?" said Warren. "Any chance it could be unarmed and just wants to chat?"

Donavan beckoned everyone to the door. "Is everyone ready?"

The group confirmed their desire to leave, except for Warren. "I'm not," he said. "One sec." He stepped over to a nearby box and opened the lid. He pulled out a bag of potato chips. "Road snack. Anyone want chips for the road?"

"Over here," said Cam as she raised a hand.

Warren fished out a bag and tossed it over. "Anyone else?"

A few '*no's*' came back, and he dropped the box on the floor. "More for me then," he said as he shoved a few bags in his pockets and walked over to David. "Okay, whenever you're ready, Angelman."

David nodded to Donovan who cracked the door open. The bright morning sun reflected off the windows from the office building across the street, and a beam of light bounced through the open door.

"Hey," protested Warren as he rubbed his eyes. "You just singed my retinas, dude."

Donovan ignored Warren's vision crisis and opened the door all the way. He ascended the small staircase and surveyed the street. Certain the area was quiet, he pulled the door closed and turned to the group. "The street's empty. We need to make our move now."

Greg smiled at Warren. "Well, you're fucked then, little brother."

Warren frowned in protest. "I've been working out the past few months. I'll be fine. I'd be more worried about you not keeping up with me." Warren grabbed his brother's belly. "Looks like you've packed on a few since I last saw you."

Amber looked up at Greg in a panic. "I can't run that fast," she said. "I don't think I can make it."

Greg gently lifted her chin and kissed her on the lips. "I'll be right with you."

"We all will," said Cam with a comforting smile. "We get through this together or not at all."

"Cam's right," said David as he looked back outside. "We'll be okay. On my lead, we go single file. Keep it low and keep it fast."

Greg reached out for Amber's hand. "We've got this."

Amber smiled as she grabbed his hand. "I know."

Warren looked over at Ashley and held out his hand. "We've got this."

"Put your hand down," said Ashley. "I'm perfectly capable of running on my own. I don't need your help."

"Not even for old time's sake?" asked Warren.

"Especially for old time's sake."

"I was just trying to be a gentleman," Warren countered as he lowered his hand.

"Everything you do under the guise of being a gentleman is two steps away from you expecting it to turn into sex."

Warren could not help but grin. "Yeah, you're probably right."

"It's time for you to move on, Warren. We're not getting back together."

"I'm the eternal optimist. Maybe you'll come around."

"Don't hold your breath." Ashley paused. "On second thought, please do."

David pushed the door open and dashed up the steps and across the empty parking lot to the building across the street. Donovan held the door as he rushed everyone outside. The rest of the group filed out behind him and snaked their way over to the sidewalk. At the tail end, Antonio stepped outside and slapped Donovan on the shoulder. Donovan crossed the street as Antonio left Jacob's and jogged over to the group.

"Okay," said David. "We to head north to Brown and turn—"

"Why don't we head down Seventh?" interrupted Warren. "It's less direct, but we'll avoid the main streets. If this thing is hunting us, shouldn't we be running in the shadows and alleyways?"

"It won't care which streets we're using. As it widens its search, it will look down every road and every alleyway. This thing moves fast, and the longer we stay out in the open, the higher the chances of it finding us.

Straight and direct is safest."

"He's right," said Cam.

David nodded. "Okay, let's keep moving."

"Wouldn't it be safer to go in the opposite direction of the church?" asked Greg. "Surely this Caretaker will be waiting for us? I know I that's where I'd be heading."

"If it follows protocol, it will sweep the church first and then widen its search. These things are highly skilled trackers. It won't take it long to put the pieces together."

"How does it know where we are?" asked Greg. "Does it have the same surveillance as Heaven?"

"We think it may have hacked into our network and mined the data," said David.

"Who the hell does your network security?" asked Ashley.

"Why?"

"They suck," said Ashley.

"I never said it was good."

"That's just fucking dandy," moaned Warren. "Once again, us mere mortals have been slammed over a barrel and fucked in the ass because a group of pretentious Gods have a bunch of made-up bullshit rules that humans are supposed to follow, without actually knowing what any of the fucking rules are."

"It's not like that, Warren," said David.

"No?"

"No," said David as he continued to scan the area.

"Why are you standing up for them, David? You were one of us. You're Oceanview."

"Are you serious? One of you?" asked David. "I'm pretty sure you hated me, Warren."

"I did, yeah, but—" Warren paused. "You know what? I'm going to write a strongly worded letter about this."

"Who to?" asked Greg.

"I don't know. The Pope?"

"I think this is out of his jurisdiction," said Greg.

"Keep it down back there," said David over his shoulder as he stopped outside Judy's Coffee Shop.

"Sorry," shouted Warren as he followed the group across the street and joined them in a small huddle.

"We're going to be wide open for the first couple of blocks on Miller," said David. He mulled over his limited options. "Antonio, run ahead and see what cover we have."

Antonio nodded. "I'll be right back." Thirty seconds later, he returned with a summary of the road conditions. "We have a few cars we can use for about three hundred yards. Other than that, there's not much to hide behind."

David mulled over the information. "We're going to move in smaller groups towards the gas station. We'll meet behind the car wash. Antonio. You and Greg go first."

Antonio led Greg from behind the wall, and they sprinted over to the first car parked on the side of the street. Once they reached their cover, Antonio looked back and offered a thumbs up to the next group and then pointed Greg to the next car.

"Celeste, you and Amber are next," said David. "Head to the first car and wait for my signal.

When the two women arrived safely at the first vehicle, he directed Donovan to lead Cam over. As Donovan led Cam away, Augustine left with Ashley.

"Okay, Warren," said David. "Are you ready for this?"

"Of course I am. I was born ready for this. The bigger question is, are you?" Warren took off across the street. "Try to keep up," he shouted over his shoulder.

The group scampered from car to car as they made their way to the gas station.

David's wrist-com crackled with static as Muriel's voice piped through. "*David, come in. Are you there*?" asked Muriel

"What's going on?"

"*It's on the tracker,*" replied Muriel from David's communications device.

"What does that mean?" asked Amber.

"We can track the Caretaker for up to a mile," said David.

"*I've got movement about eight blocks north of you,*" said Muriel.

"Which direction is it heading?"

"*East for now, and it's moving fast.*"

"That's good. That means it's going away from us," said David, relieved at the positive news.

"*It could still change direction at any time,*" said Muriel. "*I'd suggest moving a little faster.*"

David looked at the group. "Well, you heard her. This thing is moving in the opposite direction, but we're still fifteen blocks from the church.

If we're going to stand a chance of out-running it, we're going to need to pick up the pace."

The group nodded their agreement again.

"Couldn't you have ported us closer?" griped Warren.

"I won't lie," said David. "The plan has some flaws."

"No shit," said Warren.

"Groups of two again?" asked Cam.

"No, we all go at once. Time is no longer a luxury we have," said David. He looked around the corner, and seeing the street was clear, he directed the group to leave their cover. "Go."

CHAPTER 9

"This is horrific," said Lucifer as an ocean of cubicles spread out before him. He walked a step behind Death as they weaved their way through a maze of the empty indentured-servant farm. Every ten feet or so, they passed another chair surrounded by a variety of flying toaster screensavers, miscellaneous office supplies and half-full coffee cups, or half-empty coffee cups, depending on the owner's tolerance for their job and existential view of life. The two darkly dressed men were a shocking contrast to the brightness and purity of Heaven.

Death scanned the cramped workspaces as they swiftly moved through the floor. Each cubicle offered the same story. Lucifer stopped at a desk as Death continued to move ahead.

"Want a donut?" offered Lucifer from behind.

Death turned around to see the Prince of Darkness holding a box of pink glazed donuts before him. "No, I'm good, thanks," he said with a dismissive eye roll, and continued to walk ahead.

"They have sprinkles," said Lucifer optimistically as he caught up with his partner.

"You don't even know how long they've been sitting out. They're probably stale," said Death over his shoulder.

"Pfft, it's been a few hours tops, and besides, this is Heaven. Nothing is rotten here," said Lucifer as he plucked one of the donuts out of the box.

"Do you honestly believe that?"

"Sure." Lucifer smiled as he took an enthusiastic bite. He stopped walking, frowned, and promptly spat the doughy mess onto the floor.

"Ptah!" he spouted in disgust.

"Stale?" asked Death with a smile.

"Worse," said Lucifer as he wiped the vile donut residue from his mouth. "Vegan." He dry heaved as he threw the remains of the donut back into the box. "I think it's gluten-free. What kind of sad, demoralizing douchebag puts strawberry glaze and sprinkles on dry-ass, faux-dough and tries to pass it off as a sorry excuse for a donut? No donut aspires to become an abomination like this."

Lucifer picked up another donut from the box. "So, Mr. Donut, what do you have to say for yourself?" He held the donut up to his ear. "Kill me. Please," he replied in a high-pitched voice. "Duly noted," said Lucifer with an understanding nod. He dropped the offending donut onto the floor, lifted a foot, and stomped the diabolical pastry into the carpet. A moment later he tipped the box over and dumped the rest of the contents on the ground.

"Are you doing okay?" asked Death as he watched Lucifer staring at the pink and brown crumbs.

"Yeah, why?"

"You seem to be having a moment."

"I'm just righting some universal wrongs," said Lucifer as he continued to focus on his pile of pastries.

"You could have just thrown them in a trash can."

"Yeah," said Lucifer with a shrug, "But now they have to shampoo the carpets when they come back." He looked up at Death with a large grin on his face.

"If they come back," said Death. "It looks like everybody left in a real hurry."

Lucifer poked his head into the cubicle beside him and noticed a half-eaten evil donut sat accusingly on a paper plate. "They probably committed mass suicide after eating the donuts."

"It's not funny to joke about suicide."

"It's not funny to desecrate donuts, but here we are."

Death turned from the donut massacre and started to walk away. "We need to keep moving. There has been some kind of clue around—"

A muffled thud echoed from a nearby door, and Lucifer froze. He held his hand up to halt Death and pressed a finger to his lips as he cocked his head, listening intently. "Do you hear that?" he mouthed softly.

"Huh?" whispered Death, uncertain what Lucifer tried to say.

"Did you hear that?" Lucifer said, raising his volume slightly.

Death pointed to his ear and shook his head. "I can't hear you," he said, louder than Lucifer would have preferred.

Lucifer held a finger to his lips. "Shh. Dude, seriously? Are you deaf?" he whispered as he pointed to the nearby closet. "There's something in there." He took a cautious step forward and ground the rest of the donuts into the carpet.

Death looked down as he watched Lucifer sliding his foot over the floor. "You are such a child."

Lucifer grinned as he stepped closer to the door.

Another sound rang out from behind the door. "Hello?" a faint, broken voice called out. "Is someone out there?"

"I think our something is a someone," said Lucifer softly as he reached for the handle. "Hello?" he shouted back.

A slight clutter rang out, and the room fell silent.

"Okay," said Lucifer. "On three. Two—"

Lucifer reached for the door handle and inhaled. As he grabbed the knob, the door flung open, knocking Lucifer backward as a mass of floppy limbs and bright blonde hair fell out of the closet and onto the floor.

"What the fuck?" yelped Lucifer as he scrambled to his feet. "Who the fuck are you?" he asked as the man continued to squirm.

The new arrival frantically looked around the room like a rabid bunny. He scampered towards the nearest desk and disappeared underneath.

"Hello?" asked Lucifer as he stared at Death in disbelief. "What the fuck?" he mouthed silently.

Death shrugged. He was as bemused as his companion.

"Momma, is that you?" asked the timid voice from beneath the desk.

Lucifer glanced at Death and shrugged. "Momma? We're not your momma, son."

"Oh," said the stranger with a hint of sadness. "Please don't kill me," the cowering man pleaded.

"We're not going to kill you," said Lucifer. "Come on out and introduce yourself."

The man slowly peeked his head around the edge of the desk. His blonde hair was matted to his forehead, and his clothes were covered with stains.

"Hi," said Lucifer as he extended a hand to help him up, but the man pulled further away.

"Don't touch me, don't touch me," said the panicked man.

Lucifer withdrew his hand and stepped back. "Fine, help yourself up."

The man looked up at Lucifer and weighed him up. Convinced he was most likely an ally, he extended a hand. "You can help me up now."

Lucifer reached down and pulled the disheveled man to his feet. "Jesus, son. What happened to you?" he asked as he looked the poor fellow up and down.

"I'm Spencer, the executive director of the Baptist division. I used to run this division until everything went down."

"That's a mouthful. Is that an official title?" asked Lucifer.

"It's the one on the little plaque on my desk," said Spencer.

"What happened here?"

"I don't know. I went to the bathroom, and when I came out, everyone was gone. I wouldn't have been in there if Ida hadn't brought in regular donuts. She knows I have a sensitive stomach and can only eat gluten-free ones."

Lucifer frowned. "Ah, so those vile little things are yours?"

"Gluten-free is cruelty-free. They are good for your soul."

It was Death's turn to eye the newcomer suspiciously. "Are you okay?" he asked. "You look a little beat up."

"It's been a long day," said Spencer.

Lucifer stifled an unintentional laugh. "You been alone for less a day, and you already look like this? You look like you've gone feral."

"It was harrowing."

Lucifer smiled at the unfortunate man's experience. "You're a funny little fellow, aren't you?"

Spencer frowned in a mixed state of frustration and hurt. "I fail to see how my current predicament is either humorous or entertaining."

"I'm sorry," said Lucifer. "I just don't see how you could have spiraled so fast."

"I don't adapt to change well. I like my creature comforts, and they are gone. I've been forced to live like an animal."

"He's probably been eating the donuts you found," said Death.

Spencer shook his head. "No. I've been living off leftover Christmas snacks. I've eaten so many chocolate liqueurs, I think I've developed a drinking problem."

Lucifer laughed again at the unfortunate man, but judging by Spencer's wounded expression, he wasn't joking. Lucifer raised a quizzical eyebrow. "You're serious, aren't you?

Spencer nodded as a hiccup escaped his throat.

Death gently nudged Lucifer in the ribs. "Let it go," he whispered under his breath. "This guy's obviously an idiot. We have more important matters to deal with."

"Please don't leave me here alone. I won't survive another day," pleaded Spencer.

"Fine," said Lucifer. "You can help us figure out what happened around here."

"I still don't know your name," said Spencer as he extended his hand politely. "I figured he's the Grim Reaper," he said as he looked at Death.

"He is," said Lucifer with a grin. Knowing full well how much Death hated the name.

"Jerk," muttered Death under his breath.

Lucifer reached out for the shake. "I'm Lucifer."

Spencer's eyes doubled in size, and he quickly withdrew his hand before the shake could commence. "Lucifer?"

Lucifer nodded. "Pleased to meet you."

"As in the Prince of Darkness?" asked Spencer as he took a cautious step back.

"Yep. And I'm waiting for you to shake my hand. It's customary when someone offers it to you."

"That means you're Satan. As in, father to various spawn of Satan."

Lucifer nodded again. "I actually don't have any kids, but yeah, that's me."

Spencer's eyes widened further, and a scream ripped from his lungs that would make a ten-year-old girl jealous.

Lucifer and Death clasped their hands over their ears at the shrill sound. After fourteen seconds, the scream finally wound down, and Spencer gasped for breath.

"Do you feel better now?" asked Lucifer, more than a little surprised at the man's dramatic reaction.

"You can't be here, you're not allowed." Spencer frantically shook his head as if willing Lucifer away. "This is a holy place. The Angel of Darkness cannot be in Heaven. The rules forbid it."

"Rules, what rules?"

"There are protective curses placed at all the entrances to stop demons from getting in."

"I'm not a demon," said Lucifer.

"It doesn't matter. It includes you."

"So, what you're really saying is that the curse simply blocks out anyone who Gary doesn't like?"

Spencer held his hand up to his mouth in shock. "You used his name in vain!"

"That's his name, isn't it?" asked Lucifer.

"Well, yes, but you're not supposed to use it."

Death shook his head in frustration. "You can deal with this fool. I'm going to Gary's office."

"You said it too," gasped Spencer. "You can't use his name."

"Idiot," said Death as rolled his eyes at Spencer's objection and turned away from the frustrated man. "We've got better things to do."

Lucifer held up a finger to Death. "Give me a second. I'll be right behind you." He turned back to Spencer. He was starting to lose his patience with the irritating man. "Listen, Spencer, wasn't it?"

Spencer nodded.

Lucifer smiled politely. "Look, it's been nice meeting you, Spencer, but we're really in a bit of a hurry." Lucifer stepped forward to leave, but Spencer blocked his path.

Spencer brushed his hands towards Lucifer. "Shoo, shoo. Off with you, foul creature. I hereby banish you from this sacred place."

Lucifer stared at the lunatic. "Are you shooing me out of Heaven?"

"Yes. You don't belong here."

"Where do you think I started out?"

Spencer shrugged his shoulders. "I don't know. Possibly the burning pits of Hades, where all the scum and villainy are spawned."

"You're thinking of the Mos Eisley cantina," said Lucifer.

Spencer shrugged. "What's that?"

"Star Wars."

"Never heard of it. I don't watch contemporary government-funded military propaganda."

Lucifer frowned. Once again, Spencer proved he was an utter moron.

"You have no place here," said Spencer. "Never have, never will."

Lucifer knew his next words would crawl beneath Spencer's skin and send him into a flurry of objection and protest. He said them anyway. "Maybe you should brush up on your Bible studies instead of glossing over it."

Spencer's jaw fell and his eyes widened. "How dare you challenge my knowledge of the Holy tomes."

"I'm just saying—"

"HOW DARE YOU!"

Lucifer shrugged. "I just wanted you to know where I started out."

Spencer crossed his arms and turned away from Lucifer. "You are not, and never have been a candidate for Heaven."

"Nice try, cupcake. Is that what Gary told you?" asked Lucifer.

Spencer nodded. "Everyone knows this even without God telling us. Well, everyone except you, it seems."

"Well, you're wrong. I was an intern in the mailroom. Things were going great until a dozen of the female staff started a marry, fuck, kill competition. The women either wanted to marry me or fuck me, and every last one of them wanted to kill Gary. There was a disagreement about how gorgeous I am, and Gary's inferiority complex caused him to kick me out."

"You deserved to be kicked out," said Spencer. "What an abhorrent game."

Death frowned. While he was slightly prudish in nature, there wasn't a single planet that did not have its own version of marry, fuck, kill. With this knowledge, he knew that Lucifer's recollection was a tad off. "Don't you need three subjects to play—"

Lucifer smiled as he held a finger to his lips. Death rolled his eyes as he understood the goal was simply to irritate Spencer, nothing more.

"None of it matters," said Lucifer. "I'm fine with it. I'm having a good time downstairs, and I'm still gorgeous. We get a bad rap, but that's Gary's doing. He spread rumors about fiery pits, torture, and drunken orgies. Well, that last part is true."

"I can't be rescued by someone who partakes in drunken orgies," said Spencer.

"We have sober orgies, too, if you have an issue with alcohol."

"I do not want to spend my afterlife frolicking naked with people of the opposite sex."

"We have men too. Just tell me what you're into, we don't judge. Well, unless you're into kids and animals. You'll need to go somewhere else for that. We don't put up with that bullshit."

Spencer opened his mouth and inhaled, ready to scream again.

Lucifer gently placed a finger on the hysterical man's lips. "Shhh, calm your tits, sweetheart. Everything will be okay."

Spencer swatted his hand away. "Don't tell me to shhh when you are talking about depraved behavior. Heaven would not allow such heresy."

"And that is why we need to have Hell. To offset all of you closed-minded assholes, and give everyone a safe place to go, regardless of minority status. Hell isn't about criminals and deviants."

"That is exactly what Hell is about," said Spencer defiantly.

"Is this really what you believe or is that what you've been spoon-fed from years of hateful indoctrination?" said Lucifer. "Because if that is the case, you need to start thinking on your own."

Spencer crossed his arms and turned away from Lucifer. "There is nothing you can say that will make me want to join you on your quest. You are wasting your time."

"That's great. That's your prerogative." He started to push past Spencer. "We don't have time for your crisis of conscience."

"You can't honestly expect me to go with you. You can't make me."

Lucifer was done. He held no interest in helping with Spencer's moral dilemma. "That's fine. I am happy to leave your judgmental ass here."

Spencer gasped. "I am not judgmental."

"Please move. We've got shit to do. As you don't wish to shake my hand, I bid you good day. Now, please get out of my way." Lucifer nodded politely and continued after Death. "Steve, wait for me."

"Nope, not going," said Spencer as he watched Lucifer leave. "I'm keeping my happy butt right here."

"I'm not forcing you to leave," said Lucifer over his shoulder. "Do what you want. Although I'm not sure how many others will be along who will be quite as considerate."

Spencer's eyes widened at the statement. The new information drastically changed his perception on not going with Lucifer. "What do you mean others?"

"Once word gets out that Heaven is closed, there will be all kinds of unsavory folks snooping around. Looters, squatters. I mean, there may be others that stop by who are less considerate of your position and needs. People who will most likely throw you out on your ass. That's if you're alive at the end of the encounter."

Spencer held up his hand. "Wait for me, wait for me." He quickly stepped over to Lucifer's side. "What do you mean if I'm lucky?"

"Well," said Lucifer as he caught up with Death at the elevators. "Technically, you are trespassing, so who knows what the Council will do with you. They could try you for corporate espionage, conspiring for deity mutiny or worse."

"Worse?" asked Spencer. "How could any of this possibly be any worse than it already is?"

Lucifer frowned as he tried to get a read on Spencer. "They shut Heaven down. It's closed. All Christian-based followers on Earth now go directly to Hell, regardless of how they lived their life."

"Are you serious?"

"Yeah, of course I am. And do you have any idea how pissed off people get when they have spent their entire lives being good, honest God-fearing folk, only to end up being cast into the pits of Hell anyway? They do their best to avoid spending eternity with me and still wind up there. They're pissed. I'm pissed. If the Council is okay doing this, who knows what else they are capable of. I'd suggest that we come here for what we needed and get the hell out until we can get this sorted. As you can see, we don't have any more time for your personal issues."

"What are you here for?" asked Spencer. "What are you hoping to find?"

"We need to know where Gary went," said Death. "This all hinges on him."

"Gary was fired about a month ago," said Spencer, finally delivering information of use. "He's not here anymore."

"Really?" asked Lucifer as he mulled over the new twist to the story. "Do you know where he went?"

Spencer shook his head. "I didn't even know until three days ago. I haven't left this closet since everyone took off. I have a fear of being alone. My entire world is made up of barbecues and get-togethers. Without them, I'm nothing. But if the people aren't here, God's not here. No one is allowed to leave while God is in control. We could check Miley's logs in the waiting room. She keeps track of everyone coming and going. If there was a certified letter or shutdown notice, she'd most likely have signed for it."

"See, that's more like it," said Lucifer. "Now you're being useful." He pressed the already lit down button. "I need to use the bathrooms down there anyway."

"I already pushed the button," said Death.

"I know," said Lucifer. "A second push speeds it up. Everyone knows that."

The elevator pinged and the doors slowly opened.

"Are you coming, Spencer?" asked Lucifer as he followed Death inside.

Spencer pondered his options for a moment. Hang out with the Dark Prince, or return to hiding under his desk? He sighed as the painful choice became apparent. "Fine, I'm coming with you," he said as he stepped into the elevator and the doors closed. "But, if anyone asks if I'm hanging out with Satan, I'm going to deny it."

"Whatever helps you sleep at night, cupcake. Oh, and please don't call me Satan. I haven't gone by that name in years."

"I thought was your name."

"It isn't."

"Why do they call you Satan, then?"

"Funny story, actually. It was a typo I made on a Christmas card one year. I was Gary's secret Santa and apparently, I had been drinking too much and couldn't spell my own name. The rest, as they say, is history."

Spencer frowned as he considered Lucifer's excuse. "People only started using the name Santa Claus in the mid-eighteen hundreds. That was centuries after they started to call you Satan. You, sir, are lying."

"Of course I'm lying. I'm Lucifer. I'm supposed to. It's a perk of the job."

"Also, hard alcohol isn't allowed in Heaven," added Spencer.

"Not anymore," said Lucifer with a grin.

"I can see why God cast you out," said Spencer. "You're a difficult man to be around, Satan."

"You do realize that Satan is mostly used as an insult these days?"

"Of course I do. You are the devil, Satan."

"Would you like me to punch you in the face?" asked Lucifer.

"No."

"Then call me Satan one more time."

"Then what am I supposed to call you then?" asked Spencer. "Sir?"

"Just call me Lucifer or Luc. Whichever."

"Okay, sir Luc."

Lucifer laughed. "No, just Luc." He playfully ruffled Spencer's hair. "You and I are going to have an absolute blast together."

CHAPTER 10

Convinced speed was preferred over covertness, David lead the group of survivors through downtown Oceanview. One block turned to five, and five blocks turned to ten. Despite stopping to peek around corners, frantic looks at every out-of-place noise, and Warren tripping over his shoelaces twice, forty minutes later they reached the street across from the church with no sign of the Caretaker.

With the church finally in sight, David held his hand up to pause the group. "Wait here," he whispered. He slowly leaned around the corner to survey the parking lot. The yellow school bus Warren drove to the church in the final stand against the zombie-demon horde was still parked out front. "Muriel, report in," he said into his wrist-com.

"*I can't see it. It's off the tracker,*" replied Muriel from David's device.

"That's good, right?" asked Amber.

David nodded. "It's at least twenty blocks out. That means the church is clear."

"For now," said Warren, unconvinced the group would arrive at their destination safely.

"Well, that's better odds than we've had for the last couple of hours," said David. "It means it's moved on from the church, and it's expanding its search. We need to keep moving." He looked back at the group. "Keep heading east on Miller, and we'll stop at the park."

"*David, it's back on the tracker,*" Muriel's voice piped through the wrist-com.

"How close?" asked David.

"*On the edge of the range. But it's moving fast.*"

David turned to the group. "Okay, we need to pick up the pace," he said.

"*Nineteen blocks out.*"

"Are you serious?" asked Warren. "I thought you said it had a twenty-block range?"

"It does," said David. "Okay, move it," he yelled as the group took off running.

David led the team across Miller Road and into the street.

"*Eighteen blocks out.*"

"Would you tell her to shut up?" yelled Warren.

"What's wrong?" David shouted back over his shoulder.

"She's stressing me out."

"*Fifteen blocks.*"

"Fuck!" complained Warren. "How fast is this thing moving?"

"Faster than us," yelled Greg.

"*Ten.*"

"You know, giving us a countdown isn't exactly helping with my anxiety," huffed Warren.

"Faster," yelled David as the group sprinted towards a fence at the corner of Miller and Fifth Avenue.

"*Wait, it's disappeared.*"

"What?" asked David. "Repeat that."

"*It's gone from the tracker.*"

"How?" asked David as he signaled for the group to stop at the wall surrounding the downtown park, the remnants of the previous Forefather's Day event still scattered on the grass.

"*Wait, it's back at the edge of the range. Now it's two blocks. Wait, no, ten blocks. I don't know what's going on.*"

"Is the tracker broken?" asked David.

A loud thud of the tracker being hit echoed over the communicator. "*It's back to fifteen and not moving. But it's still on the screen.*"

"Any chance you could use a tracker that works?" suggested Warren.

David shook his head. "We only have one functioning. The other one wouldn't turn on."

"Has anyone up there heard of preventative maintenance?" asked Warren, once again completely underwhelmed at Heaven's collective incompetence.

"We've never needed to use them before. We found them in a drawer in a filing cabinet. I'm honestly surprised we even have one that works."

"Apparently, it doesn't," said Warren. "You want us to put our faith in turn-of-the-century tech you aren't even sure works?"

"Oh, it's way older than the two-thousands," said David.

"You're not helping your case whatsoever," said Warren.

"I tell you what, when we get back to Heaven, you can file a complaint," said David.

"You know what, I might just do that," said Warren.

"Muriel?" asked David. "Talk to me."

"*I think the tracker is working again. It's still sixteen blocks out and moving north again. How close are you?* "

"About a block," said David. He beckoned for Donovan to step over.

"What do you need?" asked Donovan as he moved up from the back of the line.

"He's on the tracker, but he's a ways off, which means we have a little more time. Head over to the church and check the entrance for any kind of traps it may have set."

"Traps?" said Ashley. "You mean like booby traps?"

'It's possible, yes," said David. "Unlikely, but I'd feel safer having one of my team check it out before we charge in there."

Donovan nodded and left the cover of the wall. He made it fifty feet before David's wrist-com crackled.

"*Wait, it's moving again.*"

"How far out?" said David.

"*Twelve blocks. Ten blocks. Eight blocks.*"

"Shit," muttered David. "New plan," he said to the group. "We break cover and head to the church."

"*ONE BLOCK!* " screamed Muriel. Her voice echoed through both the wrist-com and from down the street.

David's eyes widened as he turned towards Donovan running across the parking lot. "DONOVAN, GET DOWN!" he screamed. "IT'S HERE!"

Donovan stopped and looked around. The area was quiet. He spun to face David and raised his arms to shrug off the warning. "I don't see any—"

A crossbow bolt cut through the air and slammed into his forehead, and cracked through the back of his skull, sending a mess of brains, bone, and hair to the sidewalk. He wavered for a moment before toppling over into a lifeless heap.

"Fuck," yelled David.

"Brother!" shouted Celeste as she left the safety of cover and rushed to her fallen friend. A moment later, his body flickered and disappeared.

A second arrow erupted from an unknown origin, deadly accurate in its path. It penetrated Celeste in the left ear and quickly bridged the gap between its identical partner on the right side of her head. She dropped to the floor twenty feet from her teammate. As with Donovan, she too disappeared.

"Everybody stay back," ordered David. "It's found us."

"No fucking shit," shouted Warren. "What do we do?"

A woman's scream reverberated from the church tower. David spun in the direction of the cry to see Muriel tip over the railing and fall onto the parking lot sixty feet below. She landed with a dull splat, and like her other fellow angels, she disappeared.

David bit his lip in panic. "Shit, shit, shit," he stammered.

"What the fuck was that?" yelled Warren.

"Shit," yelled David again. He raised his wrist-com to his mouth. "Nathaniel, are you still in the church?"

"*Yeah, what's going on?* "

"It found us. Get the doors ready, we're coming in hot." He turned to the rest of the group. "We need to move now."

"What?" said Cam as her eyes widened. "That thing will kill us the second we step out there," said Cam.

"And we're most certainly dead if we stay here," said David. "We're out of options." He turned to face Antonio. "It's using a crossbow, that means it has to reload each time. I want to see how fast it takes to load its next arrow." He held out his hand towards Warren. "Quick, give me your hat."

Warren frowned with disapproval. "Oh, come on, man, that's my favorite cap."

"That's been sitting in Hank's basement for a decade," said David. "Give me the damn thing, Warren."

Warren grumbled under his breath and removed his 'Captain Planet' cap. He slapped it into David's hand. "Be careful with it."

Holding the cap by the brim, he poked it past the edge of the wall. On cue, an arrow slammed into the back of the cap. David yanked his hand back as he started to count. At ten seconds, he moved the cap out in the open again. "Eighteen, nineteen, twenty, twenty-o—" Another bolt slammed into the hat. "All right, we have twenty-one seconds," he said to the group.

"What?" asked Greg, ninety-nine percent sure of the awful plan David was about to suggest.

"It's taking twenty-one seconds to reload. If we run as a group, it won't have time to keep reloading new bolts. We'll act as your shield," said David as he pointed to his team.

"That's your fucking plan?" yelled Warren. "Throw more bodies than he can throw arrows? That's fucking terrible."

"Yeah, David," said Cam. "That's pretty weak. Surely, we have a better idea?"

David ignored the criticism. "We have twenty-one seconds between shots."

"That is not enough time to get across the street," said Warren. "It'll be able to reload."

"We're out of time and out of options," said David. "My team will protect you."

"Half your team is fucking dead," said Greg.

"I'm throwing the cap. The second that bolt hits, you run. On three, two—"

He tossed the cap onto the group six feet away, and an arrow instantly impaled it. "RUN!"

As one, the group sprinted across the parking lot.

At exactly twenty-one seconds, another bolt tore through the air and impaled Augustine's head, killing her instantly.

"Fuck," screamed Ashley as her Guardian Angel fell and disappeared.

Warren glanced to his left to see the Caretaker standing beside a car on the other side of the parking lot. "What the fuck is that?" he yelled.

"It's the Caretaker, keep running," shouted Antonio as he matched Greg's pace.

Greg looked over at the Caretaker. "He's fucking reloading," Greg shouted frantically. "Run faster!"

"How do you know it's a he?" Warren yelled back at him.

"What?" shouted Greg.

Warren panted as he headed towards the church. "Why do you assume it's a he? There are other genders it could be."

Greg held up his arms in disbelief. "Are you fucking serious? I hardly think this is the time to get into gender politics."

"I'm just saying these kinds of crass generalizations are hurting equality and—" As Warren decided to focus more on arguing with his brother rather than where he was placing his feet, he failed to notice a chunk of debris on the road ahead of him. His right foot smacked into the side of the concrete block, and he stumbled forward.

Greg was unable to react in time as he slammed into Warren and knocked him to the floor. For once, Warren's lack of attention worked in his favor. As Greg made impact, another bolt flew through the space Warren's head occupied a split second before.

Amber turned and stopped hearing the scuffle behind her. "Greg!" she screamed in panic.

"We're okay!" shouted Greg. He waved his hand and gestured for her to keep going. "Run! We're right behind you."

Antonio stopped and ran back over to Greg to help him up. "Come on!" he urged.

"Holy fuck," said Warren as he leaped to his feet. "That was close. Thanks, man," he said as he reached down and pulled his brother up. "I owe you one."

"Don't thank me, you're the one who can't focus. Let's settle up later," said Greg. "We need to keep moving."

The Caretaker let another arrow loose and it connected with Antonio's head, removing the last of David's angels.

"Fuck me," shouted Warren as he took off and sprinted towards the church, with Greg just a few feet behind him.

At the back of the group, David activated his wrist-com. "Nathaniel, who do we have left?"

"*Jebediah, Paul, and Derek.*"

"Get them out here now!" shouted David.

Nathaniel opened the church door, as Jebediah and Derek rushed out into the parking lot. A moment later, Paul rushed out to assist.

Cam and Ashley were the closest to the church door as Jebediah ran over to protect them. Blocking Ashley from the incoming arrow, his sacrifice allowed her to safely make it into the church. Derek similarly gave his life for both Amber and Cam.

The Caretaker cursed the miss under its breath as it loaded another arrow into its crossbow. It failed to anticipate the humans having other-worldly protection and growled to itself as it watched Derek collapse and disappear. Only the two male humans remained outside, and the speed they were approaching the church only allowed for one more shot before they reached temporary safety. With its bow loaded, it aimed the weapon at Warren's head, put its finger on the trigger, and fired.

Paul watched as the Caretaker released its arrow, and he dived towards Warren. The arrow hit the side of his head and covered Warren in a spray of blood and angel brains. He disappeared a second after hitting the floor, and the blood on Warren also quickly faded away.

"That's fucking gross," said Warren under his breath as the angel splatter on his face evaporated.

Warren made it across the parking lot and dashed into the church with David and Greg right behind him.

The Caretaker lowered its crossbow and marched towards the church. It pulled a dagger from its belt and threw it at Greg. The blade embedded itself into the door inches from Greg's head.

David pushed the heavy door closed behind him and pulled the large deadbolt across to lock them inside. "To the back of the church, now!" he shouted.

Greg leaned against the door to gather his breath. "Give me a second," he said as he held up a hand. A heavy slam against the door denied him his second, and he followed the rest of the group moved through the main hall to the small room at the far end of the church.

Cam pushed the door open to see a large column of white swirling light in the middle of the room. "Is this the—"

"Funnel?" continued David. "Yeah."

Greg entered the room and closed the door. "It's right behind us," he said.

"Everyone into the funnel," ordered Warren.

"No!" shouted David. "You need an angel to escort you. Else the funnel will fry you the second you touch it. Wait for me."

"We're going one at a time?" asked Warren incredulously.

"Yes," said David. "It's our only choice."

"Take Amber first. She's pregnant," ordered Greg, knowing the Caretaker could arrive at any time.

David nodded and held out a hand to Amber. "You're up."

Amber took his hand and looked at Greg.

"I'll be right up, I promise," said Greg with a smile.

"You'd better," said Amber as David stepped into the wall of energy and promptly disappeared.

Ten seconds later, David reappeared and extended a hand to Ashley.

You're next, Ash."

"I'll be right up, I promise," said Warren with a smile, mimicking his brother's pledge.

"I don't care," said Ashley. "Take your time."

Warren frowned as David and Ashley walked into the funnel. "Rude," he muttered to himself. "I was—"

A loud bang echoed from the main hall as the heavy front doors exploded off their hinges. Without hesitating, the two brothers rushed to the door and held it closed. Cam moved forward to help them with the barricade.

"Cam, you go next when he gets back," said Greg.

On cue, David reappeared as a heavy thud shook the door. Without speaking, he grabbed Cam's hand and escorted her away into the pulsing column of light.

"If the rest of his group hadn't have gotten themselves killed, this would be going much faster," griped Warren.

"They died saving your ass, Warren. We could have let it shoot you," said David as he stepped back out from the funnel. "Who's next?"

The next impact from the other side knocked Greg and Warren to the ground.

"Take Warren," shouted Greg.

The door shattered under the brutal and relentless assault, and the Caretaker climbed through the splintered wood. It looked around the room to get a bead on its quarry.

The two brothers scrambled to their feet and backed away from the creature. Their route to the funnel temporarily cut off.

In a single swift motion, the Caretaker removed both a long sword from a sheath on its belt, and another dagger, which it promptly launched at Greg.

Greg twisted as the blade sailed past his head and impaled the wall behind him. He exhaled in shock at the close call, but the situation offered little time for celebration. He turned, grabbed the knife, wall and launched it back at the Caretaker. It swatted it out of the air with a heavy steel gauntlet and advanced on the elder Hart brother. It grabbed another knife from its belt, and without looking, threw it in Warren's direction.

"Fuck," yelled Warren as he instinctively threw himself to the floor. The blade cut through the air and missed his left ear by an inch. While he was still a fair distance from athletic, Warren's reflexes certainly improved since the Oceanview outbreak.

The Caretaker swung its sword at Greg, narrowly missing decapitating him as Greg ducked and jumped away. The sharp blade cut deep into the wall and wedged firmly. The Caretaker pulled on the handle once, and meeting resistance, moved on to its next weapon. It preferred to not use a crossbow in close-quarter combat, but the irritating little humans were taking too long to die. It reached over its shoulder and unhooked its bow. It stabbed it down into a belt of arrows surrounding its left boot, loading the shaft into the flight groove. It lifted the weapon and pulled the string back.

If Warren not been fearing for his life, he would have been impressed by the Caretaker's dexterity and skill.

Greg stepped back into the corner of the room, and frantically looked around him for an escape route. "Fuck," he muttered to himself. He found himself with nowhere else to go but a nearby wooden pillar.

The Caretaker aimed at his head and fired.

Without thinking, Warren scooped up a nearby chair and threw it across the room towards his brother. The wooden seat sailed through the air and intercepted the bolt mid-flight. It crashed to the ground in multiple pieces, saving Greg from receiving an arrow in the face, and almost certain death.

"Dude, did you fucking see that?" cheered Warren, triumphant in his Hollywood-grade action.

"Thanks," acknowledged Greg as he scrambled behind the pillar. Although he did not say it out loud, he was impressed by his brother's act.

"Thanks?" said Warren. "Is that all I get for saving your life? That was fucking bad-ass."

The sudden change in position put David closer to Greg and opened an opportunity to save one of the brothers. David grabbed his hand and stepped towards the funnel.

"No!" shouted Greg. "Take Warren first."

Warren looked over at David and nodded, giving him permission to take his brother.

"No, don't," Greg screamed as he tried to wrench his hand free, but David was not relaxing his grip. "David, let me go," he protested. "I don't want to be next. Take Warren, please."

Warren looked over at his brother. "Go! I've got this. David, get him out of here."

David stepped into the funnel as the Caretaker took aim for a second time.

Warren saw the bow lift and charged at the dark creature. He slammed into its side and tackled it to the floor. As the two made impact, the crossbow fired. The bolt cut through the air and slammed into Greg's shoulder just as he and David disappeared.

CHAPTER 11

"Didn't you need the bathroom?" asked Death as he watched Spencer bouncing from left foot to right, clutching his bladder.

"Yes," said Spence as he stared at the waiting room bathroom door.

"So why are you acting like you need to pee when you could be in the bathroom peeing?"

"I can wait."

"Are you sure about that?" asked Death. "You look like you really need to go."

"I'm fine," lied Spencer.

Death smiled to himself aware of the fact that Spencer did not want to be in the bathroom alone with Lucifer. "He's going to be in there a while. Do you think you can hold it in?"

Spencer hopped from one foot to the other as he decided he could not wait much longer. For a fleeting moment he considered relieving himself in his pants.

"Just go use the bathroom, Spencer," said Death as if reading his mind.

Spencer cautiously walked over to the bathroom and pushed the door open a few inches to peek inside. Lucifer was in one of the closed stalls, so he felt a little more confident to enter. He softly walked over to one of the urinals and unzipped his pants. The second he started to pee, Lucifer's toilet flushed, and the stall door opened.

Spencer's heart rate accelerated tenfold as he turned his head ever so slightly to get a bearing on Lucifer. His skin crawled as he watched the man walk over to the sink and turned on the water.

"Hey Spencer," said Lucifer as he pumped the soap onto his hands. Spencer's conspicuous side-stare was quite apparent to Lucifer, and he smiled to himself at the man's discomfort. "Eyes forward, sport. You're peeing on your shoe."

Spencer moved his eyes to the floor to see a puddle of urine forming around his feet. He refocused his aim back on the porcelain bowl, torn between finishing the task at hand and keeping an eye on the Prince of Darkness. For the immediate future, his stretched bladder took precedence over his paranoia.

Lucifer grinned as he watched Spencer trying to pee. He finished rinsing his hands and turned off the faucet. He flicked the excess water off his fingers and turned to face his panicked bathroom associate.

Spencer closed his eyes in dread. Time seemed to be slowing down as his bladder took its sweet time evacuating. Eventually, the last drop of pee dribbled out. He frantically shook his member, desperate to tuck it back into his underwear.

"Careful," said Lucifer. "Anything more than three shakes is playing with yourself."

"I am not playing with myself," said Spencer as he zipped up his pants and walked over to the sink.

"I've figured out what your problem is," said Lucifer as he politely turned on the faucet for Spencer.

"I have a problem?" stammered the nervous man.

"You do," said Lucifer. "I think you're sexually repressed."

"Excuse me?" asked Spencer as he deliberately avoided eye contact with Lucifer and focused every part of his body on the flowing water before him. Not only was he not interested in discussing sex with a stranger, he most certainly was not interested in talking about it with Lucifer. While he was already well established in Heaven, and the chances of being sent to Hell were non-existent, he was still concerned about the eternal consequences of sin.

"You've spent your entire life believing a book that forbids sexual expression. I see how you look at me. You're attracted to me, but your religion forbids it."

Spencer's jaw fell open. "I am not attracted to you!" he said in horror.

"Oh, you can be honest with me," said Lucifer. "I've seen it a million times. I think it's kinda sad that you hold a belief with such reverence, but it doesn't allow you to be who you really are." Lucifer was not convinced that Spencer felt any homosexual cravings, but he did enjoy making the poor fellow squirm.

Spencer turned the water off and pulled a paper towel from the dispenser. "Get away from me," said Spencer as he tossed the wet towel into a nearby trash can and reached into his shirt. He pulled out a small tin whistle and held it up to his lips.

Lucifer frowned at the small device. "Is that a rape whistle?"

"Stay back, or I'll blow it."

"You'll blow what? Me, or the whistle?"

Spencer's cheeks puffed up, and he blew into the whistle, letting out a shrill single-toned, ear-piecing scream.

Lucifer held his hands to his ears as Spencer continued his ejection of air. "Fuck, man! What the hell are you doing?"

"Scaring you away," said Spencer as he exhaled into the whistle a second time.

Lucifer rubbed his ringing ears in an effort to stop the painful echo. "Please don't do that again."

"Then maybe you should keep your distance."

"Duly noted," said Lucifer as he gestured to the door. "You could be a little nicer to me, though."

"Excuse me?" said Spencer.

"You're mean."

Spencer paused at the comment. People called him many things over his lifetime, but being told he was not nice was not among them, and the statement rattled him. "I'm sorry. I'm just a little jumpy with everything going on around here lately."

Lucifer appreciated the notion. He smiled warmly as he opened the bathroom door and gestured for Spencer to leave. While he did enjoy teasing the poor fellow, he could see the man was a wreck. Both of their routines were clearly upended, and poking fun at his expense helped no one. He followed Spencer out of the bathroom into the main waiting room. "Just relax. There's nothing out here that can hurt you. Heaven is locked down. Even Death couldn't—"

The front doors to the waiting room swung open and David and Amber entered.

"Wait here," said David. "I'll be right back."

Amber nodded, and David left the room and ran back down the hallway towards the funnel.

Lucifer turned to Death standing in the middle of the room equally confused. "Uh? What the fuck was that?"

Death shrugged as Amber turned to face them. Her eyes widened as the strangers revealed themselves. "Hi?" she offered cautiously.

Fifteen seconds later, David reappeared at the door with Ashley. She looked around the room for her sister as David vanished to grab Cam. She noticed Death, Lucifer, and Spencer standing by the bathroom and backed away towards Amber, unsure who the strangers were.

David reappeared and added an equally disorientated Cam to the group. He returned to the funnel with the intention of bringing Greg and Warren back.

Fifteen seconds later, David failed to return with either of the brothers, and Amber was starting to worry. "Where are they?" she asked no one in particular.

Twenty seconds became thirty, and thirty soon became a minute.

Ashley could sense the panic on her sister's face. "I'm sure everything is fine," she said. Not entirely convinced her prognosis was accurate or true.

A minute later, David's voice could be heard coming from down the hallway. "Help me," he yelled.

Cam, Amber, and Ashley rushed out of the waiting room to the funnel. David staggered towards them, supporting the injured Greg.

"He's been shot," said David as Amber and Cam helped take Greg from him.

Greg yelped in pain as Amber noticed a black arrow in his chest, a few inches above his heart. "Oh my god," she said, her eyes full of fear.

"I'm going back for Warren," said David as he handed off Greg. "Greg needs to lay down. There's a hospitality suite on the second floor right above us. Go through the door next to the customer service window, and the elevators are straight ahead. Head to the right and the second door on the right has a room with couches and beds we can use."

Amber struggled to remember the directions as she and Cam helped Greg towards the door.

"It's okay," said Cam sensing Amber's confusion. "I remember what he said."

Greg's weight proved to be a struggle for them, and he slumped to the floor.

Lucifer rushed over to help and grabbed Greg's arm from Amber. "Here, let me help." He threw a concerned side-eyed glance at Death. The new turn of events piqued his curiosity. He was certain they were all related to the evacuation of Heaven, and he felt things were about to get interesting.

"Who are you?" asked Cam to the shockingly attractive man helping her with Greg.

"Let's get your injured friend here taken care of, and then we can work on formal introductions."

"Can we trust you?" asked Cam as they guided Greg through the door.

Lucifer smiled. "Of course you can. You're in Heaven, you can trust everyone here."

As they passed through the door, Spencer opened his mouth to disagree. Death noticed his intent to reveal Lucifer's identity and slowly shook his head. "Not now," he said quietly. "As he said, we'll do introductions later."

"Where are we taking him?" asked Lucifer.

Cam nodded to the hallway before them. "David mentioned a hospitality suite on the floor above us."

"I think I know where it is," said Lucifer as he directed Cam and Greg.

Amber walked a few steps behind them, worried sick about Greg. Her heart raced at every groan and hiss as his discomfort increased. As the elevators came into view, she rushed ahead to the panel. The nearest elevator doors opened the moment she pressed the up button and Greg was carried inside.

"I'll get the next one," said Ashley as she reached the doors. "I want to make sure Warren is okay."

Amber nodded and pressed the second-floor button as she looked back at Greg as the doors closed. Sweat started to pool on his forehead, and his skin was becoming pale and clammy. "Hold in there, babe," she said as she placed a hand on his back.

A shrill ping rang out and the elevator doors opened. Lucifer led Greg from the elevator and passed an open balcony that looked into the waiting room below. Following David's directions, they carried Greg to the second door on the right and found a room with a couch and a couple of love seats. "Over here," said Cam as she and Lucifer moved Greg to the couch.

Greg carefully sat down and swung his legs up onto the seat. He laid his head back and tried to focus on anything but the pain.

"What happened?" asked Amber.

"That fucking thing shot me as I was leaving," said Greg between clenched teeth.

"What's your name?" asked Lucifer as he crouched down next to the injured man.

"Greg."

"Pleased to meet you, Greg. I'm Lucifer. Luc to my friends."

"The Lucifer?" asked Greg.

"One and the same. How's it going?"

"I've had better days."

"May I?" asked Lucifer as he pointed at the arrow.

Greg nodded. "Just please be careful. This thing burns like a motherfucker."

Lucifer studied the arrow and rubbed his chin. "I'm going to need to pull the arrow out."

Greg tried to sit up. "What?"

"We need to get it out of you before it gets infected."

Greg slowly nodded and laid back down.

"I'm going to need you to clench your teeth. This is going to hurt," said Lucifer. He reached for the arrow, and before he made contact with the wooden shaft, Greg screamed in agony. Lucifer stepped back from Greg.

"Jesus-fucking-Christ, what the fuck did you do?" screamed Greg as saliva sprayed from his mouth.

Lucifer raised his hands. "I didn't touch it, I swear."

"Bullshit," said Greg.

"He didn't," confirmed Cam. "He never touched you."

Lucifer stepped back from Greg. "How are you feeling now?"

Greg frowned as he took stock of his pain limit. "It's actually feeling a bit better since you stepped away." He tried to prop himself up on his elbows.

"You need to lay down," said Lucifer.

"What's going on?" asked a voice from behind.

Lucifer turned to see Death waiting at the door. Ashley and Spencer stood out in the hallway flanking the entrance. "Come and look at this," said Lucifer as he beckoned Death over.

Death walked over and crouched down next to Greg. "Hi, I'm Death."

Greg grinned weakly. "Yeah, I kinda figured that. The robes gave it away."

"Is that an arrow?" asked Death.

Lucifer nodded. "Greg, I'm going to have my friend here reach for the shaft."

"Please don't," begged Amber. "That really hurt him."

"He's not going to touch it, I promise," said Lucifer as he looked at Death. "Move real slow."

Death carefully moved his hand towards the arrow, but Greg remained calm, despite anticipating a searing pain.

"Still doing okay there, Greg?" asked Lucifer.

"Actually, yeah," said Greg. "It didn't hurt. Well, not anymore that it already does."

"Move your hand away," directed Lucifer.

As Death moved his hand away, Lucifer slowly moved his own hand closer to the arrow. Greg's hands clenched into fists, and he arched his back in agony. Lucifer quickly pulled away, and Greg settled back down.

Death cocked his head and looked at Lucifer, his brain running in overdrive. "Interesting," he said. "Does anyone have a knife I can use for a minute?"

Amber's eyes widened. "No! You are not cutting it out of him!" she ordered.

Death shook his head and held up a hand to ease her concerns. "No, no, I'm not going to remove it. I just need to cut his shirt. I want to see the wound."

"I have one," said Cam as she reached into her pocket. She fished out a small knife and tossed it over to Death.

Death caught the blade and looked down at Greg. "Tell me if any of this hurts."

Greg nodded and clenched his teeth in anticipation of the inevitable torture.

Death carefully started to cut the shirt away from the area around the arrow. He pulled the ripped fabric away to see the wound was mysteriously devoid of blood or damage. Death frowned and rubbed his chin pensively. "How's the pain now?"

Greg slowly exhaled as the anticipated extra pain never arrived. "It hurts bad, but it's manageable."

Death reached out and carefully touched the flight of the arrow. "How about now?"

Greg shook his head. "No change. What did you do?"

"Nothing." Death exhaled. "I need Lucifer to touch the arrow. It's probably going to hurt, but I need to see what happens."

Cam raised an eyebrow and looked at Death at the name drop. It was the first time she heard Lucifer mentioned by name.

"Is there another way?" asked Amber before Cam could speak.

"Not if we want to figure out how to get it out of him," said Death. "Are you ready, Greg?"

Greg closed his eyes and nodded with slow unconvincing movements.

Lucifer reached out for the arrow, and a web of black, angry veins snaked away from the arrow and across Greg's torso. Greg roared in agony.

Lucifer jerked his hand away from the arrow and covered his mouth. "Shit," he muttered through his finger.

As he moved his hand back, the veins retracted and retreated towards the arrow. Lucifer frowned as he looked up at Death, trying to get a read on his face.

"Once more," directed Death. "But this time touch the arrow." He looked down at Greg. "I'm so sorry, Greg. This will be the last time, I promise."

Amber squeezed Greg's hand as if trying to transfer his discomfort.

"Honey?" said Greg between clenched teeth. "You're crushing my hand."

"Oh," said Amber as she loosened her grip. "Sorry."

With Greg momentarily distracted, Lucifer once again reached out for the arrow. The veins reappeared, and as his fingers touched the arrow, they swarmed Greg's torso. He screamed violently as the infection crawled up his neck and across his face.

Lucifer removed his hand, and the veins retracted, albeit a little slower than before. Amber gently squeezed Greg's hand as he exhaled a pained breath.

"No more," said Greg. "I can't."

"Who did you say did this?" asked Lucifer.

"We didn't," said Amber. "It was something called the Caretaker."

Lucifer looked up at Death and raised his eyebrows. Death slowly nodded his head in a solemn and silent understanding. Lucifer's eyes widened and gave Death a *'come on, you can't be serious'* look as the silent conversation continued. Death nodded his head once again.

"Is one of you going to say something?" asked Amber.

"Give us just a second," said Death as he stood up. He grabbed Lucifer by the collar and dragged him away from Greg and out of the room for some makeshift privacy.

"What?" asked Lucifer as he continued to follow Death.

Death finally stopped twenty feet away from the room. "You know what this is, don't you?" he said softly but urgently.

Lucifer frowned. "I *think* I know what this is."

"No. You know exactly what this is."

Lucifer held his hands to his temples in part confusion, part shock. "Come on, Steve, Impiety Arrows are a myth. I know it, you know it."

"And yet we're staring at one."

"It has to be something else," said Lucifer as if saying it would make it so.

"What else in the known Universe does that?"

Lucifer grimaced, desperate to come to a different conclusion. One that did not involve using mystical and forbidden arrows, used in only but the most violent situations. "Nothing."

Death lowered his voice further. "I say we pack up and leave. Forget these people, I don't know what they are involved with, but I don't want any part of it."

Lucifer shook his head. "We're already involved. Your broken lists and the extra residents in my neck of the woods confirm it."

"I didn't ask for this," said Death.

"And I did?" asked Lucifer. "We're balls deep in this now."

"None of this makes sense," said Death. "Who would send an assassin after these guys?"

"I don't know, but we have just stepped into a colossal pile of shit of epic proportions."

An agitated cough snapped their attention back to the group.

Ashley, her arms planted firmly on her hips in frustration, stared in bewilderment at the private discussion. "I really don't think this is the time for whispering," she said. "Is one of you going to tell us what the fuck is going on?"

Lucifer lowered his head and sighed heavily. He walked back into the room with Death trailing behind him. He exhaled as he faced the group. "This is some serious bullshit," he muttered under his breath. "Look, there's no easy way to say this, so I'll just cut to it. Greg's been shot with an Impiety Arrow."

"An Impiety Arrow? What's that?" asked Amber.

"It's dark magic," said Lucifer. "I'm talking really fucking evil shit."

"So, it came from Hell?" asked Ashley.

"Pfft, fuck off," said Lucifer, mildly offended at the accusation. "I promise you, we have nothing to do with this type of thing."

"I'm sorry," said Ashley. "I just assumed as it was evil that you had something to do with it."

Lucifer frowned in genuine frustration. "Why does everybody assume that all I do all day is kill and murder people? Contrary to what you've heard, nobody gets tortured under my watch. Sure, we do BDSM shit, but fuck, most of your closet Christians do that kind of kinky shit too. They're just too ashamed to admit it. What we don't do is fucking poison people and turn them into demons. This is some hardcore, Old Testament, wrath of God shit-sandwich, fuckery right here."

Ashley's ears pricked up at the mention of dark magic. "I know my way around the Bible, and I'm pretty familiar with biblical weaponry, but I've never heard of Impiety Arrows," she said. "Are you sure it's from the Bible?"

"Oh, it's not something you'll find in the Bible. God doesn't want mortals knowing about this kind of weapon doing the rounds. None of us do."

"So, it's God's weapon?" asked Cam.

"No," said Lucifer. "As much as I'd love blame him, this isn't Gary's fault." He sighed and shook his head as he mulled the facts he was facing. "I'll be honest, we didn't even think they existed." He pointed to Death. "We've heard about them, but we all assumed it was all an exaggerated myth. You know how these things go, you hear about something so absurd, so impossible, that it just doesn't make any sense."

"There's other weapons not mentioned in there?" asked Cam.

"There's a few more," said Lucifer. "But this one is the nastiest of the bunch. Whoever used this was not fucking around. Someone wanted you guys dead in the worst, most painful way possible."

"Is Greg going to be okay?" asked Amber, her concern obvious.

Death shook his head. "No, he's not."

Amber's eyes widened in shock at the blunt announcement, her hopes of good news dashed.

Ashley was not impressed at the blunt response. "Really? You know you could have softened that blow just a little bit," she said with an irritated frown.

Death shrugged. "I'm sorry, but what's the point in sugarcoating it? Saying it nicely doesn't change anything. She asked for the truth, and I gave her the truth. Would you have rather I lied about it?"

"Her fiancé is injured by some biblical weapon, and you're just indifferent. Your bedside manner could really use a polish, or are you really that callous?"

"Listen, ma'am, I'm Death. I spend all day, every day killing people. If I got all choked up over every person I've watched die who did or did not deserve it, I'd probably off myself. Being detached is part of the job requirement. My empathy went out the window centuries ago. I didn't have a choice, it had to. There is no way I could get the job done if it didn't."

Greg struggled to sit up. "Lucifer, you mentioned a demon. What about it?" asked Greg through gritted teeth, jumping on Lucifer's earlier comment.

"I'm not going to lie to you, Greg," said Lucifer. "If we don't get this arrow out of you in the next week, you're going to turn into a demon. And a pretty nasty one."

"Like the zombie-demons in Oceanview?" asked Amber, her face still dressed with concern.

"No, not even close. Those were just empty human shells with black eyes. They were kittens compared to this. I'm talking full-on fire-breathing, pointed wings, horned demon."

"That sounds fun," said Greg through a forced smile. "Can I use the carpool lane?"

Amber did not appreciate attempt Greg's humor at such a serious moment. "That's not funny." She turned towards Lucifer and Death. "Why can't we just pull it out?"

"I can't," said Lucifer. "It requires two of us to remove it."

"There are two of you, I don't understand," said Amber.

"No, Death can't remove it. It has to be me and Gary pulling it at the same time."

"Gary? Who's that?" asked Amber.

"You mean God, don't you?" said Cam.

Lucifer nodded.

"Then you are *the* Lucifer, aren't you?" asked Cam.

Lucifer nodded again. "I'm sorry, where are my manners?" He bowed politely and stretched out an arm before him. "Lucifer Morningstar at your service."

"You are fucking gorgeous," Cam blurted out. She didn't even bother to catch herself.

Lucifer smiled. It was not the first time he heard such compliments from either sex. "That was eloquent," he said with a grin.

"You expect me to apologize?" asked Cam as she stared at the ridiculously good-looking man standing in front of her. "They really weren't shitting when they called you Heaven's most beautiful angel, were they?"

Lucifer smiled for a second and raised a knowing eyebrow. "Nope, but I never tire of hearing it. You're not hard on the eyes either." Cam's demeanor immediately caught him off guard, and he found himself mysteriously drawn to the woman.

Cam blushed at the compliment. "Thanks," she said. In an effort to distract from her mild embarrassment, she tried to change the subject. "Hell, even that guy can't keep his eyes off you." She nodded over to Spencer, standing at the back of the group with his eyes fixed on Lucifer.

"Oh, he's just pissed that he thinks I'm the Anti-Christ. Personally, I never even met Christ when he was alive, so how I can be anti-Christ make no sense. It's like being anti-broccoli without ever eating it. Therefore, in his eyes, I need to be cleansed."

"I'll cleanse you," Ashley said with a sly grin.

Cam looked over at her and mock scowled. It seems she faced competition for the Devil. "Hands off bitch, he's mine."

"We'll see." Ashley returned the playful banter.

"Okay, ladies," said Lucifer. "I appreciate the compliments, but I don't think this is the time or place."

"Don't flatter yourself," said Ashley. "You're not really my type." She winked at Cam. "I'm just fucking with you. He's all yours."

"Do I get your names?" asked Lucifer with a smile.

Cam raised her hand. "Cam."

"Pleased to meet you, Cam," said Lucifer.

Ashley and Amber introduced themselves, and Lucifer politely nodded his welcome.

"Who are your friends?" asked Cam.

Lucifer pointed to Death. "This lovely fellow over here is my esteemed colleague, Death."

"As in the Grim Reaper?" asked Ashley.

"As in Death," said Death. "Please don't call me that."

"Why not?" asked Ashley.

"Because I don't like it."

"I thought—" started Ashley.

"You thought wrong," interrupted Death.

Lucifer gestured toward Spencer, who remained remarkably quiet the entire time. "And this delightful little sprite is called Spencer. We go way back, don't we?"

Spencer inhaled and let out one of his trademarked pre-teen screams. The high-pitched wail continued for five seconds and then ten.

Before it reached fifteen seconds, Lucifer placed his hand over Spencer's mouth. "Okay, sweetheart, calm down. You're going to scare out gues—"

Spencer bit down hard on Lucifer's hand.

"Ow! Motherfucker." Lucifer ripped his hand away. "You bit me, you asshole." He looked down at the bloody bite mark on his hand. "And you drew blood."

Spencer wiped the back of his hand across his lip to see a small trickle of blood on his skin.

"How does it taste?" asked Lucifer.

The realization hit Spencer like a truck. "Oh my god, I've ingested demon blood!" His cheeks puffed up as he dry heaved.

Amber started to get agitated at the derailing of the issue of Greg. "If you guys are done flirting and goofing around, how do we get this arrow out of Greg?"

"My apologies," said Lucifer. "Gary and I must remove the arrow at the exact same time. The mix of good and evil allows it to pull free with the poison. If either one of us pulls it on our own, Greg dies instantly."

"Even if God does it on his own?" asked Amber

"Especially if God does it. He's the evil one."

"He is not!" exclaimed Spencer, shocked at Lucifer's brazenness. "You, sir, are the evil one. The Bible says so, and I won't hear anything to the contrary."

Lucifer winked at Spencer. "Oh, you know you love me."

Spencer held his hands to his mouth in protest. "I do not!"

Lucifer grinned again. He enjoyed winding Spencer up. "It really doesn't have to be simply good and evil. It's more about polar opposites. Light, dark, right, wrong, angels, and demons. I was cast from Heaven and my wings removed, so now I'm the opposite of God."

Cam stepped forward. "I hate to be the one to bring this up, but where is God? Can't we just go to see him?"

"He's gone," said Lucifer.

"What do you mean he's gone?" asked Cam.

"That's why Death and I are here," said Lucifer. "Something is going down, and we're still trying to piece it all together. Heaven's been evacuated, God is missing, and now we find out someone has sent a Caretaker after you. We're all stuck in the middle of something big."

"You've heard of Caretakers?" asked Cam.

Lucifer nodded. "We have, but they aren't supposed to carry anything like an Impiety Arrow."

"Amber?" called Greg.

"You need to rest, love. We're trying to figure this all out."

"Where's Warren?" asked Greg.

In their rush to flirt with Lucifer and decipher the arrow, the group neglected to notice that neither Warren nor David returned from the church.

CHAPTER 12

Cam and Ashley sprinted back to the elevator and returned to the waiting room. As they pushed the door open beside the customer service window, David was already crossing the room.

"Where's Warren?" asked Ashley, her face already showing signs of concern.

David shook his head. "He wasn't there when I went back."

"Where did he go?" asked Ashley, visibly shaken that something may have happened to her ex.

"I don't know. There were signs of a struggle. I found more arrows in the wall, but they were both gone."

"Did the Caretaker get him?" asked Cam.

David shook his head again. "I don't know. I didn't see the scorch marks like we found with Lee and Reverend Ellis. But neither one of them were there." David saw the pain on Ashley's face but was unable to offer words of comfort. "I'm sorry, Ashley, I doubt he was strong enough to fight the Caretaker. None of us were. If we didn't have the angels, we'd all be dead."

Ashley nodded. She understood the gravity of David's words. "Did you leave the church?" asked Ashley.

"Of course," said David. "I went outside, and I shouted and looked."

"So why was the Caretaker gone?" asked Cam.

"I don't know where it went. If I were to guess, I'd say it couldn't complete its mission and left to report its findings."

Ashley knew David made sense, but it did little to help her accept the inevitable. "We have to find him," said Ashley. "Take me back down there, and I'll help you."

"We can't," said David. "It's too dangerous. I don't have enough people to protect you. Until we can figure out what is going on, the only place you're safe is right here. I can no longer protect you in Oceanview."

Ashley closed her eyes. While her feelings remained the same towards Warren, she wished she'd chosen her last words to him more thoughtfully. "Take your time," she said.

"Excuse me?" said Cam.

"The last thing I said to Warren was take your time. I didn't mean it this way."

"Don't do this to yourself," said Cam. "This isn't your fault." She turned to David. "So, what do we do now? We need to tell Greg."

"I'll do it," said Ashley.

"Are you sure?" said David.

"Yeah. It needs to come from me."

David nodded. "Is everyone still upstairs?"

"Yeah," said Cam. "We found some other people you should probably meet."

♦♦♦♦

"Where's Warren?" asked Greg as Ashley walked into the room.

Ashley looked at Death and Lucifer and nodded towards the door, indicating they should leave. Lucifer placed a gentle hand on Ashley's shoulder as he followed Death out of the room. Greg struggled to sit upright as only Amber and Ashley remained.

Ashley exhaled softly as she took Greg's hand. "He's gone," she said.

"No," said Greg. "He can't be. David went right back for him."

"He wasn't there," said Ashley. "The Caretaker wasn't there. The church was empty."

Tears welled up in Greg's eyes as survivor's guilt tore through him. "It should have been me. I told him to go first. He should have gone through first. I should have stayed and protected him. It was my job. It's my fault he's gone."

Amber squeezed his hand. "It's not your fault," she said, knowing her words of comfort would offer little solace to Greg's grief. If the brothers switched places, he would be the one being mourned, and she would be consoling Warren as her heart was torn from her chest. She hated herself for the battle of emotions she experienced. "I'm so sorry," was all she could muster.

Greg collapsed back onto the couch as the pain in his shoulder became too intense. The fight in the church replayed over and over in his head as he tried to find an ending where both brothers would make it out alive. He was furious with David for taking his choice away from him.

♦♦♦♦

Outside in the hallway, David watched as Lucifer and Death exited the lounge.

"Who are you?" asked Lucifer.

"I'm David."

"Just David?" asked Lucifer.

"First hierarchy Guardian Angel David."

"That's a rather pretentious title, isn't it?" asked Lucifer.

"Don't blame me," said David. "I didn't ask for it. Hell, I'm an atheist. I shouldn't even be here."

Lucifer's eyebrows lifted. "Oh, you're that David. I've heard all about you."

"In the flesh. Well, mostly. I'm guessing you're Lucifer" David nodded towards Death. "And judging by the robes, you're Death."

"You're quite astute," said Lucifer. "Who are these guys? Why are they so important?"

"They're the Oceanview Seven," said David. "We had some issues with God a few months ago."

"Ah, those guys," said Lucifer as more pieces of the puzzle slipped into place. "Well, this is starting to make a bit more sense then."

"You've heard of them?" Asked David.

"Oh, yeah," said Lucifer. "Who hasn't? We've all heard of the Oceanview Seven. It's considered Gary's greatest blunder. However, I think you might be three short, aren't you?"

"No, the Caretaker got to them. There's only four left. It's been a rough day."

"What happened?" asked Death.

"By the time I knew the Caretaker was out there, it had already killed two of them. It killed the third while we trying to escape the church."

"We can't let the rest of them leave until we figure out what's going on," said Lucifer. "There's too much at stake."

David stepped further away from the room to get out of earshot from Cam and Ashley. He nodded for Lucifer and Death to join him. "I need you two to be straight with me. What's going on with Greg?"

"What do you mean?" asked Lucifer. "He was shot."

"I know he was shot," said David. "I saw the black smoke around the wound. The only weapon that does that is an Impiety Arrow."

"That's exactly what it is," said Lucifer. "I'm surprised you've heard of them. I thought that stuff was kept secret."

"I wasn't a hundred percent sure, but you just confirmed my suspicions."

"But how did you find out about them?" asked Death.

"Well, I'm still under a twelve-month probation period," said David. "I'm not allowed to go most places in Heaven, so I spend a lot of time in the archives reading and studying

"I bet you found some good stuff in there," said Lucifer with a smirk.

"Oh, you know I did," said David with a knowing grin. "There's all kinds of fun things you won't find in the Bible. I also know that Impiety Arrows are the weapons of demons. The Caretaker is not a demon."

Lucifer would be lying if he said that the thought never crossed his mind. "I think we're dealing with something far more sinister than it seems. We need to figure out who wants these people dead."

"And fast," said David.

"How long does he have?" asked Cam, who quietly walked up behind them.

The group turned to face Cam, as Ashley and Amber joined her.

"And please be honest with us," said Amber. "We don't have time to sugar coat it."

"We have one hundred and sixty hours," said Death.

"That's specific," said Cam. "Why that amount?"

"A hundred and sixty-eight hours is seven days," said Lucifer. "The Universe has this colossal boner for the number seven. Even Hell got lumped with the seven circles."

"Aren't there nine?" asked Cam.

"Yeah, but I'm not really much of a conformist, so I added heresy and lust to bump it up a bit. Besides, nine is my lucky number."

"Really?" said Cam. "I was born September ninth."

"Is that so?" said Lucifer with a smile.

"Uh, still not the time, guys," said Amber. "We have more important things to discuss."

"Sorry," said Cam as she caught herself

"What is our plan?" asked Amber as she directed the conversation back on track.

"I don't know about you two," said Lucifer as he gestured to Death and Spencer, but I think we should start in Gary's office."

Death nodded in agreement. "He uses his computer for everything. It's as good a place as any."

"We can't get up there," said David. "I already tried, but the elevator's locked."

Lucifer fished the janitor's I.D. card from his pocket and waved it in front of him. "One step ahead of you. I've got us covered."

David shook his head. "That won't work. General janitors don't have access."

"Who would then?" asked Lucifer.

"All department heads have access to his receptionist," said David. "They need to be able to stop by."

As one, the group turned to face Spencer.

"What are you looking at?" asked Spencer as he spun around to check if someone was standing behind him.

"The man who is going to get us up to Gary's office," said Lucifer.

Spencer pointed at his chest. "Me?"

Lucifer nodded.

"How?"

"With the I.D. badge hanging around your neck." Lucifer pointed at the lanyard in the middle of Spencer's chest. "The one next to your rape whistle."

"Why do you need a rape whistle in Heaven?" asked Cam.

"Because Lucifer made me uncomfortable when we were in the bathroom earlier today," said Spencer as his hands moved to his whistle and held it for support.

"He's not afraid to use it too," said Lucifer. "The fucking thing is really loud."

"He made me blow it," said Spencer.

"The whistle or Lucifer?" asked Cam.

Lucifer smiled as Cam mirrored his earlier comment to Spencer. "Oh, I like you."

Cam smiled as Lucifer held out his hand towards Spencer and gestured for him to hand over his badge.

Spencer shook his head. "I don't think my moral compass would allow me to assist the Devil in violating God's personal office space."

"Just give me the badge. You don't have to come."

Spencer shook his head in defiance and clutched the badge against his chest.

"Would you be happier back in the closet we found you in?" asked Lucifer.

Spencer shook his head once again. "I'll come. Someone needs to keep an eye on you.

"What can we do?" asked Cam.

"I can go check the waiting room security camera footage," suggested David. "Maybe there's something there?"

"I wouldn't bother," said Death. "Apparently, Miley turned the cameras off years ago. She didn't want the added responsibility of switching out the tapes."

"I'd rather you waited here," said Lucifer. "Until we know what we're facing, I don't want to take any unnecessary risks."

"I thought Heaven was supposed to be safe?" said Ashley.

"I'm just being cautious," said Lucifer as he turned to walk towards the elevators. "We'll be right back," he shouted over his shoulder.

Death and Spencer followed Lucifer, leaving David with Ashley, Amber, and Cam behind.

"I don't like standing around doing nothing," said Ashley as she watched Lucifer round the corner and disappear. "I feel like we should be doing something useful."

"He's right. We need to wait here," said Cam.

"No," said Ashley. "We need to be looking too."

"Do you know your way around?" asked Cam. "Because I certainly don't. This place is immense. The worst thing we can do is split up. We just need to hope they find something useful in God's office, because if they do, they won't want to be wasting time chasing us down when they get back. The best thing we can do is wait here."

"I feel useless," said Ashley.

"We all do," said Cam. "But we have to trust them."

"Trust them? We don't even know them." Ashley was getting frustrated at the lack of progress and the feeling of being inadequate.

"Lucifer seems nice," countered Cam.

"Really? You can tell that with your track record of men?" said Ashley. She cringed as soon as the words passed her lips. "I'm sorry. I didn't mean—"

Cam smiled sadly. "It's okay," she said. "I take a lot of value in the opinion of a woman who dated Warren."

"You married him," said Ashley.

"For three months. You stayed three years."

"Ouch," said Ashley. "And touché."

"Are you two done?" asked Amber. "We have more important things to be worrying about."

Cam and Ashley mumbled their apologies to each other.

Spencer hesitated when they reached the elevators. "I don't think I should go up there. And even if I let you up there, his office is probably locked."

"Stay, leave, it really doesn't matter to me, just buzz us up to his floor," said Lucifer with a shrug as he continued to walk away. "We don't have time to deal with your existential crisis, but we are getting into God's office with or without you." He stopped at the elevators and pressed the call button.

A moment later, the doors opened, and Lucifer and Death stepped inside.

Spencer reached into the elevator and waved his I.D. badge in front of a black box beneath the vast panel of floor numbers. He pressed the button labeled executive and stepped back out of the elevator. "This will take you directly to his office."

"You're not coming with us?" asked Lucifer.

Spencer shook his head. "God doesn't like it when I go into his office. He'll write me up for trespassing again."

"But God isn't here, is he? He won't know," said Lucifer. "It will be our little secret."

"We're not allowed secrets in Heaven. He'll know. He always knows," said Spencer.

"Because he's omniscient?" asked Death.

"No, because he has a camera in his office."

"He probably keeps back issues of Playboy in his desk and doesn't want anyone to find them," suggested Lucifer.

"That is an abhorrent thought." Spencer paused. "If you do happen to find them, please dispose of them properly. We can't have that kind of smut where there may be children present."

"Okay, well, we'll catch you later, Spencer, leader of Baptists."

"You're coming back for me, right?"

"No," said Lucifer as the doors started to close.

Two inches before the doors met in the middle, a hand was thrust in the gap triggering the safety sensor. The doors reopened and Spencer stepped inside. "I've changed my mind."

♦♦♦♦

The elevator slowed down and stopped. The doors chimed and opened to reveal Nancy's empty receptionist desk.

Lucifer stepped out and pointed to the slightly ajar door behind the desk. "It's open," he said softly. "Watch your step."

Spencer hesitated as Lucifer and Death moved ahead. "I think I'm just going to wait here. I'm not comfortable going into his office."

"Suit yourself," said Lucifer as he walked over to the door and stopped, straining to hear any out-of-the-ordinary sounds. Hearing none, he cautiously pushed the door open. God's office was quiet and mostly dark, shy of a small lamp on his desk. A half-finished cup of coffee sat beneath the light source, and a stack of papers were spread over the work surface.

"What happened here?" said Death.

"I don't know. It looks like someone left in a hurry." Lucifer nodded towards a filing cabinet by the door. "Take a look in there, I'm going to check out his desk. There must be something around here. You don't just stomp into Heaven and kick everyone out without leaving a paper trail of some kind." He scanned over God's desk and pulled on the top drawer. Finding it locked, he moved to the bottom drawer. It slid open to reveal a row of folders. "Hey, Spencer," said Lucifer as he pulled out a folder and scanned through the contents. "He's got naked pictures of your mom. Can I have them?"

Spencer poked his head into the office and puffed up his chest in weak defiance. "He certainly does not. How dare you sully the memory of my mother."

Lucifer grinned as he turned his attention back to the desk. "It's okay, I don't need them."

Spencer scowled at Lucifer. He was not amused by his vulgarity.

"I already have most of them, and she looks kinda frumpy in the ones I don't have."

"You are disgusting," said Spencer as what may be considered rage started to bubble within him.

Death glanced over at Spencer to see him flapping his arms in frustration. He shook his head as he crossed to the French doors on the other side of the office. "Really?" he asked Lucifer. "Do you have to taunt him like that?"

"What? I'm just trying to keep the mood light given the situation at hand."

Death reached the doors and pushed them open. He stepped out onto the balcony and looked at the Earth floating below. "I can see why Gary likes it up here," said Lucifer as he followed him out. He leaned on the railing and looked down. "That's one hell of a view."

"Freeze," said a disembodied male voice. The man stepped partially from the shadows aiming a pistol at Lucifer and Death, his face hidden. "State your business here and choose your next words wisely."

Death and Lucifer promptly raised their hands in surrender.

"Whoa," said Lucifer in a panic. "We're unarmed. We're here to find Gary."

"Gary?" asked the voice. "How do you know his name?"

Lucifer stepped backward in the hope of finding a light switch.

"I said don't move," said the voice.

"I'm just trying to find a light switch," said Lucifer. "We're old acquaintances."

The light flicked on from somewhere else in the room, and Lucifer squinted while his eyes adjusted.

"Raphael!" said Lucifer as the light washed over the room and identified the mystery occupant. "How's it going, man?"

"Luc? Steve?" asked Raphael, God's trusted right-hand man. "Thank goodness. I was worried it was someone dangerous."

"Hey!" protested Lucifer. "We can be dangerous, can't we, Steve?"

"I mean hostile," said Raphael in his half-assed defense.

"We're not the one pointing a gun," said Death.

"Sorry," said Raphael, realizing his gun was still trained on the two men. He lowered it and placed it on God's desk.

"You're allowed guns in Heaven?" asked Lucifer, surprised to be staring down the barrel of a pistol.

"No, absolutely not," said Raphael as he held up the weapon. "It's a cigarette lighter." He flicked the ignitor and a small flame popped up. "It's completely useless as a weapon, but it looks the part."

"You're allowed cigarettes in Heaven? Since when?"

"No, but Gary is," said Raphael as he placed the lighter on the desk.

"He's God. He can bend the rules a little."

"Must be nice," said Lucifer.

"What are you two doing here?" asked Raphael, getting the conversation back to the pressing matters at hand.

"Really, Raph?" asked Lucifer. "I think you know exactly why we're here. We're trying to find out what happened, and why every one of your residents suddenly became my residents. It's a little crowded down there, and it's kinda pissing me off."

Raphael appeared to be genuinely surprised at the revelation. "Everyone went to Hell?"

"Yep," said Lucifer.

"Oh, shit. I'm so sorry. I had no idea that would happen," said Raphael.

"You did this?" asked Lucifer.

"Not intentionally."

"But why did everyone leave?" asked Death

"I enacted Protocol Nine," said Raphael.

"And that is?" asked Death.

"It's a mass evacuation order," interrupted Lucifer. "We have the same contingency option in Hell, but I've never used it as I thought it would be kind of a dick move to send all my people up here. It's a pretty drastic measure, so something spooked you. What was it?"

"The council got wind of the whole atheist in Heaven thing and put Gary on leave while they investigated. No one knew. He just slipped out later that night and disappeared. The Council was supposed to send a replacement, but no one ever showed. I've been trying to keep things running ever since. Things were going okay until I got locked out of the panic room."

"What's in the panic room?" asked Death.

"It's a room at the back of Gary's office. It has a terminal with a lock on it. Once a month, we have to send a check-in status to the Council. If we don't check-in, they assume we've abandoned the place. It's just a button on a control panel, nothing complicated." He nodded towards Lucifer. "You should know, you have the same thing in Hell."

"Yeah, either I press it, or I have Scooter do it. There's a couple of people who can handle it, but it's just in my office. I don't have it locked up."

"And that's the problem. Gary doesn't like to delegate responsibilities," said Raphael, fully aware of the lameness of his argument.

"Surely you have a contingency plan in case leadership becomes temporarily indisposed?" asked Lucifer.

Raphael shook his head. "There's a proposal sitting on Gary's desk waiting for a signature to diversify leadership."

"How long has it been sitting there?" asked Death.

"Eight-hundred and ninety-seven years."

"Are you serious?" asked Lucifer.

"Yeah. After he left, we couldn't sign purchase orders or contracts. I'm amazed we held on as long we did. Gary has all the passwords and login information locked in the panic room."

"You don't have them in a backup location, in case, you know, Gary runs away?" asked Lucifer.

"Or fired?" added Death.

"Our database has been hacked several times. Gary felt our network security was only as strong as our weakest employee. Believing he was the safest person in Heaven, he limited access to only himself. My hands have been tied."

"Is that why I found his desktop password on a piece of paper under his keyboard?" asked Death.

Raphael shrugged. "What can I say? Sometimes he's a moron. As we couldn't send the check-in, the Council sent a notice of eviction. So, until we can find Gary, foreclosure proceedings are moving ahead, and we're being kicked out in two weeks."

"He didn't give you any kind of clue where he could be hiding?" asked Lucifer.

Raphael shook his head. "To be honest, until this morning, I'd just been focusing on keeping things running. I didn't have time to figure out where he went. I visited the waiting room to see if Miley had seen him leave, but she was gone."

Death walked over to Lucifer. "Do you have things under control here?"

"Sure, why?"

"I'm going to visit Miley."

"You know where she is?" asked Raphael.

"Yeah, she's my temp at my office. I'll see what she knows. I'll be right back," said Death as he walked to the elevator.

"Can't you just teleport?" asked Lucifer.

"Nope. I'm not allowed to. I have to go to the hallway outside the waiting room."

Lucifer watched Death leave and turned his attention to the office.

He picked up a manila folder labeled David from God's desk. He flicked through the numerous inserted pages within and skimmed over the text. "I can't believe he let in an atheist."

Raphael nodded. "I wasn't his greatest moment."

"What in the fuck was he thinking?" asked Lucifer.

"It just kind of happened," said Raphael. "He didn't do it on purpose."

Lucifer walked over to the open French doors. He stepped outside and looked down at the Earth. "You don't think he'd be down there, do you?"

"It's possible," said Raphael. "He does have a soft spot for the locals. But it's a big planet, this doesn't exactly narrow it down a whole lot, even if he is there."

"Has he ever spoken of a vacation spot, or somewhere he'd like to go?" asked Lucifer. "Hawaii? Disneyland? Wyoming? Surely something has come up in conversation."

"No," said Raphael as he shook his head. "He's never mentioned it."

"He has a locked drawer in his desk, any chance you have the key?"

"I don't have any keys for his office," said Raphael.

"Give me the gun," said Lucifer as he extended his hand.

"It's not a real gun," said Raphael as he passed it over.

"I know it's not. I want to see if I can jimmy the drawer open." Lucifer jammed the lighter on the edge of the drawer and pulled sharply. The drawer popped open, and Lucifer was in. He rummaged through assorted passwords on sticky notes, pens, and scraps of paper. Towards the back of the drawer, he found a small envelope. He pulled it out and opened it to find a birthday card for Nancy he forgot to give her four years prior. Lucifer dropped the card back in the drawer and stood up.

He started to turn away as God's computer dinged. Lucifer moved the mouse to wake up the monitor. In the middle of the screen was a calendar reminder advising of The Phoenix Open the following weekend. "Hey, Raph, any idea what The Phoenix Open is?"

"No idea," said Raphael. "Why?"

"Because that's where he's going to be next week." Lucifer started walking towards the office door. "I think we have our lead."

"Make sure this door doesn't close," said Raphael as they exited the room.

"Why?" asked Lucifer.

"Only the leader of Heaven can unlock it. Yet another ridiculous spell put in place to keep things secure. If the door closes, we can't get back in until we find Gary."

"Is there anything else we need in here?" asked Lucifer.

"I'm not sure," said Raphael. "But I'd like the option if it comes down to it."

Lucifer frowned as they entered the receptionist area outside God's office. "Where did Spencer go?" he asked no one in particular.

"Who?" asked Raphael.

"Spencer," said Lucifer. "Tall, lanky guy. Blonde hair, kinda dainty. He was with us when we came in."

"Baptist Spencer?"

Lucifer nodded. "Yeah, that guy. You know him?"

"I do. How is he still here? Other than the janitor, I didn't realize anyone else was left."

Lucifer shrugged. "He said he was in the bathroom when everyone left. We found him hiding in a closet. He's been following me around like a reluctant puppy."

"I'm under here," said Spencer meekly from beneath Nancy's desk.

Raphael was mildly confused by Spencer's behavior. "Why are you under the desk?"

"I was hiding. Just in case."

"From what?" asked Raphael.

"From whatever was in God's office."

"Well, it's safe to come out now," said Lucifer. "There's nothing here that can hurt you."

"I'll be the judge of that," said Spencer. "Unlike some of you people, I am not comfortable charging recklessly into an unknown situation. I prefer to stay safe until I can evaluate things."

"Suit yourself," said Lucifer as he shook his head and walked over to the elevator. "We're leaving."

Spencer's head popped up over the desk. "Wait, you can't leave me," he said as the men entered the elevator. He rushed over to the doors and stepped in before they could close on him. The thought of being left alone again outweighed the discomfort of associating with Lucifer. At least for the meantime. As the elevator descended, he wobbled slightly and held onto the wall to steady himself.

"You okay there, sunshine?" asked Lucifer.

"I think I have a hangover," said Spencer as he rubbed his throbbing temples.

Raphael frowned. "How is that possible? We don't have hard alcohol in Heaven."

"I found fruitcake in the desk," said Spencer.

"Oh," said Raphael, still confused. "I don't understand. How do you get drunk from fruitcake?"

"He's an idiot," said Lucifer.

"I heard that," said Spencer.

"I wasn't whispering," said Lucifer smiling. "Come on, we're going back to the lounge."

Death appeared in front of his office door and looked down upon his flowers with sad eyes. Knowing Miley was waiting for him in Susan's place removed any joy he once held for his quaint garden. "Come on, Steve, you can do this," he said to himself as his half-assed pep talk did little to motivate him. He inhaled a quick succession of breaths as he pumped himself up to face his replacement secretary. "Sixty seconds, and you're in and out. You've got this." He inhaled sharply and pushed the door open, the small bell above the door announcing his arrival. From the rear office, Death could hear the phone ringing.

"We're closed," shouted Miley from the back as the phone continued to ring.

Death frowned as he shut the door behind him. "Excuse me?"

"I said we're fucking closed. I'd suggest taking a number, but we really don't care if you come back or not."

Death picked up his pace as he stormed to the back room. "What in the hell, Miley?" he asked as he walked up to her computer.

"Huh?" said Miley as she lowered her nail file and looked up at Death. "What are you doing here?"

"Why are you saying we're closed? We're not closed. We're never closed."

"Who are your customers?" argued Miley. "Nobody ever comes here but the water guy. I don't even know why you have an office."

"Because it's peaceful," said Death. He pointed at the phone. "Are you going to answer that?"

Miley placed her nail file on the desk and glared at Death. "No, I'm not. You never gave me a job description, genius. You forced me to improvise."

"And by improvise, you mean not answering the phone and telling anyone at the front door to go away. Did you let Darren in with the water jugs?" He pointed to the empty water cooler.

Miley shook her head in utter disinterest. "No. I thought that was him at the door again when you came in. He was a persistent little shit."

"Dammit, I'm grandfathered in on those prices, on the condition I accept bi-weekly delivery. You've just ruined that. I'm not made of money, you know."

"I guess you're not grandfathered anymore then, are you?" Miley picked up her nail file and continued to sand down her red talons.

Death noticed the monitor was dark, and the computer was asleep. "Have you at least been checking the email?"

"No. I can't even find Minesweeper on this piece of shit computer, so I've been surfing porn."

Death turned his lip up in both irritation and disgust. "Please don't surf porn on Susan's computer. She won't appreciate that."

"Well, hopefully, she doesn't have an active webcam. She really won't appreciate that," said Miley with a gigantic grin. She winked suggestively at Death.

"You are vile, you know that?"

"Flirting won't get you anywhere with me, pasty boy. Why are you back here anyway? Have you come to spy on me, you pervert? You were probably watching the webcam, weren't you?"

Death's jaw dropped and, for a rare moment, was speechless. No pithy comeback, no backhanded comment, just silence. Watching Miley pleasuring herself on the internet was on a rather extensive list of things he would like to avoid experiencing in this life, or any other for that matter.

"Oh, relax, you pale bastard. This is more woman than you could ever handle," Miley said as she rubbed her hands over her breasts. "Weren't you supposed to be off gallivanting around Heaven like some kind of deranged white knight?"

"That's why I'm here." Death looked away from Miley and walked over to his private office. "Where's Gary?" he asked as he retrieved a key from beneath his robes and unlocked the door. He disappeared inside and quickly closed the door behind him.

"How the fuck would I know?" Miley shouted from the other room. "Do I look like his babysitter, Grim? He doesn't ask my permission when he wants to leave. That's Nancy's job. I don't have the time or desire to follow his every move."

Death stepped over to his desk and unlocked the side drawer. Inside sat his collection of Blood Cards. The lot was considerably smaller than the one he owned during the Oceanview disaster, but he still kept a few on hand. With the speed things were escalating in heaven, he felt having an extra or two would be beneficial if the situation spiraled further.

"What are you doing in there?" shouted Miley.

"None of your business," said Death as he removed the cards and locked the drawer.

He exited his office and quickly locked the door behind him.

"You know I can pick locks, right? I'll be in there snooping around the second you leave."

Death stopped at Miley's desk. "You run the front desk for Gary. No one gets in or out without you seeing it. It's your job to keep track of who's coming and going. Surely you saw something."

Miley rolled her eyes at the suggestion she actually does what is expected of her. "Just because it's my job, it doesn't mean I'm doing it. Heaven has a non-discipline policy, so as long as I do the bare minimum, I'm golden. No one complains."

"Just this one time in your life, please do something helpful," pleaded Death. "A lot is riding on this. We have to find him."

Miley shrugged with indifference. "This really sounds more like a you problem than a me problem. I'm not sure what I get out of this if I help you."

Death exhaled. He needed to change his tactics. "If we can't get Gary back to Heaven, everything you love is gone. All of it. Your daily routine, your cushy job."

Miley squinted at Death. "I see what you're doing, Grim and I don't like it."

"Is it working?" asked Death.

"Yes."

"Good. So where did he go?"

"He left about a month ago with his golf clubs and never came back," said Miley.

"Really?" Death never expected her to say something that could be construed as remotely useful and was surprised at her response. "Did he say where he was going?" he pressed.

"What part of me saying he left with his golf clubs was straining on that tiny little brain of yours? He was going to play tennis."

Death's moment of optimism was fleeting as Miley returned to her usual snarky self. While he did not have an exact location of God's whereabouts, he did know he was not hiding in Heaven.

CHAPTER 13

Death stepped out of the elevator into the second-floor hospitality area. Cam, Ashley, and David were sitting in the lounge waiting for a report on anything that vaguely resembled hope.

Ashley sat up as she spotted Death walking towards them. "Did you find anything?" she asked.

"Gary left with his golf clubs," said Death. "But I don't know exactly where—"

"He's going to something called The Phoenix Open," said Lucifer as he entered the room, closely followed by Raphael and Spencer.

"Phoenix Open tickets? How did he score those?" asked Cam.

"You know what that is?" asked Lucifer.

"It's a golf tournament," said Cam.

"I'm guessing it's in Phoenix, Arizona," said Lucifer.

"Actually, it's Scottsdale," said David. "I went a couple of times over the years. It's one of the rowdier stops on the PGA Tour. Think Happy Gilmore but with less hand-to-hand combat."

Death seemed confused at the reference. "I have no idea what you're talking about."

"You've never seen Happy Gilmore?" asked Lucifer. "How the hell have you not seen it?"

"I don't watch movies," said Death. "I'm far too busy for that."

"It's a classic," said Cam as she started to quote the movie. "Why won't you don't you just go home? That's your home! Are you too good for your home?"

"Apparently, Gary is," said Lucifer with a smile.

Death whistled to get the conversation back on target. "Okay, so that's half the problem solved. We know he's in Arizona and probably in the Scottsdale area," said Death.

"So that's our plan. We go to Scottsdale and find God," said Lucifer. "We bring him back here and get that arrow out of Greg."

"Simple as that, eh?" asked David.

"How many people do you think live in Scottsdale?" asked Death. "It's a big city."

Lucifer shrugged. Population estimates and projections were not his forte.

"At a rough estimate, I'd say about two hundred and fifty thousand," said David.

"Ah," said Lucifer, his plan a little more flawed than he hoped. "That's a lot of people."

"Yeah, but he could also be in Phoenix," added David adding more logistical fuel to the fire. "The cities are really close to each other. So that's not out of the question."

"And how many live in Phoenix?" asked Lucifer.

"About one-point-seven million," said David.

"Okay," said Lucifer. The number was not ideal, but it was better than no hope at all.

"But if you include the Greater Phoenix area, there's at least twenty-five more towns and cities. Gary could be in any one of them."

Death rolled his eyes as the chances of finding God diminished, "Dare I ask how many?"

"We're probably looking at four-point-five million. Give or take," said David.

Cam frowned as she failed to see how the group would be able to find a needle in a haystack of needles. "How are we supposed to locate one person in five million?"

"I might be able to help out with that," said Raphael. "Follow me."

Amber hesitated as the group walked away. "I'm going to stay here with Greg," she said.

Ashley pulled her sister in for a hug. "We'll find him."

Raphael directed the others towards the elevators and pressed the down button. As Heaven was devoid of residents, the car was already waiting, and the doors opened instantly. Raphael stepped inside and swiped his ID badge below the bank of floor numbers. A row of previously invisible numbers instantly appeared.

"Ooh," said Lucifer as he rubbed his hands together in glee. "Hidden floors. Now I'm really excited."

♦♦♦♦

"What the hell is this?" asked Cam as the elevator doors opened and the group stepped out into the expansive room. She held numerous expectations of Heaven, but a telephone help desk center was certainly not one of them.

Lucifer looked at his surroundings as a broad smile crept across his face. "Now this is some cool shit."

Raphael opened his arms and gestured to the sea of desks and computers spread out before him. "Welcome to Invocation."

"Invo-what-what?" said Cam.

"This is a surveillance room," said Ashley in a matter-of-fact tone.

"Excuse me?" said Raphael.

"You heard me," said Ashley with the slightest of smiles.

"How do you know?" asked Cam. "Nothing's turned on."

"Two things," said Ashley. She held up a single finger. "One, I work in building security. I know surveillance gear when I see it." She raised a second finger. "And two, he called it Invocation. It's the process of invoking something or someone for assistance." She turned to Raphael. "You're using this to spy on Earth, aren't you?"

Raphael opened his mouth to speak as Ashley took a seat in the nearest chair.

"How are you doing it?" she asked before Raphael could answer the previous question. She reached up and flicked on a monitor.

"Uh, we're—"

"Holy shit, you're using cameras and microphones to watch us. It's—" started Ashley.

"Look, I know what you're going to say," said Raphael. "Even Gary disappro—"

"—fucking brilliant," said Ashley with a massive grin. "I assume you use it to listen to prayers?"

Raphael was visibly taken aback at the statement. "I—"

"Oh, come on," said Cam. "There's no way they use surveillance equipment for something as personal and private as prayer."

Ashley shrugged as if answering the most obvious question on record.

"Why else would Heaven need a surveillance system if it wasn't for answering prayers?"

Raphael sighed at how easily Ashley was able to uncover one of Heaven's deepest and darkest secrets. "Yes, we listen to prayers."

"I knew it," said Ashley. "This is totally ripped off from The Dark Knight. It's creepy as all fuck, but I love it."

"Thank you," said Raphael, still in a mixed state of shame and appreciation. "We've had it for a while. We only implemented it during the Oceanview crisis. We used it to find patient zero."

"Sure you did," said Ashley as she studied the system.

"I'm serious," said Raphael. "We added it into our new hire orientation when we realized there was no way of tracing the source of the outbreak."

"That's quite the invasion of privacy," said Ashley "And God was okay with this?"

"He had no idea this place existed."

Ashley smiled. "So even Heaven has plausible denial. Cute. Did you continue to use it after Oceanview."

"I... er—" spluttered Raphael.

"You guys are fucking creepy," said Ashley.

"Do you—" started Cam.

"I morally object to this," interrupted Spencer as he finally spoke up.

"You would," dismissed Lucifer. He looked over at Cam. "Please continue."

Cam smiled at Lucifer's defense. "Do you have a vetting process?" she asked Raphael.

"What do you mean? For prayers?" said Raphael.

"Yeah. I mean, you can't act on all of them. There must be some process that determines which ones you listen to."

Before Raphael could respond with a reasonable answer, Ashley moved on to the next logical elephant in the room. "How did you hear prayers before invocation?"

Raphael's eyes widened at the question. Ashley at once asked and answered one of religion's heaviest questions. "I—" His lack of comment said everything Ashley needed to hear.

Cam pointed to Ashley, her eyes wide. "Now there's the million-dollar question."

"You never listened to prayers, did you?" accused Ashley. She was not asking.

"No. We didn't," said Raphael.

"What?" said Cam in disbelief. "Then who was I praying to every time my life went to shit?"

"Not us," said Raphael. "Sorry."

"This is priceless," said Ashley. "I'm not sure sorry is going to cut it. There's going to be a lot of seriously pissed off people if they find out."

"Yeah, that's savage," agreed Cam. "And crushingly disappointing. Do you think we can use this to find God?"

Raphael nodded. "That's the plan."

"Can you search by address?"

"Sure," said Raphael. "We can search by address, zip code, or coordinates. Why?"

"Ash, can you punch in my address?" asked Cam. "I'm curious about something. One-oh-eight-one west Adams Road."

Ashley tapped a few buttons, and a live feed from Cam's kitchen appeared on the screen. Shane, Cam's previous overnight house guest sat at her kitchen table eating her cereal, just as naked as the last time she saw him.

Cam snarled at the image in front of her. "That motherfucker. I told him to leave this morning. That piece of shit."

A moment later, an equally naked woman walked into the frame and stopped next to Shane. She planted an affectionate kiss on his cheek as Shane slapped her bare ass.

Cam frowned. "What the fuck?"

"Do you know her?" asked Ashley.

"Nope. Looks like he was fucking someone in my bed. Gross." She looked across with Raphael. "Can he hear me?" asked Cam.

Raphael shook his head. "No."

Cam was anxious to speak with her unwanted guest. "Can we broadcast audio to him somehow?"

"It's a listen-only system," said Raphael. "Audio only goes one way. Pretty much all surveillance cameras lack audio. It's a federal crime to record conversations in the US."

Ashley raised an eyebrow.

"Why do I get the feeling that you are about to contradict me?" asked Raphael.

"It's not a federal crime. In most states, you just need knowledge or consent from one party."

"Well, it's not a feature we connected as we never intended for two-way audio."

"Bullshit," said Ashley. "You just need to reroute the audio source and—" She paused. "The system is already configured to communicate both ways." She studied the controls again. "It's just muted from an admin account. I can unlock it if I have the password." She spun in her chair and looked at Raphael. "You know, for a pious bunch, you lie to each other a lot. What's the password?"

"Heaven."

"Are you fucking serious?" asked Ashley at the lame password announcement. "Capital H?"

"All lower case."

"Jesus, you suck," said Ashley as she typed in the substandard password. "No wonder you started the zombie apocalypse. Your network security policies are fucking terrible." She pressed another button and leaned back into her seat. "Okay, mics are hot."

Cam leaned into the microphone. "Hey, Shane."

On the screen, Cam watched Shane spin around as the voice piped into the kitchen. "*Who's this*?"

The naked woman stepped back from Shane as she too tried to locate the source of the audio.

"It's Cam. Remember, we fucked last night, and then I told you to leave?"

"*Oh, yeah*," said Shane.

"Why are you still in my kitchen?" asked Cam.

"*I thought you said this was your house*?" asked the naked woman with an increasing level of concern in her voice.

In the video, Shane frantically tried to usher the naked woman out of the room. He nonchalantly turned back to the camera. "*Oh, hey, how ya doing*?"

"Itchy," said Cam.

"*Huh*? *What do you mean by itchy*?" asked Shane from her kitchen as the naked woman slowly crept back into the frame. Shane brushed her away from the camera as if not being able to see her would be enough to calm Cam down.

"Oh, I've had another herpes flare-up again," said Cam with a grin. "If you're going to be staying, can you at least make yourself useful? My doctor just called in refill a prescription to Walgreens. If you want to go pick it up for me, she said that there should be enough cream for both of us."

"*WHAT*?" screamed the woman from off-camera as she charged at

Shane, her fists balled and flying at his head. "*You gave me fucking herpes? What the fuck?*"

"*I don't have—*" said Shane as he tried in vain to block the torrent of slaps.

Cam tapped the mic one last time. "Shane, get the hell out of my house and take your herpes-ridden fuck-puppet with you." Cam fell back into her seat as a smile exploded from ear to ear.

"Girl, that was savage," said Ashley as she raised a hand and hi-fived Cam.

"That was amazing," said Lucifer with genuine sincerity.

"Are you two done?" asked Raphael. "We do have more pressing things going on here."

"Oh, right," said Ashley as she spun in her seat and faced the monitor. "Let's go find God."

"It can be a little tricky to select the cameras," said Raphael as Ashley clicked on a map of the US and zoomed in on Arizona.

The screen immediately filled with red dots. Each one connected to a unique camera or microphone. "I think I've figured it out," she said as she settled into the software.

"I see that," said Raphael as he straightened up and watched Ashley take control of the situation.

"Even with access to all these cameras, there's almost four million people," said Death. "How are we supposed to find one person?"

"Standing around griping about it probably isn't the best way to get started," said Cam. "Pull up a chair and help us look."

"You heard the pretty lady," said Lucifer as he looked at Death and Spencer. "Let's start spying on people."

"It's not spying," said Raphael weakly.

Cam smiled and patted the chair next to her and looked at Lucifer. "All yours if you want it?"

"I would love to," said Lucifer with a smile as he sat down next to Cam and studied his workspace. He picked up the computer's mouse and moved it to the left side of the keyboard.

"Not set up to your satisfaction?" asked Cam.

"Nah, I'm a leftie," he said with a smile. He was, in fact, not a leftie at all and simply wanted an excuse to put his hand closer to Cam's.

Ashley circled a group of cameras, and the screen changed to a live video feed of the first camera.

Cam flexed her fingers, ready to type. "Where do you want me to start?" she asked her fellow voyeur.

"Start at I17 and work your way east," said Ashley as she clicked on the next camera icon and the video changed. "Lucifer, take south. Spencer north-east and Death, you can take south-east.

As the group settled into the locations, Ashley continued her own search.

Click.

New video.

Click.

New video.

The images rapidly changed from traffic cameras, to cell phone selfies, to ATM feeds, from high-definition images, to low-resolution grainy and pixelated. And for the next four hours, the group cycled through thousands and thousands and thousands of different cameras.

After thirty minutes of clicking, Lucifer's hand brushed gently against Cam's, and an electric charge she had not felt in years coursed through her body. She looked over at him. His eyes remained focused on the screen, but she could see a slight smile.

Death experienced a close call at around the ninety-minute mark, but the man turned out to be a God impersonator spinning a sign for a tax filing company, but other than that brief moment of hope, their search turned up nothing.

♦♦♦♦

For two, days the team sat in Invocation and spied on Arizona. In between caring for Greg, Amber made sure the group enjoyed an endless supply of coffee to keep them alert. Greg drifted in and out of consciousness, but Amber stayed by his side as she watched the man she loved succumb to the effects of the deadly arrow.

On the twentieth hour of surveillance, Amber arrived with another round of coffee. "Anything?" she asked hopefully as she delivered her tray to the group.

Ashley turned to look at her sister. "Not yet. I'm sorry. We've scanned hundreds of thousands of cameras."

Amber nodded. She knew they were running out of time, but begging them to move faster seemed fruitless. They were already doing the best they could. Pushing them further would benefit no one. She would have to put her faith in that God would show up before Greg could no longer be saved.

Cam looked up as she watched Amber leave the group. Beside her, Lucifer clicked his tongue in frustration as he pressed the wrong button on his mouse again. She blushed ever so slightly as she realized he was not using his dominant hand and simply wanted to be closer to her.

As the group continued their desperate search, a small spark of hope was smoldering on the Earth below in the most unlikely of places.

CHAPTER 14

"Have you ever had a secret so big that the entire world would think you were insane if you said it out loud?" Warren asked the burly bartender standing in front of him. He had not suffered a violent death at the hands of the Caretaker, in fact he was quite alive and well. He was depressed for sure, but he was breathing.

"Listen, son," said Griff as he placed a beer in front of Warren. "I'm a bartender. I've been one for forty-seven years and I've heard it all a thousand times over. My poppa was a bartender before me, and he heard a thousand stories, and his poppa was a bartender, and he heard a thousand more. I promise you, there isn't a yarn you could spin that I haven't been told before." He wiped his hands on his apron. "So, if you want me to think that you're insane, you better have a real good one hidden deep down in your pocket."

"This is a big one," said Warren as he reached for his beer.

"Lay it on me."

Warren sighed. "I've seen God."

Griff rolled his eyes and turned his attention to the rows of spirits behind him. "Come on, son, you're not even trying." He commenced turning a few bottles to display the various brands before picking up a cloth.

"It's true. I was face to face with him, and we spoke to each other."

"Okay, god boy. What did you say to him?" said Griff as he wiped down the rear bar.

"I shot him."

Griff turned back to face Warren, his interest piqued. "You met a god—"

"Not a god, *the* God." Warren interrupted.

"You met *the* God, and the first thing you did was shoot him?"

Warren nodded solemnly. "Yeah. Not my greatest moment, if I were being honest."

"And may I ask why you shot him?" asked Griff with a raised eyebrow.

"I thought he was a zombie-demon."

"A zombie demon?" said Griff, pausing between words.

"Zombie-demon," said Warren enunciating the faster speed. "There's a hyphen."

"Right. Whatever."

"We'd been dealing with an outbreak in our town. And then, after I volunteered to be his sacrifice to save the planet, he killed David instead, and took him to Heaven."

Griff placed his cloth on the bar and wiped his hands on his apron. His stare never left Warren. "David?"

"Yeah, and he was an atheist, so who the fuck knows the implications of that."

Griff continued to eyeball Warren with growing suspicion.

Warren looked down at his chest. "What, do I have something on my shirt?"

"Let me get this straight. You met God and thinking he was a demon zombie—"

"Zombie-demon. There's a hyphen."

"Thinking he was a zombie-demon, you shot him. Then you offer to be his sacrifice, and instead, he kills an atheist. Am I on the right track here?"

Warren nodded. "Yeah, sounds crazy, eh?"

"Nah, it doesn't sound crazy."

"Really?" Warren's face lit up as he took a sip from his beer. The validation helped calm his nerves somewhat.

"It is crazy." Griff reached across and plucked the beer out of Warren's hands. "I think you've had enough."

Warren was incredulous as he reached out to get his glass back. "This is my first beer."

"And you've had enough. Do you even listen to yourself? You sound like a grade-A raving mad lunatic. Zombie-demons? Christ, son, whatever you're smoking, you might want to lay off it. It's turning your brain fucktarded."

Warren settled back into his seat and sighed. "Greg used to call me fucktarded."

"Greg? Is he your therapist?" asked Griff, hoping the deranged man was at least getting mental health support.

"He's my brother."

"Who is also your therapist?" asked the bartender hopefully.

"No, we own a repair shop together. We fix cars."

"And has your brother seen God and more of these so-called zombie-demons?"

"Oh, yeah, in fact, he helped me kill my first one."

"You killed one?"

"We slammed its head in a dumpster, and I jumped on the lid until we cut its head off. He also saw my first headshot."

"You shot one?" asked Griff.

"Not one. Lots."

"And where is Greg now?"

"In Heaven."

"He's dead?"

"Oh, no. David came back to Earth and started taking us to Heaven to escape the Caretaker."

"The Caretaker?"

"Yeah. He was sent to Earth to kill us for seeing God."

And where did all of this happen exactly?"

"Oceanview," said Warren.

"Where's that?" asked Griff

"Here in Arizona."

"Arizona?"

"Yes," said Warren.

"Our Arizona?"

"Yes," said Warren again.

"On Earth?"

"Yes, on Earth. Where the fuck else would Arizona be?"

"Watch your tongue, son," threatened Griff.

"It's up north, west of Flagstaff," said Warren.

"Never heard of it. You sure about that?"

"Of course I'm sure. I lived there my entire life."

Griff turned to the rest of the bar. "Anyone here heard of Oceanview, Arizona?" he said with a raised voice.

Scattered *'no's'* and *'where's'* came back in reply.

"See? No one's heard of it."

An older man in a plaid shirt and baseball cap raised his hand as he rose from his seat. "I've heard of it."

Griff scowled at the man. "Sit down, Frank. You think the earth is flat and the election was rigged."

"It is and it was," the old man said rather sadly as he sat back down. "I have proof."

"You also think that vaccines cause you to pick up radio waves with your brain."

"They do. Abraham Lincoln talked to me while I was eating breakfast this morning."

Griff looked back at Warren. "See, the only person here who has heard of your imaginary town is a senile old man—"

"I can hear you, you know. I'm old, I'm not deaf."

"Sorry, Frank. What I meant to say was, the only person here who has heard of your imaginary town is this charming and equally fucktarded old man."

Frank's smile quickly arrived and passed after the insult.

Griff turned back to Warren. "I think it's time for you to go home, son. You're lucky I've never heard of Oceanview. I'd hate to have to call the cops for multiple homicides."

Warren slid off his chair. "Yeah, some days I have a hard time believing it myself. What do I owe you for my three sips of beer?" he said as he pulled out his wallet.

Griff shook his head. "It's on me. I'd suggest putting the money towards a shrink. I think your head's broken."

"Can I have a sandwich?"

"No."

"Chips?"

Griff pointed at the exit. "Don't push it, son. I think it's time for you to leave."

Warren nodded his thanks and headed for the door.

"Did you forget something?" Griff shouted after him.

"Huh?" Said Warren. His minding cast back to Hank shouting at him the last time he left Jacob's after a few too many drinks and refusing to turn over his keys. However, on this occasion, he was not intoxicated. He had never been more sober.

Griff held up a small canvas bag. "Your purse."

"It's not a purse," said Warren as he walked back over to the bar. "It's a satchel."

♦♦♦♦

The front door to the bar opened, and Warren stepped outside. He exhaled a heavy breath as he stopped to collect his thoughts. His shoulders slumped as hopes of heading back to his car with a full stomach were dashed. "I'm not crazy," he muttered softly as he fished his keys from his pocket. "I did see God. And I shot him." He put the key in the driver's side door lock and struggled to unlock it. "And his stupid-ass zombie-demons fucked up my car door." He strained as the key finally clicked over and the door unlocked. Warren hesitated before opening the door as he pulled his cell phone from his pocket. "Call Greg," he said to the device as it auto-dialed his brother. The phone promptly returned a rapid series of beeps just as it did the previous three hundred times he tried. His brother was currently a long way from quality phone service. "God-dammit, Greg, where are you, man? Answer the phone."

He opened the rear door and stared inside the car, reviewing its limited contents. A blanket and pillow were bundled up on the backseat, along with various fast-food wrappers and empty soda cans. The vehicle became his primary residence since his forced eviction from Kim's house. He owned few possessions since leaving Oceanview, and now he owned even less. Warren sighed as he climbed into the car and pulled the door closed behind him. He placed the satchel on the floor and pushed it under the passenger seat. It took him a moment to adjust the pillow and wadded-up blanket to form something that vaguely resembled a bed. He laid down on the pillow and pulled the blanket around his neck.

Sleep greeted Warren unusually fast as his mind failed to make any sense of the recent events. Despite drifting away so easily, Warren slept fitfully. For more than an hour, he tossed and turned and mumbled in his sleep. His dreams danced with visions of the Caretaker shooting Greg and his brother's screams as the arrow pierced his shoulder, moments before disappearing with David. He felt helpless and alone, and his visions did little to quiet the demons chipping away at his sanity.

♦♦♦♦

Warren's first experience with consciousness began with him rolling off the seat onto the floor, followed by a loud *clang* of chains hitting concrete. "The fuck?" he yelled from beneath a tangle of limbs and blankets. He thrashed and twisted as he kicked the covers off and crawled back onto the seat. He reached for the handle and pushed the door open. Below him, the ground was quickly moving away as the car started to lift from the rear. He leaned out of the door to see a tow truck hoisting the car into the air from its rear end. "The fuck?" he said again as he pulled himself out of the car and dropped to the ground. "Hey, what are you doing, man?" shouted Warren over the mechanical din of the truck retracting the chains. "This is my car," he said as he stood up and brushed himself off. The man at the controls stood with his back to Warren as he worked the chain.

Warren walked over to the driver, waving his arms to get his attention. "Hey, asshole, what are you doing? That's my car."

The repo-man finally turned to face Warren. His dark aviator sunglasses covered his eyes. "You're in a no-parking zone, pal."

"No, I'm not," said Warren.

The repo man pointed at a sign and the wall of the bar. "Yes, you are."

"No. I'm in the spot next to a no-parking sign. I'm not parked illegally. Give me my damn car back." Warren lost enough in recent months. Losing his car would be the final straw. "This is all I've got left, please, don't take it."

"You should have thought about that before parking illegally."

"I'm not parked illegally."

"Well, it's a proxy towing for dangling your toe over the line," said the driver as he walked over to the rear of Warren's car.

"What fucking line?" asked Warren, rapidly losing his patience. "I've broken no laws."

"I know your type. You use a technicality to make sure the rules don't apply to you."

"What technicality? I'm parked next to the fucking sign."

"The longer you argue with me, the bigger the fine gets," said the man as he tugged on the chains to test them.

"Now you're just being a dick. I didn't do anything wrong."

The "What can I say, it's a slow day. I don't make the rules."

"Apparently, you do," muttered Warren.

The driver pulled a screwdriver from his pocket and flicked the tip of it across the trunk of Warren's car, scratching the paint. "Oops," he said as he walked around the opposite side of the vehicle.

"What the fuck man, watch the paint. I've already had to get the damn thing fixed after the zombie-demon—" He caught himself before finishing the sentence.

The tow truck driver paused and looked at Warren. He immediately lowered his head and turned away. "Arguing isn't going to make this any less painful."

Warren stared back at the man for a moment. He cocked his head as he analyzed the stranger. There was something familiar about him. "Don't I know you from somewhere?"

The man shook his head as he remained facing the opposite direction. "No, I don't think so."

"Yeah, I'm pretty sure I do." Warren

The man finished checking the chain and rapidly moved towards the front of the truck.

"Wait," shouted Warren. "Come back here. Who are you?"

Warren moved towards the driver as he climbed into the cabin. "Hey, I'm talking to you." He grabbed hold of the man's leg before he could close the door.

The man turned around and looked at Warren. "Get the hell off me, human."

Warren's jaw immediately fell open. He would recognize the God who tried to kill him in Oceanview anywhere. "Gary?"

God froze as he recognized Warren. He would recognize the man who he tried to sacrifice in Oceanview anywhere. "I have no ideas who that is." God jerked his leg away from Warren's grip and slammed the door shut.

"Motherfucker," said Warren as he fell back from the door.

The truck pulled forward with Warren's car still in tow. Warren lunged at his departing vehicle and grabbed hold of the hood. He climbed onto the roof and slid down on the rear windshield onto the trunk. "Stop the truck," yelled Warren as he reached for the chain suspending the car.

God turned sharply as the truck pulled out of the parking lot in the hopes of dislodging his stowaway.

"Shit," yelped Warren as he lost his balance. He grasped for the tow chain, barely clinging on. The truck straightened up as it pulled onto the street, and Warren climbed onto the bed of the truck. He carefully made his way over to the cabin and reached around the side for the passenger door handle.

God swerved again, and Warren grabbed the side mirror as he struggled to maintain his grip. He placed a foot on the running board and leaned his head into the half-closed window. "Let me in," he shouted.

"No," said God as he focused on the road ahead. "Get off my truck," he said as he glanced over at Warren.

"Pull over, I just want to talk," yelled Warren.

"No," said God again. "We have nothing to talk about." The traffic light ahead turned red, and God pressed hard on the brake pedal. "Dammit," he muttered. As the truck slowed and stopped, the engine volume died down, and the two men no longer needed to shout.

Inside the truck, God realized the other door was unlocked and frantically stretched out over the seat to try and lock it. Warren beat him by a microsecond and opened the door.

He climbed in and sat down next to God. As he pulled the door closed, he immediately jumped into interrogation mode. "Talk to me, please," begged Warren. "I need answers."

God promptly removed his glasses and turned to stare at Warren. Nothing happened. He continued to stare a moment longer before turning his attention back to the windshield. "Shit," he muttered under his breath.

"What?" asked Warren. "What's wrong?"

"Nothing," said God as he dropped his glasses into the breast pocket of his overalls and turned his attention back to the red light.

Warren's eyes widened as God's intentions became clear. "You dick," he shouted. "You were going to kill me."

"No, I wasn't," said God. "Why would you say that?"

"Because you took off your glasses, and the only time you take off your glasses is to kill people with your laser vision."

"I don't have laser vision."

"Well, whatever the fuck you call it, your eyes kill people. You told us at the church."

God turned away from Warren, frustrated at the discovery of the loss of yet another of his powers and desperate for the traffic light to change. "Well, it looks like it doesn't work now anyway, so it doesn't matter."

"You're an asshole," said Warren. He tilted his head and raised an eyebrow as he put the pieces of the puzzle together. "So, if you can't laser kill me, that means something has happened." Warren paused as he weighed up the possible reasons God may have been rendered powerless. "Do some magic."

"I don't do magic."

"Don't or can't?" asked Warren.

"What does it matter?"

"Because they imply two vastly different things. Saying don't means you chose not to. Can't means someone has taken it away."

"You're an observant little shit, aren't you?" said God as he waited for the light to change.

"What can I say, I people watch." Warren eyed God accusingly. "What happened to you?"

"I don't want to talk about it. I have places to be."

"So do I, Gary."

God sighed at the blatant disrespect. "Please don't call me that."

"Oh, no can do there, buddy," said Warren. "At this moment, you are human like the rest of us. You've lost the privilege of being called God. Until that has changed, you are nothing more than Gary, and I am going to use the ever-loving shit out of it." Warren paused. "Gary."

"I'm going to remember this," said God. "When I get my powers back, you and I are going to have words that you may find uncomfortable and given your desire to go to Heaven when you die, disappointing."

"Bring it, Gary. I'm already having doubts about where I want to spend my afterlife anyway. Gary."

"Oh, I am going to smite the ever-loving shit out of you."

"And here comes Old Testament Gary," said Warren as he rolled his eyes. You should take after your son, he was much nicer to people."

"And look where that got him," said God.

Warren reached forward and opened the glove box.

"What are you doing?" asked God as he continued to wait for the traffic light to change. A moment later, the red light switched to green, and God pulled away.

"I want to see what it says on your registration."

God reached over and tried to grab Warren's hand. The truck swerved dangerously as he pulled on the steering wheel.

Warren nodded at the road ahead. "You may want to focus on the road. You're going to kill that grandma."

God looked up to see an old lady crossing the street and jerked on the wheel to avoid squashing her. He glanced back at Warren as he corrected his course.

Warren continued to rummage through the glove box and pulled out the vehicle's registration. He glanced over the document and paused. He turned to God with a raised eyebrow. "Edgar Jackson?"

God stammered for an answer. "I—"

Warren smiled. "You stole this vehicle, didn't you?"

"No, I didn't," said God.

"Who's Edgar Jackson?"

"That's my alias to protect my identity."

Warren pulled a truck driver's ID card from the glove box. "Are you sixty-three and black?" he asked in reference to the picture on the laminated card, who was quite obviously not God.

"What is that noise?" asked God.

"What noise?"

"When I brake." He pulled over to the side of the road and stopped. "I think the running boards is loose again. You probably dislodged it when you climbed on the truck. Can you open the door and see if it's separated?"

Warren opened the door and looked down at the step below him. I don't see any—"

God leaned over and pushed him out of the truck.

"Hey!" protested Warren as he stumbled to keep his footing. "You dirty bastard!"

God pulled the door shut and slammed the lock down. He pressed his foot on the gas pedal and pushed it to the floor. While the truck could not accelerate at the speed God desired, it was enough to pull away from Warren and put some space between them.

Warren stepped back as the truck pulled away, but he remained standing in the road. The car behind him honked in annoyance at the obstacle. Warren turned to see a taxi trying to pull around and flagged the driver down.

"Where to?" asked the driver as Warren climbed in the back seat.

Warren pointed to the tow truck ahead of them. "Follow that truck."

The cabbie's eyes widened at the order. "I have waited my entire life to hear a passenger say that. Hold onto your butt, this may get bumpy."

Thirty minutes later, after never once breaking twenty-seven miles an hour, the driver looked bored and disheartened as he lazily followed God's tow truck. He pursed his lips and made a frustrated rumble.

"Everything okay?" asked Warren.

"I just thought my first high-speed chase would be more exciting."

"I'd get used to this guy disappointing you. He's rather good at it."

"Who are we following? Your lover's ex? The man your wife is cheating with?"

"God."

The driver glanced up at Warren in the rearview mirror. "God?"

Warren nodded as he noticed the rosary beads and cross hanging from the mirror.

"Yeah. Long story short, he was kicked out of Heaven, and I need to bring him home. Or at least follow him until Lucifer can catch up with him."

"You're working with Lucifer to catch God?"

"Yeah, crazy huh—"

The driver slammed on the brakes and thrust Warren forward into the back of the passenger seat.

"Ow," griped Warren. "What the hell, ma—"

"GET OUT OF MY CAR!" the driver screamed.

"Come on," said Warren.

"You are a servant of the Devil, and you have no place in my sanctuary."

Warren opened the door and climbed out of the cab. "Your sanctuary smells like Cheetos and ketchup," he yelled as the driver pulled away.

Once again, Warren found himself dumped off on the side of the road. However, despite his ride being cut short, about fifty feet ahead, he saw God pulling his truck through a gate leading into a tow yard. "Holy shit," he said as he broke into a sprint, desperate to get to the gate before God could close it.

His fortunes could not quite extend to another victory, as God closed the gate and stepped back as Warren slammed into it. Warren reached through the railings, but God stood three inches out of his grasp.

"Please. Can we talk?" asked Warren.

"There is nothing for us to talk about," said God.

"There is plenty for us to talk about. Can you let me in just for a few minutes?"

"I'm most letting you come in for a few seconds."

Warren looked at God. "I thought we were cool."

"No, Warren. We are definitely not cool. Not even remotely."

"I'm just wanting to make sure this isn't going to affect my chances of getting into Heaven."

"Warren. The first time we met, you shot me," said God. "So that's one strike for you right out of the gate."

"Yeah, well, the first time I met you, you tried to sacrifice me. The second time, which if you're keeping count, was less than an hour ago, you tried to kill me with laser eyes. I think that pretty much makes us even."

"Did I ruin your favorite suit?" asked God.

"No."

"Then we're not even. Your chances of going to Heaven are pretty much zero."

"I've been to church hundreds of times. You said that going just once is the basic criteria for heaven. Surely hundreds of times gives me some wiggle room?"

"No, not really. Your options are Hell or Missouri."

"Why Missouri?"

"I hate Missouri."

"These are crappy options. Why are you a tow truck driver anyway? You had a really good thing going in Heaven." asked Warren.

"Have you ever towed a car before?"

Warren shook his head. "I can't say that I have."

"Well, you should, it's fucking awesome." He spun and gestured to all the cars around him. "This yard symbolizes despair and disappointment."

"This goes against everything you're supposed to be. You're stealing people's shit, and by the looks of things, you enjoy it."

"How could I not? The looks on their faces when they see me pull off with their precious vehicle in tow is priceless. *'Oh, please don't take my car', 'I'll give you money'*, and my absolute fucking favorite, *'dear God, please don't let him take my car'*. Do you have any idea how hard it is for me to keep a straight face?"

"Look, are you going to give me my car back or not?"

"Not." God turned and walked to the office building behind him and opened the front door.

♦♦♦♦

Inside the office, God pushed the door closed behind him and threw his keys on a nearby desk. He pulled the accompanying chair out and flopped down into the seat. With a heavy sigh, he lifted his hands to his face and rubbed his throbbing temples. He exhaled heavily as he removed his sunglasses and placed them down next to his keyboard. He never expected the humans to find him at all, let alone so quickly and he frowned as he replayed the last few hours back through his mind. Was there a chance he had been lax and somehow given a clue to his hideout? Or was it just some deep universal cosmic bullshit karma that Warren's car was the one he has decided to tow? He cursed his misfortune under his breath and flicked on the security monitor on his desk.

Through the outside camera, he watched Warren standing in front of the gate kicking rocks. "Please go away," said God softly. "I just want to be left alone."

He enjoyed the change in pace that driving the truck offered him. It was the first time in thousands of years he did not have subordinates asking him for direction. There were no fires to put out and no atheists wandering the halls, and he certainly did not have to worry about whether his lists were right. All he needed to worry about was finding a car and towing it away. It would not be the first time he worked his way from the ground up and held no issue repeating the journey, even if he was a little rusty.

God's promotion in Heaven was not under the most ideal of circumstances. He certainly did not start in the CEO position. In the early days of his arrival, he was called Gary the Intern. He started out in the mailroom sorting through ancient tablets and scrolls that needed to be delivered to various low and middle-level managers. This was Heaven in its infancy, before the Witnesses and Joseph Smith fan club cluttered up the hallways forcing various expansions to be added to the Kingdom of Angels. Before Miley choked any smidgen of optimism new arrivals held for an afterlife of peace and salvation.

The previous Executive Director was a man called Nigel. And, truth be told, nobody liked Nigel because he was an insufferable dick. And his dickish behavior became a destructive spiral. The more people disliked him, the bigger dick he became, and the bigger dick he became, the more people disliked him. This hate-hate relationship with his residents eventually came to a head one morning when God innocently advised Nigel that he was signing a purchase order in red ink instead of the required black.

"Excuse me?" said Nigel as he looked up from his desk at the person daring to critique his work.

"I said you're using the wrong pen," said the man who would become God.

"Is this the face of a man who gives a shit about the color of ink?" Nigel circled his face with a finger.

"No," said Gary.

"Is this also the face of a man who thinks the opinions of a hopeless, fuck-wit of an intern hold any kind of value?"

God slowly shook his head. "No," he said quietly. "But accounting will simply send it back to you so you can resign it with the proper colored ink."

Nigel slammed his pen down on his desk in a fury and looked up from his seat. "How long have I worked here?"

God shrugged. "A thousand years."

"Ten. Ten thousand years. And how long have you worked here, George?"

"Gary," corrected God.

"Oh, Gary, is it? Well, excuse the shit out of me."

God smiled. "It's okay—"

"I did not ask for your opinion, Garth. That's the problem with this place. It's too full of pathetic nothings who think their opinions mean anything to me."

"I thought you created us in your image."

Nigel turned to face God, his face flushed red with rage. "What?"

"I—"

Nigel reached up and grabbed God by the ear. "Come with me, peasant." With his free hand he snatched the purchase order from his desk.

Nigel stood and pulled God by his lobe. He pushed his door open and walked past Nancy's desk.

"Sir?" asked Nancy as she cautiously rose from her seat.

"Quiet!" yelled Nigel as he dragged God out of the room and down the hallway towards the elevators. "This doesn't concern you."

"You're hurting my ear, sir," protested God.

"Another word from you, and you'll be cleaning my personal toilet with your toothbrush for an eternity. And I have irritable bowel syndrome." He stabbed at the down button and waited for the car to arrive.

Ding.

The doors slowly opened, and Nigel pushed God inside. "You can explain yourself to fiscal," he seethed.

Two minutes later he was standing in front of Janet, the head of the fiscal department, holding the purchase order in one hand, and God's ear with the other.

"Can I help you, sir?" she asked politely as she looked at God squirming in pain from Nigel's grip.

Nigel slammed the paper down on the desk. "Larry, here—"

"Gary. Ow—"

Nigel twisted his hand and by proxy, God's ear. "Larry says that PO's need to be signed in black ink. I've decided to do it in red. I'm in charge and I like red."

"That may be, but he's not wrong, sir. It is supposed to be black. Red doesn't show up properly on the scanner."

"Why don't we have a better scanner?" asked Nigel.

"Because you're brand loyal and told us to buy an Epson."

"So, you're saying that this is my fault?"

Janet shrugged. "By proxy, yes," she said as she threw his fancy words back at him.

Nigel clenched his jaw. "So, you're saying that Jeff is right, and I am wrong?"

Janet nodded. "I am."

Nigel let go of God's ear and stared at him intensely. "I don't like you, you annoying little shit. If you think you can do the job so well, you do it. I quit."

And that is the rather bland story of how Gary O'Donnell became God and the most worshipped and loved man on Earth. Calling it underwhelming did not seem to do it justice. Those expecting an epic tale of a young man overcoming impossible odds to become the leader of all Christianity and its various offshoots were sorely disappointed. Sensing this to be a potential issue to readers seeking excitement, the first action Gary took as the new and improved God was to remove the book of Nigel from the Bible, and the opening verse '*In the beginning, there was Nigel, there was only Nigel, and Nigel was lonely*' was no more.

CHAPTER 15

Deep in the bowels of Invocation, the main elevator doors slid open, and Amber stepped out carrying a fresh carafe of coffee and a mug. A thin trail of steam wafted from the cup as she walked over to Ashley sitting at a nearby terminal. She placed the cylinder on the desk and stopped behind her sister.

Ashley's focus was aimed squarely on the monitor in front of her, as she continued to methodically cycle through endless camera feeds. As soon as she confirmed God was absent from the image, she clicked on to the next one and resumed her search.

"Hey, sis," said Amber softly as to avoid unnecessarily scaring her. "I brought you a surprise."

Ashley spun in her chair to see Amber holding out the mug proudly before her. "What is it?" she said as she took the steaming drink and sniffed it.

"I bet you've never had Holy Hot Chocolate before. Truth be told, it tastes pretty much the same as Earth hot chocolate, but the name is cool." Despite trying to act casual, her eyes were red from hours of crying and lack of sleep.

Sadness swept over Ashley's face as her sister's grief became apparent. "Oh, sweetheart." She said as she placed the mug down on the desk and stood to embrace Amber.

Amber wrapped her arms around Ashley and rested her head against her shoulder. The two sisters stood still for a moment, struggling to hold onto a moment of peace in the unfolding chaos. Amber sighed heavily. "I can't lose him, Ash, he's my entire world. I don't know how I'll carry on without him. We have a baby to raise, I can't do it on my own."

"We're not going to lose him, and your kid will have both parents for a long time to come. We're going to find out where God is hiding, and we'll bring him back to Heaven. We'll fix this." Ashley was uncertain if she believed her words.

"When did you last take a break?" asked Amber as she glanced at the monitor.

"I don't know. Maybe nine, ten hours ago," said Ashley.

"Why don't you go take a rest. I can take over and continue the search," offered Amber.

"I can't walk away. We need to find him."

"I'm not asking or expecting you to walk away," said Amber. "You just need a little downtime to recharge. If you collapse, you won't be of use to anyone. Go take a nap. Cam and I have this under control."

"I tell you what," said Ashley, give me an hour, let me finish my hot chocolate, and I'll take a break. Deal?"

Amber nodded at the offer. "Deal."

Ashley sat back down in her seat and commenced her holy voyeuristic channel surfing.

Amber gently squeezed Ashley's shoulder. "I'll be back to check on you."

At Lucifer's desk located two seats to the right, a private message notification popped up on his screen, and he leaned in to read it. The message came from Death's computer four seats down who sat to the left of Ashley and Spencer.

What if we can't find him?

Lucifer frowned as he typed out his response. *What do you mean?*

What do we do if we can't find Gary?

Lucifer paused and considered the question. *I haven't thought that far ahead.*

I have.

Of course you have. Lucifer waited for a follow-up message that never arrived. *And? Don't keep me hanging.*

If this goes wrong, I think we should just say forget it to the whole damn thing and disappear.

Lucifer frowned at the pointed response. *We need to find him. We're stronger together. The longer we're apart, the easier it will be to pick us off.*

Not if we leave.

Lucifer gave Death a side-eyed glance as he typed his response. *See, that is why you need to have me on board.*

Why?

Checks and balances.

What do you mean by that?

Lucifer smiled to himself. *I mean, I'm here to stop you fucking off and leaving the rest of the Universe to deal with this shit.*

Oh, you mean the exact same thing that Gary did?

Lucifer pondered Death's comment for a moment. He was correct, Gary had simply just fucked off, and left everyone else to sort his shit out. *Yeah, just like that I guess. But, as the saying goes. Two wrongs don't make a right.*

Are you really going to throw that hippy dippy nonsense at me? You're the Prince of Darkness. Don't tell me you have a moral compass?

Lucifer smiled to himself. *Honestly, Gary can fuck right off. He's ruined my routine. I had a good life, and he fucked it up. I used to know what I was doing tomorrow, next week or next year. I had a routine. And his antics fucked it up. But I'm not walking out on this. Not on Greg, or any of these people.*

Especially the hot blonde to your left, huh?

Lucifer smiled again. *That's none of your business.*

You are so transparent.

I am not.

You're blushing. Death grinned to himself.

Don't you have a god to find? Lucifer looked to his side and made brief eye contact with Cam. He quickly diverted his eyes back to his computer.

Another private message popped up on Lucifer's screen. This time it was from Cam. *Thank you.*

For what ? replied Lucifer.

For not giving up on us.

How did you know?

I could see your screen. Sorry. Cam glanced at him and smiled. *Oh, and you're blushing.*

♦♦♦♦

"Come on, man," pleaded Warren as he leaned against the fence of God's tow yard. "Please let me have my car back."

A hundred feet inside the yard, amidst numerous towed or wrecked vehicles, God walked towards an RV carrying his bag of golf clubs. He whistled to himself as he ignored Warren's plea. Stopping at the rear ladder, he hoisted his bag over his shoulder and climbed up onto the vehicle's roof.

"I can see you," said Warren.

God leaned over and placed a bright yellow golf ball on the roof. He arched his club back and swung.

The ball sailed through the air in the direction of Warren.

"What the fuck?" said Warren as he leaped back from the fence and instinctively ducked.

The ball slammed into a parked car behind him with a loud *clang,* leaving a dent in the driver's side door.

"Hey!" he screamed at God. "What the hell, dude?"

"Fore!" shouted yelled God from the top of an RV in the middle of the yard.

"You're supposed to yell that before you hit the ball," Warren protested loudly as he stood back up.

"Not when I'm aiming for you, I don't," said God, as he continued their loud conversation. He crouched down and placed another ball on the roof. He studied where Warren was standing and moved the ball back six inches. Not that the position would make much of a difference, he still sucked at golf. He swung again, but this time his aim was off, and the ball sailed well wide of his target.

"Fore," screamed God a second time.

"Why are you trying to hit me?" shouted Warren.

"Why are you following me?"

"Because we need you back in Heaven."

"Are you kidding me?" He swung his club again, and another ball flew through the air. "I don't do that anymore. I've moved onto greener pastures."

Warren ducked as the third projectile skimmed over his head. "Goddammit, would you stop it?"

"No. Fore," said God as he placed a fourth ball on the roof.

Warren jumped back as the ball careened past his head.

"Fore," yelled God again.

"Can I least get my car back, please?"

"Do you have three hundred dollars?"

"What for?"

"Towing fee. Look at the sign on the gate."

Warren looked at the sign attached to the gate beside him advising him of a two-hundred-dollar retrieval fee.

"The sign says two hundred."

"That was yesterday," countered God.

"I can see my damn car from here," said Warren, pointing to the vehicle twenty feet away. "I can walk in and grab it. You literally don't have to do anything to help me."

"No," said God. "You can't have it."

"Just let me take it."

"Come back with three-hundred and fifty dollars, and it's yours."

"You just said it was three-hundred."

"Read the rest of the sign. The price is variable if you argue with me."

Warren leaned in closer to the sign. "No, it doesn't."

"No? Oh, well, it's supposed to." God sent the next ball directly at Warren's car and left a decent-sized dent on the rear passenger side panel. "Oops."

"Now you're just being an asshole," shouted Warren.

God placed another ball before him and swung at Warren. "Fore—" he yelled as the ball careened through the air. "—Hundred," he added with a smile.

Warren sighed in frustration. "You're a dick, Gary. Is there an ATM machine around here anywhere?" he asked. "I'll get you your damn money."

"ATM," replied God.

"What?"

"It's just ATM. The M stands for machine. Calling it an ATM machine is redundant."

Warren shook his head and turned away from the fence. "Thanks for nothing, ass."

"I'm just trying to help you," shouted God with a broad grin. "Knowledge is healthy."

"Asshole," Warren muttered to himself again as he turned away from the fence. He gave the street a once over and determined there were no ATMs in his general vicinity. He stepped into the street as another golf ball sailed through the air beside him and hit the building across the street with a loud clink.

♦ ♦ ♦ ♦

In the basement of Heaven, the team continued to scan their screens for any sign of God. Upon verifying one camera was clear, they would click on their mouse and cycle over to the next image. In rapid succession, they each skimmed over traffic light cameras, security cameras, and cell phones as they spied on the greater Phoenix area.

"I need sleep," said Spencer, his eyelids hanging low. "I can't stay awake much longer."

Raphael rubbed his eyes and yawned. "Me too. I'm going to miss something if I'm not careful."

Death had long since passed out and snored loudly from his seat. At least one of them was getting some much-needed rest.

Ashley sighed. She too, felt the effects of no sleep and stress, and coffee no longer provided any benefit. "We should have done this in shifts," she said.

"It wouldn't have made any difference," said Cam. "There are hundreds of thousands, if not millions of cameras to go through. We'll be lucky if we can get through half of them."

"What are you saying?" accused Ashley.

Cam realized her words sounded like she was giving up. "I'm not saying we won't find him, Ash. We just have a lot of ground to cover and not a lot of time to do it."

"I didn't mean to jump on your shit. I'm tired, I'm scared, and my heart is breaking for Amber."

"Well, I don't think things are looking very positive at all," said Spencer. "Simple math says we don't have enough time to scan through all of the available cameras."

Lucifer leaned back in his chair and looked over at Spencer. "You got drunk on fruitcake, so you don't get an opinion."

"He did?" asked Cam.

"Oh yeah," said Lucifer. "Isn't that right, Spencer?"

Spencer turned his attention back to his screen and continued his search.

♦♦♦♦

Warren's search for an ATM turned up empty, and as his quest led him further away from the tow yard, he became more despondent. He noticed an old lady sitting at a bus stop across the street making an obvious attempt to avoid eye contact with him. Oblivious to her concerns of a strange man heading her way, he ran over to woman.

"Ma'am," Warren asked the silver-haired lady standing at a bus stop.

"Is there an ATM nearby? My phone's not getting a signal." He held up his phone to signify his distress.

The old lady continued to look away from Warren.

"Ma'am, can you hear me? I'm looking for an ATM."

She looked Warren up and down, and deciding that the frazzled man was a mugger, she swung her purse at his head. "Help!" she screamed as she swung again. "I'm being attacked!"

Warren covered his head as he backed away from the deranged old coot. "You're fucking crazy, lady. I'm not hurting you. I'm just —"

Thump.

"—asking—"

Thump.

"—if you know where—"

Thump

She planted another direct hit on the side of Warren's head. "Ow!" he yelped as the zipper caught him on his cheek and left a thin bloody mark.

She arched her arm back for another strike as Warren turned away. "Go away, you thug."

Warren shook his head as he backed off from the frantic woman. He barely made ten steps when an empty Coke can bounced off the back of his head. He grimaced as he struggled to maintain his composure. "I'm already leaving."

"Keep walking, pervert," she yelled after him as she dug through the nearby trash can for another soda can.

"I'm not a perv—" said as another empty soda can whizzed past his head. He crossed the street and left the crazy old lady to herself.

After fifteen minutes of walking, Warren saw the familiar stagecoach logo of a Wells Fargo bank on the opposite side of the street. He exhaled in relief and jogged over the busy road to the ATM. "Are you a sight for sore eyes," he said as he inserted his card into the slot and punched in his PIN.

The machine thought about his action for a moment and asked if he wanted to make a withdrawal. Warren pressed the yes button and requested four-hundred dollars. The machine once again considered his request, but this time decided to deny him any further advancement.

"Oh, come on," griped Warren as an insufficient funds message popped up on the screen. "How am I supposed to get my car back?" He backed out of the withdrawal screen and requested a balance update. He was three dollars short of his desired amount. "Of course," he muttered under his breath.

While his attention was focused on the bank, a different elderly lady joined the line behind and politely coughed to encourage him to speed things up.

Warren turned to face the woman. "Ma'am, I've come up twenty dollars short on my account, and I need to get my car from the impound. I need four hundred and I only have three-eighty. Is there any chance you would consider loaning me twenty bucks, please?"

The old lady ignored his request and continued to stare past him.

"Ma'am?" Warren asked politely again.

The lady looked away and continued to dismiss him.

Warren sighed and turned back to the machine. "Miserable old hag," he mumbled under his breath as he returned his focus to his lackluster bank account.

"Excuse me?" asked the old lady. "What did you say?"

Warren decided to ignore her and continued to stare at the screen.

She tapped him on the shoulder. "I asked you a question, young man."

Warren sighed as he turned around to face the woman. "Which part would you like me to repeat?" he asked, his voice laced with annoyance. "The loud part where I politely asked you, to your face, for assistance, and you chose to ignore me? Twice. Or the part where I was facing away from you and I insulted you under my breath, and you suddenly gained superhuman hearing? I just want to be clear which part I need to repeat for you."

"I beg your pardon! You don't have to be rude."

"And you don't have to choose to have selective hearing when you would rather be a bitch, than help someone who asked nicely."

"You youth today are disgraceful," the woman protested.

"Oh, fuck off," Warren paused. "Wait, do you hear that?" He held a hand up to his ear. "Someone somewhere needs a boomer to go ask for a manager. You'd better hurry."

Warren returned his attention to the ATM so he could pull out what money he did have. He hoped that he could possibly negotiate with God as he was only a few dollars short. He pressed the cancel button and watched as the screen processed his command. The balance warning disappeared, and Warren let out a heavy sigh. He pressed the cancel button again and waited for his card to be ejected so he could repeat the process. The screen remained still with his card deep inside the mechanics. Warren pressed the button again.

Warren slammed his hand on the glass. "Give me my fucking card back, you electronic douche-canoe," he yelled as the screen went black. "Great," he muttered under his breath and turned away.

Beep.

"I'll beep you, you motherfucker." He slapped his hand against the screen and the monitor to life.

"Sir, can you please hurry up? I am in a rush," said the old woman.

Warren, his frustration rising, turned to the old woman and jabbed a finger towards her face. "Not a good time," he said as he diverted his attention back to the card-munching robot. "I need my fucking car back."

Cam's eyes slowly closed as the claws of sleep started to grasp hold of her. As her head tipped forward, she snapped upright, jolting herself awake. The glare of the monitor stung her eyes as she looked at the rest of the group and realized she was the last one standing. She stole a quick glance at Lucifer and smiled. The man was gorgeous even when he slept.

She rubbed her face and resumed her review of the camera feeds on her screen. After a series of eight mundane traffic cameras and a cell phone video of a drunk group at a roadside bar, a familiar face filled the frame. She instinctively clicked next, and the feed changed. "Wait," she said as she realized her mistake, and clicked the back button on the screen. The face filled the screen again. She paused as she looked at the man staring back at her. "Holy fuck," she blurted out, almost dumping her coffee in her lap.

"Did you find him?" asked Ashley as she spasmed in her seat and suddenly awoke.

"Nope," said Cam as she turned her monitor towards Ashley. "I found this."

"Holy fuck!" shouted Ashley.

At her sudden outburst, everyone else in the room suddenly awakened from varying stages of sleep.

"What?" asked Lucifer.

"It's Warren," said Ashley. "He's alive."

"Holy shit," said David. "Where is he?"

Cam leaned into the screen to read the camera identification number. "A Wells Fargo ATM in south Phoenix."

Ashley turned to Raphael. "Is there a way we can communicate with him?"

Raphael nodded. "We can hear him, but we can only talk to him through chat. Click on the camera, select ATM as the output, and click on text chat."

"Good enough," said Cam as she followed Raphael's directions as she watched Warren turn away to argue with the woman behind. "We can make this work."

♦♦♦♦

Warren was rapidly losing his patience, both with the ATM and the old crow hassling him. After offering a few more choice words to the impatient woman behind him, he once again looked back at the screen. The picture remained black for a moment longer, before a single yellow word appeared.

Warren?

Warren raised an inquisitive eyebrow. "Yes, I know who I am, thanks very much." The text disappeared, leaving a black screen. A moment later, more yellow text appeared.

Warren, are you there?

Warren looked down at the screen, unsure how to communicate with the phantom messenger. "Yes, I'm still here. Give me my debit card back." He was uncertain why he was talking to a computer he knew could not hear him. "Why am I even talking to you? You're a fucking machine."

We can hear you through the ATM.

"You can?" asked Warren with a hint of confusion.

Yes.

"We? Who is this?"

It's Cam.

Warren frowned, certain someone was screwing with him. "I know there's a fucking cam. I'm looking right at."

No, it's Cam. I'm here with Ash.

"Right," he said. "Quit fucking with me."

It's me, Warren. I promise.

"If it's really you two, tell me something that only I would know."

You cheated on Ash with her best friend.

Warren's eyes widened. "Holy shit, it is you. How did you find me?"

There's a camera in the ATM. We can see you.

"Where are you?" asked Warren.

We're still in Heaven. We're here with Amber and David.

"Where's Greg? Is he okay?" He waited as Cam typed her response.

He's hurt. The Caretaker shot him. We need to find God and bring him back to Heaven. Lucifer can't get the arrow out on his own.

"Lucifer?"

Yes.

"You mean as in the Devil?"

Yes.

"Well, you can tell him I've already found God," said Warren.

You have???

"Yes."

Are you serious?

The old lady behind him was losing her patience with the man talking to the ATM. "Sir! I need to use this. Please, hurry up."

Warren turned and held up a dismissive hand to silence the woman. "I'm kinda busy right now. You should have thought about that when you were rude to me." He lowered his hand as he returned to the conversation.

"Sir!" she protested.

Without taking his attention away from the ATM, Warren raised his right hand behind him and extended his middle finger.

Warren ? Have you really found God?

"Yes, I found God. Why would I lie about that?"

How?

"He was trying to tow my car."

Why was he towing your car?

"He said I was illegally parked outside a bar, but I wasn't. He was just being a douchebag again. And then he tried to kill me with his stupid laser vision, but it doesn't work anymore."

Are you drunk?

Warren frowned in frustration. "No, I'm not fucking drunk."

Why was he in a tow truck?

"Career change, I guess. He's still kind of a dick, though."

Can you get back to him?

"Yeah. I followed him to the tow yard. I know exactly where he is. He's locked behind a gate about five blocks south of here."

Can you climb over this gate?

"Not without tearing myself to pieces on razor wire."

Warren, I could kiss you.

Warren smiled at the statement. He was hoping Ashley was behind the keyboard. "Ash?"

No, it's Lucifer. I'm typing now.

"Are you female?"

No.

"Oh."

We need to you persuade him to come back to Heaven.

"How am I supposed to do that? I'm not exactly his favorite person these days. The fucker tried to kill me with his truck and then tried to hit me with golf balls."

A hand tapped Warren on the arm to encourage him to turn around. Without looking at the finger's owner, Warren shrugged it off and continued his discussion with Lucifer.

The stranger placed a firm hand on Warren's arm. "Sir?" a younger female voice asked, clearly not belonging to the old lady.

"What?" Warren asked with a frustrated tone as he turned around.

"Are you okay, sir," Police Officer Luna Martinez asked as Warren made eye contact with her.

Warren seemed surprised to see the cop. "Uh, yeah, I'm fine, officer. I'm just in the middle of something kinda important."

"These people have said you're having a conversation with the ATM machine," said the officer.

"It's an ATM."

"Excuse me?"

"Sorry, it's something God told me," explained Warren." Look, I'm trying to stop a demon invasion again. So, if you don't mind, I need to get back to talking with Lucifer. He's waiting for me."

"Who did you say is helping you?" asked Martinez.

"Lucifer."

"A Lucifer, or the Lucifer?"

"The," said Warren.

"I see. You said demon invasion again. This isn't the first time you've stopped a demon invasion?"

"No."

"Did Lucifer help you the first time?"

"No, God did. Well, he kinda did. He mostly just made things worse than they already were." Warren pointed at the ATM. "Look, I really need to get back to this."

"Uh huh. I'm going to need you to come with me."

"What? I'm not doing anything wrong."

"It's just for an evaluation. We want to check the old noggin to make sure you're okay."

"I'm not crazy."

"You say that, but you're talking to Lucifer through an ATM machine. The facts are telling me a very different story."

"It's an ATM," repeated Warren as he turned his back on Officer Martinez and resumed interacting with the screen.

Warren? Is everything okay?

"I'm still here," said Warren "The crazy old bitch behind me called the cops."

"I'm going to need you to turn around and place your hands behind your back," ordered Officer Martinez. "I'm not going to ask you again."

Warren looked back at the officer. "You're arresting me? On what grounds?"

"Disturbing the peace."

He turned back to the screen. "I'm not disturbing the peace. I'm trying to talk to Lucifer through the ATM." At that moment, self-awareness washed over Warren as he realized how utterly insane he sounded. "Shit."

"Turn around. I won't ask you again."

"Do I get my phone call if you arrest me?" asked Warren.

"Why? Do you need to call God?"

"No. I don't have his phone number. He never gave it to me."

Cam watched the events unfolding on the monitor with an open jaw and wide eyes. She flinched as Warren's head was slammed against the ATM camera and the police officer pulled his hands behind his back.

"*You have the right to remain silent*," Martinez's voice rang out through her headset.

"*Lucifer needs me to find God,*" said Warren, opting to not remain silent and, in fact, succeeding in making things worse.

"Well, fuck," said Cam as she dropped her headset on the desk.

"What's going on?" asked Amber as she stepped off the elevator with a fresh cup of coffee, intending to change shifts with her sister.

"Warren just got arrested," said Cam.

"Excuse me?" said Amber. Not entirely sure what she's just heard.

"Oh, shit," said Cam, realizing Amber was not fully up to speed on the recent developments. "We found Warren."

"You did?" Amber's jaw fell open.

"Yep, and that's not even all of it. He found God. We're going to save Greg."

The information was too much for Amber to process, and the hot mug slipped from her hands and smashed on the floor, splashing coffee everywhere. "Oh, my God," was all she could muster.

Ashley rushed over to help her sister, who appeared to be moments away from collapsing. "Careful there, sis," she said as she stepped over the puddle of coffee and put her arm around Amber.

"Is he really alive?" asked Amber.

Ashley nodded. "He is."

"Is he okay?"

"Yeah," said Ashley. "Aside from the whole getting arrested thing."

"What happened?"

"Long story, but he gave us God's location. We know where he is."

"What do we do now?" asked Amber.

Lucifer raised a hand. "I'm going to head down there and bring him back home."

"I'll go with you," said Cam as she tried to join in on Lucifer's adventure. "I could use a break from this place, and it would be a great chance to get to know the famous Lucifer."

Lucifer smiled at her before letting her down. "As much as I'd love that, it's far too risky."

"Shouldn't that be my choice?" asked Cam, a little disappointed at his rejection. "I want to help my friend."

"He's right," said Raphael. "The Caretaker could still be looking for you. It doesn't know that Lucifer was involved."

"If we can get my ring working, I can teleport down there, grab Gary and be back in five minutes."

Raphael cringed. "I'm afraid it won't be as easy as that. When we enacted the shutdown protocol, it blocked all angels from teleporting to earth."

"Does that mean me?" asked Lucifer.

Raphael nodded. "Afraid so."

Lucifer shrugged off the hurdle. "So, you still consider me an angel then?" He smiled at the revelation.

Raphael stammered as he tried to explain himself.

"Oh, relax. I'm just fucking with you. I don't care if I'm an angel anymore. I'll just take Death with me then. It's no big deal."

Death raised an eyebrow. "How did I get roped into this?"

"Because I need someone else who can teleport who isn't an angel," said Lucifer

Raphael was not finished putting a wet blanket on Lucifer's plans. "You know Death's not allowed to teleport angels."

"Can we teleport when we're down there?"

Raphael shook his head. "Same rules. Death can, you can't."

"How was David able to move down there when he grabbed the Oceanview people? He's an angel."

"He's kind of an anomaly," said Raphael. "He's a guardian angel in training. He had to come back through the funnel. The funnel is the only way up or down."

"What about the closet that Death and I used to get up here?" asked Lucifer. "That still works."

"Gary can't use it," said Raphael.

"Why not?" asked Lucifer. "He set it up."

"He put a filter on it to only allow lesser staff to use it."

"What a dick," said Lucifer.

"Besides, it only has two access points. Death's office and Hell."

"You could have just said that," said Lucifer. "The lesser staff comment was unnecessary."

"Why can't Death go on his own?" asked Cam. "Wouldn't it be faster if he's the only one who can teleport?"

Lucifer shook his head. "Convincing Gary to come back is not going to be easy. He's not going to listen to Death."

"What about David?" asked Cam.

"Especially not David."

"What makes you think he'll listen to you?" asked Ashley. "The last time I checked, the two of you weren't exactly on speaking terms."

Lucifer removed the glove from his right hand to reveal the same black veins that he saw on Greg wrapped around his palm. "Because I have proof that I'm not lying."

Cam gasped at the revelation. "Are you—"

"Going to turn into a demon?" finished Lucifer.

Cam slowly nodded.

"He's already a demon," mumbled Spencer as he woke from his nap.

"And good morning to you, sunshine." He turned his attention back to Cam. "Once we cure Greg, this will all go away," said Lucifer, trying his hardest to look confident.

"And if we don't?"

"Well," said Lucifer. "We're not going to let that happen, are we?" He hoped his tone and smile masked the fear he was feeling. He turned his attention back to Raphael. "The only way I can get Gary to come back is to show him my hand. His first duty is to his flock, whether he wants to admit it or not. Once he sees one of them is infected, he'll have no choice but to come back. So, with the fact I can't teleport, what are my options?"

"Use the funnel to get down to Oceanview," said Raphael.

"Then what?"

"You'll need to secure transportation."

"What, you mean like a car or something?" asked Lucifer.

"Yeah. It's just over a two-hour drive. It shouldn't take you long to get there. We can still wrap this up quick." Raphael reached into his pocket and pulled out a wrist-com. He tossed it over to Lucifer. "You'll need this to talk to us."

Lucifer smiled as he caught the device and strapped it to his arm. "All right then," he said. "Let's go, Death, we have a job to do."

"Excuse me? We?" asked Death.

"Oh, you're still coming with me. We're going on a road trip," said Lucifer as he walked towards the elevator. "I need the company."

"I'm company," said Cam.

"I'm sorry," said Lucifer. "I meant someone immortal. Just in case things go bad. Keep the coffee warm, I'll be back before you know it. Maybe I'll bring you a gift."

Cam's eyes lit up at the suggestion. "A gift?"

"Yeah, maybe like a kitten or something." He paused. "Do you like kittens? Of course you do. Everyone loves kittens, right?" He said before Cam could respond. "Do you like kittens?"

Cam blushed again at the mild flirting. "I love kittens."

"Then I'll bring you one back."

"Hurry," she said.

"I'll be back before you know it." He waved goodbye as he entered the elevator.

Death muttered under his breath as he followed Lucifer inside. "You're embarrassing me."

"One more thing," said Raphael.

"Now what?" asked Lucifer.

"You can't just charge in there and lay all of this on him. You know how he gets, he's going to freak out. We need to prepare him for this."

"I'll do my best, but I'm not good at delivering bad news," said Lucifer.

"It's not the news, it's the courier."

"The fate of humanity is at stake, and he needs to prepare himself because he doesn't like the people delivering the news, not the news itself?"

Raphael paused. "Pretty much, yeah. I never said he was logical."

"You know what they say, Raph?" said Lucifer as the doors started to close.

"What?"

Lucifer shrugged. "If you don't like the smell of the cheese, go back to the cow."

"What does that even mean?" asked Raphael as the doors closed.

"I have no idea."

Five minutes later, Lucifer and Death departed the main waiting room and headed towards the funnel at the end of the hallway.

"Wow," said Lucifer as he stopped and overlooked over the edge of the funnel into the seemingly bottomless hole. "So, I'm supposed to just jump in?" he said, suddenly unsure of taking the leap.

"Yes," said Death.

"I don't know. That's a long way—"

Death placed a hand on Lucifer's back and pushed him into the hole. Death smiled to himself as he prepared to jump. If he needed to take part in this stupid mission, he was at least going to try and make the most out of it.

CHAPTER 16

"You're a dick, Steve," griped Lucifer as he stumbled over a mangled janitor's cart. "Why do you push me, you asshole?"

Death smiled. "It looked like you were having a moment of hesitation. I figured I'd give you some assistance."

"Well, I wasn't ready," said Lucifer as he looked around at the debris scattered around the base of the funnel. "What the hell is all of this shit?"

Death looked around at the pile of garbage they were standing on. "The old man was throwing things down the funnel."

"Why would he do that?" asked Lucifer.

"Because he's a moron," said Death.

"I can't believe you fucking pushed me. Ass."

Death continued to smirk at Lucifer's reaction as the two men stepped down from the pile of junk and looked around the empty church.

Lucifer nodded towards an arrow buried deep into a nearby pillar. A small wisp of black smoke circled around the shaft. "Well, we're definitely in the right place," said Lucifer. "That's an Impiety Arrow."

Death pointed to another lodged in the back of a pew. "There's another one."

Lucifer noticed two more in the wall. "This creature wanted the survivors dead in the worst conceivable way. We're lucky only one of them got shot."

Death nodded in agreement as Lucifer looked around at the various God-praising memorabilia scattered around the church and grimaced.

"Are you okay?" asked Death.

"This place is gross," said Lucifer as he looked at the crosses and pictures of Jesus.

"I'm betting Gary's house looks exactly the same way," said Death. "But with more candles and motivational posters."

Lucifer smiled at the thought. "Do you really think he has crosses on his wall after what happened to his kid?" asked Lucifer.

"He's oblivious enough, so who knows." Death walked towards the door and into the main hall.

Lucifer gave the art one final look and followed after Death. "See, now I want to get an invite to his house to see for myself."

Death smiled. "We need to find a car."

"Theft is my specialty. I can hotwire any—"

"No need." Death snapped his fingers and promptly disappeared.

"That teleporting shit is going to get old really fast," said Lucifer as he sat down on a pew and waited for Death to return.

Ten minutes later, Death reappeared, dangling a key chain in front of his face. "Ready?" he said as he tossed the keys to Lucifer. "You're driving."

"Damn right I am," said Lucifer as he stood and followed Death out of the church.

♦♦♦♦

"You're kidding, right?" said Lucifer as he stared at the chestnut brown, beat-up, piece of shit 1981 Chevy Cavalier parked on the street outside. "I'm not getting into that. I'm going to catch Tetanus."

Death's smile faded. He hoped for a more positive response from his upcoming travel companion. "I want us to be inconspicuous. I figured if I stole something new, it would garner too much attention. We need to fly under the radar. Gary can't see us coming, else he's going to run."

Lucifer walked around the car, taking in every dent, "This is so far under the radar, our bellies will be scratching gravel." He leaned into the passenger window and looked inside. "Are you changing your robes?"

Death frowned. "No. Why would I do that?"

"Well, I hate to burst your bubble, chief, but unless you change, we won't be inconspicuous. You stand out worse than I do."

"I like my robe," said Death. "Don't try to change me. Besides, I'll keep my hood up most of the time. No one will be aware of me. I'll fly under the radar."

"Don't be so touchy," said Lucifer as he hooked a pinkie finger under the door handle and carefully opened the door. He tried to avoid touching the frame as he slinked into the driver's seat.

"And you need to quit being such a baby," said Death as he opened his door. "It's not that bad."

"I wish you'd have let me get the car. We'd be riding in style."

"And in less than an hour, we'd be sitting in a jail cell after the GPS blasts out our location."

"That wouldn't be the worst thing. It'd be better than being seen in this crapmobile"

"This car doesn't have GPS, so unless we, meaning you, do something stupid, then we're off the grid. No one is tracking us, and we can do our job in peace."

"It doesn't mean I have to like it," said Lucifer as he pulled on his seat belt. It jammed and refused to expand more than a few inches. "I can't help but feel I'm not going to live long enough to regret this."

Death smiled as he put on his working seat belt. Lucifer started the engine and pulled away from the church.

"What the hell happened here?" asked Lucifer.

"Gary happened here," said Death as they turned onto Seventh Street.

"Bullshit," said Lucifer.

Death frowned. "What do you mean? An army of flesh-eating zombie-demons tore through the town."

"Yeah, I know the details. But the key word here is flesh-eating. Not concrete-eating. Has no one ever questioned that the entire town crumbled in less than six months? I've never seen decay like this."

"When Gary called the zombies back to Heaven, he demolished half of the town. Why do you think everyone left? There was no way he could bring back that many people without considerable structural damage. Between that and the damage that happened during the outbreak, the town was uninhabitable."

Lucifer pulled onto Sonora Street and headed east, carefully moving around various wrecked vehicles and piles of rubble. "I feel like we need a montage scene or something," he said cheerfully as he flipped through the radio stations.

"A what?"

"You know, a scene where we do a bunch of shit together and then laugh and joke about it over some music.

"Shit?"

"Yeah. Get ice cream, race go-carts, ride donkeys. That kind of shit."

"Go-carts? Yeah, sorry, I don't do *shit*." Death finger quoted the curse for emphasis.

"Look, this is going to be a really long drive. I'm just trying to lighten the mood a little."

"Well, you'll have to forgive me, I'm not used to having a fellow passenger. I prefer to travel solo," said Death as he focused on the road ahead.

Lucifer stopped on the next station as a country guitar twang played from the speaker. His eyes widened with excitement. "Don't tear my heart, my achy breaky —" he sang enthusiastically.

"No!" Death stabbed at the radio and turned it off. "That is out of the question."

Lucifer grins. "You know, if your magic robe could allow you to carry passengers, we wouldn't have to drive." He turned the radio back on and stopped as *Ticket To Ride* began to play. "There, that's more like it."

"I wouldn't have put you as a Beatles guy," said Death.

"No?"

"I figured you'd be more of a Death Metal kinda fan."

"Wow, thank you for playing into that stereotype. I happen to like the classics."

"You know, speaking of The Beatles, I always wondered why Lennon never went up to Gary. With all the good he did for the world, there's no way he legitimately went down to you."

Lucifer looked away and focused on the road ahead. "Yeah, that's weird, huh?"

Death furrowed his brow as he started fitting the pieces together. "You didn't have anything to do with that, did you?" he said as he looked directly at his traveling companion.

"No," said Lucifer. "I really need to focus on driving."

Death continued to stare at his companion as he tried to coax a confession from him.

"Fine. I may have pulled some strings," said Lucifer as he shrugged, trying to avoid a direct answer.

"No, you didn't," said Death. "That's impossible."

Lucifer nodded. "Guilty as charged."

"How? The lists are infallible."

"Yeah, but Gary's database isn't."

And the last piece of Death's mental puzzle fell into place. "Did you hack into Heaven's database?"

Lucifer grinned at the suggestion. "Never."

"Do you know about many protocols you violated doing that? Seve—"

"Eighty-four. Eighty-five depending on whether you consider The Beatles a pop or rock band."

"I —" Death was uncertain how to continue.

"Come on, Steve, I'm the Devil. I have ways around things. People expect me to do this kind of shit. Why would I disappoint the masses? So, fuck, yeah, we got Lennon. You think I'm wasting him on Heaven?"

"Who else did you take that you weren't supposed to?"

Lucifer thought about it for a moment. "Well, George, obviously. I'm waiting for Paul and Ringo, although I think McCartney might be immortal. Can you imagine how excited my people will be when I bring the Fab Four back together? Hey, you want some presale comp tickets for the next show?"

Death paused at the offer. His mind said no, of course he did not want tickets for a fraudulent concert. It would not be proper to be seen taking favors from either one of his clients. His mouth, however, disagreed. "Yes, yes I do."

Lucifer smiled again. "Wow, I didn't think you'd agree to that. I'll hook you up."

"Who else?"

"We have an entire concert pavilion. It's like Coachella but with less drugs. We have Cobain, Presley, Hendrix, Winehouse, Joplin, Mercury. It's a fucking party down there. I've also called dibs on Jagger and Sir Elton."

Death found himself in a stunned silence as Lucifer blatantly admitted fudging the system to his benefit.

"Oh, don't look at me like that," said Lucifer. "You know Gary doesn't deserve talent of that magnitude. If I'd had more notice about our road trip, I could have made us an epic mixtape of new songs."

"New songs?"

"Yeah, they're all still recording. Hell has some of the best studios in the universe. Last year, Lennon wrote a song called 'Everything will turn out okay', and it's probably the most beautiful song ever written. We nurture creativity."

"Why do we even need a mixtape? We're driving."

"We need road trip music."

"You're bound and determined to make this trip as uncomfortable as possible, aren't you?"

"Yep," said Lucifer with a grin.

"You still blame me for all of this, don't you?" asked Death.

"Yep."

"Would another sorry cut it?"

"How many sorry's do you think it would take to erase dealing with Gary?"

Death smiled. "Yeah, I suppose you have a point. But you don't get off lightly either. You had issues with your list too."

"Yeah, that'll teach me to rearrange my filing system. Lesson learned."

The first thirty minutes of the drive passed by with little excitement and it appeared Death and Lucifer would make good timing to Phoenix. However, the following twelve miles proved to be a much different beast.

The brake lights on the big red Ford truck in front illuminated for the fiftieth time in three minutes, and Lucifer let out his fiftieth sigh. He tapped his fingers on the steering wheel in frustration. His patience had long since worn thin, and his agitation was annoying Death.

"Can you stop sighing?" asked Death.

"We've been stuck in traffic for an hour, and we've barely moved a mile. If we could teleport, we wouldn't be stuck in traffic. And if we weren't stuck in traffic, I wouldn't be sighing."

"So, what you're saying is—"

"It's Gary's fault," said Lucifer. "Can you find us a shortcut on the map?"

"Yeah, in about ten feet, take a left."

Lucifer looked out of the driver's side window to see the edge of the mountain ten feet from the other side of the road. "You're funny."

Death glanced over at Lucifer and raised an eyebrow. "And you're asking stupid questions. It's single-lane traffic on the side of the mountain. Where would you suggest we turn?"

Lucifer turned to look at Death as the car started to move again. "We really need to work on your attitude," he said with a smile.

"Brake," said Death. "BRAKE!"

Lucifer slammed on the brakes, missing the trailer hitch on the truck in front by an inch. "See, that was also Gary's fault."

The brake lights disappeared for the briefest of moments and quickly returned.

"Come on!" yelled Lucifer as he reached over and slammed on the horn again. "Get a fucking move on, we're in a hurry. We have lives to save."

"Calm down," said Death. "You hitting the horn and yelling isn't going to make them move any faster."

Lucifer punched the horn again. "It might."

Honk.

And again.

Honk.

"It makes me feel like I'm doing something," said Lucifer.

Honk.

The driver's side door to the truck in front swung open, and a large bald man stepped out. He wore a white tank top revealing his intimidating and abundant muscles and what were likely redneck prison tattoos.

"Oh, for fuck's sake," said Lucifer. "We really don't have time for this."

"Good going, Luc," said Death as he tried to avoid eye contact with the large man advancing on them.

The man reached Lucifer's window and tapped a thick hairy knuckle against the glass. "Roll down the window, asshole," he commanded.

Lucifer cranked the manual window control and the glass lowered two inches. "Hello," he said cheerfully.

"Keep going," ordered the man as he pointed down.

Lucifer turned the handle, and the windows closed again. "Sorry," he lied as he lowered the window all the way down. "Technology, eh? Am I right?" he said with a smile. "I wanted a car with electric windows, but my friend here—"

"I don't give a shit about your friend. Are you the one who keeps honking at me?"

Lucifer pointed to his chest. "Me? You mean this horn?" He pointed at the steering wheel.

"Honk it one more time," said the gruff man. "Go on, I fucking dare you."

Death closed his eyes in anticipation and dread. "Don't do it. Don't do it. Don't do it. Don't do it. Don't do it," he muttered as Lucifer slowly moved his hand to the horn. "Luc, don't. Please, don't. Please—"

Lucifer smiled to himself and slowly and cheerfully tapped the horn.

Honk.

"Lock the d—" Death started as the man ripped the driver's side door open.

"Hi," said Lucifer. "How are—"

The man reached into the car and grabbed Lucifer by the scruff of the neck. He yanked him from the vehicle and held him a foot off the ground.

"Hey, watch the suit, man. Scotchgard doesn't get Neanderthal out of wool."

The man roughly set Lucifer down on the tarmac as his fingers formed a fist. "I was going to ask you to give me a reason to not punch you in your smug little face."

"Glad I saved you the effort," said Lucifer.

"But if I have to listen to one more word come out of your prissy little mouth, I'm going to rip your tongue out instead."

Lucifer reached out and tapped the man gently on the nose. "Honk!" he said with a playful grin.

The man pulled his arm back, ready to swing.

"Not the face! I really like my nose."

"Shut the fuck up," the man said as he swung his fist at Lucifer's face.

The punch landed hard on Lucifer's cheek, and he stumbled backwards into the car door. He paused as he regained his composure and straightened his jacket. "Are you done?" He brushed his hand across his lip and wiped off a drop of blood.

The man ground his fist into his other hand. "Oh, I'm just getting started."

"Traffic's moving," shouted Death from the passenger seat.

"I'm a little tied up," said Lucifer as the man grabbed him by the neck again.

"You doing okay?" asked Death.

"Yeah, I got this." Lucifer grabbed the man's fingers and started to bend them back.

A second and even larger man climbed out of the passenger side of the truck and waddled over to Death's side of the car.

"Steve, incoming!" shouted Lucifer.

"It's okay," shouted Death. "My hood is up, he can't see me."

"Get out of the fucking car," the larger man ordered Death.

"Shit," muttered Death as he frantically tried to take off his seat belt, regretting boasting about it being functional. It seemed Lucifer was not the only one losing their abilities.

In one smooth gesture, the man opened the door and pulled Death from the car, slamming his head onto the hood of the car.

Lucifer turned to face his assailant and smiled.

"What are you smiling about, you little shit?" said the Ford driver. "You know what I'm about to do to you."

"What is going to happen is put me down, wipe your greasy fingerprints off my jacket, turn around, and toodle your Budweiser and KFC-ridden ass back to your penis-compensation truck, and pretend you were never stupid enough to get out of your vehicle. How does that sound, sport?"

The man clenched his fist for a second time and swung it at Lucifer's face. Lucifer raised his hand and caught the punch mid-swing. The man seemed taken aback at the speed his victim moved.

"Uh, uh," said Lucifer as he shook his head. "The first one you get for free. I'm not giving you two." He raised his arm and punched the man square in the face.

Dazed, the man dropped Lucifer and staggered back. He took two clumsy steps and fell to the floor as consciousness left for a brief vacation.

"You doing good over there?" asked Lucifer as he rubbed his neck.

"No!" screamed Death as he struggled with the other man.

"It looks like he can see you," shouted Lucifer.

"Really? You think?" Death pushed the man away and took a step towards the passenger door. He reached through the window and pointed at the console between the seats. "Blood Card."

The man grabbed Death from behind and squeezed his throat.

"Where?" asked Lucifer.

"In the cup holder," gasped Death.

Lucifer looked down to see half a dozen Blood Cards. "No magic, that's cheating."

"Give me the fucking card," said Death.

"Whoa, watch the words, potty mouth." Lucifer reached over and picked up one of the cards. He held it out as Death's arm was wrenched back outside "For fuck's sake," said Lucifer as he climbed out of the car and walked over to the two feuding men. He held out the card before him.

Death's eyes widened as he realized Lucifer's intentions. "No! You can't use—"

Lucifer tapped the card against the man's arm.

Splat!

The man promptly exploded into a bloody mess.

"Dammit, Luc," said Death as he looked down at the gooey bloodstain on the tarmac. "I'm the only one who can use Blood Cards."

Lucifer pushed the toe of his shoe across the bloodied mess. "I know.

I'm surprised that even worked."

"It didn't work. You made him explode," said Death incredulously.

"Isn't that the same thing?" asked Lucifer.

"No, it's not the same thing. Blood Cards are supposed to be a peaceful transition between this world and the next. They aren't supposed to make people explode. Now I have extra paperwork to do. Get back in the dammed car." Death was close to losing every last bit of his shit.

"You're sexy when you're angry," said Lucifer with a sly grin as he climbed back in.

"Uh uh," said Death. "You're not driving anymore. Out."

"Fine," said Lucifer as he stepped back out on the road and switched sides with Death. "I want the working seatbelt anyway."

Both men traded sides and climbed back into the car. Death reached over his left shoulder for his own restraint and pulled, but the buckle refused to budge.

"Told you," said Lucifer as he put on his seat belt with a loud click. "Safety first," he said as he patted his chest.

"I hate you," said Death.

"Are we forgetting something?" asked Lucifer.

"Huh?"

"The people behind us?" Lucifer tapped his temple. "You need to do the mind thingy."

Death rolled his eyes and opened the door. "I'll be back," he said as he once again left the shitty brown car and walked over to the vehicle behind them. "Hi folks," he said with a forced smile.

The poor driver and passenger in the car sat frozen in place, their eyes wide and their mouths open in shock.

Death pointed to the rear door behind the driver. "Can I come in??"

The driver slowly nodded as Death opened the door and sat down behind the two occupants.

"Look, I know what you think you just saw, but I assure you, you didn't." He placed a hand gently on each of their shoulders, and their eyes glazed over. "Do we have an understanding?"

The two nodded their heads slowly.

"The truck on the other side of the road has broken down. Traffic will pick up again shortly. Enjoy your trip." Death climbed back out of the car and headed back towards Lucifer. "It's not called mind thingy," he said as he closed the door. "It's called cleansing."

"Kinky," said Lucifer.

The vehicles in front of the red truck started to move and Death pulled around it. Traffic finally started to pick up pace, and thirty minutes later, they were back up to the full speed limit.

Lucifer pointed at an upcoming freeway sign indicating an imminent gas station. "I need a soda."

"Yeah, me too," said Death. "That sounds like a good idea." Death promptly disappeared.

"Son of a bitch," screamed Lucifer as he scrambled to grab the steering wheel as the car suddenly found itself without a driver.

Death reappeared holding a sixty-four-ounce unsweetened iced tea and a rather proud look on his face. He took a long sip from the straw as Lucifer stared at him. "What?"

"The fuck, dude? Where's mine?" asked Lucifer as he released the steering wheel to Death.

"Oh, you wanted one?"

"Uh, yeah. It was my suggestion. You know? When I said need a soda. Of course I wanted one."

"Be right back."

"No, don't —"

Death disappeared again, and Lucifer once more reached for the steering wheel. Moments later Death reappeared, clutching a small bottle of Diet Pepsi.

"Will you stop that!" yelled Lucifer. "You're going to get me killed."

"Oh, relax, I was only gone a second." Death passed the soda over to Lucifer.

Lucifer stared at the bottle. "I can count at least a dozen things wrong with this. When have I ever said I liked Pepsi? You do know who brews this shit, right?"

Death shrugged.

"Mormons."

"No, they don't," said Death. "That's an urban legend."

"Let's just say that Pepsi is more of a Gary drink, but as you didn't get me anything else." Lucifer cracked open the can and took a swig. He promptly spat it out back into the bottle. "And it's fucking warm."

"Sorry," said Death, not at all sorry in the slightest.

"Why didn't you get cold ones?"

"I thought I did. They must have just restocked." Death, in fact, did not look in the refrigerator. He simply grabbed a bottle from a nearby stack not yet been displayed for purchase.

"And why do you get a sixty-four-ounce, and I get a twenty? I'm thirsty too."

"I can get you a cold one if you like?" Death pointed to the gas station coming up ahead of them.

"No. We're going to do this the old-fashioned way. We're going to pull over and go inside in person."

Lucifer pitched the bottle over his shoulder into the back seat and a muffled yelp came from behind them.

"The fuck?" He tilted the rearview mirror down and pointed it at the backseat. "Pull over," he directed Death.

"We're almost at the gas station." Death craned his neck to look into the back seat as he guided the car off the freeway and into the gas station parking lot.

Lucifer climbed out of the car and stepped over to the rear passenger door. He pulled the rear door open to see a pile of blankets covering the back seat.

"You can come out now, Spencer," said Lucifer.

The pile of fabric stirred, but nothing appeared.

"Spencer, I know you're in there. If you don't come out, I'm going to start punching the seat. Hard."

The blankets slowly parted as Spencer's head peeked out. "Hi," he said with an awkward innocence

"What the fuck are you doing here?" asked Lucifer

"I'm sorry. I overheard you saying you were going to go find Gary, and I wanted to help. I jumped down the portal thingy before you left. But I got nauseous on the way down and went outside to vomit. I got weak and found this car and decided to lay down in the back until I stopped feeling dizzy."

"I guess you're lucky that Death has a shitty taste in cars then," said Lucifer.

"What's wrong with this car?" asked Spencer. "It looks nice."

Lucifer glanced over at Death and grinned. "Told you it was a bad choice."

Spencer straightened his shirt as he stepped out of the car. "I need to stretch my poor legs."

Lucifer frowned. "So why do you care about what happens to Oceanview? You're not vested in this."

Spencer shrugged. "Heaven is all I have. Without it I'm nothing. I miss the barbecues and the singing."

"Singing?" asked Lucifer. "So that's why there's a fucking kumbaya sing-along going on in my throne room?"

"We love to sing our hymns," said Spencer. "It brings us peace and enlightenment."

Death started to laugh at Lucifer's glorious misfortune.

Lucifer turned to him and scowled. "Fuck off. It's not funny, Steve. They are horrible house guests."

"Yes, it is. You have a cavern full of choral Baptists."

Lucifer rolled his eyes in irritation. "We're getting drinks and snacks. Are you coming with us?" he asked Spencer.

Spencer pondered the question for the briefest of moments and nodded his head. "I want Moon Pies. I can feel my blood sugar levels dropping"

"I thought you were vegan?" asked Lucifer.

"I am vegan and gluten-free. Moon Pies are banana flavored, which makes them fruit."

"They have wheat flour in them. Which has gluten," argued Lucifer.

"Fruit cancels out gluten," said Spencer defiantly. "Fruit cancels out all kinds of horrible things."

"And you're an idiot," added Lucifer. He picked up one of the snacks from the shelf and analyzed the ingredients list. "These things actually expire? I thought they were immortal like Twinkies."

"Of course they do," said Death. "They expire like everything else."

Lucifer shrugged with indifference. "I didn't even think they had an expiration date. I thought it was just a space-filler to make a store look more stocked than it really is. I can't believe people really eat this shit."

"Have you ever eaten one?" asked Spencer. "They're truly delightful."

"Yes," said Lucifer. "Once. It was horrible. It's a cake of lies. It tastes like failed dreams and poverty. But whatever floats your boat."

"What can I say? I have specific tastes," said Spencer.

Lucifer opened the door to the gas station and gestured for Spencer and Death to enter.

The clerk behind the counter frowned as the two darkly dressed men and Spencer walked into the door. He watched the suspicious character walk around the store as they picked out snacks and ducked into freezers.

"I didn't think people could see you with your hood up?" Lucifer asked Death as he browsed a display of potato chips."

"They shouldn't," said Death. "I think this whole Heaven issue is screwing my abilities too."

"Great, you get to suffer with me then," said Lucifer as he selected a bag of Doritos and immediately put them back down. He growled to himself as he studied other bags.

"What's wrong?" asked Death.

"I miss having three options," said Lucifer.

"Huh?" said Death.

"There's too many choices."

"Just pick one. I don't think the clerk wants us here."

Lucifer looked up to see the clerk staring at them with his arms crossed. Lucifer leaned into Death. "I know this isn't the greatest time to mention this, but do you have any money?"

Death looked at Lucifer in frustration. "No. I assumed you had some cash in that expensive suit of yours."

"I haven't needed cash in centuries. I think all I have is my lucky doubloon and I don't think the exchange rate is too favorable on those at the moment."

"Then how are we supposed to pay for all of this?" asked Death.

"How did you get the sodas before?"

"I stole them."

"Well, I can't teleport," said Lucifer. "Could you lift your robe and use it like a basket?"

"Absolutely not. I am not showing my legs to anyone. They haven't seen sun in centuries."

"Can't you just teleport these out to the car?"

"And how will you get out with the clerk watching you? He probably has a shotgun."

"We could, you know—" Lucifer whistled and nodded towards the door. His intentions to run quite clear.

"Really?" asked Death.

Lucifer grinned. "Yeah. Beer run without the beer. I could also grab beer and make it an official beer run."

"Do you really think I can run in this robe?"

"Run where?" asked a voice behind them.

The pair turned around to see the store owner squaring off in front of them. They were not as inconspicuous as they hoped.

"Excuse me?" asked Lucifer politely, feigning ignorance.

"Run where?" the man asked again.

"The bathroom," lied Death. "I've drank too much soda."

"Uh, huh." The gruff man folded his arms. He looked at the groceries the two men were holding. "Are you going to pay for those?"

"Of course we are," said Lucifer.

"How?"

"With money," said Lucifer.

"Show me."

"Here, hold these," said Lucifer as he handed his supplies over to the store owner. He started to pat down his pockets looking for his non-existent wallet.

Death lowered his head and coughed softly. "What's Spencer doing?" he whispered under his breath as he nodded towards their cohort walking past the counter out of the store owner's field of vision.

Behind the surly man, Spencer was huddled by the water display glancing around suspiciously.

"He's not particularly good at being inconspicuous, is he? He looks like a criminal," said Lucifer in equally hushed tones. Lucifer watched Spencer slink towards the door with a container of salt and six bottles of water and smiled as the thieving Baptist disappeared with his loot, along with his hypocrisy, out of the door.

The store owner coughed as Lucifer stopped patting his pockets. "You two Halloween freaks need to get the hell out of my store. Now."

Death also handed his snacks over to the man and followed Lucifer to the exit.

Lucifer walked ten feet from the door and held out his hand. "Keys," he demanded.

"I thought I told you I was driving," said Death.

"You were. And then you started teleporting. I'm supposed to be Heaven's most beautiful angel. I'd like to keep it that way, please. I don't need a face full of glass."

Death chewed on his lip as he contemplated the request.

"I tell you what, you let me drive, and you can control the radio," offered Lucifer.

"You know I don't really listen to music," said Death as he reluctantly handed over the keys to Lucifer.

"What about me?" asked Spencer.

"What about you?" said Lucifer as he walked to the driver's side of the car.

"I can drive."

"Yeah, that's cute," said Lucifer as he dismissed the announcement. "Get in the back, princess."

Spencer scowled as he climbed into the back of the vehicle and immediately put on his seat belt.

Lucifer pulled away from the gas station, and the group continued their journey towards Phoenix. As they made their way south, Lucifer's lack of sleep became more apparent as his braking became heavier, his swerving more erratic, and his use of the horn more frequent.

"Would you mind slowing down a bit?" asked Death.

"Steve. I haven't slept in three days. You're lucky I don't fall asleep and wrap this car around a tree."

"Do it. I'll just teleport. The only person you'd kill is Spencer."

"Excuse me?" said a distressed Spencer from the back seat.

"I can live with that outcome," said Lucifer.

"I object," whined Spencer.

"You don't get a say in this," said Lucifer. "And speaking of you, what were you stealing—"

Spencer wrapped an arm around Lucifer's neck and pinned him to the seat. As the car swerved, Death grabbed the steering wheel to keep it from hitting the car beside them.

"Spencer!" protested Death. "What are you doing?"

A moment later, Spencer poured a bottle of water over Lucifer's head.

Lucifer struggled to break away from his assailant's grip. "What the fuck, dude?" he spluttered as he spat out water that ran into his mouth.

The car swerved again as Lucifer turned his attention back to the road. He wiped his sleeve across his face to remove the water that dripped down from his forehead. "Spencer, I'm going to kill—"

A second bottle of water was dumped over his head and Lucifer swerved again.

"Jesus Christ, what are you doing?" shouted Lucifer.

"Benediction of the salt," said Spencer.

"What?"

"Benediction of the salt. It's a holy ritual that—"

"I do believe he's trying to exorcise you," said Death with a grin.

"The fuck?" said Lucifer.

Spencer poured more water into the palm of his hand and flicked it at Lucifer. "Most cunning serpent—"

"That's it." Lucifer let go of the steering wheel and leaped into the backseat. Death quickly teleported to the driver's seat to avoid driving headlong into oncoming traffic.

Spencer squealed as the Prince of Darkness collided with him and knocked him over. Spencer flicked more water at his assailant as Lucifer reached for the plastic bottle and promptly used it to smack Spencer on the forehead.

"You shall no more dare to deceive—"

Smack.

"—ouch, deceive the human race—"

Smack.

"—ouch, persecute the Church, torment God's elect and sift them as wheat—" Spencer rubbed his red forehead. "Stop hitting me!"

"Stop exorcising me!" shouted Lucifer.

"I can't! I must do the Lord's work," said Spencer as he tried to wrestle the bottle back from Lucifer. "I'm doing this in the name of God."

"God doesn't even like you," said Lucifer.

Spencer immediately stopped struggling and stared at Lucifer. "Why would you say such an awful thing?" He fumbled for another bottle and unscrewed the cap.

"No, you don't", said Lucifer as he reached for the bottle and smacked Spencer on the head with it.

"Stop hitting me!" wailed Spencer.

"Pull the car over," ordered Lucifer. "I'm throwing this moron out."

Death pulled the car off the freeway and skidded to a halt. The rear driver's side door flung open, and Lucifer climbed out. "Get out," he said as he shook the water off his suit.

Spencer slowly stepped out of the vehicle clutching his bottle of water. He poured more water onto his hand and flicked it at Lucifer. "The power of Christ compels you!" He flicked more water at Lucifer, hitting him square in the face.

Lucifer screamed and grabbed at his face. He stumbled forward and dropped to the ground. "Oh, my god, it burns. It burns. What have you done to me?"

Spencer's eyes widened, and he rushed over to Lucifer. "I'm so sorry, Mr. Lucifer, sir."

Lucifer turned to Spencer and grinned. "Just kidding."

Spencer scowled and immediately dumped the rest of his water over Lucifer's head.

"Are you fucking serious?" Lucifer straightened up.

Spencer backed away as Lucifer moved towards him. "I said the power of Christ—"

"That's Catholicism, you moron. Baptists don't exorcise, you silly little tit," said Lucifer.

"I don't care. I'm switching teams for the good of humanity." Spencer raised his hand to flick more water as Lucifer closed the distance between them. Lucifer swatted the bottle out of his hand, and Spencer squealed and fell to the floor in the fetal position. "Don't hurt me, spawn of hatred."

A passing car slowed down as the passenger raised her cell phone and snapped a picture of the scene. Lucifer frowned as he watched the amateur paparazzi pull away. "Get up, Spencer. You're drawing attention." He reached down and offered him a hand.

Instinctively, Spencer slapped his hand away. "I can get up perfectly well on my own, thank you very much."

The squabbling duo walked back to the car. Lucifer stopped at the driver's side door to see Death at the wheel.

"Nope," said Death. "Passenger seat, back seat, or trunk. Pick one, you're not driving anymore."

Lucifer returned to the passenger seat as Death pulled away once again, and the group commenced their quest.

"Are you okay, Spencer?" asked Lucifer to a pair of deaf ears. "Spencer? Are you ignoring me now?" He waited for a response that never arrived. "Spencer?"

"I'm not ignoring you," said Spencer as he deliberately looked away and avoided eye contact. "I'm simply making the decision to not speak to you. There is a difference."

"Fine. I get to pick the music."

Spencer continued to stare out of the window.

Lucifer flicked through the stations and stopped at the loudest, heaviest music he could find. "Ooh, Megadeth, "said Lucifer as the opening riff to '*Peace Sells*' began. "I love this song." He turned around to face Spencer and started singing. "What do you mean I don't believe in God? I talk to him every day." Lucifer stopped singing and held his hand to whisper to Spencer. "I don't. He's an asshole. And he won't take my calls."

Spencer continued to stare out of the window.

Lucifer continued to sing. "What do you mean I don't support your system? I go to court when I have to." He held up his hand again. "I really don't. Jury duty is for losers."

Spencer jammed his fingers into his ears. "I can't hear you."

Lucifer grinned and turned back to the radio. "Fine, no Megadeth. I wonder what else we have." He skimmed through more channels and stopped on something louder and heavier and even more offensive to

Spencer's lightly plugged ears. "I bet you're a Cannibal Corpse person, aren't you?"

Spencer's eyes widened to impossible sizes as the thrashing guitars and drums that spawned directly from the darkest depths of the bowels of the earth erupted from the speakers. "Turn it off! Turn it off!" he screamed. "I'll talk to you!"

Lucifer smiled and turned the radio off. "See, was that so difficult?"

"I really dislike you."

A movement in the rearview mirror caught Death's attention. He looked up to see red and blue flashing lights behind them. "Well done, fellows. We've got company."

Lucifer looked in the side mirror. "Dammit. I told you to stop fucking around, Spencer. We really don't have time for this." He pulled the car over and opened the glove box in the hopes of finding insurance or registration, but his search came up empty. "I don't suppose you took the time to get a driver's license over the past few thousand years, did you, Steve?"

Death looked at Lucifer and clenched his jaw. "Really?"

"Hey, you're the one who insisted on driving. I figured you planned this a little better."

A firm tap echoed on Death's window, and he turned to see a cop standing outside the car. Death dutifully lowered the window and smiled. "Hello," he said politely.

"License and registration," demanded the cop.

"You didn't say please," said Lucifer as he leaned forward and waved at the cop. "My friend is a stickler for good manners. You should ask him again."

The cop lowered his sunglasses and stared into the car. "I won't ask you twice."

"About that. I—" Death started.

"He doesn't have those," said Spencer from the back seat. "He probably shouldn't be driving."

Lucifer stifled a laugh as Death's eyes widened at the sudden unnecessary announcement.

"Really?" said Death as he turned to face Spencer. "Are you serious right now?"

"I have to tell the truth," said Spencer. "I can't let you lie to a police officer." He leaned forward so the cop could see him clearer. "I think he might be here illegally," he said as he pointed at Lucifer. "And they both stole from a gas station."

"Motherfucker," said Lucifer as he lunged at Spencer.

The cop reached down and unclipped the strap holding his gun in place. He removed it from his holster and pointed it at Death. "Every one of you, get out of the car and put your hands behind your head. You're under arrest."

CHAPTER 17

Sweat pooled on Greg's brow as he twisted and thrashed around on the couch. Amber was no longer able to hold his hand as his erratic movements became more aggressive, and she was forced to retreat to the door, and looked upon him from the opening.

A light cough came from behind her. She turned to see Ashley standing in the hallway.

"How is he doing?" asked Ashley.

Amber shook her head. "He's getting worse. Have you heard from anyone?"

"Lucifer checked in about thirty minutes ago. They got stuck in traffic north of Phoenix for a while, but they seem to be making progress now. We're hoping they contact God in the next hour or so."

"What about Warren?"

"We lost track of him after he was arrested. I think we're going to focus on bringing God back so we can fix Greg first, and then we'll go find Warren."

"Warren," mumbled Greg from the couch. "Take Warren first. No, not me. Take Warren." He rolled over and returned to unconsciousness.

Amber inhaled in a frail effort to remain calm. "We're running out of time. Greg is getting worse by the hour."

Ashley looked at the concern on Amber's face and placed a loving hand on her shoulder. "We'll get him healed soon."

Another cough from behind announced David and Raphael's arrival. Amber and Ashley turned to greet them.

"Have you heard from them?" asked Ashley.

"We have a problem," said David.

"Now what?" asked Ashley. "I thought things were moving again?"

David bit his lip as he tried to find a delicate way to drop the news.

"David?" asked Ashley. "What happened?"

"They got arrested," said David.

The color drained from Amber's face as her hopes of saving Greg were hindered once again.

"Who?" asked Ashley.

"All of them," said David.

"Please tell me you're kidding," said Ashley. "We can't afford another setback."

David shook his head. "Spencer tried to exorcise Lucifer in the car, and they were arrested for reckless driving."

"Spencer? What is he doing there?" asked Ashley. "I thought he was here with us?"

"Apparently, he sneaked out when no one was looking," said Raphael.

"So now what do we do?" asked Amber.

"I'm going down to find them," said Raphael.

"We're going down," added Cam.

"What?" said Amber, her eyes wide. "You can't. It's too dangerous, the Caretaker is still out there."

"David can't teleport anymore, and Raphael can't drive. I'm not going to ask Ashley to leave you. I'm the only logical option."

Amber stepped over and wrapped her arms around Cam. "I won't forget this."

Cam kissed her gently on the cheek. "We'll be back by tonight."

The jail cell door slammed shut in Spencer's face with a loud clang. He starred at the bars as Death and Lucifer walked over to one of two benches at the back of the sparse room and sat down next to two rough and heavily tattooed fellow inmates.

Spencer turned around to look at the two other inmates, and his face flushed white as he judged them based on their tough exteriors. He spun back to face the cell door. "Please, you have to let me go. You've made a terrible mistake," he shouted as he grabbed hold of the bars. He waited for a response. "Hello?" he pleaded.

"Shut up, curly," shouted a distant cop. "Yelling won't help you."

Spencer glanced over at the two inmates and pressed his back against the bars. He watched with terrified eyes as Lucifer extended a hand to the nearest man.

"Hi," said Lucifer cheerfully. "I'm Lucifer." He offered his hand to the man.

"Pitbull, but my friends call me Phil," said the fellow prisoner as he grabbed Lucifer's hand. "This is Shank."

Lucifer leaned across Pitbull and reached out to greet Shank. He smiled as the obviously drunk man struggled to grab his hand. "A pleasure."

"S'up?" the intoxicated man slurred.

"Nice place," said Lucifer cheerfully. "What are you in for here?"

"My esteemed acquaintance here was driving drunk," said Pitbull.

"So why did they arrest you?" asked Death.

"I was the one who stole the car," said Pitbull with a sly grin. "What about you guys? What did you do?"

"We associate with an idiot," said Lucifer.

"They can arrest you for that?" the inmate asked as he raised an eyebrow, genuinely contemplating the possibility.

Lucifer nodded towards Spencer. "Well, he's an idiot, and I'm locked up because of him. So yeah, it would certainly seem that way."

"Would you like me to k— k— kl hm?" Shank stammered incoherently.

"I'm sorry, what did you say?" asked Lucifer, amused at how fast the situation appeared to be escalating.

Spencer spun to face the bars and grabbed hold of them with white knuckles. "Help! Someone's going to kill me," he yelled. "Please, help me!"

"Sit down and shut up," shouted the cop from down the corridor. "We'll get to you later. Screaming won't speed things up."

Shank frowned at Spencer's freak out. "I said, would you like me to c— c— call him an idiot? I can do that. I'm good at calling people idiots." He looked down at his hands and focused intently on his fingers. "These tiny little snakes move around a lot," he said as he wiggled his fingers. "I wonder if they're poisonous." He pressed a finger against his thigh and waited. "Nope."

"Sit down, Spencer," said Lucifer. "We ain't going anywhere for a while."

"No, no, you don't understand. I'm too fragile for prison. I won't make it a day." Spencer raised his hands to his head as he plunged into a dead-on panic attack. "Hello? Is anyone else out there?" he shouted as his terrified voice raised an octave. "Help!"

"Shut up!" yelled the cop.

"Please let me out," Spencer yelled again.

A moment later, the police officer stepped up to the bars. "I told you to shut up, cupcake. Another peep from you, and I'll make sure you get the chair."

"Do you have a chair?" asked Spencer. "I'd like that, please. There's no more seats left."

The officer pointed to the bench next to the other inmate. "Sit there, or sit on the floor."

"But it smells like urine and dropped soap," protested Spencer

"Sit. Down," said the cop. Dainty inmates annoyed him, and Spencer was by far one of the daintiest people to pass through his jail.

Spencer inhaled sharply as he considered his options. He slowly rotated to face Pitbull. With his jaw clenched tight, he walked over, and stopped in front of him.

"What do you want?" the gruff man asked as he looked up at the blonde oddball.

Spencer let out another heavy breath and reached down for his belt. "I'm doing what I must."

Pitbull frowned as he watched Spencer loosen his belt and unzip his pants. "What are you doing?" He turned his head towards Lucifer, but his eyes remained fixed on Spencer. "What's he doing?"

Lucifer shrugged. "I have no idea, but I'm vested now."

The man turned to Death. "What about you?"

Death shrugged. "I'm with him. I'm curious to see how this plays out now."

Spencer paused and sighed. Frustrated at the need to explain the obvious, he pushed his khakis around his knees. "I've heard how rough prison sex is. Please be gentle, I don't want to rip my favorite trousers."

"This is county jail," said Lucifer. "You are not getting raped here."

"Prison rape happens at all levels of incarceration," said Spencer as his pants completed their fall to the ground. "Everyone knows that. I'm just trying to be proactive and protect my property."

Pitbull raised an eyebrow as Spencer slid his fingers into the waistband of his boxer shorts and pulled them down.

Their attention was drawn to the cell door as an officer approached with a set of keys. The cop stared at Spencer standing in front of Pitbull with his pants and tighty-whities dropped around his ankles. He thumbed the radio on his shoulder. "Ed, I need some assistance with a pervert in cell three."

♦♦♦♦

"Rough night, sweetie?" asked the smiling waitress as she placed a plate of borderline-incinerated bacon and over-easy eggs on the table in front of God.

"Huh?" asked God as he glanced at the perfectly cooked breakfast, although mildly curious about the small pool of water on the plate.

"The sunglasses. It's a bit late for those. I'm guessing you had a bit too much fun last night?"

"Oh yeah, right." God slowly lowered his shades and placed them on the table. He was still struggling to get used to being able to look upon humans without setting them on fire.

"Can I get you anything else? I recommend the coffee for the post-party incapacitation. Extra black will cure almost any ailments."

"My ailments are more of the pain in the ass kind."

"Oh, you have diarrhea?"

"What? No, I don't have diarrhea. I mean—" God paused. "Do you have tea?"

"Iced?"

"Ew," protested God as he raised his upper lip in disgust at the thought of cold tea. "Do you have hot?"

"Sorry, love, we don't have that."

"It's the same as iced tea, but you use hot water instead."

"We only use our hot water for coffee and sterilizing food we drop on the floor."

God looked back down at the small puddle of water on his plate and furrowed his brow. "Well, that answers that," he muttered to himself.

"We have coffee."

"I'll just have orange juice, thanks."

God picked up his fork and casually poked at the food before popping a piece of floor bacon into his mouth. An hour passed by as the contents of his plate slowly disappeared and his glass of juice diminished. A little past noon, he looked down at his watch and flagged the waitress as she passed by his table. "Can I get my check, please?"

"No need," she said with a smile. "Someone took care of it."

God frowned in curiosity. No one knew he was there. "Who?"

The waitress stepped aside to show Raphael standing at the register alone looking at God.

God sighed in frustration and lowered his head as Raphael walked over to his table.

"Hello, Gary," said Raphael as he pointed to the empty seat across from God. "May I?"

"No."

Raphael ignored God's objection and sat on the empty seat.

"How did you find me?" asked God, cutting to the chase.

"Invocation."

"I didn't say you could sit down."

"Can I get you fellas anything?" interrupted the waitress as she returned to the table.

"No, he's leaving," said God as he stood from his seat. "And so am I." He stepped away from the table and stomped over to the front doors.

"Gary?" shouted Raphael as he followed God from the restaurant. "We need you to come back."

God waived a dismissive finger above his head as he pushed the front door open and walked outside towards his truck. "Save it, Raph, I'm not interested."

"Gary, please," begged Raphael as he followed him across the parking lot.

God stopped at his truck and looked down at the ground. "No, I'm out. I'm done. They punished me. Remember when that happened? I do. It went something along the lines of *'hey, Gary, thanks for your thousands of years of service, but we're moving in a different direction'*. So that's fresh."

The radio crackled, and a distant voice rang out. "*Anyone in the vicinity who can take a vehicle to impound*?"

God opened the cab door and reached inside for the radio. "This is truck seven. What's going on, Mary?"

"Henry's truck broken down again. Can you meet him at the north station as soon as possible and take the payload off his hands?"

"Roger that," said God as he threw the radio on the seat. He turned back to face Raphael. "You wasted your time coming here. I'm not going back."

"We need you," said Raphael. "Something's happened."

"That ship has sailed, Raph. I'm sure whatever it is, you can handle it. You've shadowed me long enough. You'll figure it out." He climbed up into the truck. "I've gotta go. People to meet, cars to tow, lives to ruin."

Raphael sighed as he watched God close the door and pull away.

"Where's he going?" asked Cam from behind.

Raphael turned to see her walking towards him. "He's not coming."

"What! Are you just letting him leave? We need him."

"He needs more time," said Raphael.

"Time is not a luxury we're blessed with," argued Cam. "What are we going to do?"

"Gary is a stubborn fool," said Raphael. "We'll need to be a bit more persuasive. His tow yard is only a few miles from here. We'll head there and wait for him. He'll show up eventually."

♦♦♦♦

Spencer's pants around his ankles stunt earned him a couple of hours in an interrogation room until it could be determined he was not a credible threat. He was returned to the cell and resumed sitting as far away from the rest of the group as possible. As he focused his attention on the door and the freedom that lay beyond it, Pitbull enthusiastically showed Lucifer his extensive collection of devil tattoos.

"I got this one at a shop on Long Beach," said Pitbull as he rolled up his sleeve to reveal a large devil face tattoo on his left forearm. He pulled the sleeve up further to reveal a second tattoo of a large grinning devil riding a bright yellow wasp. "I got this one in London when I was a bouncer for a rock club."

"I'm flattered," said Lucifer as he looked at his portrait. "That's some good ink."

"I've always loved the Devil," said Pitbull thoughtfully. "Although, I gotta say you don't look like what I expected."

"No?" asked Lucifer with a smile.

"No. You're way better looking than I thought you'd be. I figured you'd be more red. And have wings and horns, you know?"

"I get that a lot," said Lucifer.

Shank blinked and turned his attention back to Lucifer. "How do we know you're the Devil?" he asked as he focused intently on every word he spoke. "You could just be saying that for attention."

Pitbull nodded. "My esteemed colleague does have a point. Can you prove you are who you say you are?"

"Of course I can," said Lucifer. "I can tell you the happiest moment of your life."

Pitbull frowned at the underwhelming offer. "How does that prove you're Satan? If anything, it makes you more Christian than evil."

"How so?" asked Lucifer.

"Well, isn't happiness God's realm? Why would the Devil care what makes us happy?"

"Are you a religious man, Pitbull?"

Pitbull nodded. "I am."

"What denomination?"

"Catholic."

"So, what's the first thing you do when you go to church?" asked Lucifer.

"I confess."

"To what?"

"My sins."

"Okay," said Lucifer. "So why is the religion of love spending any time focusing on the bad things in your life? Wouldn't you want to focus on the good stuff?"

"Whoa, that's deep, man. I didn't think of it like that," said Pitbull. His mind genuinely blown. "Yeah, I guess you're right."

Shank blinked once in genuine disbelief.

"I focus on the good things," said Lucifer. "Here, give me your hand, and I'll show you."

Pitbull reached out and offered Lucifer his palm.

Lucifer placed it between his own and closed his eyes. "Your favorite memory is Super Bowl forty-one. You got a phone call from your wife about the birth of your daughter."

"Yeah, I remember that. The Colts won. It was the greatest day of my life."

"Do me," said Shank as he rose to unstable legs and shoved his hand in front of Lucifer.

Once again, Lucifer reached out and placed Shank's hand between his and he closed his eyes. He smiled as Shank's memory popped into his head. "Your favorite day was from three years ago. You were at Taco Bell, and they put an extra soft taco in your party pack." Lucifer paused and opened his eyes. "Really? That's it?"

Shank stared at the ground as his entire Universe was unceremoniously flipped on its head. "Whoa," was all he could muster.

"Screw this," said Death as he stood up sharply and interrupted the casual banter. "We don't have time for this nonsense. I'm going to find the keys and get us out of here." He nodded his head and disappeared.

The inmate stared at the empty spot Death previously occupied and frowned in confusion. "Uh." He turned to face Lucifer. "Did he just—"

"Disappear? Yeah, he does that all the time. It's really fucking annoying when he does it while he's supposed to be driving." He noticed the man's confusion. "Don't worry, he'll be back, and we'll get out of here."

"Why couldn't he just teleport us all out of here?" asked Pitbull.

"He can only teleport himself at the moment. He lost some of his abilities since God went missing."

"Oh," said Pitbull. "That makes sense," he lied. It did not make any sense whatsoever.

Lucifer looked at Spencer as they waited for Death to return. Ten seconds turned to thirty, and soon became two minutes.

"He must be having a hard time finding the keys," suggested Spencer.

"It's not that big of a station," said Lucifer. "Something's wrong."

A moment later, Death reappeared outside the cell holding the keys in his hand. He breathed heavily as he jammed the key into the lock. "We need to hurry, I don't know how long—"

A cop stepped up from behind and jammed a taser into Death's ribs. A loud crack of electricity erupted as he shoved 50,000 volts into him. Death gasped for air and convulsed as the electric current surged through his body. The cop kicked the cell door open and pushed Death inside. He stumbled two paces and fell to the floor unconscious.

Spencer looked at the open door and stood from his seat.

"Spencer? What are you doing?" asked Lucifer as his blonde companion bolted for the exit.

The cop pulled the door closed as Spencer reached the bars of the door, and in one swift motion, moved his tazer to the door and activated the device. The electricity struck Spencer with a loud pop. Spencer squealed and dropped to the floor.

The cop turned to Lucifer and pointed the weapon at him. "How about you, sunshine? Do you want to be next?"

"Nah, I'm good, mate," said Lucifer as he held up his hands. "You've already made this the best day of my life. I'm quitting while I'm on top."

Death started to stir and painfully climbed to his feet. He noticed Spencer on the floor next to him. "What happened to him?" he asked as he shuffled back over to the bench and flopped down next to Lucifer.

"The same thing that happened to you, but way funnier," said Lucifer with a grin.

"Is he okay?"

Lucifer shrugged. "I guess we'll see, won't we. So, what do we do now?"

Death parted his robe to reveal his left hand. "I still have a key," he said with a grin.

"You sneak!" said Lucifer. "I must be rubbing off on you."

"Not likely," said Death. "You're a bad—" A light purring echoed from beneath the seat, and Death stopped talking. "Did you hear that?" he asked.

"Hear what?" said Lucifer as he cocked his head to listen. "I don't hear anything."

"That sounds like a— "

"Kitten!" said Lucifer, his voice rising an octave as he dropped to his knees and looked under the seat.

Curled up on the floor was a small cat no older than six months. "How did you get in here, you adorable little fuzzball?" asked Lucifer as he reached for the miniature feline and plucked it out.

"I hate cats," said Death as he scooted away from Lucifer.

"Of course you do," said Lucifer as he held the kitten up to his face. "How can you hate this cute little ball of fur?" he said as the kitten licked the tip of his nose."

"I'm allergic, and cat hair is a nightmare to get out of wool. Keep it away from me."

"Pay attention to the grumpy man," said Lucifer as he nuzzled the purring animal.

"Where did you find a cat?" asked Spencer as he sat up and rubbed his head.

"Under the bench," said Lucifer. "How are you feeling?"

"Like someone electrocuted me," said Spencer. "You can't keep a cat you just found."

"Sure I can. He's a prison cat and prison cats are fair game. I can give him a loving home." Lucifer planted a kiss on the kitten's head. "I think I'm going to call him Nipples," said Lucifer as he ran his hand across the kitten's back.

"Lucifer! You can't call a kitten, Nipples," said Spencer. "That is grossly inappropriate."

"Why not? Everyone has them."

"Well, I don't. I'm allergic."

"I mean nipples, Spencer, not kittens."

"I know."

Lucifer opened his mouth to retort, but found no words that would make sense. Spencer was clearly an imbecile.

While the group argued about the logistics of a nipple allergy, things in Heaven continued to go downhill. In the previous hour, Greg's condition rapidly deteriorated. His violent transformation accelerated faster than the previous three days combined. As Demon-Greg thrashed around on the couch, Amber was forced to leave the room as it was no longer safe to be alone with him. She watched her fiancé through the slim glass window in the door, painfully aware they were running out of time to save him.

CHAPTER 18

Lucifer chewed on the inside of his lip as he contemplated his next move. Another hour passed, and the group was no closer to breaking out of their cell. Although Death found a key to open the cell, there were six armed police officers between them and the front door, and while Lucifer used to be bulletproof, he was uncertain if the recent events affected that. Spencer was another variable, and he did not rate the man's chances of making it out alive. He knew his options were limited and if they were going to stand a chance of saving Greg, he was going to have to take drastic measures. Fortunately, he still held onto a few secrets he could call upon in extreme circumstances.

"If I do something to get us out of here, I'm going to need your word that you won't say anything to Gary."

Death shrugged. "I don't care what do you. You know I don't like the guy. In fact, the more it could potentially upset him, the happier I will be."

"Fair enough," said Lucifer as he looked over at Spencer. "How about you?"

"You know I have the inability to lie," said Spencer.

"Do you want to stay in jail?"

"If God asks me what you did, I will be forced to tell the truth."

"I'll take that as a yes for now," said Lucifer as he stood and walked over to the cell door.

"I didn't say yes," objected Spencer.

Lucifer dismissed him with a brush of his hand as he stopped at the door. "Steve, throw me the key," he asked Death.

Death tossed the key over to Lucifer, and without looking behind him, Lucifer raised a hand and caught it.

"Officer?" called Lucifer.

A moment later, one of the officers approached the door. "What do you want?"

Lucifer leaned into the bars and lowered his voice. As he blinked, his eyes changed from hazel to a deep red. "I need you to unlock this door and escort me and my friends from this cell."

The officer nodded as Lucifer passed him the key. "Understood."

"You are going to erase any record of our presence here, and we are leaving this station as free men."

The officer nodded once again. "Understood," he said as he unlocked the door and pushed it open.

Lucifer turned to face the rest of the cell's occupants. "Gentlemen, if you'd like to follow me."

"Does that include us?" asked Pitbull.

"Of course it does," said Lucifer. He bent down and reached out a hand. "Nipples," he called out. "Time to go." He made a clicking sound with his tongue and his new kitten companion crawled out from beneath the bench. He scooped the animal and gestured towards the exit.

Everyone except Spencer stood and followed Lucifer into the hallway.

"Come on, Spencer," said Lucifer. "Move like you have a purpose."

"I'm not leaving," said Spencer defiantly.

"What?"

"I have never had so much as had a parking ticket, but here I am sitting here in prison. I now have a rather significant blemish on my record. I do not want to add prison break to my rap sheet."

Lucifer held zero interest in playing Spencer's passive-aggressive mind game. "Fine, stay here. You're not exactly mission critical at this point."

"You can't make me leave."

"I know," said Lucifer as he disappeared from sight.

Spencer looked around the empty cell. "Nope. Not leaving." He tapped his left foot rapidly on the floor as he waited for someone to come for him, but as the seconds ticked by, it became quite apparent that they left him to fend for himself. "Wait for me," he yelled as he jumped to his feet. "I've changed my mind."

As the officer navigated the hallway, a voice called out from another cell. "Hey guys," said the mysterious man. "Any chance I could come with you?"

"Sorry, we're busy," said Death as he passed the cell.

"It's critical I get out of here," said the man.

"Sorry, sport," said Lucifer backing up Death's rejection. "We're in a hurry and can't carry any extra baggage."

The man sighed. "Look, I know this sounds weird, and I promise you I'm not drunk, even though it sounds like I am," said the man, his voice laced with desperation. "But I'm on a really important mission to bring God back to Heaven. Life as we know it depends on it."

Lucifer frowned as he stopped and looked towards the voice. "Say that again."

"I'm on a mission to find God and bring him back to Heaven."

"Warren?" asked Lucifer, recognizing his face from the ATM's built-in camera.

"Yeah," said Warren. "How do you know who I am?"

"I saw you on the ATM. We were sent down to do the same things as you."

"You have? Who are you?" asked Warren.

"I'm Lucifer."

"Holy fuck nuggets," said Warren with his usual grace.

"This one too, Officer," shouted Lucifer as he flagged down the cop and pointed to Warren.

The officer released Warren from his cell and led the group downstairs to the lobby and to the front door. "You're free to go, gentlemen," he said as he pushed open the front door and gestured outside.

Lucifer approached the door last and stopped before leaving. "We need a vehicle," he said as his eyes glowed red once again.

The officer pointed to the parking lot. "Feel free to take anything you want. The key box is on the wall by the door."

"Much appreciated," said Lucifer as the officer stepped back inside and closed the door.

Warren was still buzzing about being rescued by Lucifer and pointed to Death. "Who's that?" he asked, hoping what he was assumed was correct.

"He's Steve," said Lucifer.

"Oh, I thought he was the Grim Reaper," said Warren.

Death sighed. "I'm Death."

"Isn't that the same thing?" asked Warren.

"No."

"I knew it was you," said Warren. "You look just like him. But what is it with you lot and anti-climactic names? Fucking Steve? That doesn't exactly scream Grim Reaper, does it?"

"Listen, you mortal dimwit, don't push me. I can snuff you out faster than you can blink."

Warren held up his hands in defense. "I'm sorry, it's just that you don't look like a Steve to me."

"What do I look like?"

"Pasty," offered Warren with a grin. "Some sun couldn't hurt."

"What about us?" asked Pitbull, interrupting the squabble. "Do we get a car too?"

"Help yourself," said Lucifer. "What's theirs is yours."

Pitbull and Shank stared at each other for the briefest of moments as the offer sank in. Broad grins spread over their faces as they realized that not only were they free, but they could also commit grand theft auto with zero consequences.

"Isn't that our car over there," said Death as he pointed to a tow truck pulling away, towing their shitty brown Chevy Cavalier behind it.

The driver leaned out of the window and raised his middle finger towards them.

Death frowned. "Is that—"

"That motherfucker," yelled Lucifer as he sprinted after the tow truck.

The chain on the back of the tow truck lowered, and the car dropped to the asphalt with a loud crunch. The hook disconnected, and the truck pulled away faster without the heavy load holding it back.

Lucifer reached into his pocket and pulled out the keys. He tossed them over his shoulder in the general direction of Death. "Get the car," he shouted over his shoulder. "Gary's mine."

"What should I do?" shouted Death as Lucifer sprinted away.

"Catch up with me."

In the cabin of the truck, God glanced over at his side mirror to see Lucifer running behind him.

"Stop the truck, Gary," shouted Lucifer as he chased down the vehicle.

"No!" God yelled out of the window as he increased the distance between them. "Idiot," he muttered to himself as he turned his attention back to the road, just in time to see the traffic light ahead switch to amber as the car in front started to brake. "No! Don't stop," he pleaded as he pressed on the brake pedal and his truck stopped. "We could have both made that, you stupid asshole."

Only one car passed in the other direction as God waited for the light to change. He tapped on the steering wheel as his attention bounced between the mirror and the traffic light. "Damn it," he said as Lucifer quickly closed the gap between them. There was no way he was going to outrun Lucifer if the light did not turn green. He looked either side to confirm no cars were coming and slowly lifted his foot from the brake pedal.

"Oh, no you don't," muttered Lucifer under his breath as the truck started to pick up speed again. He gave one final push and leaped at the driver's side door. "Stop the fucking truck, Gary," Lucifer shouted breathlessly as he leaned across God to try and snatch at the keys from the ignition.

"What the fuck are you doing?" protested God as he swatted at Lucifer's hands. "You're going to get us both killed."

"If I die, you're coming with me. Now pull over and give me the fucking keys."

"Get off my truck!" said God as he slapped Lucifer's hand in a lame effort to break his firm grip.

"No, pull over!"

God struggled to keep the steering wheel straight as he reached over to the passenger seat and fumbled for his lunch bag. His fingers found the strap and, in one fluid motion, swung it at Lucifer's head.

"Ow," Lucifer protested as the bag slapped him in the face. "Fuck it." He grabbed the steering wheel and pulled hard. The truck swerved to the left and careened across the road. It slammed into a tree with a loud crash and stopped. Lucifer was thrown off the vehicle and landed on the ground with a heavy thud. He remained motionless while he waited for the air to return to his stressed lungs.

"What is wrong with you?" God shouted from inside the cabin. "You wrecked my truck," he whined as an aggressive cloud of steam sprayed up from the fractured radiator. He pushed the tweaked door open and stepped down towards Lucifer, who was slowly climbing back to his feet.

Lucifer inhaled as he tried to regain his breath. "Well, if you'd cooperated when I asked, instead of flooring it, you'd still have a truck." He nodded over to Death pulling up behind them. "Thankfully, we still have our car, so you're coming with us."

"No, I'm not," said God.

"This isn't up for discussion," said Lucifer.

"Good. Then take me back to my yard and we can all be on our merry way."

"You're needed in Heaven," said Lucifer. "Things are starting to unravel."

"I left Raphael in charge. Everything is fine."

"No, Gary, everything isn't fine. It's about as far from fine as you can get. Raphael couldn't handle the responsibility. He got locked out of the panic room, he couldn't press the check-in button, the Council got involved, and they shut it down."

"They shut heaven down?"

"Yeah."

"Wow. I didn't see that coming," said God. "I thought I left everything in good hands."

"Well, you didn't," said Lucifer. "And you know what happens when haven gets shut down?"

God shook his head.

"They sent everyone down to me."

"Everyone?"

"Yes, everyone," said Lucifer. "I have all kinds of unsavory characters in Hell now, and it sucks, and there is no end in sight. The old-time members are getting upset, and when they get upset, I get upset. Last year I told Steve that hell was like Dick Clark's New Year's Rocking Eve, but with more strippers and coke. Now it's more like a congressional hearing. Hypocrites, heathens, and douchebags all shouting and cursing at each other. If Trump dies before this is sorted out, I quit. I can't handle that orange asshole."

"Why would you think he's coming to me?" said God. "I don't want him either."

"You know, going to church and all that shit. It's your rules, Gary. We need you to help get your prized creation back in order, and we can't do it without you."

"My creation?" said God. "I couldn't give two shits about my creation. I went down there to help them, and the bastards shot at me. One of them fucked up my suit. I liked that suit. To be honest, they hurt my feelings. So, if I can get back at the little fuckers by towing their cars, I'm all in."

"That seems a little petty," said Lucifer.

"Have you read the bible? It's kind of my thing." God sighed and turned away. "Why are you even here?"

"We need your help. Something is going down in Heaven, and we need you back."

"I'm not interested," said God. "Come back when you're selling something different."

"Oh, for fuck's sake, we don't have time for this," said Lucifer as he slid the glove from his hand and raised his palm to God.

God stared at the web and bit his lip, deep in thought. "Is that—"

"It is," said Lucifer.

God's eyes widened as he tried to process what he was looking at. "No, uh uh." He shook his head as if trying to will away the image. "That's not real." His face wore a mask of genuine fear and as the color drained from his skin, he became frail, almost human. "That can't be real. It's impossible," he said as if saying it out loud would somehow make the words true.

Death threw a frustrated glance towards Lucifer, unable to mask his disapproval. "We were supposed to build him up to that, Luc."

"Yeah, well we don't have a whole of time to discuss this," said Lucifer. "We need to stop walking on eggshells and get this sorted out. The stakes are way too high now."

Lucifer looked back at God as he lowered his hand and placed it back into his glove. "I'm afraid it is quite real, and we really need your help, Gary. Please, I'm begging you."

Were Lucifer's plea come at any other moment, on any other subject, God would have ridiculed him until his last breath. However, humor and mockery were the furthest items from his thoughts. Instead, he simply nodded. "Let's go back to my office, and maybe we can talk."

Lucifer and God walked over to Death's car and stopped at the passenger side door.

"Shotgun," said God as he reached for the door handle.

"No. You get in the back behind me," said Lucifer as he slapped God's hand off the handle. "You can sit next to Spencer and keep him company."

"Who?" asked God as he opened the door and climbed inside.

"Hello, sir," said Spencer cheerfully as God sat down next to him and pulled the door closed.

"Oh, for fuck's sake, why are you here?"

"I was coming to help them find you," said Spencer.

"Hello again," said Warren as he leaned forward and waved at God.

God sighed at the unexpected and wholly unwanted reunion. "I don't suppose me objecting is going to change the outcome of this, is it?" He struggled to hide his irritation at being forced to ride with the four people he hated the most in his life.

"Not in the slightest," said Lucifer as the car pulled away. "So why are you a tow truck driver anyway? It looks like you'd get greasy."

"Why not?" asked God, his voice laced with defense. "What's wrong with being a tow truck driver?"

"Hey, I'm not judging," said Lucifer. "I just don't understand why you'd want to."

"Are you kidding me?" said God. "This is the first vacation I've had in over three thousand years. I don't have to answer to anyone but myself."

Lucifer was unclear on how his situation could be considered a holiday from his routine. "But you took a job towing cars. You simply went from one job to another. How is that a vacation?"

"The difference is it is on my terms. My world, my rules. And this is really messing with my world."

"Wanna play Slug Bug?" interrupted Spencer with the unbridled enthusiasm of a ten-year-old on a road trip. "It'll make the time go by faster."

"That sounds like a great idea," said Lucifer with a broad smile, knowing full well it would get under God's skin.

"You lay one finger on me, and I will punch you so hard, you'll become one with Warren," said God as he looked out of the window to avoid eye contact with Spencer.

"I was just trying to pass the ti—"

"Slug Bug," yelled God as he punched Spencer on the arm.

"Ow. I didn't see one," said Spencer as he rubbed his arm.

"It was there," said God. "We just passed it."

"You're supposed to point it when you see—"

"Slug Bug," yelled God again and punched Spencer for a second time.

Spencer scowled at him as he rubbed his progressively aching shoulder. "I didn't see that one either."

"Honor system," said God.

"That's not really how the game—"

"Slug Bug," said God as he delivered a third blow. "Right there," he added as an afterthought.

"I don't think that was a Bug. It looked like a BMW."

"Are you sure? It looked like a Bug to me."

"No, I'm fairly sure that wasn't a—"

"Slug Bug," yelled God again as he intentionally punched Spencer in the same location.

"Ow," squealed Spencer, his arm feeling like it was on fire. "That was a motorcycle. Do you even know what a Bug looks like?"

"Yeah?" said God with a smile. "Of course I do." He pointed to a large eighteen-wheel truck that quite obviously was not a Bug. "Slug Bug," he shouted as he punched Spencer again.

"I don't want to play with you anymore," said Spencer as he crossed his arms and turned away from God.

As Spencer's gaze wandered outside, a bright yellow VW bug slowly, almost purposefully drove past. His eyes widened in panic, and he instinctively grabbed his arm and pulled away from God. "No!" said Spencer, as if disciplining a bad puppy.

God smiled and turned away from Spencer. Spencer let out a sigh of relief and turned back to the window.

"Slug Bug," whispered God as his fist made impact for the sixth time.

♦♦♦♦

The remainder of the drive passed by in silence as Lucifer drove the group back to God's tow yard.

As the car approached the tall metal gates, God leaned between the front seats and squinted at another car parked out front. Cam and Raphael stood beside their vehicle, patiently waiting for the rest of the group to arrive.

"Hey, it's Cam," said Warren breaking the awkward silence. He was happy to see a friendly face.

"Are you serious?" asked God as Lucifer stopped the vehicle. "Did you need to bring the entire crew with you?"

"I didn't know they were coming," said Lucifer. "I'm as surprised to see them as you are."

"This feels like an intervention," said God as he pulled the door handle and climbed out of the vehicle.

God walked over to Raphael with long, irritated strides. "You're persistent."

"We've known each other for thousands of years. Please hear us out," pleaded Raphael.

"I already know. Lucifer showed me his hand."

"He was supposed to build you up to that," said Raphael.

"Raph, in case you haven't noticed, I've lost everything. My kingdom, my flock, my secretary, all of it gone because some asshole decided I'd violated some obscure rule. And now you lot show up with an infected black hand. So, if it's all the same to you, I need some time to process all this."

Raphael was not done trying to persuade him. "We don't have time. We wouldn't be here if it wasn't important."

"I just drove with the four people who annoy me the most. It's like some higher power intentionally brought every person who irritates me and dropped them in one spot."

"You don't mean me, do you?" asked Spencer, a little offended at being grouped with people God did not like.

"Especially you," said God.

Spencer took a step backward at God's dismissal. "Gary, please."

God raised an eyebrow at Spencer's brazenness "What did you call me?"

"Sorry, I meant God."

"You used my name in vain."

"It was an accident," said Spencer.

"What are the rules about using my name in public, Spencer?"

"Don't?"

"Exactly."

While God argued with Spencer about the public use of his name, Lucifer sided up next to Cam as they walked into the yard. "What are you doing here?" he asked. "This could be dangerous."

Cam shrugged. "We saw you get arrested, and Raphael thought you needed help. He needed a driver, so I volunteered to come with him," she said as if stating the most obvious thing in the world.

"Couldn't bear to let me out of your sight, could you?" said Lucifer with a cheeky grin.

"Not in the slightest," said Cam with an equally large smile. She playfully bumped against his shoulder. "Can't let you save the Universe without me, can I?" She noticed his kitten curled up in Lucifer's arm. "You found one?"

Lucifer nodded. "I told you I would bring you a gift."

"Holy fuck, that is adorable."

"Cam, meet Nipples."

♦♦♦♦

Five minutes later, God was seated at his desk with the rest of the group staring at him as they waited for him to speak. His silence was not due to stubbornness or a desire to be difficult. He simply did not know how to process the information. Everything he thought he knew about the Universe had been flipped on its head. "How did it happen?" he finally asked.

"Caretaker," said Lucifer.

God shook his head. "Bullshit. That's impossible, it wasn't a Caretaker. That shit on your hand is from an Impiety Arrow."

Lucifer raised an eyebrow in mild surprise. "So, you recognize it then?" He was uncertain if God knew what caused the black infection.

"Of course I recognize it. I fought for centuries to make these things disappear. They're vile and have no place in a civilized universe."

"This is far from a civilized universe," retorted Lucifer.

"That may be so," said God. "But I don't need to be contributing to its delinquency." He dismissed the conversation with a wave of his hand. "But this is moot. It can't be an Impiety Arrow as Caretakers are not allowed to carry them. There is only one entity capable of wielding such a weapon."

"Please don't say a zombie-demon," said Warren hopefully.

"According to legend, it's Mephistopheles," said Lucifer.

"What's that?" asked Warren.

"A greater demon," said Lucifer.

"Great. Of course he is," said Warren, his voice tinged with defeat. "Why wouldn't he be?"

"No way," said God. "If was here, we'd know it. The guy leaves a trail of destruction a thousand miles wide."

Lucifer frowned as he processed the information. "True. Then this begs the question, how can a Caretaker carry an Impiety Arrow, and who gave it to him?"

God studied Lucifer for a moment. "And the bigger question is, why did you touch it? Why were you even around such a weapon?"

"I didn't know what it was until I touched it," said Lucifer. "Someone sent the Caretaker after the Oceanview survivors, and he shot one of them with it"

"Why send a Caretaker after a tiny bunch of insignificant humans?"

Cam contentedly stroked her kitten as she listened to the discussion unfolding. "Um, you know these insignificant humans can hear you, right?"

"My point is sending a Caretaker to kill a human is like using a planet to hammer a nail. It's ridiculously over the top. Humans aren't exactly difficult to kill."

"We can still hear you," said Cam.

God rolled his eyes in frustration as he struggled to get his point across. "Bacteria can kill you. The smallest organization on the planet can snuff you out in seconds. You're squishy." He turned back to Lucifer. "Don't say you disagree with me. You know I'm right. This is way too heavy-handed. What's going on with the human who was shot?"

"He has a name," said Warren. "It was my brother, Greg."

Lucifer held up to hand to calm Warren. "This isn't helping, Warren." He focused his attention back on God. "I can't take the arrow out on my own. I need you to help me."

God exhaled and rubbed his chin pensively. "Where is it?" he said, finally asking the long overdue question.

"It's still in Greg's shoulder," said Lucifer.

God shook his head. "Not the arrow. The Caretaker."

Spencer decided it was also his time to speak. "I think I have a hangnail," he said as he held up his hand.

Warren shrugged his shoulders as he ignored Spencer's medical crisis and responded to God. "Oh, you don't need to worry about that. I took care of it."

"What did you say?" said God as he turned to face Warren.

"I said I think I have a hangnail," said Spencer again.

"Not you, Spencer," said God. "No one cares about your damn finger."

Spencer raised his index finger to show his micro-sliver of loose skin. "I'll have you know I was in prison, and it's well documented that they never clean the cells. Who knows what infection is coursing through my veins."

God raised his hand to Spencer. "Shut up," he said.

"Excuse me!" said Spencer, a little hurt.

God turned back to Warren. "What did you say?"

"I said I took care of it," said Warren.

Warren reached into his satchel and pulled out a severed hand clutching a white orb.

"What the fuck is that?" asked Cam.

"It's a hand," said Warren.

"Of course it's a fucking hand, but whose is it?" pressed Cam.

God's eyes widened as he studied the severed extremity. He held a hand up to his mouth as he put the pieces together. "Oh, you didn't?"

Lucifer frowned, confused at the cryptic discussion. "Did what? What did he do?"

"He killed the Caretaker," said God. "You did, didn't you, Warren?"

"I did," beamed Warren, quite proud of his accomplishment. "I took that fucker to the cleaners."

God shook his head. "No. No you didn't. Please tell me you're joking."

"Why would I joke about something like that? I'm quite proud of it. I wish Greg could have seen—"

"Why the fuck did you kill it?" interrupted God. "You had no right to do that."

Warren raised an eyebrow and looked at the rest of the group, who appeared equally confused. "You're kidding, right? There was a monster kicking its way into our church. It shot my brother. It fucking killed Lee and Ellis. The fucker was trying to kill me. You bet your ass I put it down. We fought. I killed it. End of story."

"Do you know what you've done?" asked God.

"Yes. I killed the thing that had already murdered two of us and was trying to finish the job. You're welcome," said Warren. "You could be a little more grateful."

"No, no, no, no," said God as he held his hands to his head. "Sorry, Luc, I'm out. You lot are on your own." He picked up his jacket and turned to the door.

"Where are you going?" asked Lucifer. "I need your help."

God stopped. "You never said anything about killing the Caretaker." He turned to face Warren. "I can't believe you fucked the Universe again."

Warren stabbed a finger towards God. "Fuck you, Gary. Yes, I fucking killed it," he said as he turned his finger towards his own chest. He then pointed to the rest of the group. "There isn't a person in this room who would have done anything differently. I ended this and I saved us. I don't understand why this is such a big deal. I killed the thing that was trying to kill us."

"Because a human is not supposed to be able to kill a Caretaker. Only gods, angels, and demons can do that."

"Well, it killed the angels David brought with him, and there wasn't a god around to help. Which seems to be pretty typical these days. My options were pretty limited."

God grabbed his keys off the table. "This means it failed its mission. Something bad is about to happen. I'm leaving and getting as far away from this as I can. I suggest you seriously consider doing the same."

Lucifer stepped in front of the door.

"How did you kill it?" asked Lucifer. Arguing about why it happened seemed pointless. He was more interested in the how.

"I pulled one of those arrows from the wall and stabbed it in the eye."

"So why weren't you there when David came back for you?" asked Cam.

"When I killed it, the entire room flashed white, and I found myself back at my ex-girlfriend's house. It was like the entire previous twelve hours had been erased. She then threw me out a second time. It's been a shitty few days."

"So why do you have its hand?" asked Spencer. "That's really disgusting."

"I figured no one would believe me if I said I killed it, so I grabbed a souvenir. I'm not sure what the ball is though. It wasn't glowing like that earlier." Warren pried the stiff fingers apart to free the orb.

"No, wait!" yelled God as he held up his hands. "Don't touch it!"

God's protest was too little, too late. The ball rolled out of the dead hand and dropped onto the floor with a loud clink. The group stared at it as they waited for something to happen. A second changed to ten, change to thirty, but the ball remained dormant.

"Can we breathe yet?" asked Cam cautiously.

"I don't know," said God, uncertain of what could occur.

"How about now?" asked Cam.

"I don't know," said God for a second time. "Maybe?"

"You're a bit jumpy for someone who says I don't know a lot," said Cam trying to lessen the tension.

"Yeah, what are we waiting for?" asked Warren. "It doesn't seem to be doing anything."

God bit his lip as he waited pensively for the ball to do something. "I guess it wasn't what I thought I was it was."

Warren was more than a little confused at God's reaction to a harmless orb. "It's just a ball."

And then it started to spin.

"Oh, fuck me sideways," said God. "It's exactly what I thought it was."

"What is it?" asked Warren.

"It's a Herald," said God.

"And what is that?" asked Warren.

"A messenger of the gods," interrupted Lucifer. "This is bad. This is really bad. They never carry good news."

A seam appeared on the equator of the ball and a second across the top, splitting the upper second in half. The two quarters lifted away, and a glowing white light started to emit from its core. "Welcome to Herald version seven, software update 54.29," said a calm and body-less voice.

"Oh, look, they speak English," said Warren. "Ain't that a tad convenient?"

"Shh," ordered God. "It translates to whichever language the viewer speaks for ease of use."

"Greetings, exalted viewer, and insignificant humans," the voice continued.

"Well, this is not off to a promising start," said Cam as she rolled her eyes.

"Due to the recent violations of celestial codes 7293171226a and 864528363b. You have been scheduled for termination."

"What?" screamed Cam. "Are fucking serious? There's something else coming for us now?"

The mysterious voice was not finished. "At the behest of the Council of Deities, you have been chosen for combat against four unbeatable champions. We wish you luck and Godspeed to your next life."

"Oh shit," said Lucifer. "They've invoked Operatio Equus Quattuor."

"What is that?" asked Warren. "I don't speak French."

"It's Latin, you idiot," said God. "It's Operation Four Horse."

Warren shrugged. "Still not helping."

"Did you ever listen in church?" asked God.

"Always," said Warren. "Except when it was boring. And it frequently was."

"It's the Four Horseman," said God.

"Oh, those guys. I think Johnny Cash sang about them. I didn't realize it was an actual thing."

"Yes, it's an actual thing," said God. "And they will not stop until every one of us is dead. Then they will kill everyone you have ever met, and then everyone they have ever met. And so on, and so on until everyone is dead. The Earth isn't safe, Heaven isn't safe, and neither is Hell." He turned to Raphael. "Raph, is the force field up?"

Raphael shook his head. "No, we had to turn it off to allow us to use the funnel to get down."

"So, Heaven is exposed?" asked God.

"Until we can get back through the tunnel. Yes," said Raphael.

"Fuck."

Lucifer stood up, concern suddenly covered his face. "I've got to make a call. I need to protect my people." He pulled his communicator out of his pocket as he stepped away from the group. "Scooter, are you awake?" he said into the device.

The device remained silent.

"Scooter?"

Static erupted from the device and after a few seconds gave way to the din of techno music. "*Hello*?" shouted Lucifer's number two.

"Scooter, it's me."

"*Oh, hey! Whatcha need, boss*?"

"Get the force field up. No one in, no one out until I give the order."

No answer came from the communicator.

"Scooter?"

"*Voop, voop, voop*."

"Are you voguing again?" asked Lucifer.

"*Maybe*," said Scooter.

"Not the time, Scoot. Try to focus. This is really important."

"*The new EDM mix tape just came in and it's off the fucking hook. People are loving it*."

"Put down the glowsticks for ten minutes and get the force field up," said Lucifer. "The music needs to wait. I'll check it out later."

"*I thought you'd be excited*," said Scooter. "*What's going on*?"

"I don't know, but I want to be ready for when I do."

"*Right, boss*." The call went silent for a moment. "*Hey, Fister, boss man wants us to put the force field up*." The device rustled again as Scooter resumed his discussion with Lucifer. "*Done. When you coming back*?"

"Not for a while," said Lucifer. "Remember no one in or out," he ordered before ending the call. He turned to face Raphael. "So, what do we do?"

"We need to get to Oceanview and use the funnel," said Raphael. "And I suggest we move fast."

"I have a minivan I towed yesterday," said God. "It should fit the seven of us."

"I think we should take two cars," said Raphael. "It may help distract them a bit."

"He's right," said Lucifer.

"I'll go with Raphael," said Warren.

"Shotgun on the minivan," shouted Spencer with a level of enthusiasm unnecessary for the severity of the situation.

Now that God was fully aware of the severity of the situation, he moved considerably faster than before. It took less than five minutes to retrieve the keys and bring the minivan to the front of the yard. As the van pulled onto the street he looked up at the rearview mirror, knowing this was likely the last time he would see the place. Truth be told, he missed Heaven, but it would be a while before he would be comfortable admitting it to anyone.

"How long do we have until the Horsemen show up?" asked Cam, interrupting God's thoughts.

"We don't know," said Lucifer. "We're in uncharted territory now."

CHAPTER 19

Throughout history, villains have come in all shapes and sizes. Sometimes they are child-eating clowns, other times, they run for political office, and some are software developers who create manipulative social media networks. The penchant for evil deeds can appear from the oddest of places and have the strangest of effects. The Bible certainly held no shortage of bad guys. There was Adam and Eve, the two naked parseltongues, the dude who wrote Leviticus that hated gay people and fabric, and the wise man who showed up at the manger with Frankincense without verifying if Jesus possessed any childhood allergies. However, the most famous and recognizable biblical villains were the Four Horsemen of the Apocalypse.

While this little gang of undead deviants was typically associated with the end of the world, and all of that fire and brimstone hubbub, they actually served a much more intricate role in day-to-day operations. Sure, they showed up at the end of the world from time to time, but their specialty was hunting, and they were frightfully good at it.

Ripped from the darkest corners of the darkest nightmares, all four featured similar terrifying appearances. Their faces were thin and skeletal, and their eyes sickly and bloodshot. Various pieces of distressed ancient leather armor covered a tattered black robe, and their gauntlets were made of rusted metal. A thin belt wrapped the top of their right boot, and six knives were evenly spaced around it. Each Horseman was cursed, or blessed depending on your cup capacity perspective, with a unique weapon. Pestilence's tool of choice was a bow carved from the crushed spines of a hundred human male children. On his back, he carried a quiver full of unending arrows. His aim was impeccable, and anyone unfortunate to be caught in his sights seldom lived to tell the tale of their encounter.

War held a sword. There was nothing particularly interesting or unique about the blade. It was just a run-of-the-mill sword. However, coupled with War's ability to throw the weapon and use some otherworldly ability to recall it with his mind, it became a rather formidable weapon.

Famine originally carried a pair of scales, which, while looking cool on ancient scrolls and greeting cards, were utterly useless in combat. Many scholars who studied the Horsemen understood the scales to represent the way that bread would have been weighed during a famine, while others interpreted them as the scales of justice. The more granola analysts saw it as the struggle to maintain a healthy work life balance. But, regardless of intent, clobbering an opponent with a balancing device did little more than irritate them, and certainly failed to incapacitate any foes. It only took three major battles for Famine to toss them aside and choose a more practical weapon and changed his weapon to an ax.

Death, not to be confused with the Grim Reaper Death, was originally supposed to carry a scythe, but he chose to give it up for a variety of reasons. Trying to swing it from a horse proved cumbersome and quite difficult to operate. After he accidentally killed his first three horses and was forced to conduct business with a missing pinkie finger on his left hand, Death subsequently changed his primary weapon to a more manageable spear. As with War, he was able to recall the weapon with his mind.

No Horsemen could be considered complete without their titular steed. Although biblical historians decided that the horses were unique colors, the truth was that they were all simply just plain old horses. Dead, decayed, and quite bony in parts, but just horses. There was nothing that really distinguished them to the casual observer. Their uniqueness came in the color of their saddle.

Pestilence rode a horse with a white saddle. Green or a murky brown would have made more sense, as one typically does not associate disease and plague with the shade of white. War's horse was adorned with a blood-red saddle that was more fitting to his name. Famine's horse carried a black saddle, and Death's was a pale whitish brown. This upset Death as his favorite color was black, but Famine called dibs first as he was lumped with the lamest weapon.

These villainous creatures reared their ugly heads up at numerous moments over the centuries, each time causing death and chaos to those around them. Now, all four of them set their targets on terminating the Oceanview Five.

♦♦♦♦

We're closed," shouted Griff, the grumpy bartender, as a loud bang echoed from the front door of the bar. "Come back later." He continued to wipe a towel around a dripping wet beer glass and gave the outside visitor no more thought.

Another much louder bang echoed off the door, and the glass slipped from Griff's hand. "Son of a bitch," he shouted as he stepped back from the shattered mess. "Go home, you drunk bastard," he shouted. "I said we're closed. We open in an hour. And if you don't let me finish getting set up, it's going to be longer than that, and I'm going to water your drinks down." He grabbed a nearby broom and started to sweep the glass into a pile. After three strokes of the brush, the persistent visitor hammered the door for a third time. Griff gritted his teeth and threw his broom to the ground in anger. He walked to the end of the bar towards the front door. "For the last god dammed time, I said we're—"

The door exploded off its hinges, and a dark character on a horse entered the bar. Griff ducked down behind the edge of the bar to shield his face from the cloud of splinters that scattered across the room. He reached for his shotgun beneath the register and pointed it at the new visitor as he stood up. "Maybe I stuttered, son. I said we're closed."

Pestilence swiftly removed a knife from the belt around his boot and launched it at Griff. The blade slammed into his hand and pinned it to the wall. The shotgun fell to the ground with a loud clatter. Griff screamed as the rider dismounted and walked over to the bartender. He tilted his head as he looked at the injured man. He ran a pale finger across the bar and brought it up to his mouth. A black tongue appeared from behind a set of rotten teeth and licked the length of the digit. "Where are they?"

"Who?" said Griff as he grimaced in pain." Where are who?"

"The hunted. One of them was here. Where are they?" asked Pestilence

"I don't know who you're talking about. There's no one here."

The terrifying visitor sniffed the air as he stepped closer to Griff. "The Oceanview brother, he was here. I can taste him. Where is he?"

Pestilence twisted the knife, and Griff screamed out in pain. While Griff was a complete bad ass in his bar, he suffered a remarkably low pain tolerance, and tears welled up in his eyes.

"Wait," pleaded Griff. "Oceanview? Did you say Oceanview?"

"Speak fast, mortal."

"There was a guy who said he was from Oceanview. He was saying all kinds of crazy shit. Stuff about demons and God. Real crazy stuff."

Pestilence ripped the knife from Griff's hand, and the shaking man collapsed to the floor. "He told you about God?"

Griff nodded his head frantically as he clutched his bleeding hand. "Yes, yes, he did. He said he saw him at a church, and he helped fight demon-zombies or something."

"It's unfortunate he did that. You know too much now." Pestilence flicked the knife and sliced Griff across the throat.

Griff grasped at his neck as a fountain of blood poured from the wound.

A door opened six feet away, and Dean, a boy of fourteen entered the bar from the back room. "Griff, I took out the trash, is there—" he stopped dead in his tracks as he tried to process the scene before him.

Pestilence stormed over to the boy, grabbed his throat, and lifted him off the floor. The boy screamed and struggled as Pestilence's gaze penetrated his soul. The Horseman leaned into his face and licked the boy across the cheek. The child screamed as a reddish-brown infection spread across the saliva track and coursed through his body. His skin turned yellow, and small, pus-filled wounds appeared all over his skin. The wounds split open as his skin cracked and oozed blood. The violent pain mercifully ended, and his body went still.

The first of the Four Horsemen arrived in Phoenix.

War, the second Horseman to appear, did so at the Wells Fargo ATM where Warren previously held his one-sided discussion with Lucifer. This proved to be a bit of an inconvenience for Gladys Hamilton, as she was in Pestilence's way. She was analyzing her meager bank balance to determine how much she could afford to pull out for her lazy and ungrateful granddaughter. For the fourth time in as many weeks, the good-for-nothing girl wiped out her own back account on what amounted to little more than unnecessary trinkets and silliness.

As she studied the various banking options on the screen, a large shadow fell across her. "Just a moment," she said sweetly. "I'm just getting some money for my granddaughter." She completed her transaction, retrieved her sixty dollars, and turned around. "Children today—"

The money and receipt slipped from her hand as she stood face to face with War. He removed his sword and relieved Gladys of her head. As her body-less noggin bounced on the ground, War sniffed the air as he sought out invisible traces of Warren's location. Sensing his prey moved on, he climbed back on his horse and continued his quest.

♦♦♦♦

As the Horsemen slowly expanded their search to track down the Oceanview Five, Horseman Death appeared outside the gate of God's tow yard. His horse immediately started to scrape and dig at the ground and wound itself up into a wild frenzy. Horseman Death climbed down and sniffed the air, expecting to find Warren's scent. He cocked his head as he detected something else. Something strange. Something entirely unexpected. "Brothers," he whispered softly. Despite the other Horsemen not being close by, they heard him through a deep telepathic connection, making face-to-face interaction unnecessary. "The human has been here, and he's headed north."

"I will pick up the trail," said Famine.

"There is something else, brothers," said Horseman Death. "Another scent. One unexpected."

"Who is it?" War's body-less voice drifted back to him.

"It seems their God has joined them," said Horseman Death.

"Are you certain, brother?" asked Pestilence. "There are grave ramifications to this accusation."

"I am sure," said Horseman Death.

"He's not supposed to be here," the voice of Famine drifted back to him.

"He knows the penalty for interacting with humans," agreed War. "The rules are clear."

"And for that, he must die," said Horseman Death.

♦♦♦♦

"Shouldn't we be driving a little bit faster?" asked Death, noting their slower than expected progress getting to the freeway.

God shook his head as he focused on the road. "We can't draw attention to ourselves. The last thing we need is to get pulled over by the police."

"We'll be okay," said Spencer as he turned around in the passenger seat to look at Lucifer. "Lucifer can just do that thing he did at the police station."

"What do you mean?" asked God.

Lucifer grimaced as Spencer offered up his secret ability and stopped petting the kitten in his lap. While avoiding any eye contact with God, he looked at his pious and loud-mouthed travel companion. His eyes flashed red as he spoke. "What Spencer means is I can talk my way out of almost anything."

Under Lucifer's trance, Spencer nodded in agreement. "Exactly. He can talk himself out of anything."

Lucifer's eyes returned to normal, and he leaned back in his seat. However, his action was not lost on Cam.

"What did you just do?" she asked under her breath.

"I'll tell you later," he whispered with a smile.

"Did you bring any weapons?" asked God, unaware of Lucifer's hidden ability.

"Why would we have weapons?" asked Death.

"Weren't you expecting to fight the Caretaker?"

"Yeah, but we didn't have a lot of time to prepare for this," said Lucifer. "We're kinda making this us as we go."

"You're right on that one," agreed Death.

Lucifer looked over at Spencer. "Do you still have those water bottles in your backpack?"

Spencer nodded and pulled the bag from his shoulders. "I think so, yes."

As Spencer dug through the bag, Lucifer offered his kitten to Cam. "Can you hold him for me?"

Cam gleefully pulled the cat to her chest. "Of course."

Spencer pulled out an empty bottle. He tossed it on the rear floor as he pulled out two more bottles of water of varying contents. "Which one?"

"I'll take the half-empty one." Lucifer smiled as he reached out for Spencer's bottle.

Spencer pulled it away from Lucifer and held it against his chest. "Do you have to be such a negative Nancy?"

"Excuse me?"

"Why does it have to be half-empty? Why can't it be half f—"

Lucifer snatched the bottle from Spencer's hand. "Give me the fucking bottle."

"You are so rude," protested Spencer. "Just because you're thirsty, it is not an excuse for you to be impolite."

"I'm not thirsty, you half-wit. I want to make more holy water."

"Well, I don't have any salt left. We can't make anymore," said Spencer. "But I do have these." He opened his bag to reveal eight more bottles inside.

"How many did you steal?" asked Lucifer.

"It's not stealing when it's the Lord's work," said Spencer indignantly.

"Why did you make holy water?" asked God.

"This idiot tried to exorcise me with stolen water on the drive down here," said Lucifer.

"He does know that theft invalidates holy water, right?" asked God.

"Apparently not," said Lucifer.

Spencer ignored the review of his exorcism and returned the focus to Lucifer's plan. "How can we do the benediction of the salt without salt?" he asked, the panic rising in his tone. "This is a terrible idea."

Lucifer pointed at God. "Who's driving the damn van, Spencer? I'm quite sure Gary can bless this." Lucifer held up the bottle of water in God's direction. "What you do say, Gary?"

"Is it name brand or generic?" asked God as he focused on the road.

"Smart Water?" said Spencer as he displayed the label.

"That'll work," said God.

"Why does the brand matter?" asked Spencer.

"The cheap shit dilutes the magic. It makes it less potent."

Gary reached over and held his hand over the water. "Oh, frail synthetic vial of overpriced mineral extracted fluid, plucked from the bountiful teat of this earth, consider thine blessed and holy."

"Really?" said Cam as she rolled her eyes. "If you're not going to take this seriously."

"Is it blessed?" asked Spencer, ignoring Cam's skepticism. "Did it work?"

"Of course it didn't. That's not how it works," said Warren as he looked over at God. "Can you get us holy water or not?"

"The short answer is yes, I can make holy water. But it's not as simple as blessing it. I need to process it."

"I don't understand," said Spencer. "What do you mean by process?"

Death shrugged. "Don't look at me. This isn't my area."

Cam shrugged in equal confusion. "I have no idea what's talking about.

I'm still coming to grips with the fact I'm in a car with Lucifer, Death, and God."

God looked up at the rearview mirror again and winked at Lucifer. Lucifer smiled to himself.

Cam noticed the brief interaction, and the unspoken suggestion became apparent. "Oh, for fuck's sake, dude. He means he needs to take a piss to create holy water," said Cam cutting to the chase.

"That's gross," said Spencer, his face washed with confusion and disgust.

"Yep," said God. "Luckily, I forgot to go before we left. Body of Christ equals bladder of God, or something like that. I don't make the rules," he said as he fumbled for his zipper. "Can someone help me? I can't steer and pee in a bottle at the same time."

Lucifer shrugged. "I ain't doing it. I volunteer Spencer as tribute."

"What?" protested Spencer. "I am not touching his God parts."

"My what?" said God.

"Your holy pee-pee. I'm not touching it. That's sacrilegious."

"You called shotgun," said Lucifer as he quickly removed himself from the equation. "That's the risk you take when you're up front."

"I second that," said Death.

"Third," said Cam.

"All those in favor indicate by saying aye," said Lucifer.

"Aye," said everyone in the van except Spencer.

"The aye's have it," said Lucifer as he offered Spencer the empty bottle. "You'll need this."

"This is vulgar," said Spencer as he hesitantly grabbed it.

"Better hurry," said God. "I can't wait forever."

Spencer carefully reached over and placed the bottle between God's lap, refusing to make eye contact with his boss's genitals. "Is it out yet?"

"No," said God. "It's stuck. I need your help."

Spencer muttered a prayer under his breath and reached over to help God remove his penis.

God looked down. "You're going to need to hold it to put it in the bottle, or I'm going to get pee on my pants."

"Oh, my goodness," whined Spencer as he turned away, desperately trying to avoid eye contact. "This is sacrilegious," he griped again. He reached his hand in the general direction of God's crotch and helped guide his penis into the bottle.

"Ahhh," said God as he started to relieve himself. "That is so much better."

Spencer's breathing started to get heavier as the bottle slowly filled and the urine threatened to spill.

The car swerved sharply as God pulled on the steering wheel. The water in the bottle sloshed around.

"Eww, you almost peed on my hand!" protested Spencer.

"Sorry, I thought I saw a dog," lied God. "Hold the bottle still, Spencer. Don't get my pants wet."

"I'm trying," said Spencer frantically.

The car swerved again, and Spencer squealed. "Oh, my goodness, I've got pee-pee on my hand."

Lucifer laughed at Spencer's misfortune.

"It's not funny, Mr. '*I volunteer Spencer as tribute*'," said Spencer. "He just peed on my hand."

Cam raised a hand to her mouth to stifle a laugh.

Swerve.

"OH, MY GOODNESS, IT HAPPENED AGAIN!"

Swerve.

Splash.

Scream.

Spencer furrowed his brow as the vehicle swerved again. "Why did you swerve? There weren't any cars to avoid." He turned to face God.

God continued to focus on the road ahead, but he grinned from ear to ear. "Oops."

"Sometimes you are not a nice person," said Spencer, as close to an insult as he was capable."

"Oh, you know you love me," said God with a grin.

"At the present moment, that is certainly debatable," said Spencer. "Are you finished yet?" he asked, clearly frustrated at getting played by his boss.

"Yes," said God, barely holding back a laugh.

Spencer pulled the bottle away and screwed the cap on.

"Can you tuck me back it?" asked God. "You kinda left me flapping in the wind."

"No, I most certainly cannot."

As God adjusted himself, Spencer passed the bottle back to Lucifer. "Your holy pee-pee water."

Lucifer grabbed the bottle, lowered the window, and immediately tossed it outside.

Spencer gasped as he watched the container sail out of the window.

"Why did you throw the bottle away?"

"It was full of piss," said Lucifer. "We don't need it. It's disgusting."

"That was our holy water. What are we going to do now?"

Lucifer held up the previous bottle God blessed. "We're going to use this."

"I thought it needed to be processed?" said Spencer.

"No, I just needed to pee," said God. "I didn't want to pull over."

Lucifer vigorously shook the bottle of water, and it started to fizz. "See," he said with a grin. "Holy water."

"I hate every single one of you," said a frowning Spencer as he crossed his arms in a huff and slumped back into his seat.

While the group laughed at Spencer's misfortune, they failed to notice a new figure appear on the road a dozen cars behind them.

Famine, the last of the Four Horsemen, had arrived.

Phoenix Police Officer Martinez was suffering from an existential crisis. Part of her wanted to indulge the boredom of monitoring traffic on the northbound I-17 freeway, randomly selecting which drivers to pull over for various minor infractions. Anything bigger required more paperwork than she felt like completing. Her other more dominant half wanted to continue savoring her favorite Philly Cheesesteak sandwich from Freddie's World-Famous Subs and Wings.

Her criteria for choosing the driver whose day she was going to ruin was a deeply scientific method, perfected from years of studies and analysis. With her squad car pulled off to the side of the freeway, her automatic plate reader scanned the vehicles passing by. She coughed as she prepared to execute her selection.

A car barreled past. "Eeny. Expired plates. Boring."

The next car quickly followed, and she ran the next set of plates through her computer. "Meeny. Driving without insurance? Nope."

She scanned the next vehicle. "Miny. Expired license." She looked down at the computer one more time. "And moe. Unpaid speeding ticket. Perfect. And easy."

She reached down to put the car into gear and saw her sandwich basking on the passenger seat. "Oh, how could I neglect you, my delightful steak-filled marvel." She picked up the sub and bit off a huge chunk. Savoring the cheese-covered meat for a moment, she gently chewed and swallowed, licking her lips as she smiled to herself. If life could be better, she dared anyone to prove it.

Her radio crackled to life, and she contemplated placing her food back on the seat. "*Any officers present on northbound I17, please check in*."

The sandwich-munching officer ignored the call and continued to worship her delicious treasure.

"*Martinez, are you still in the vicinity of the thirteen-thousand block of I17?*" said the female dispatcher.

The sub continued to win Martinez's attention as her taste buds were rewarded for her negligence.

"*Martinez, I know you're there*," said the dispatcher, her voice laced with irritation. "*We can see your cruiser's GPS location*."

The officer looked at the radio, her mind a torrent of potential decisions.

"*Martinez, put down your damned sandwich, and pick up your damned radio*."

The hungry officer sighed as she lowered her sandwich, picked up her radio, and thumbed the talk button. "This is Martinez."

"*Thanks for taking the time out of your busy day to join us*."

Martinez ignored the dig. "What do you have for me that's better than my steak sub?"

"*We have reports of a 693 heading your way*."

Martinez frowned and glanced into her side mirror. A 693 warned her of a reckless driver, and she scanned her surroundings for any signs of a threat. "That's a negative on my end. How far away?" she asked, unconvinced it was more important than her delicious, but slowly getting cold, sandwich.

The radio sat silent a moment. "*Uh, hold on just a moment. We have an update on that*."

Martinez shrugged and picked up her sandwich for another bite.

"*It looks like we now have a 646*."

Martinez looked around for signs of suspicious activity. "That'f alfo a negatife," she mumbled with a full mouth of bread, cheese, and steak.

"*No, sit tight. We're getting an updated status*." The dispatcher paused. "*We're getting a report of a 10-70*."

As the radio fell silent once more, the air filled with sounds of chewing teeth, lip-smacking, and swallowing.

Martinez leaned into her windshield for a closer look. "I don't see an improperly parked vehicle," she said as she took another bite.

A moment later, a car fell from the sky and landed on its roof in the road in front of her with a loud crash. Glass sprayed out from the shattered windows and pinged against Martinez's vehicle.

Martinez promptly spat out her sandwich onto the dashboard. "What in the Kentucky fried fuck?" she yelled.

"*What was that*?" asked the dispatcher in a voice a tad calmer than Martinez.

"A fucking car just fell out of the sky." Martinez opened her door and stepped out onto the side of the freeway.

A second later, another vehicle crashed onto the far side of the freeway with a loud metallic crunch causing other cars to either swerve around or crash into it, furthering the chaos.

The sound of a car's horn screamed out, and Martinez leaped back against her vehicle's door as God's van, closely followed by Raphael's car, ripped past her at a speed far higher than the freeway allowed. "Holy shit," said Martinez as she climbed back inside and pulled the door close. Her heart pounded at the back of her throat at the near-miss.

Martinez's radio was not finished with the random distress calls. "*We're also reporting a 702, an 803, a 586, a 917, 916, a 647, a 918, and a 585.*"

The flurry of numbers warned her of a speeding vehicle, an animal at large, illegal parking, an abandoned vehicle, a city code violation, a suspicious person, an insane person, and a traffic hazard.

Martinez flicked on her lights and siren and prepared to take off after the perpetrators. Her radio cracked one more time as the dispatcher called in a miscellaneous animal incident. Martinez looked to her left just as War, the third Horsemen rushed by, carried by his undead horse. She stared at the radio, blinked once in disbelief, reached down, and turned it off.

War whipped the reins of his horse and spurred his decayed mount to run faster. God's van was slowly increasing the gap between them, and War was determined to not lose sight of his quarry. He raised his left hand and the car beside him lifted off the tarmac. The helpless driver inside pulled his hands from the steering wheel as he looked around in panic. War flicked his wrist and sent the car flying towards God.

"Fuck," screamed God as the car crashed in front of him. He steered hard to the left and narrowly avoided a collision. A moment later, another car crashed before him.

The sudden drop in speed allowed War to narrow the distance between them.

"He's getting closer," yelled Cam

"Give me a bottle," ordered Lucifer as he reached a hand towards Spencer.

Spencer dug into his bag and pulled out a bottle of holy water. Lucifer lowered the window as he grabbed the liquid and unscrewed the cap. As he prepared to throw the bottle at War, God swerved again, and Lucifer dropped the bottle.

"Fuck," screamed Lucifer. "Give me another," he said as he reached behind him.

His aim on the second bottle was flawless, and the bottle crashed against War's steed and splashed water across its face and torso. Wafts of smoke drifted from the body as if acid was eating away at its remaining dead skin. The horse whinnied as it stopped running and rose on its hind legs. War struggled to main his grip and struggled to guide the horse back onto all fours. He unsheathed his sword and tossed it into the air.

A moment later, Death, the last of the Four Horsemen, and certainly not the Grim Reaper, charged past. He reached up and caught War's sword and returned his spear to his back. Horseman Death yanked on his reins and continued the chase.

"Does anyone have a visual on Warren and Raph?" asked Lucifer as he looked out of the windows on his side of the van.

"He's two cars over and about a car behind," said Cam.

Lucifer nodded as he turned to non-horseman Death. "Steve, can you teleport into a moving target?"

"If I focus, I can." Death squinted at Lucifer. "Why do I have the feeling you're about to suggest something reckless?"

"You flatter me," said Lucifer.

"That was not a compliment."

"Spencer, give him a bottle," demanded Lucifer. "Steve, port over to Raphael's car, and we'll hit him from both sides."

"On my way," said Death as he took the bottle from Spencer and disappeared.

God looked out of his side window and spied Raphael's car coming up beside him. "Let's do this," he shouted as he saw Death reappear in the back seat of the other vehicle.

Lucifer leaned out of his window as Raphael pulled up beside him. In the other vehicle, Death handed the bottle over as Warren lowered his window to face Lucifer.

"On my command," shouted Lucifer.

Warren nodded his understanding as Horseman Death ran between the two vehicles.

"Now!" screamed Lucifer.

The two bottles of holy water sailed through the air and collided on either side of the horse. The water quickly ate into the undead steed, and it started to lose its footing. As Horseman Death lost his balance, he crashed into the side of Raphael's car. Warren fell back into the car and slammed into Raphael, causing the car to swerve.

In one last desperate act, Horseman Death swung War's sword at the vehicle. The blade sliced through the front fender and severed the axel. His horse collided with the side of the vehicle and buckled under the pressure, throwing Horseman Death into the air. He deftly flipped off the horse and landed with a hand and knee planted firmly on the tarmac, his sword stretched outside beside him. Cars honked as they swerved around him to avoid impact.

The fallout of the sword's impact on Raphael's car was immediate and devastating. The front right wheel tore away from the car and bounced down the road, slamming into the windshield of another car, killing the driver instantly. As the front of Raphael's vehicle collapsed, the rear end launched high into the air.

"Grab Warren," yelled Raphael. "Get him to the other vehicle."

Death nodded, wrapped his arms around Warren, and ported him back to God's minivan.

As Warren's rescue commenced, the vehicle flipped end over end over end, with crunch after sickening crunch. Parts of the damaged car separated from the body and launched into a dozen different directions, peppering the freeway and traffic with debris. Sparks flew as it skidded on its roof and crashed into the side barrier. Horns honked as panicked drivers tried to swerve around the various disabled vehicles. A plume of smoke wafted up from the wrecked vehicle, and various fluids and coolants poured out.

God watched the accident in terror and quickly pulled his foot off the accelerator. As the minivan slowed down, Death appeared in the back and deposited a shaken Warren into an empty seat. He looked up at Raphael's car and time seemed to stop. As other drivers tested their reflexes swerving around Raphael's wrecked vehicle, not everyone was as fortunate. The driver of a large red truck barreling down the freeway did not swerve to the left, or to the right. In fact, he did not react at all. He slammed into the back of Raphael's car at seventy-five miles an hour, and the two hunks of metal disappeared in a fiery explosion.

"NO!!!" screamed God as he watched his eternal friend perish. "Go get him!" he shouted at Death. "Bring him back."

"I can't," Death yelled back. "You know I can't port angels. There's nothing I can do."

"GO GET HIM!" cried God as tears welled up in his eyes. "Please, you have to."

"I CAN'T," shouted Death. "He's gone."

"We've gotta go," said Lucifer as he pointed to Horseman Death climbing to his feet.

"Fuck," screamed God as he slammed his foot on the accelerator and left their pursuer behind.

CHAPTER 20

The second hand of the clock in meeting room 2e ticked loudly as Amber looked up for what felt like the thousandth time. She knew her frequent glances would not speed up the group returning, but she lacked much else to occupy her time. The fear of losing Greg tore at her soul and she used anything to distract her from the pain in her chest.

After a violent outburst of thrashing limbs and spit, Demon-Greg finally fell silent and lay still on the couch. Amber watched him for thirty minutes and seeing no signs of movement, she crept back into the room fearing the worst. She stood by the door watching his chest for any sign he was still breathing. In the past hour, his skin turned an off shade of grey and felt clammy to the touch. The last time his eyes were open, the whites were pink and angry. Greg was not recovering, and the longer the team took to return, the more Amber's heart continued to ache. A loud hissing breath escaped his lungs and she let out a heavy sigh of relief. He was still alive, but for how much longer was anyone's guess.

♦♦♦♦

Traffic barely moved for two hours as various traffic accidents and road construction caused delay after unwanted delay. In an effort to avoid the main freeway, God decided to take a less-traveled path to Oceanview. While they quickly lost the Four Horsemen, their progress ground to an agonizing halt once again as they sat waiting at another lengthy construction zone.

With what could only be described as borderline nihilism, the orange-clad construction worker swatted at his stop sign, sending it into a chaotic spin. The sign rapidly oscillated between stop and go as it started to slow down, and eventually decided to end on displaying stop.

This sudden change in notification forced the approaching minivan to slam on its brakes and skid to a halt. The sign operator looked up at the van to see God yelling at him from inside.

"He can't hear you, Gary," said Lucifer as God paused for breath.

God pressed the horn. "I bet he can hear that."

"Hitting the horn isn't helping anyone. It's not going to make the traffic move any faster," said Lucifer.

"Ugh, humans are so annoying. They sit here in their prissy little cars lining up like a bunch of lemmings," moaned God.

"Hey, humans in earshot," said Warren from the rear seat.

"And you're annoying," said God. Although he was mostly referring to the sign gatekeeper. "Come on, you pedantic little peon," he yelled as he punched the horn.

Honk.

Warren opened his mouth to retort, but thought better of it. God witnessed his closest friend die and was entitled to some time to grieve. Even if he was acting like an asshole.

Honk.

The construction worker locked eyes with God and slowly raised a middle finger.

"Dick," muttered God to himself. He lowered his window and leaned out to face the man. "We're in a hurry. Can you just let us go?"

"No," said the gruff construction worker. "My job is to control traffic."

"There are no cars coming the other direction," said God. "There is literally no other traffic."

"There might be."

"Are you fucking serious?" asked God. "I can see the end of the construction zone from here."

"Yes."

"This isn't helping," said Spencer, in a lame and misguided attempt to calm God down.

"What?" said God as he turned to face his annoying passenger.

"You might try being a little bit nicer to him," said Spencer.

God muttered under his breath as he looked back at the man outside. "Please get the fuck out of the way," said God.

"No," said the sign holder.

"That's not what I meant," said Spencer.

God rolled his eyes in frustration and raised the window. The construction worker started to turn the sign to go, and the minivan started to creep forward. The sign-holding sociopath quickly flipped it back to stop, and God hit the brakes again. The man turned the sign a quarter rotation, and God's foot instinctively lifted off the brake. With a face-spanning grin, the man turned the sign back to start.

"Motherfucker!" screamed God as he mashed the horn again. "I'm going to kill him."

"Not without your laser vision, you're not," said Warren.

"But I can run his ass over."

"Vehicular manslaughter is not going to make this trip any easier," said Warren.

The sign spun one more time, and the stop direction faced God. He clenched his teeth and made a mental note to smite the man when his powers returned.

A rumble of a distant explosion echoed, and Cam turned to look out of the rear window. "I think we've got company."

Lucifer followed Cam's gaze to see a ball of fire and smoke erupt into the sky a few miles behind them.

"We're sitting ducks here," said Death. "We need to do something."

"We need to get off the road," said God. "Staying here is a bad idea."

"Off-roading in a minivan down the side of a hill isn't much better," countered Warren.

"We leave the vehicle and go on foot. We can get down there easy enough," suggested God.

"You want us to go outside?" asked Cam, not liking what she heard. "If we can't outrun them in a car, how do you think we can outrun them on foot?"

"How are we supposed to get back before Greg turns?" asked Warren. "We can't run to Oceanview. We're still seventy miles away."

God pointed to the grassy area at the bottom. "We need to get out in the open. Trust me, I have a plan."

With no one suggesting a better alternative, Lucifer offered his support to maintain unity within the group. "Everybody out," said Lucifer as he removed his seatbelt. "We're following Gary and going on foot."

Spencer gasped at the continued use of God's real name. "You're not supposed to call him—"

"SHUT UP, SPENCER," God and Lucifer yelled in unison.

Warren pulled the rear door open and leaped out of the van. He held the door as he assisted Cam, Lucifer, and Spencer onto the ground.

"I've got Nipples," shouted Lucifer as reached in and scooped up his kitten.

"Over the barrier," ordered God as he dashed across the road and jumped over a small barrier designed to keep traffic from going over the edge of the slope.

"Hey!" yelled the construction worker. "What are you doing? Get back in your van. You'll block traffic."

God stopped and turned to the man in the vest. "Are you a praying man?" asked God.

"Yeah, why?"

"I'll remember this."

"What's that supposed to mean?" asked the construction worker as the team walked by. "HEY! WHAT'S THAT SUPPOSED TO MEAN?"

"Shut the fuck up," shouted God over his shoulder.

"What the fuck did you say to me?"

Spencer paused with one leg over the barrier and looked back at the man. "He told you to shut the fudge up. Well, he didn't exactly say fudge, but you get the general—"

The man dropped his sign and took a step towards Spencer. "I'm going to fuck you up, you prissy little bitch."

Spencer squealed and concluded climbing over the railing.

The group carefully ascended the side of the hill, and quickly made their way down.

"Lucifer, can I borrow your wrist-com?" asked God.

"Sure," said Lucifer as he removed his electronic communicator and tossed it over.

"Anyone there?" asked God into the device.

"*Who's this*?" asked David from the far end.

"Who do you think it is? It's Gary."

"*Oh, hey Gary,*" said David. "*Sorry, there's a bit of static. Greg's running out of time. How are things looking down there*?"

"Not good. Raph's dead."

David stayed silent for a moment. Raphael had always been one of the more patient members of Heaven and was far more accepting of him being a misplaced atheist than many others he met. "*What happened*?"

"Our guests caught up with us and killed him," said God. "We're not going to make it to the funnel in time. I need you to head down to the basement and do something for me."

"*You mean the floor you banned me from and said I was never allowed to enter?*"

"Yes. That one."

"*So, I'm assuming you want me to power up the focused matter transmitter?*"

Lucifer's ears pricked up at the sign of classified information.

"How do you know about that?" asked God with genuine surprise.

"*Because I ignored you and went down there anyway,*" said David. "*I'm not especially good at this angel following directions stuff. I thought we'd covered that?*"

While David's confession irritated God, he was grateful he did not have to detail the ins and outs of the device he was hiding.

"What's a focused matter transmitter?" Lucifer asked casually.

"Nothing," said God.

"No, I think it is. I think the expression on your face when he brought it up means it is a very big something. What is it?"

God bit his lower lip as he considered his limited options. "Shit," he muttered to himself. "It's a device used to transport matter from one place to another," said God.

"You mean like a teleporter?" asked Warren.

"Yes," said God. "That's exactly what it is."

"So why don't you just call it a teleporter?"

"Because we felt it was more appropriate to call—"

"You really need to stop with these pretentious names. It's not impressing anyone," said Warren.

"Do you want to save Greg or not?" asked God, his voice tinged with irritation.

"You have a fucking teleporter?" asked Lucifer, a little surprised to hear Heaven was still hiding secrets for him to discover.

God sighed in resignation. "We do."

"Since when?"

"A while," said God.

"Do you know how many laws that violates, Gary?" asked Lucifer.

"Seventeen. Eighteen if you include the one about the potential to creating alternate timelines and multiverses."

"Why didn't we use it as soon as we found you?" asked Warren. "We'd already be safe in Heaven and wouldn't have the Four Fucking Horsemen of the Apocalypse chasing us. and Raphael would still be alive."

God sighed. "One of the reasons I was fired from Heaven was using it when I came to Oceanview."

"Why does it matter?" said Warren. "You said yourself that you don't want to go back to Heaven. Who cares if you use it again?"

"I—" God paused. Warren in all his annoying self did in fact present a valid point. It seemed he did want to go back to Heaven after all, and his denial cost him a dear friend.

♦♦♦♦

Ashley rested against the door frame watching over Greg and Amber with a heavy.

A polite cough echoed behind her. She turned to see David walking towards her.

"I need your help in the basement," said David.

"Sure," said Ashley. "What's down there?"

"There's a teleporter, and we're going to bring our people back. I guess we need to learn how to use it. You in?"

"Fuck yeah, I'm in," said Ashley."

Minutes later, David and Ashley stepped off the elevator into the teleporting room. The device was a sight to behold. Two giant metal rings rotating around a semi-sphere sat above an expansive control deck. A short flight of steps allowed users to climb up into the sphere.

"Holy shit," said Ashley. "How are we supposed to use this?"

David shrugged his shoulders as he lifted the wrist-com to his mouth to continue his discussion with God. "So how do I power up this thing? Is there a manual?"

"*No*," said God.

"Of course not," said David.

"*On the main console, you should see a series of six red switches.*"

David quickly scanned the control panel for the highlighted items.

"There," said Ashley as she pointed to a small row of covered switches.

"Okay, found them," said David.

"*You have to prime the charging coil before we can start the rings. Flip the switches in this order. One, four, three, six, five—*" God paused a moment. "*No, wait. One, four, three, six, two —*" God paused again.

"Whenever you're ready, Gary," said David, his voice dripping with Sarcasm.

"*Calm down, I'm thinking.*"

"I'm calm," said David. "Just let me know when you're ready to save the universe. I'll be here."

"*Four, one, five, two, three, six.*"

"Are you sure?" asked David.

"*Yes.*" God paused once more. "*Four, one, five, three, two, six.*" Another pause followed. "Maybe."

David heard God exhale over the wrist-com.

"*Two, four, one, six, three, five.*"

David remained silent, expecting yet another change.

"*Are you there?*"

"I am."

"*Did you flick the switches* ?"

"Do you have the right order?"

"*Of course I do.*"

"Okay then, here goes." David started to lift the switch covers and press the buttons, calling out each number as his hand moved back and forth. "Two." Click. "Four." Click. "One" Click. "Six." Click. "Thr—"

"*Wait. Five is next.*"

"You said three."

"*Yeah, but I meant five. Then three.*"

Ashley threw David an uncomfortable look. "He's not instilling me with much confidence," said Ashley softly.

"Me either," said David as he pressed the last two buttons, and the switches went dark.

"*What's going on* ?"

"Nothing," said David. "It didn't work."

"*Shit. Did you press the green start button?*"

"No," said David.

"*Well, how is it supposed to power up if you don't press the start button?*"

"Because you didn't tell me to."

Ashley shrugged and pressed the button. The device made a soft grinding sound. Then a loud *clunk* echoed around the room. "That doesn't sound healthy."

David followed Ashley's shrug with one of his own. "I have no idea what a teleporter sounds like."

Slowly the rings started to spin, and the sphere lifted off the pedestal.

"I think we've got it," said David.

♦♦♦♦

God waved a hand and ordered the group to stop. "Okay, the

teleporter's up. We need to stand still so they can get a lock on us. Does anyone have a phone?"

"Yep," said Warren as he pulled his from his pocket and lifted it up. "Why?"

"The teleporter will use it to triangulate our position." God held up his wrist-com. "David, you should see a blue square button labeled seek."

"*Got it.*"

"Press that and look for a signal spiking in the nine thousand range. That should be the wrist-coms."

"I see it."

"Do you see the pulsing signal next to it?"

"Yep."

"That's Warren's phone. Use the arrows and select the signal. Press the green enter button, and it will lock onto us."

"If you're going to use it, hurry up," yelled Cam. "We've got company."

The group followed her gaze to see the Four Horsemen charging along the road above.

"Everyone, huddle up," said God.

The group squeezed together to form a tight ball.

"Closer," shouted God. "Make sure everyone is in."

Spencer backed away from the group and prepared himself to run from the Horsemen.

"Spencer!" yelled God. "Stop moving, you moron! We're not coming back for you if you fuck around."

Spencer took a cautious step towards the huddle. "I'm sorry," he said. "I'm claustrophobic."

"Grab him," God ordered Lucifer.

Lucifer grabbed Spencer by the scruff of his collar and pulled him towards the group. "We're good," he shouted.

"Okay, David," said God. "It's now or never."

"*We've got a lock.*"

"Punch it!" shouted God.

"Hold onto your butts," said Lucifer as the air crackled around them.

"I can't breathe," said Spencer as the group huddled together. "You're crushing me," he whined as a blue ball of energy materialized in the air and surrounded them.

"Spencer, relax," said Lucifer. "This will only take twenty seconds. It'll be over before you know it."

"I can't, I can't," said Spencer as he started to hyperventilate. He placed his hands on Lucifer's back and pushed backward.

"What are you doing?" screamed Warren, as he and Cam stumbled away from the group as Spencer pushed them away.

"Okay, I can breathe—"

A loud electrical crack erupted, and the group disappeared, leaving Warren and Cam staring at a singed section of grass.

"What the fuck?" shouted Cam.

Warren looked up at the road to see the Horsemen sniffing around their minivan. "Head for the trees," he ordered.

In the teleportation room, the giant metal rings started to rotate as the blue ball of energy started to form. A moment later, God, Lucifer, Death, and Spencer materialized out of thin air. The group was certainly smaller than the one Ashley expected to be standing in front of her.

"Where's Cam and Warren?" asked David. "The sphere was big enough for all of you."

Despite her anger with Warren, Ashley's heart stuttered when she noticed he was missing again. "What happened?"

Lucifer turned to face Spencer. "Yeah, Spencer, where are they? Wanna tell her what just happened?"

"I—" stammered Spencer.

"What he's trying to say is that he pushed them out of the bubble right as we were about to teleport," said Lucifer, his voice with anger.

"Are you fucking serious?" yelled God. "Do you know how dangerous that is?"

"What's wrong?" asked Spencer as Lucifer shooed him out of the teleporter. "What did I do?"

"If they were stuck halfway in the bubble, only half of them gets transported," said God. "It would have cut them in half."

Collective yelps and groans burst from the group as they looked around to see any signs of blood or extra limbs on the floor.

"You are a fucking idiot, Spencer. What were you thinking?" said God.

"It's okay. I don't see anything," said Lucifer with a relieved sigh. "Looks like you got really lucky, Spencer."

"I didn't mean to," said Spencer. "I became claustrophobic and couldn't breathe. It was an accident."

"Want me to go back and get them?" asked God.

"No," said Lucifer. "I need you here to help me with Greg. I'll go back for them once we're done."

"We have to go back for them," said Ashley.

"I know we do," said Lucifer. "I'm worried as much as you are, but they're safe for now," said Lucifer, not being entirely honest. "We need to focus on Greg first, then we bring them home." He hoped the look on his face masked his true concerns. As he escorted God to Greg's location, deep down he was terrified that Cam and Warren were anything but safe.

♦♦♦♦

Cam and Warren stood with their backs pressed tight against a pair of thick tree trunks. The rest of the group was gone, and the Four Horsemen zeroed in on their location.

Cam stole a side glance at Warren and placed a finger to her lips to silence him. She held up four fingers and pointed over her shoulder to indicate the presence of the Horsemen. Warren nodded his understanding and remained quiet.

Pestilence's horse sniffed the ground, frantic in its quest to locate its prey. It dug at the dirt as they drew closer to Cam and Warren. Twenty feet away, the horse stopped as it reached the singed ground where the teleporter previously activated. The horse's head darted back and forth as it tried to pick up the smell of the humans, but the smell of the burning grass masked any other scents, and the trail went cold.

Pestilence yanked on the reins of his horse, and the group galloped away, leaving Cam and Warren to exhale in relief. Ten more minutes passed before they felt comfortable enough to step away from their respective trees and determine their next move.

"That was too close," Warren.

"Yeah," said Cam. "We need to keep—" She paused and tilted her head. "Can you hear that?"

Warren tilted his head and focused on the distant noise. "It sounds like a train."

"It is," confirmed Cam. "There's got to be a track nearby. We need to find it."

Warren looked through the tree line ahead of them. "Over there. Come on."

They sprinted through the trees and up a small embankment to see a set of train tracks stretching out into the distance in both directions.

However, neither could see evidence of a train.

"Shit," said Warren. "Did we miss it?"

Cam squatted down and placed a hand on the track.

"What are you doing?" asked Warren.

"Figuring out what direction the train is heading." She felt the track a moment longer. "It's coming this way."

"How can you tell?"

"I can feel it through the tracks. The vibrations are getting stronger," said Cam. "How fast can you run?"

"Fast enough," said Warren.

"Fast enough to jump on a train?"

"I'll guess we'll find out," said Warren with a grin. He waited for Cam to laugh, but it never arrived. "You're serious?"

CHAPTER 21

"Are you ready?" asked Lucifer as he reached for the door handle.

God slowly nodded his head. "As I'll ever be," he said in a not entirely convincing tone.

Lucifer pushed the door open and gestured for God to enter. God puffed up his cheeks and exhaled as he took a cautious step into the room. Greg stood in the corner facing the wall, the shadows masking the full extent of his transformation.

"I've got this," said God with a little more confidence. "I've never met a demon I couldn't expel from Heaven. Isn't that right, Luc?"

"Just because you demonize me, it doesn't make me a demon, you ass," said Lucifer as he momentarily contemplated letting Greg eat God.

Demon-Greg slowly turned to face God and revealed his true form. His skin as grey as stone and his black, empty eyes bore deep into God's soul. A pair of leathery wings started to stretch out behind him.

"Nope. Let me out, Luc. I didn't sign up for this," said God as he pushed past Lucifer and bee-lined for the nearest meeting room door.

"Where's he going?" asked Amber as God stormed past her.

"I don't know," said Lucifer as he watched God disappear inside and slam the door behind him. "Watch Greg," he directed Death. "I'll be right back." He crossed the hall to the closed door and banged hard on the wood. "Open the damn door, Gary," he yelled as he hammered his palm against it.

"Nope," said God from the other side. "I'm not coming out."

"Don't think I won't kick this door in," threatened Lucifer. "We have a job to do."

"I've changed my mind, I'm not going to do it," said God.

Lucifer was losing his patience. "Dammit, Gary. Get your ass out here now. We are running out of time."

"You just said he was shot with an Impiety Arrow," said God from behind the door. "You said nothing about him being a Dark-Demon."

"I kinda figured that Dark was implied when I said Impiety Arrow. You know what these arrows do, and you know what is going to happen to Greg. I could really use your help expelling it."

"I didn't realize he was this far along in the process."

"Well, had you not fucked off and left us with our balls flapping in the wind, we would have fixed this earlier, and we wouldn't be dealing with a fucking Dark-Demon. So, get your ass out here before I come in and drag you out by your hair."

"That's not my problem," said God. "This sounds more like a you issue, than a me issue."

"Fine," said Lucifer. "Then I'm going back to Hell, and you can figure out a way to get rid of a Dark-Demon on your own. I'm sure Spencer would be a great asset."

"What?" asked God from behind the door.

Lucifer remained silent as he waited for God to get his act together.

The door slowly opened, and God peeked his head out. "You wouldn't."

"Try me," said Lucifer. "The teleporter is still working. I can be back in Hell in five minutes sipping a margarita and eating nachos."

"I'm not strong enough to do this," said God.

"Neither am I," said Lucifer. "But together we will be. I can't do this without you, I need your help."

God visibly struggled with the choice, before settling on common sense. "Fine. Let's just get this over with."

"Okay then, good. We're back on track." Lucifer once again gestured towards the demon room.

"Can you say that again?" asked God as they walked back towards Greg's room.

"Say what again?"

"The part where you said I can't do this without you."

"Fuck off," said Lucifer.

God grinned slightly as he poked fun at Lucifer.

Death stepped out of the room and cleared the way for the two men to re-enter. God rolled his eyes and muttered something about Lucifer's mother under his breath.

"I heard that," said Lucifer. He smiled as the two men entered the room.

Demon-Greg had diverted his attention back to the corner and stood facing the wall.

Lucifer carefully closed the door and turned to God. "Follow my lead, and this will be easy. Just stay behind me."

God nodded as he eyed Demon-Greg with caution.

"Good morning," said Lucifer.

Demon-Greg ignored the greeting and continued to breathe heavily.

"I was wondering if we could have our human back, please?"

The creature turned to face him. "There is no human here," it said as its eyes started to glow red as its gaze bore into God. "I know everything about you, Gary."

God's eyes widened at the mention of his name. "Fuck this," he said as he turned and left the room for a second time.

"Dammit," said Lucifer as he followed God back outside. "Gary, wait," he said as he closed the door.

"Are you fucking serious?" said God incredulously. "This thing is creepy."

"He's mind-fucking you," said Lucifer.

God shook his head like a scared child. "I really don't want to do this. There has to be another way."

Lucifer placed his hands on God's shoulder in an act of gentle reassurance. "Look, I know you're scared of demons. I get it, and truly, I understand, but I can't do this without you. If we don't get the arrow out of Greg fast, the turn will be permanent, and that will bring down a demon problem the likes neither of us has ever seen, and I will be powerless to stop it. So, Gary, please, I'm asking, neigh, begging you to help me."

The edge of God's mouth turned up ever so slightly. It was the face of a man struggling to be brave in the face of pure unadulterated fear. "You're begging me?" he asked as his voice cracked.

"Enjoy the moment," said Lucifer with a comforting grin. "You won't get it again."

God nodded and inhaled deeply, pumping himself up for the confrontation. "All right, let's purge this asshole." He pushed past Lucifer, opened the door, and stormed back into the room.

"What are you doing?" asked Lucifer. "I said follow my lead!"

Demon-Greg slowly turned around the face the two men.

"Listen, you demon fuck—" started God.

Demon-Greg's cheeks puffed up as he stared at God. His head thrust forward, and a stream of yellow vomit erupted from his mouth.

God leaped back as the viscous fluid landed square in the middle of his overalls and splashed onto his face. "Son of a bitch! He fucking barfed on me," he yelled as the yellow matter dripped down from his chin. He turned and spat onto the floor. "And I think I got some of it in my mouth." He wiped his face on the sleeve of his shirt. "I need mouthwash."

"Not the time, Gary," said Lucifer. "Grab his right arm."

The two men charged at Demon-Greg, and each grabbed an arm. They pushed him from the chair and knocked him to the floor.

"Keep him still," shouted Lucifer as he struggled to kneel on Demon-Greg's left arm and grab the arrow.

Demon-Greg thrashed and bucked the two men off him.

Lucifer scrambled to his feet and dove back on top of the monster. "Come on, Gary, put your back into it."

"I'm trying," said God as he jumped back onto Demon-Greg.

Despite their weight, they struggled to keep the writhing creature down.

"We need help," said God.

"Yep," agreed Lucifer. "Everyone, in," he shouted towards the door.

Amber and Death stepped into the room and looked at the struggling duo.

"Steve, grab his legs. Amber, grab this arm," yelled Lucifer as he turned to face God.

Amber rushed over to Demon-Greg and pinned his arm down, putting all her weight on the thrashing limb. Death entered the room and stepped over to Demon-Greg's legs. A moment later, Ashley and David appeared at the door.

"What can we do?" asked David.

"Help Steve pin his legs down," shouted Lucifer. "Ashley, help Gary with his arm. I need him to help me with the arrow."

The two new assistants dove onto Demon-Greg's limbs and pinned him down. Each one struggled to keep him still.

"Berrish cor ganna shaa," shouted Demon-Greg. "BERRISH COR GANNA SHAA!"

"What is he saying?" asked Amber. "What language is that?"

"Isn't it obvious?" asked a newly arrived Spencer. "It's the tongue of the Devil."

"What did you say?" asked Lucifer as he turned to face Spencer.

"I said he's speaking the tongue of the Devil."

"Can you translate it," asked Ashley.

"Can we focus on Greg?" pleaded Amber, her soft voice lost in the chaos.

"No," said Lucifer as he fought to get closer to the arrow.

"Yes, you can," said Spencer.

"No. I can't fucking translate it because I don't speak fucking Demon. I don't understand what he's fucking saying."

"Guys—" started Amber again, but was quickly interrupted.

"Maybe you've simply forgotten," suggested Spencer.

"Maybe I should shove my foot up your ass and see what ancient languages you can remember. How does that sound to you?" asked Lucifer.

"Uncomfortable," replied Spencer.

"CAN WE PLEASE FOCUS ON GREG?" screamed Amber. This time her voice was perfectly clear. "STOP FUCKING ARGUING."

Spencer stepped back, shocked at Amber's sudden outburst, but she was right. He lowered his head and stepped back.

Lucifer nodded his apologies to Amber and locked eyes with God. "Ready?" he said as he grabbed his hand.

"No. I'm really not," said God. "Is this going to hurt?"

"Nah," lied Lucifer as he thrust both of their hands onto the shaft of the arrow. "Not a bit."

The pain was instant. God screamed as black smoke wafted up from the arrow. "It's burning!" he yelled as Lucifer squeezed his hand tight. "What the fuck? You are a lying sack of crap."

"Do not let go of the arrow," ordered Lucifer. "You will kill all three of us. Now pull!"

"I hate you," cursed God as they pulled on the arrow.

Demon-Greg bucked and thrashed as the arrow slowly slid out of the wound.

"I know," said Lucifer as he clenched his teeth. "One. Last. Pull."

With a final yell of determination, Lucifer and God yanked the arrow. It slid from Greg's body with a wet hiss.

Lucifer and God fell to the floor as the cloud of black smoke thickened and swirled around Greg. The others backed away, uncertain what was happening inside the smoke. An arm penetrated the maelstrom and disappeared. A moment later a leg punched through. As it retreated into the cloud, a loud scream pierced the air.

"Greg," cried Amber, her voice tinged with panic. "What's happening?"

"He should be turning back into your fiancé," said Lucifer.

"Should?" asked Amber pointedly. "You said this would work."

"In theory, yes," confessed Lucifer. "I've never done this before."

The smoke started to dissipate and slowly revealed a body curled up on the floor. It was Greg in all his former human glory, all signs of his demon possession gone.

Without hesitating, Amber rushed over to him. "Sweetheart?" she asked as she crouched down to cradle his head. "Can you hear me?"

Greg started to stir and opened his eyes. "Amber?"

Amber smiled and kissed him on the forehead.

"What happened?" asked Greg.

"You went full-on demon, dude," said Ashley. "Horns, wings, and all that shit. You looked kind of a badass."

"And you puked on God," said Death with a smile.

Lucifer watched the happy reunion and smiled at a job well done.

"You are a lying bastard," said God as he turned to face Lucifer, clutching his burning hand to his chest. "You said it wouldn't hurt. You lied to me."

"Yep," said Lucifer.

"Why?"

"Because I lie. I thought that was obvious by now."

"You don't have to be so good at it."

"If I'd told you it hurts, would you have done it?" asked Lucifer with a knowing grin.

"Probably."

"Really?" asked Lucifer with a grin.

"No," confessed God. "I have a low pain tolerance."

"There you go then. That's why I lied to you. How's your hand doing?" asked Lucifer with genuine concern.

"What do you think? It hurts." He held it up for Lucifer to see. It was red and swollen as though suffering a minor burn. "Doesn't yours?"

"Not really," lied Lucifer for a second time.

Ashley walked over to God and gently grabbed his wrist. "We should get some ice on that."

"That sounds nice," said God with a smile, but he continued to face Lucifer. "You held onto the same arrow that I did. How come your hand isn't hurting?"

Lucifer smiled. "What can I say? I must have a higher pain tolerance than you do."

"I guess years of BDSM parties will do that to you," said God.

"You're funny" said Lucifer with a grin.

Spencer raised an eyebrow. "What's a BDSM party?" asked Spencer.

Lucifer grinned and placed a gentle hand on Spencer's shoulder. "Oh, my poor, sheltered, hobgoblin. It means Biscuits, Danish's, Sandwiches, and Marshmallows."

"Oh, you mean like a picnic?"

"I don't know if I'd say it's like a picnic," said Lucifer. "More of a buffet of delights."

"I'm ready to go now," God said softly to Ashley. Talking of sex still made him incredibly uncomfortable, so he gladly let Ashley steer him away from the group to the nearby breakroom and away from the discussion.

Lucifer was not finished toying with Spencer. "Yeah, that's exactly what I mean. As a Baptist, you'd love it. Once all this has blown over, you should stop by Hell, and we can get a buffet going for you."

"I'm not sure if I'm comfortable going to Hell for this. Would you consider bringing one up to Heaven?"

God stopped dead in his tracks, waiting for Lucifer's inevitable positive response.

A broad sweeping grin stretched across Lucifer's face. "Are you kidding me? I would be fucking delighted to host a BDSM party in the Baptist division. Just tell me when."

God turned and stabbed a finger at Lucifer. "The holy fuck you are."

"I believe that was a direct invitation from an ambassador of Heaven," said Lucifer. "No take-backs."

"How does that feel?" asked Ashley as she placed an icepack on God's red hand.

"Nice," said God. "Thank you for wanting to help me."

"That looked like it hurt."

"It did," said God. "I don't understand why it didn't hurt Lucifer."

"Oh, I'm certain it did. He winced when he touched it. I think he was just trying to act tough in front of everyone."

God smiled at the comforting thought.

"Thank you for helping my friend. I owe you one," said Ashley as she continued to hold God's hand.

"How so?" asked God.

"Greg means the world to my sister, and she means the world to me. So, by proxy, your kind gesture to Greg was a kind gesture to me. I feel like I owe you."

"Think nothing of it," said God with a slight smile. "You don't owe me anything. It was my pleasure."

"You are a terrible liar," said Ashley. "I know you said you didn't want to do it, but you did it anyway. Actions always speak louder than words in my book."

God frowned. Unsure how to answer her.

"We haven't been formally introduced. I'm Ashley." She held out her right hand to shake God's, but realizing it was his bad hand, she switched to her left.

"I know who you are," said God. "I remember you from the Oceanview church."

"You do?" asked Ashley with a raised eyebrow.

"Of course. How could I not? You're beautiful."

Ashley's jaw dropped. It was her turn for a stunned silence.

"Knock, knock," said Lucifer from the open door. "I hate to interrupt, kiddos, but we need to get the teleporter fired up again."

"Can it wait until I fixed Gary's hand?" said Ashley. "His skin is still pretty raw."

Lucifer clenched his teeth. "I'm sorry, we need to go get Cam and Warren right now. It can't wait."

Ashley let go of God's wrist and stood up. "What's going on? Are they okay?"

"No," said Lucifer. "When we left, they were being chased by the Horsemen."

"What the fuck?" said Ashley. "You said they were safe. You lied to us." She turned to face God. "You both did."

Lucifer noticed God cringe at the accusation. "We had no choice. I needed you to focus on the task at hand. I needed everyone's attention to be focused on Greg. Now that he's okay, we can turn our attention to the next issue and save your friends."

Ashley nodded. "Does Amber know?"

Lucifer shook his head. "Just you two and David."

"What about Spencer?" asked Ashley.

"I've threatened him with bodily harm if he speaks to anyone," said

Lucifer.

"Good," said Ashley. "Let's keep it that way. I don't need her feeling guilty. She's been through enough"

"I'm going down personally," said Lucifer. "I will bring them both back, I promise. Trust me, I'm as stressed about this as you are."

Ashley noticed the sincerity in his eyes and nodded softly. It seemed he was falling for Cam more than he let on.

CHAPTER 22

Warren and Cam lay on the wooden floor of the train car, hypnotized by the rhythmic clacking of the wheels on the tracks. The perimeter of the trailer was lined with large wooden crates, leaving a small empty square in the middle of the room.

"What are you thinking about?" asked Cam, breaking a fifteen-minute silence.

"I don't know. My head is all over the place at the moment," confessed Warren.

"I hear that," agreed Cam. "It's been a hell of a week."

Warren stared at the roof a moment longer. "What's Heaven like?" he asked.

"You don't want to be surprised when you get there?" replied Cam.

Warren rolled over to look at Cam. "Yeah, I do, but I also don't want to be let down either. God hasn't exactly lived up to my expectations so far. You know what I mean?"

"Yeah," said Cam with a smile.

"I guess I shouldn't be surprised, though. If we were made in his image, then it should be a given that he'd be a bit of a dick too."

"That's pretty deep," said Cam.

"You can't tell me you weren't a bit disappointed when you met him."

"I didn't have any expectations, to be honest. I guess I never really gave it much thought. I never believed in all that."

"But I saw you in church all the time in Oceanview," said Warren.

"I wasn't there for God. I was hoping to find an eligible bachelor," said

Cam with a sad and distant smile.

Warren grinned at the confession. "In Oceanview?"

"I know, right?"

"Really? I was the town's most eligible bachelor, and I was an asshole."

"Oh, don't be so hard on yourself," said Cam. "You had your moments. Even through our briefest of marriages."

"Yeah," laughed Warren as he cast his mind back to their short union. "What were we thinking?"

"That we were bored and lonely. It seemed right at the time."

Warren smiled. "We could have hooked back up after the divorce."

"No. Because I dated idiots, not assholes, and you were still an asshole," grinned Cam.

"Ouch," said Warren with mock distress.

"You cheated on your ex."

"Fair point," said Warren.

"Did you ever cheat on me?" asked Cam.

Warren shook his head. "Nope," he said with genuine honesty.

Cam smiled at the response. He held no reason to lie to her so many years later.

"Can I ask you a question?" asked Warren.

"Sure."

"Did I miss a threesome with you and Deb?"

Cam smiled. "Yep."

"Dammit."

"Four times."

Warren groaned in annoyance. "Aw, come on. Seriously? Wasn't that technically cheating on me?"

"Nope. I told you to come home and that I had a surprise waiting for you. You told me one more round of pool and you'd be home. That's what you get for staying out playing pool with your brother every night and neglecting me."

"You know, you've changed since you left," said Warren, his tone becoming more serious.

"Yeah? In what way?"

"You just seem more confident. More self-assured." Warren paused. "It looks good on you."

Cam frowned. She was uncertain if it was a genuine compliment or a sad attempt to flirt with her. "Are you hitting on me?"

"Not at all. I used to see you every night at Jacob's, watching every guy who walked into that bar. And I'd see your heart break a little bit more each time they'd leave. It hurt seeing that happen to you over and over. You deserved better." It was indeed a compliment.

Cam smiled at Warren. "I have better now. Things finally ended up going the right way for me. It took getting the hell out of Oceanview to sort my shit out. I left all my ghosts there."

"Doesn't running just make your ghosts follow you?"

"That's just it. I wasn't running. After the town fell, there was nothing left to stay for. There was nothing to escape. That chapter of my life ended, but I got closure on it. I didn't leave with my baggage. I was able to get a fresh start. Between the insurance money and the money Donald left me, I wiped my slate clean. I said my peace and left. I went back to school, got some education under my belt, and rebuilt my life."

Warren smiled. "That's really good to hear," he said. "I'm happy for you."

"What about you? Where did you end up?"

"If I were to be honest, I never really got over Ashley," said Warren as he rolled back over and stared at the roof. "I know it sounds clichéd, and I know I fucked it up, but she was the one. I see Greg and Amber, and all I can think is that it should have been me and Ash. But me being me, I couldn't let that happen and I sabotaged it."

"You think you can ever fix things with her?"

"Not this time. If I was just dead-weight, I think you can grow and climb out of that. The insurance money we got from Oceanview would have helped me with that. But, ultimately, she deserves to be with someone better than me. You should never forgive someone who cheats on you. And to be honest, I'd question her if she did. I fucked up. I still want her in my life, and even if we stay friends, I'll consider myself lucky."

"Look at you all grown up," said Cam as she playfully nudged Warren in the ribs.

"I haven't changed that much. Certainly not as much as you have. It's good to see someone come out of this for the better." Warren pondered life for a moment. "Do you still think about what happened in Oceanview?"

Cam sighed. "I try not to, but I feel that is a disservice to those we lost. But I'd lose my mind if I dwelled on it. I've had to shut it out for my own sanity. What about you?"

"Every damn night," said Warren. "I don't sleep well these days. I've lost twenty pounds because I don't eat. Hell, how do you think I can fit in my old pants I found at Jacob's? I'm a complete mess."

"I thought you liked fighting the zombie-demons? You joke about it enough."

"I was terrified," admitted Warren. It was the first time he made the confession out loud, and his honesty surprised him. "I put up this smart-ass, not-give-a-shit exterior, but I was terrified. I've hidden my fears behind my mouth, and I started way before the zombie-demon outbreak"

"You need to be yourself. You're allowed to be scared."

Warren sighed. "I don't even know who that is anymore. I saw my friends eaten alive. I killed my barista at Starbucks."

"Kevin?"

"Yeah."

"He was fucking terrible," said Cam. "He fucked up my order every single time I went through the drive-through," she said as she cast her mind to the countless moments she needed to get out of her car and go inside to complain.

"Maybe he liked you and just wanted an excuse to see you in person?" offered Warren. "He was really shy."

"I didn't have time for that passive-aggressive bullshit. Fucking up a woman's coffee is not a smart way to make an impression. I know I was desperate to be loved, but fuck, if I can't count on you to make me a quad shot espresso, we don't have much to build on."

Warren smiled. "See, you did have standards after all."

"Yeah, I guess I did." Cam paused a moment. "I stabbed a woman in the eye with the heel of my shoe."

"Goddamn," said Warren.

"Yeah, I was attacked after Lee dumped me on the side of the road to go home to his wife. I was so fucking angry with him."

"Was she a zombie-demon?"

"Of course she was. I wasn't wandering around stabbing random women in the face."

Warren chuckled. "Fair enough." His serious demeanor quickly returned. "I heard his wife died in the outbreak. Did you guys get to talk before we left Oceanview?"

Cam shook her head. "And now I can't even clear the air with him. I never wanted him to die. I never wanted any of them to die. I can't even believe he's gone. It's like the Universe hasn't fucked us in the ass enough. Every day seems to be getting worse."

Warren smiled sadly. He enjoyed talking to a woman so blunt and to the point. The three months spent with Kim were pleasant, but she was not exactly what he'd call exciting or edgy. No tattoos, one piercing in each earlobe, and seldom cursed. In fact, the complete opposite of what attracted him to Ashley, and his interaction with Cam made him miss his Oceanview ex so much more.

"Do you think they are coming back for us?" asked Cam.

"They'd fucking better," said Warren. "I don't think the two of us could take on the four horsemen on our own. I'm sure they'll be back once they've fixed up Greg. Then we can go up there and hang out in Heaven." Warren paused. "I wonder if we'll get to meet anyone when everyone comes back from Hell," said Warren as he mused about the long-lost people from his life.

Cam's ears pricked up at the suggestion. "You really think we'll be able to meet people?"

"Maybe?"

"I want to see my dad," said Cam.

"Yeah? Both of my parents are gone, but given the choice, I'd like to see my mom again."

"Yeah?"

"Yeah. My dad was always so hard on me. He always treated me like I was inferior to Greg, no matter what I did or what I achieved. I was never good enough. In Greg's defense, he never gave up on me, even after my dad died, long after my dad had long given up on me. But my mom? When I was around her, she made me feel like I was the only person in the world."

"That's how my dad made me fe—"

They both felt the train jolt and held their breath as it slowed. The rumbling of the wheels started to die down as Warren stood and walked over to the sliding cargo door.

"I think we're here." He grabbed the handle, and carefully inched the door open. "Let's g—"

Warren froze mid-sentence. Pestilence, his bow aimed at Warren's heart, sat astride his undead horse outside the door.

"Fuck," muttered Warren as he yanked the door closed.

"What's wrong?" asked Cam.

"We've got company," said Warren as a crossbow bolt slammed into the door, from the outside, ejecting a shower of splinters into the car.

"They found us?" said Cam.

"I don't think they ever stopped chasing us." Warren walked over to the opposite door and slid it open.

War stood on the other side, starring at Warren and Cam. It slowly raised its sword as Warren closed the door.

"Fuck," said Warren again.

Cam looked around the trailer for an alternate exit. "What about the roof?" she asked as she pointed to a hatch above them. "If we stay low, we might be able to crawl out and head to another car."

"I don't like heights," said Warren. "The last I went up on a roof, I got stuck and had to spend the night in the cold spooning Greg."

"Huh?"

Warren was wandering. "Nevermin—" A loud bang echoed from the door and cut off Warren mid-sentence. "You know what? The roof sounds like a great idea to me. Help me move one of these crates over, and we can jump up."

Cam and Warren stepped over to the nearest crate and pushed it towards the hatch. Cam hopped up onto the box and pulled the release catch. She pushed the hatch open and poked her head outside. "All clear," she whispered as she looked back down at Warren. "Come on." She climbed out of the car and dropped into a prone position.

Warren's head popped up, and he followed Cam's lead. Cam pointed to the end of the carriage and gestured for them to climb down. The two crawled on their stomachs, elbow over elbow, to the end of the car.

Cam stopped and looked over the edge at the coupling below. Remaining silent, she pointed down, made a U shape, and then pointed back up indicating the need to drop down and climb up to the other car.

Warren nodded his understanding as he spun around and started to slide over the edge.

Cam held her hand up to stop him. "Wait."

"What's wrong?" said Warren as he pulled himself back up.

"We might have a bit of a problem."

Warren cautiously looked over the edge of the train to see that War and Pestilence were joined by Death and Famine. "Well, shit."

"We're surrounded," said Cam, her voice laced with panic. "You think we could jump down and outrun them?"

Warren shook his head. "They kept up with a train. We'll be dead before we hit the ground." He carefully pushed himself up to see over the edge of the car and immediately made eye contact with Famine. "Shit," he muttered as he ducked back down.

Famine removed a sword from a sheath on his saddle and climbed down. "I can see you, mortal. There's no point in hiding."

Warren and Cam slowly stood up. "Hi," said Warren cheerfully.

"You're surrounded, human," hissed Famine. "You've got nowhere to go. Climb down, and I will kill you both. Quickly."

"What are my other options?"

"I will climb up, and I will kill you both. Slowly."

"What kind of choices are those?" asked Warren. "Is there an option where you don't kill us?"

"No."

Warren looked at Cam. "Any ideas?"

Cam shook her head as she reached for Warren's hand. Warren looked at her with a sad, knowing smile. Neither said a word, there was nothing left to say. The end was inevitable.

"Have it your way, mortal. Make your peace."

The air around Warren fluttered as Lucifer appeared out of nowhere. "Hey kids! Miss me?" he said with a smile.

Cam's jaw dropped in shock and excitement. "You came back," she said as she wrapped her arms around him.

"Of course I did," said Lucifer

"Man, am I happy to see you," said Warren. "But I ain't hugging you."

"Your timing is perfect," said Cam as she smiled at the new arrival. "What kept you?"

"Oh, you know, humans to save, demons to purge, the usual." He winked at Cam. "It looks like you made some new friends. Ready to go?"

"Stand aside, Lucifer," said the Horseman standing beside Famine. "We have no conflict with you. The mortals are our target."

Lucifer clenched his teeth together and inhaled. "I'm afraid that's going to be a big no from me."

"We have clearance from the Council to expunge anyone who stands in our way, human or otherwise."

"Yeah, see, that's not going to work for me either," said Lucifer.

"Stand clear of the mortals, fallen angel. This is your last warning." The Horsemen pointed his spear towards Lucifer.

"Sorry, I didn't catch your name," said Lucifer.

"I am Death."

Lucifer cringed. "Ooh, yeah. That's going to be awkward. See, I already know someone called Death, and if I tell everyone that Death just tried to kill us, then they are going to think it was the real Death, and that's just going to confuse them."

"I am the real Death," hissed Horseman Death.

"Yeah, but you came along second. Therefore, I'm going to need to give you a nickname, so I don't confuse the two of you. I think Horsey-Death is—"

"SILENCE!" yelled Horseman Death. "What kind of games are these?"

Lucifer shrugged. "The stalling kind. I needed a minute to get Warren's phone triangulated." He held up his wrist-com. "Ash?"

"*Ready,*" her crackled voice replied.

Warren and Cam nodded.

"Call it in," said Lucifer.

Warren lifted his phone and speed dialed Ashley. "Ash?"

"*Are you guys ready*?" she asked from the great unknown.

"Hit it," said Warren.

"No!" yelled War. He launched his blade as a glowing blue orb appeared around the trio. The sword cut through the air and missed the disappearing group by a microsecond.

♦ ♦ ♦ ♦

Ashley watched the spinning orb as the velocity increased. As the discs reached their maximum velocity, the images of Warren, Cam, and Lucifer started to appear. A loud mechanical groan echoed from the device, and the lights dimmed for the briefest of moments. When the light returned, only Lucifer and Cam remained in the orb teleporter and the rotating rings were slowing down.

"Where's Warren?" asked Ashley.

Lucifer and Cam looked at each other, unsure why their trio had been reduced by thirty percent.

"He was right here," said Lucifer.

"Fuck," said Ashley as she flicked on the intercom.

♦ ♦ ♦ ♦

On the grassy field, Warren appeared six feet in the air and fell hard onto the ground. "Ow," he protested as he stood up and brushed the grass from his winded chest. Before his breath fully returned, his phone buzzed in his pocket. He fumbled to pull it out and quickly answered it.

"*Where are you*?" asked Ashley as he accepted the call.

"About two hundred feet from where you picked me up," said Warren.

"Where's Cam and Lucifer?"

"*They're here. They made it,*" said Ashley.

"Well, at least some of us did. What happened?"

"*We don't know,*" said Ashley. "W*e lost power briefly, and the machine reset. It's back on now, and we're going to try again. In three, two—*"

On one, the blue energy cloud reappeared and surrounded Warren. With a loud crack, he disappeared.

A moment later, he reappeared five hundred feet further down the plain. At least this time he landed on his feet. "You know I hate the feeling of teleporting, right?" complained Warren.

"*We're trying to get you here, but we keep losing power,*" said Ashley.

"Well, get it back on. They're coming after me again," said Warren. A distant neighing turned his attention to the chasing Horsemen closing the distance between them.

"Ash?" said Warren, his voice raised in pitch.

"*We're trying.*"

"Try harder."

War raised his sword and swung it at Warren's head as another ball of energy started to form around him.

"Shit!" yelled Warren as the sword arced towards him.

The familiar loud electrical crack rang out, and Warren disappeared as the sword cut through the air his head occupied a moment before. A second later, he popped up a thousand feet further away. "That one was better, but they're still coming."

The Horsemen quickly located his new position and immediately took off after him. Warren was now in a race for his life to return to Oceanview and with each failed teleport, his odds of survival diminished.

♦ ♦ ♦ ♦

"We're pulling too much power," said God as he looked at a computer monitor. "This machine was not designed to be used this many times in one day. It needs to cool down between jumps. We've never used it this much before."

"We don't have time to wait," said Ashley. "Warren's in trouble. Can we reroute power from somewhere?"

God shrugged. "I'm sorry, I don't know. Commercial electrical is way outside of my field of expertise. This project was Raph's baby. I know just about enough to use the basic teleport controls." He turned to Lucifer.

"Do you have anything like this in Hell?"

Lucifer shook his head. "Honestly, I've never had anyone who wanted to leave bad enough to justify me building anything like this. Don't you have an operating manual or something?"

"We do," said God. He stepped back and looked at the cabinets beneath the control terminals. He reached down to the nearest one and pulled the door open. He removed a giant three-ring binder at least twelve inches thick and dropped it on the terminal with a loud thud. "One manual of three thousand eight hundred and sixty-seven pages. Feel like some light reading?"

"I'll pass," said Lucifer.

"Can we just keep rebooting and trying smaller teleports?" asked Ashley.

"We could, but we run the risk of overheating the turbine and frying it," said God.

Ashley smiled at him and playfully slugged him on the shoulder. "See, you do know how to use this thing."

God shook his head and pointed to a nearby sign advising overuse of the turbine to prevent overheating. "Not exactly," he said. "But thanks for the vote of confidence."

"What happens if we do that?" asked Lucifer.

"There's a fail-safe that shuts it all the way down if overheats," said God.

"How long does it take to recover from a full shut down?" asked Ashley.

"About three days," said God.

"Three days? Warren doesn't have three hours. How long can we keep running it before it shuts all the way down?"

God looked at the temperature gauge on the side of the machine. "We have about four more jumps before this thing is toast."

"Is that enough to get him back?"

God remained silent.

"Gary, can we get him home?" pressed Ashley.

"Possibly. But we need to get the protective force field up before the Horsemen find us," said God. "I don't know if we have enough power to run both." He bit his lip as he looked down, contemplating his limited options. "How far away is Oceanview?"

"About six miles," said Ashley.

"Then we need to get him as close as we can before we lose all power," said God. "He's running out of time."

♦ ♦ ♦ ♦

Warren continued to sprint across the field as the Horsemen picked up their pursuit.

His phone chirped as Ashley's voice piped through. "*Warren?*"

"Please tell me you've got some good news?"

"*The teleporter keeps overheating and it needs some time to cool down between jumps.*"

"I'll keep running then," said Warren.

"*We may have a problem.*"

"You mean this isn't already a problem?"

'*We only have about four jumps left. The further you can run between jumps, the machine can cool down a little, and the further I can get you on the next jump.*"

"What about the Horsemen, Ash? I can't outrun a fucking horse. Has anyone thought about that?" Warren hesitated. "You can get me back up there, right?"

Ashley remained in a silence similar to God's.

"Ash, can you get me back?"

"*We're not sure. It's going to be close. We're getting a force field ready to surround Heaven and protect us from the Horsemen,*" said Ashley.

"Heaven has a force field?" asked Warren.

"*Yep, but we don't know if we have enough power to run both at once. We'll get you as close to Oceanview as we can. The funnel is still active in the church. If you can get to it, we'll send David down to bring you back.*"

This was not the news Warren expected to hear, but given his current predicament, it was far from the worst news he could have received. "This is the best plan you've got?"

"*We have no other way of getting you back.*"

"Not gonna lie, Ash. It sucks ass." Warren sighed. "Get me as close as possible, and I'll figure out the rest."

"*Just don't let those things follow you to the funnel. We're pretty they are able to use it if they find it.*"

"Are you trying to make this difficult because I cheated on you?" asked Warren, only half joking.

"*Don't make it personal, Warren, I want you back up here with us.*"

"I'm sorry, I didn't mean—"

"*Head's up, we're porting again.*"

Warren disappeared and reappeared two more times, putting four miles between himself and the Horsemen.

♦ ♦ ♦ ♦

God raised his hand as he waited for the system temperature to drop. Every second that ticked by felt like an hour. Finally, the gauge lowered from the last red bar to tick over to yellow, but green was still a few bars away.

"Are we good?" asked Ashley.

"No," said God. "That's why my hand is still up."

"Dammit," said Ashley. "We're almost there." She paused as she waited for God to lower his arm.

The gauge dropped to the first green bar, and God lowered his arm. "Do it."

Ashley punched the switch. The silver rings rotated for one cycle and froze.

♦ ♦ ♦ ♦

The blue orb flickered around Warren as he started to disappear.

♦ ♦ ♦ ♦

A high-pitched screech of metal on metal bounced around the room, and a large puff of smoke erupted from the middle of the device.

"Shut it off!" shouted God. "SHUT IT OFF!"

Ashley hit the switch again. The system powered down, and the room fell silent. "What happened?"

"It's toast," said God.

"I thought we had four more jumps?" protested Ashley.

"Not anymore," said God. "I'm sorry."

"*Ash, are you there?*" asked Warren through the intercom.

♦ ♦ ♦ ♦

Warren reappeared half a mile away in the middle of a quiet road. He turned around to get his bearings and recalibrate his internal compass.

"*Are you okay*?" asked Ashley.

"Yeah. I've got a bit of distance. I'll see how far I can get on foot until the next jump." Ashley remained quiet. "Ash?" he said into his phone. "Are you there?"

"*The teleporter is down,*" she said.

"Are you serious? You said I had four more jumps."

"*That's all we can do. How far did you get* ?"

"Not far enough. I'm still about two miles from Oceanview," he said into his phone. "I'm at Enrique's gas station on Cholla Road. I think I can make it, but these things are fast. I might not be able to outrun them. Maybe we can invite them in for coffee and talk it over?"

"*Warren,*" said Ashley. "*This is serious. Please don't fuck this up.*"

"Hey, it's me," said Warren with a grin. "Just remember, if I die out here, it's your fault."

"*Warren!* "

"I'll see you in thirty."

He disconnected the call and looked around. In the lot in front of the gas station, a boy of about ten rode his bike in ever-expanding circles while he waited for his mom to come out of the store. Warren jogged over to the child and stopped. "Hey kid, can I buy your bike?" he said with a smile.

The boy thought about it for a moment as he summed up the jumpy man in front of him. "Sure."

"How much?"

"How much you got?"

Warren raised an eyebrow at the unexpected hustle. "Let me sit on it to see how it fits, and I'll make an offer."

The boy climbed off the bike and offered the handlebars to Warren. "Here, try it."

Warren swung his leg over and sat on the seat. While it was certainly a child's bike, it was big enough for him to ride.

"So, what's it worth to you?" asked the boy.

"My undying gratitude," said Warren as he started to pedal away. Throughout his life, he occasionally committed various underhanded deeds, but stealing a child's bike was a first.

"Hey," yelled the boy as he watched Warren race away. "That's my bike! Mom!" he screamed as he turned to run to the store. "Mom!"

"What's wrong, young man?" enquired a female voice from behind. "Is everything okay?"

The boy turned to see Officer Martinez looking out of her squad car's driver's side window. He pointed at Warren disappearing down the road. "That man stole my bike."

"Stay here, young man. I'll get it back."

♦ ♦ ♦ ♦

Warren pedaled as fast as the little wheels would allow as he headed towards Oceanview. He made it another hundred feet before a siren sounded behind him. He looked over his shoulder to see the cop car behind him. "Shit," he muttered under his breath.

"Pull over," said Officer Martinez from her car's loudspeaker.

Warren ignored her command and continued to move the bike forward.

Martinez sighed and pulled around Warren as he pedaled frantically. She lowered her passenger window as she drove parallel to him. "Sir, can you pull over, please?" It took her a moment to recognize Warren from the ATM. "You again? Aren't you supposed to be in jail?"

"Lucifer and Death broke me out. Aren't you out of your jurisdiction?"

"I really need you to pull over, sir."

"I can't, I'm being chased. They're coming for me, and I need to get home."

"Who's chasing you? There's no one behind yet. And where's home?"

Warren gestured further down the road. "Oceanview."

"Never heard of it."

"What do you mean? It's two miles from here. Look." He pointed to an approaching street sign that had directed him to Oceanview for as long as he could remember.

Martinez let her foot off the brake as she let Warren pull ahead. Moments later, Warren reached the sign and climbed off the bike. It pointed the way to Williams and Phoenix, but the location and direction of Oceanview were gone.

"I don't understand," said Warren as he scratched his head. "Where did it go?"

The police car pulled up next to Warren, and Officer Martinez climbed out of the car. "As I said, your phantom town doesn't exist."

"This is bullshit," said Warren. "It was here a couple of weeks ago." He jumped back on the bike and took off again

Martinez sighed as she returned to her vehicle. It was time for her to bring the lunatic into custody. "Sir?" she said. "I need you to pull over and get off the bike."

Warren continued his trek down the familiar road. He passed the usual landmarks, the giant pine tree with one side dead, the power transformer, the collection of utilities boxes. He stopped his bike at the mile marker and looked around. The road he would typically turn onto was no longer there. The only thing before him was a large grassy field. It was as though the town never existed. "What the hell?" he said to himself.

Warren furrowed his brow and turned his bike towards the field. He pedaled off the edge of the road, but he never made it onto the grass. The air around him shimmered and glowed bright blue. He pushed forward for ten more seconds and broke free onto a thin road. The familiar way to Oceanview stretched out ahead. "What in the ever—"

"—loving fuck is going on?" continued Officer Martinez from behind him.

Warren turned to see the cop getting out of her car. Her face, a mask of shock and confusion.

"What the fuck was that?" she asked.

"My guess is that it was a force field."

"A force field? Really?"

"It certainly seems that way," said Warren. "See? This road leads to my town. I'm not crazy."

Martinez did not go for her handcuffs or a weapon. Instead, she beckoned Warren over to her side. "The jury is still out on that. We need to talk."

Warren walked over to the Officer. "Can you give me a ride into town? We can talk on the way."

"Not yet. I'm going to need some answers, and pronto. You said someone was chasing you? I'm assuming that wasn't a lie either?"

Warren shook his head. "No. I have some rather nasty characters on my tail. If you can get me to town, I'll answer anything you want, Officer—"

"Martinez, but I think given the current predicament, we can move to a first-name basis.

"Warren," he said as he offered a friendly hand.

"Luna," she said as she pointed to the passenger side door. "Get in."

Warren opened the door and climbed into the car. "I've never been in the front of a cop car before. I'm usually in the back."

"You've been arrested before?"

"Oh yeah, lots," said Warren. "Hank would always call the cops, so I didn't drink and drive when I tried getting in my car."

"I'm just going to ignore that," said Luna as she pulled away. "Who's chasing you?"

"The Four Horsemen," said Warren.

"Did you piss off some jockeys?"

"No, something a bit more biblical."

Luna chuckled. "What, you mean as in '*of the Apocalypse*'?"

Warren nodded. "Yep."

"Get the fuck out of here. The bad guys from the Bible?"

"Yeah, those guys. Crazy huh?"

"You know, thirty minutes ago, I'd probably have tazed you for being a public nuisance, but considering we just drove through an invisible wall, my mind is opening up to new experiences."

"Yeah, it's been a wild few months."

"Where are we going again?" asked Luna.

"Oceanview."

Luna frowned. "At the border of the Sonoran Desert?"

"Yeah, the founder was an asshole."

"Are you sure it's here?"

"Yeah, once we get past these trees the road will curve to the right, you'll see it."

Moments later, the car exited the small grove of trees, and Oceanview appeared in the distance. Or at least what remained of it. As they got closer, the scope of the damage became more apparent.

"What happened here?" asked Luna as she glanced around at the ruins of the town.

"The shorter version is God accidentally unleashed an army of zombie-demons and pretty much killed everyone."

"That's the short version?" said Luna with thinly veiled surprise and confusion.

"Yeah."

"That's pretty loaded for a short version. You said zombie-demons, right?"

"Yeah, they're kinda like zombies as they like to eat people, but they have those weird black eyes like demons, so we decided to call them zombie-demons. Could we have come up with a better name? Probably. But at the time, we were more worried about being eaten than naming them."

"How long ago did you say this happened?"

Warren tilted his head as he crunched the numbers. "Six months or so. Give or take."

"And the town has decayed this much so fast? That doesn't sense."

"And a force field surrounding it does?"

Luna shrugged. "Fair point."

"But, yeah, it does feel like the town is rotting." Warren looked at the decay around them. "Take the next left."

"Where are we heading?"

"The church."

"It's a bit late for prayer, isn't it?"

"I'm not going there to pray, Luna," said Warren with a smile. "There's a portal in the back of the church that leads directly to Heaven. Wanna come with me?"

"Get the fuck out of here."

"I'm serious. Besides, it's safer than facing the Horsemen. They're probably coming after you now anyway."

Despite Warren's previous ever-expanding teleporting leaps, the Four Horseman managed to run but a mile or two behind, and quickly closed the gap.

The young boy at the gas station recently whining about his stolen bike discovered new things to complain about when War showed up and promptly decapitated his mom. As Enrique, the gas station's namesake, ran out with his shotgun, Horseman Death threw a knife at his head. His noble charge lasted approximately nineteen feet, and he collapsed on the ground beside Famine. With the witnesses gone, the Horsemen continued their hunt.

Minutes later, they arrived at the invisible Oceanview barrier and stopped at the side of the road.

War's horse started to whinny and scratch at the ground. "He came this way," said War. "But the trail ends."

Famine climbed down from his undead horse and crouched down on the ground. He picked up a handful of dirt and held it up to his decayed nose. It inhaled sharply and licked the remains from the palm of his hand. "This way," he said as he pointed to the field, unaware of the force field that surrounded the town.

"Are you certain, brother?" asked War. "There are no tracks past the road."

Famine mounted his horse and pulled on the reins. "I am certain. I can smell them."

He guided his horse towards the field. The wall shimmered as he disappeared inside.

The remaining Horsemen looked at each other and followed Famine through the barrier.

A few seconds later, War emerged on the other side to see Famine surveying the area. "I was a fool to doubt you, brother," said War as he emerged. "You always see the way. Where do we go from here?"

Famine pointed to a group of trees in the distance. "This way." He jerked his reins, and the horse broke into a sprint.

♦ ♦ ♦ ♦

"Turn right here," said Warren. "Third house on the right."

"Did you live here?" asked Luna.

"Yeah," said Warren.

"What do you need to pick up?"

"We need to hide your car?"

"Excuse me?"

"We need to hide your car," said Warren." We can't let them see us use the portal."

Warren jumped out of the car and jogged over to the garage door. He pulled it up, and Luna pulled forward.

"Do you think they even made it through the wall?" asked Luna as she opened the car door and quietly climbed out. She exited the garage, and Warren pulled the door down before her.

"Oh, I'm certain of it."

On cue, a distant horse neighed, announcing the Horsemen's arrival.

"Shit, they're already here. Time to move," said Warren.

"How did they catch us?" asked Luna. "How fast do they move?"

"Fast."

"How far is the church from here?" asked Luna

"Just over a block." He pointed to the house across the street. "Over the gate and over the back wall."

Luna nodded, and the duo took off running. As expected, the gate was locked and required climbing. The last time Warren scaled gates and walls, he was being chased by a hoard of zombie-demons. Since that time his dexterity improved somewhat, and he was able to keep up with Luna as she effortlessly cleared both barriers.

They dropped down on the sidewalk. Despite the plan being logical, staying out in the open concerned Warren as he glanced around for cover. He nodded to the Oceanview central bus stop fifty feet away. "Follow me and keep low."

Warren and Luna crouched and dashed over to the bus stop. An acrylic sign housing a torn poster promoting the town's shitty football team still occupied the side of the stop. The church was visible behind the closest house.

Luna pointed to the front of the church. "Are we going in through the front door?"

"No," said Warren. "We can't risk going through the lobby. It's too visible from the parking lot. If we use the cars as cover, we can get to the back of the church from here. There's a small door on the far side. The bushes will cover us."

Warren pointed to a nearby red van. "Head to the van. If the street is clear, we run."

They stepped out from the bus stop to the red van and immediately ran to the wall behind the church. They easily hopped over and dropped down into the parking lot across the street. Warren's phone buzzed once again.

"*Are you close*?" asked Ashley.

"We're at the church," he said softly.

"*David's already at the funnel waiting for you,*" said Ashley. "*We're good to go when you are.*"

"Good," said Warren. "They're right up my ass."

"*What* ?" asked Ashley.

"The Horsemen are right behind me," said Warren. "We're going to be cutting this real close."

"*Warren!*" protested Ashley. "*You led them to the funnel* ?"

"I didn't have a lot of choices."

"*Why did you do that* ?"

"Because they were chasing me, and I'm tired of being the only one left down here to fend for myself."

"*Warren, they can use the portal,*" said Ashley.

Warren's heart sank. "What?"

"*The Horsemen can use the portal. You're leading them right to us.*"

"Great, now you tell me," said Warren. "It would have been handy to have known this ten minutes ago."

"*You need to lead them away,*" said Ashley.

"It's too late, Ash. I'm already here."

"*Have they seen you yet*?"

"I don't know."

"*Then move fast.*"

Warren looked over his shoulder towards Luna. "This way," said Warren as he ran to a row of bushes that led to the back door. He pushed it open and beckoned Luna inside. He carefully pushed the door closed and walked into the back room.

Luna's eyes widened as she stared at the column of blue light. "Wow," was the only comment that filtered to her mouth. It was certainly a sight to behold for uninitiated human eyes.

"Hi," said David as he stepped out of the funnel, breaking Luna's hypnosis. "Who are you?"

"Don't worry, she's with me," said Warren. "She helped me get here. She's cool."

Luna looked down at the pile of junk on the ground near the base of the funnel. "What is all this?"

Warren shrugged. "I have no idea."

"Are you sure we're in the right place? It looks like someone has been throwing garbage down here."

"That wouldn't surprise me," said Warren. "When you meet God, you'll understand."

David smiled. "Who's going first?"

"How do we use it?" asked Luna.

"Just hold onto David and just step inside," said Warren. "At least that's what we did last time. Want me to go first?"

"Nah, I've got this." Luna inhaled as she stepped towards the light and wrapped her arms around David.

"Close your eyes and hold tight. This moves fast," said David as they walked into the light and disappeared.

Warren exhaled as he waited for David to return. His mind wandered to his first attempt to use the funnel and the rude interruption of the Caretaker that nearly killed his brother. He hoped things would be a little less chaotic this time.

A loud bang echoed in the main hall of the church and jerked Warren back to the present. His deadly pursuers had caught up with him, and Famine's horse kicked in the heavy oak front door. They would be on him in less than a minute.

"Fuck," hissed Warren as the whinnying of the undead horses advanced on his location. He rushed over to the back room door and locked it. "Where are you, David?"

A moment later, David reappeared from the funnel. "Ready?"

Warren held a finger to his lips to silence David. "Our friends are here," he whispered.

David nodded and beckoned Warren over to him. Warren jumped away from the door and wrapped his arms around David. Both men stepped into the light and disappeared.

CHAPTER 23

Luna clutched her stomach as the white light surrounding her disappeared. She looked around the hallway to get her bearings as nausea ripped through her body.

Another flash of light appeared from behind as David and Warren stepped out of the funnel.

"Are you okay?" asked Warren as he placed a supportive hand on her shoulder.

"I feel like my stomach has been thrown in a washing machine."

"It'll pass quickly," said David. "We need to get out of the hallway. We're not safe yet."

David led the group down the hallway to the waiting room doors. As they rounded the first corner, the funnel rippled, and the first of the Four Horsemen stepped out of the light.

David turned the last corner to see Ashley standing by the open door. "Took you long enough," she said with a smile. Her attention then moved to Luna. "Who the hell are you?"

"Luna," said the newcomer as she entered the waiting room to see Lucifer, Cam, and Spencer standing nearby. "And you are?"

"Ashley. We'll do the rest of the introductions later," said Ashley. "Everyone, get in." She raised her wrist-com to her mouth. "Okay, we're in," she said. "Bring the shield up."

A loud neigh echoed through the hall, and the group turned to face in its direction.

"They're here," said Warren.

"Guys, where's the force field?" asked Ashley with a little more urgency. "They found us."

Through the vertical blinds, War could be seen charging down the opposite hallway.

"GUYS?" shouted Ashley. "Where the fuck are you?"

"*Working on it,*" said God from the communicator.

"Work faster," said Ashley.

"*Work damn you!*"

"Gary?"

"*COME ON!*"

"GARY?"

In the hallway, War whipped his reins and spurred his horse into a full-on sprint. All the occupants of the waiting room could do was wait with bated breath as the inevitable massacre approached.

Cam reached down and grabbed Lucifer's hand.

Lucifer gently squeezed it and locked eyes with her. "He'll get it up. Trust him," he said.

♦ ♦ ♦ ♦

"Goddammit!" yelled God as he slammed his hands on the deck. "Work, you mother fucking piece of archaic shit."

The control panel emitted another loud clunk, and the device jumped back to life in a flash of lights and sound.

A scream rang out from the radio.

"ASHLEY!" he shouted in panic.

♦ ♦ ♦ ♦

The shield materialized around the waiting room as War's horse crossed the threshold. The shimmering wall sliced into his mount and severed the animal's head with a wet squish. War and the rest of his horse crashed into the wall in an explosion of electricity and sparks.

The horse's severed head skidded across the floor and came to a rest at Spencer's feet. The lifeless creature stared up accusingly at the group.

"What the fuck?" screamed Cam.

"Oh, my goodness!" squealed Spencer as he kicked at the head. Despite the feebleness of his strike, Spencer's foot penetrated the skull, and his shoe disappeared inside. The poor man was not amused. "Oh, my goodness, my foot's stuck!" He ripped his foot back from the head. Black and brown slime and sinew clung to his shoe as the gooey substance formed a puddle on the floor. "Oh, my gosh, I've got undead horse brains on my shoe! Somebody, help me!"

He fell to the floor and dramatically tried to crawl away from the ghastly head.

"Oh, man. I'm sorry, dude. You're fucked," said Lucifer. "It's probably got acid for blood." He winked at Cam as he watched Spencer scramble across the floor like a dying swan.

"Get it off me. GET IT OFF!" screamed a distraught Spencer.

"What the fuck is that?" asked God as he stepped into the waiting room.

"It's War's horse's head," said Warren. "It got stuck in the force field when it came up. Shoink!" he said as he made a slicing action with his right hand and mimicked the head being severed.

"Gross," said God as he turned his nose up at the sight. "What's wrong with him?" he asked as he looked at Spencer.

"He's an idiot," said Lucifer.

"What is he crawling away from?" asked God.

"His foot."

"Does he realize it's still attached?" asked God.

"No idea. He's an idiot." Lucifer turned to Spencer. "Dude, you can get up now. Your foot's fine."

"You said it had acid on it," said Spencer as he stopped crawling.

"Is it burning?" asked Lucifer.

"No." He paused. A moment later, two plus two finally made four. "Ah," he said as he climbed to his feet.

"Do I need to amputate?" asked Lucifer.

"No. I'll be perfectly fine," said Spencer.

"Who's our new guest?" asked Lucifer as he politely smiled at Luna.

"Where's Greg?" asked Warren before anyone could answer. There would be time for introductions later.

"This way," said Ashley as she opened the door and gestured for Warren to enter. "And who are you?" she asked Luna, still unclear who the newcomer was.

Warren paused. His urgency was not an excuse for being rude. He turned to the group and pointed to Luna. "I'm sorry. This is Officer Martinez. She helped me get here."

"Hi. You can call me Luna."

"Luna," said Warren. "This is Ashley, Cam, Death, Lucifer, Spencer, and God." He pointed to each person as he went through the roster.

The group waved their hello's as Luna's jaw dropped at the earth-shattering introductions. It was not every day she found the opportunity to meet God, Lucifer, and Death, especially all in the same day.

Warren turned to Ashley. "Lead the way."

"They're on the floor above us. The elevators are this way," she said as she pointed to the rear door marked private.

As they crossed the waiting room to the door, Warren glanced around at the sterile environment. "This looks like my dentist's office," he said, woefully unimpressed with the decor. "I hope the tour gets better than this."

"It's certainly not what I expected," said Ashley as she directed them down the hallway to the elevator lobby. "I'm glad you didn't die."

"Me too," agreed Warren. "There were a few moments there where I didn't think I was going to make it."

"What happened to the Caretaker?" she asked as the elevator arrived.

"I killed it."

"Shut the fuck up. No, you didn't."

Warren raised his eyebrows and smiled. "Yeah, after it attacked us. I stabbed it in the eye with one of its arrows."

"You're serious." Ashley smiled, surprised at how impressed she was at Warren's unexpected bravado.

The elevator stopped, and the doors opened.

"How's he doing?" asked Warren as he stepped out.

"He's still sleeping," said Ashley. "He's been through a lot, but he's going to be okay. He just needs time to recover."

As Warren reached the small room holding Greg, he tapped gently on the door to avoid scaring Amber. "Hey, future sis, how's it going?"

Amber turned towards Warren and smiled. She rose from her chair and met him with a warm hug. "Thank God you're okay. We were so worried about you."

"How's he doing?" said Warren as he nodded towards Greg.

"Keep it down. He's still resting, but he's getting better."

Warren rolled his eyes. "He needs to get up." He was not the type to coddle his older brother, even if he was recovering from a close call with death. "Oi, wake up, you lazy shit," he shouted.

"Warren!" protested Amber angrily. "Let him sleep. He needs to rest."

Greg stirred as his eyes slowly opened. He squinted as his eyes adjusted to the room, and Amber slowly came into focus. He smiled at the comforting vision.

Amber rushed over to his side and placed a hand on his chest. "I'm sorry it was Warren. I tried to stop him and let you rest."

"He's alive?" said Greg as she struggled to sit up. "Is he here?"

"He is."

"I need to see him."

Amber placed a gentle hand on his shoulder. "Take it easy," she said. "You've had a rough few days."

"How's it going, drama queen?" asked Warren with a sly grin as he stepped around Amber and waved at his brother.

Greg looked past Amber to see Warren standing at the end of the couch. "Where have you been?"

"The usual. Killing demons, saving your ass. How are you feeling?"

"Like I've been possessed by a demon."

"You look like shit. I'm glad they fixed you before I got back. If things got much worse, I was going to stab you between the eyes with a crowbar to put you out of your misery."

Greg laughed at his brother. "I see you haven't changed a bit while I was out."

Warren shrugged. "You weren't out that long. Besides, I can't take the risk of more demons coming, can I?"

Greg frowned and looked back a Warren. "Wait, you were actually going to stab me in the head?"

"Yeah. Of course I was. You wouldn't have done the same for me?"

Greg pondered the option for a moment. "You're probably right. However, I would have waited until you had fully turned into a demon first." He stretched his arms and yawned. "So, what have I missed?"

"Well, I killed the Caretaker."

"Really?"

"Yeah."

"On your own? With no one's help?"

"Yes, on my own."

"Cool. Thanks, man." Greg held up his fist, and the two brothers bumped their knuckles together. "What else?"

"We went to Phoenix, got my car towed, got arrested, broke out of jail, found Gary, he pissed on Spencer's hand, and I've been chased by the Four Horsemen of the Apocalypse."

"Oh." There was little more for Greg to add as he processed the barrage of information. "How long was I out?"

"About a week."

"And in that time, you managed to summon the Four Horsemen?"

"Yeah. It's been a hell of a day."

"And what do they want?"

"To kill us."

Greg nodded. "Of course they do. Is there anything around here that doesn't want us dead?"

Warren shrugged. "Yeah, it does seem to be becoming a bit of a trend, doesn't it?"

"So, what's the plan?" asked Greg. "I assume they are coming after us?"

"They're already here," said Warren.

"I take it you led then here?" said Greg.

"Yeah," said Warren. "But it wasn't intentional."

"You've been through a lot," said Amber. "You can sit this one out if you want. None of us are going to judge you for that."

"I will," said Warren.

"I wouldn't expect anything less," said Greg with a smile. "Where's Gary?"

"He's in the bathroom cleaning up," said Warren. "You threw up all over him. It was fucking gross."

Greg cringed. "Really?"

"Yep. I'd pretty much rate your chances of going to Heaven as zero."

"Was he in his white suit that you put the bullet hole in?"

"No," said Warren. "He was still wearing his towing overalls."

"Huh?" said Greg, failing to understand his brother's description.

"Yeah, he's a tow truck driver."

"Oh," said Greg as he struggled to process the information. "What's going on now?"

"Everyone is hanging out in the lounge outside. We really don't have much of a plan going."

"Help me up," said Greg.

"You need to rest," said Amber. "You've been through a lot."

"I just wanna know what's going on. Can we leave? Are we stuck here? If God and Lucifer are both here, surely one of them has a plan."

♦ ♦ ♦ ♦

The room was quiet as Amber and Warren entered, supporting Greg between them.

Ashley noticed their arrival first and stood to greet them. "Hey," she said with a warm smile. "Welcome back to the land of the living."

"How are you feeling?" asked Lucifer as he looked up from the couch.

"Better. Thanks to you and God, from what Amber told me. I owe you one," said Greg as he hobbled over to the nearest empty couch.

Lucifer dismissed the suggestion with a brush of his hand. "You don't owe me a thing. Glad you're on the mend."

Greg noticed Cam snuggled up next to Lucifer. "What's the story with you two?" he said with a raised eyebrow.

Cam smiled as she looked up at Lucifer. "What can I say? He's growing on me."

Greg enjoyed seeing Cam so happy and nodded his approval as he hobbled over to the nearest chair and sat down. "You two look good together," he said with a smile.

"Good to see back," said David who was standing next to a realistic looking, but nevertheless faux electric fireplace.

"Thanks," said Greg. "I'm indebted to all of you. Warren tells me we're facing the Four Horsemen now?"

"Yep," replied Lucifer.

"Well, that escalated quickly," said Greg

"Seems to happen a lot around here," said Ashley.

"Are we talking full-on biblical Four Horsemen, or something different?" asked Greg.

"Yeah, it certainly seems like it," said Lucifer.

"So, War, Pestilence, Famine and Death?" asked Greg.

"Yep," said Lucifer. "Seems like Famine is the leader, but Death is the really nasty one. He doesn't give a shit who dies or how painfully it happens."

The group turns to face Death.

"Hey, no relation," said Death as he raised his hands in defense. "It's not exactly an uncommon name."

Warren frowned. "You're saying it's the same as John?"

"I suppose so," said Death.

"So now we have two people called Death?" said Warren. "This is going to get confusing. Are you sure you want us to keep calling you Death?"

"Yes," said Death. "That's my name."

"Yeah, you're going to need a new name," said Lucifer, knowing full well it would irritate Death.

"What can we call you?" asked Warren. "I'm getting confused over which Death is coming to kill us."

"Both of them will be if you keep comparing me to the other Death," said Death.

"There is an obvious solution," said Lucifer. "We could call you the Grim Reaper."

"You can shut up," said Death as he pointed a finger towards Lucifer.

"It would just be temporary until this all blows over," said Warren. "It doesn't have to be a permanent change."

Death gestured to the entire group. "The first one of you who calls me The Grim Reaper gets stabbed. We are not changing my name. Do I make myself clear?"

"Okay, calm down," said Warren. "It was just a suggestion. "I'm just trying to prevent people from getting confused."

"He does have a point," said Cam. "I'm already confused."

"Maybe we could put it to a vote?" suggested Spencer.

Rumblings of approval and agreement filled the room.

"Do I get a say in this?" asked Death.

"Of course," said Greg. "All those in favor of calling Death The Grim Reaper, raise your hand."

Everyone in the group lifted an arm in agreement.

"Opposed?" asked Greg.

Death raised his arm as he looked around the room for any semblance of support.

"The ayes have it," said Greg.

"I hate every single one of you," said Death.

"Relax, Grim," said Warren with a smile. "It won't be forever."

Death looked at Warren and snarled. "Wait until your time is up, sunshine. I have complete control over where you go when you die."

Warren frowned at the suggestion. He was not ready to die yet. "We could just call you Steve," he suggested.

"Why would we call him that?" asked Greg.

"Because that's his name," said Warren.

"Wow," said Greg.

Death turned to look at Greg. "What do you mean, wow?"

"Nothing. I just expected something a little more dramatic than Steve."

"Well, I happen to like my name," said Death. "And besides, I was here first. Why are we changing my name?"

That's a fair point," agreed Lucifer.

"We could call the other one Britney," offered Warren.

Greg frowned. "Why would we call him Britney?"

"Well, Horseman Death carries a spear. And I just thought Britney Spears."

Lucifer shrugged at the suggestion. "Works for me. And it'll probably piss him off too, so that's a plus."

Death nodded his agreement. "Good, thank you. All I want is just a little respect now and again."

Warren looked over towards Lucifer. "So, what's your story?" he asked.

"My story?" said Lucifer. "What do you mean?"

"I mean, why were you cast out of Heaven?"

"I thought you knew all about the Bible?" said Ashley.

"I do, Ash, it's in Ezekiel 28, but seeing as everything else I thought I knew has turned out to be wrong, I figured I'd get clarification on some other things that have been bothering me." He returned his attention to Lucifer. "Tell us what really happened."

Lucifer looked up as he contemplated his response. "Warren's not wrong. Most people refer to either Ezekiel or Isaiah 14, but my ejection actually happened in Revelation 12:7."

David's ears pricked up. "The dragon fight?"

Lucifer nodded. "Yep."

"What's the dragon fight?" asked Cam, unfamiliar with dragons in the Bible.

"And there was a great battle in heaven, Michael and his angels fought with the dragon, and the dragon fought and his angels," said David.

"That sounds fucking cool," said Cam. She turned to face Lucifer. "You never told me you've seen a dragon."

"I haven't," said Lucifer. "It's just one more thing misquoted or mistranslated."

"That's a pretty big thing to get wrong," said Warren. "How do you mistake something for a dragon?"

"Oh, a dragon was involved," said Lucifer.

Warren's frown showed he was not following along.

"It happened during a game of Scripple."

"What's that?" asked Cam.

"It's like Scrabble, but the letters are cut out from scripture. I used to play with St. Michael all time. One night we got drunk and made a bet that if I lost, I'd leave Heaven. I used the word Dragon, and that dirty motherfucker simply added an S to the end and got a triple word score. My vision was blurred, and I thought I had the last S, but it was a Z. A big shouting match ensured, I called him an illiterate cheat, and he called me retarded Judas. I was able to get in a couple of punches before security told me to gather my things and threw me out of Heaven."

Warren frowned as Lucifer wrapped up his story. "You're fucking with us, right?"

Lucifer smiled and shook his head. "I wish I was."

"Is everything lame in Heaven?" asked Warren. "That story is just sad."

Lucifer smiled. "Yeah, it wasn't my greatest moment. But I can't complain. Hell has been an absolute blast."

"All this excitement is making me sleepy," interrupted Spencer as he stood from the couch. "Does anyone else need coffee?"

Cam raised a hand. "Me."

"Same," shouted Lucifer.

Spencer nodded and walked towards the kitchen area and straight into a freshly dressed God carrying a cup of tea.

"Careful," griped God as he carefully steadied his cup, narrowly avoiding a spill.

"Whoopsie," said Spencer. "These corners can be a doozy." He disappeared into the kitchen behind God.

God sighed and looked down at his settling cup of tea. "Fucking Spencer," he muttered under his breath.

"Would you like some coffee?" asked Spencer as he reappeared around the corner and slammed a hand down on God's shoulder, causing him to jump and dump half of his tea across the front of his jacket.

"Seriously?" asked God as he looked down at the brown mess.

"I'll take that as a no then," said Spencer as he disappeared back into the kitchenette.

God placed his cup on a nearby table and walked over to the closest bathroom, cursing under his breath along the way. He pushed the door open and disappeared inside.

As with Earthly laundry, time was of the essence in order to remove stains from white clothing, and God flicked the water on and grabbed a paper towel.

"Do you always wear white when you throw coffee on yourself?" asked Ashley from the door behind him.

God looked down at his stained jacket, unsure of how to respond.

"Do you always walk into men's bathrooms unannounced?"

"Sometimes. It depends on who's in there. Let me help you with that," said Ashley as she took the cloth from him. "Take your jacket off before it seeps through to your shirt."

God obediently removed the white coat and handed it over to Ashley. "It's not coffee, it's tea. If that makes any difference?"

"Not really," said Ashley. She ran the towel under the warm water and dabbed it onto his jacket, blotting at the stain. "The trick is to get to the stain before it gets a chance to dry. Do you wear anything other than white?"

"No, I have an image to uphold," said God. "Besides, it's steeped in centuries of tradition. Lucifer wears black. I wear white. That's how it is. People would lose their collective shit if they saw me walking around in black."

"Do you like black?" asked Ashley.

God raised a curious eyebrow. No one had ever asked him that before. "What does that have to do with anything?"

"Everything. Do you like wearing black?"

"I used to," said God with a sad, distant smile. "Many, many years ago."

"Then stop doing what people expect of you. How long have you been in charge of Heaven?"

"Thousands and thousands of years. I've lost count, to be honest."

"When was the last time you did something that went against what people expect of you?"

God genuinely pondered the question. "It's been a while."

"Then do something for you for a change. I think you'd look good in black."

God smiled at Ashley, obviously flattered. "Really?"

"Yeah, I think the salt and pepper hair and a black jacket looks hot together."

"I'll have to consider that." God beamed and straightened his posture slightly. Many years had passed since he was last complimented on his looks. He was not a bad-looking guy by any stretch of the imagination, but there was an unwritten law in Heaven that you do not flirt with the boss. So, the masses treated him as a leader rather than a potential romantic opportunity.

Ashley handed his jacket back over to him, and he held it up. The brown tea stain was no smaller, in fact, it looked like it may have grown slightly.

"Er—" started God.

"Yeah, it's fucked," said Ashley with a smile.

God looked down at the jacket and tossed it into a nearby trash can. "I think I'd rather try a black one." He opened the bathroom door and gestured for her to leave. "After you," he said politely.

♦ ♦ ♦ ♦

Death was pacing the floor with a hand on his chin as Ashley and God returned to the group.

Cam smiled as she noticed God's confident stride. One that generally came from receiving an uplifting comment. She raised an inquisitive eyebrow to Ashley, who smiled and shrugged in mock denial.

"What's going on?" asked God.

"He's coming up with a plan," said Lucifer.

"Is he going to do anything other than walking?" asked Amber.

Lucifer shrugged. "I have no idea. He's been pacing the room for ten minutes. Surely that's enough time to come with something."

Death stopped pacing and turned to face the group, his right eyebrow raised with enthusiasm. "I've got it," he finally said.

The group looked up at him, their attention piqued.

"Well?" asked Warren, "Spill it."

"We hide," said Death.

"Where?" asked Cam.

"Here," said Death.

"Aren't we already doing that?" asked Lucifer. "That seems a little lackluster to me."

Warren turned his lip up in confusion. "Really? It took you an hour to decide that the best plan of action is to simply do exactly what we are doing now?"

"Leaders sometimes have to make difficult decisions, and these decisions take time."

"This was not a difficult decision," said Warren. "In fact, I don't think you could have put any less effort into it if you had tried. I've come up with better plans, and my plans are usually terrible."

"Well, I can't fight them," said Death. "Someone else will have to."

"Why?" asked Warren. "This is your fight too."

"Because I'm scared of horses. I'd be a liability to the team if I froze," said Death, as he crossed his arms like a petulant child.

"That is a terrible excuse," said Ashley.

"Yeah, it's pretty weak," agreed Lucifer.

"Well, I don't see what the deal is. We have plenty of food and water, and there are board games in the break room. We can just out-wait them."

"They are immortal, Steve," said Lucifer. "That could take a while."

"So are we," said Death.

"I'm not," said Warren.

"That's unfortunate for you," said Death.

Warren turned to Greg. "I don't know about you, bro, but if the only option we have is waiting until all the mortals die, I'm going out fighting."

"Yeah, I'm with Warren on this," said Greg, still in minor discomfort from his ordeal.

"We could play board games to pass the time," suggested Spencer.

Warren frowned as he pondered the suggestion. "Fighting a squad of undead horsemen or playing Scrabble? Count me in!"

"Oh, I don't play Scrabble," said Spencer. "There are too many opportunities to use curse words or other offensive phrases. It's far too risqué and risky."

"Oh," said Warren. "Clue?"

"And role play as a murderer? No thank you."

"Sorry?"

"A game of lies. Saying you're sorry, but you're not really sorry."

"Operation?"

"Pretending to be a surgeon."

"Is there anything you can play?" asked Warren.

Greg raised a hand to interrupt the discussion. "Before we figure this out, I was wondering if there was there somewhere I can get a snack around here?" asked Greg. "Turning into a demon has made me hungry."

"There's a bunch of vending machines three floors above us," said David. "Want me to go?"

"I'll go," said Warren. "I want to check out Heaven a bit more. This might be my only chance."

David nodded. "It's down the hall to the right of the elevators."

"Don't start the games without me," said Warren.

♦♦♦♦

Warren stared at the rows of candy hiding behind the glass as he tried in vain to make a decision. He knew Greg would want a Snickers, but his own selection was going to be a bit more challenging. As he scanned the individual rows, he quickly noticed that most of the available sweets were old and discontinued candy. "Holy shit, Hubba Bubba Dr. Pepper gum," he said with a massive grin as he gazed up at the crimson red package sitting above a sticker that read L9.

Warren pulled a quarter from his pocket and hesitated before dropping it in the slot. Above the coin slot, a small sign announced, '*All Earth currencies valid*'.

"I wonder—" said Warren, as he dropped the coin back into his pocket and fumbled around again. He pulled out a Chuck E. Cheese token and slid it into the machine. The mechanics clicked as it processed the coin. An LED display lit up above the slot and announced one credit available to use. "Fucking score," said Warren triumphantly as he pressed the L button. "Bring daddy the goods," he said as his finger moved over to the 9 and stabbed at it gleefully.

The coil holding the coil rotated for half a spin and stopped before the gum could fall off the end.

"Are you kidding me?" Warren muttered to himself. "All of the fucking engineers in Heaven, and they still can't make a vending machine that doesn't break? Give me candy, you thieving piece of pious garbage." He delivered a swift kick to the bottom of the machine.

A muffled groan echoed from a nearby room. Warren turned in the direction of the noise and cocked his head and listened. Ten seconds passed, but no other sounds came. He returned his attention to the vending machine holding his candy hostage. "Where was I?" he said as he placed his hands on the side of the machine and tried to shake it. The candy refused to leave its nest. "Asshole," he muttered and planted another swift kick to the metal base. A second later the groan sounded out again.

"Hello?" said Warren as he stepped back from the vending machine.

His greeting was met by another loud moan.

Warren decided the vending machine was a lost cause and exploring the sound would be infinitely more exciting. "Hello?" he asked as he crossed over to the door. He pulled on the handle, but the doors did not move. "Hello?" he asked again. Hearing no response, he leaned into the door and put an ear against it. No other sounds came from behind. Warren shrugged as he stepped back.

He looked up to see a vertical deadbolt at the top of the door and reached up to pull it down. He opened the door and looked inside. The room was dark, and he pulled up his phone to cast a light on the room. Seeing nothing, he flicked the phone off and closed the door. As it clicked shut and he started to push the deadbolt back into place, something charged against the doors and knocked him backwards.

A small blonde woman in her early thirties rushed out with her eyes closed and wildly swinging a Bible. "Stay back, foul creature of sin. My lady parts are not available for your pleasure or recreation."

Warren ducked as she swung the Bible at his head. "Calm down, lady," he said. "I'm not here for your lady parts, I promise."

The woman opened one eye and looked at Warren. "You speak English?"

"Yes."

"So, you're not a demon?" she said as she lowered her Bible.

"Demons can speak English," said Warren.

"So, you are a demon?" She raised her book and threw it at Warren's head.

Thankfully her aim was poor, and her arm was weak, and the heavy book landed on the floor five feet in front of Warren. One foot away from the woman.

"I'm here with God. We're trying to save Heaven," said Warren, changing his tactics. "Who are you?"

"God's back?" she asked, ignoring his question.

"He is. I'm Warren," he said as he politely extended a hand. "I was getting snacks for my brother."

"Cindy," she said as she gingerly offered the same.

"Nice to meet you, Cindy," said Warren. "I'm heading back downstairs if you'd like to join me? We're about to start playing some board games."

♦♦♦♦

David was the first to notice Warren's guest as he sat upright in his seat. "Who's this?" he asked.

"Everyone, this is—" started Warren.

"CINDY!" screamed Spencer as he stood and ran over to the surprised woman.

Cindy's eyes widened as the gangly blonde man dashed over to her. "Oh, my goodness! SPENCER!" she replied with equal enthusiasm. "You're alive!"

Spencer stopped two feet in front of her. "May I hug you?" he asked politely.

"Permission granted," she said.

Spencer awkwardly wrapped his arms around her and gave her a gentle hug, patting her on the back two times. He stepped back a few seconds later.

"You still have your whistle," said Cindy, pointing at the silver device hanging around Spencer's neck.

"I never leave without it." Remembering his manners, he turned to the confused group. "Everyone this Cindy. She is my second in command in my division. I could not be blessed with a more competent and, may I pay you a compliment?" he asked politely.

"Of course you may," said Cindy.

"A more charming right-hand man. Sorry, I mean woman."

Cindy gave the group a small wave. "Hello."

Lucifer pointed to an empty couch. "Pull up a seat and join us," he said. "We're about to play Go Fish."

"Oh, I can't play that. I'm a vegan."

Clearly Cindy was just as hopeless as Spencer.

Game night in the reception room moved forward with varying degrees of success and the large pile of games in the center of the room was slowly shrinking. Four rounds of Go Fish were scrapped when God eventually confessed that some of the cards were missing, and Clue was short-lived when it was also discovered that God previously marked all the cards and guessed the murderer every time.

"How come it's Gary cheating and not you?" Spencer asked Lucifer as he packed the game away in its box.

"Why do you assume I'd be the one cheating?" said Lucifer as he took a swig from a wine bottle. "I'm not the one with a fragile ego."

"Are you referring to me?" asked God.

"Yeah," said Lucifer. "Are you denying it?"

"No," said God with a smile. "I like winning."

"I bet I could beat you," said Ashley with a sly grin.

God opened his mouth to retort, but instead flushed bright pink.

"You are adorable when you blush," teased Ashley.

"Why don't you grab another game, Spencer?" said Lucifer as he hit the bottle of wine again.

"Would it kill you to use a glass?" asked Spencer as he put Clue away and rummaged through the cabinet looking for a new game.

"Probably," said Lucifer as he passed the bottle to Cam, and she took an equally enthusiastic swig.

"And where did you find wine anyway?" asked Spencer.

"It was in a desk in the hallway outside. It's weak as all fuck though."

"You shouldn't be rummaging through people's desks," said Spencer. "It's a sin to steal."

"Isn't it also a sin to hide contraband in Heaven?" countered Lucifer.

"That was mine," said David.

"Of course it was." Spencer clenched his teeth and turned back to the cabinet. "Why doesn't that surprise me? The wine is for special occasions. Only department heads are supposed to have access to it. Of which you are not one." He moved his attention back to the stack of board games. "How about Pictionary?" he asked as he pulled the box out and showed the group.

"I don't care," said Lucifer. "Just pick something Gary can't cheat at. But put me on his team just in case he does."

"Okay," said Spencer as he removed the board from the box.

"Let's play immortals versus humans," said God. "Luc, Spencer, Cindy, David you're on my team. The rest of you are on the other."

"Hey," objected Death. "Why aren't I on the immortal side?"

"The humans can use your help," said God with a grin.

"Why can't David join them?" he moaned.

Spencer set up the easel and paper as Cindy carefully unpacked the game.

"Ready?" asked Spencer.

"Let's draw this!" said Cindy. She rolled the dice across the table. "Three," she squealed as she moved her token to a green square. She picked up a card from the top of the deck and glanced down at it. "Ooh, this is a difficult one. Wish me luck."

Spencer clenched his fists together in excitement. "You've got this, sweetie."

Cindy blushed as she picked up the marker and stood up. "Ready," she said. Her face full of grim determination.

Ashley flipped over the timer. "And, go."

Cindy drew an oval blob.

"Bee In your bonnet," yelled Spencer triumphantly a second later.

"Yep," beamed Cindy as she held up the card.

"Oh, come on!" griped Ashley as she flipped the barely moved timer back over.

"How the fuck did you guess that?" asked Warren.

Cindy poked her tongue out at Warren. "Don't be a sore loser. Green does not look good on you. Stop sinning and start winning." She passed the dice to Death. "Your turn."

Death rolled the dice and opened his mouth to read the result.

"Four," said Cindy before Death could speak.

Death moved his token and drew a card from the deck. He looked down at the word he needed to draw. "Oh, for fuck's sake," he muttered in a rare moment of obscenity as he slammed the card down. "I want another card," he said.

Spencer shook his head. "Nope, that's against the rules. You have to play the card."

Death yanked the cap off the marker and readied himself to draw on the whiteboard.

Spencer flipped the timer over. "And go."

Death frantically started to draw the outline of a crude skeletal head, but the group remained silent. He added a jaw and the nasal cavity. He turned to his teammates and held out his hands, waiting for someone to talk.

Warren shrugged. "I have no idea."

Death sighed and continued to draw. It was not until he added two eyes and some teeth that the team woke up.

"Oh, it's Halloween," yelled Amber.

"Skeleton," shouted Cam.

Death shook his head as he continued to draw and added a cape to the character.

"Zombie-demon," shouted Warren.

"Satan?" offered Spencer from the other team.

"What?" complained Lucifer as he turned to face Spencer. "I look nothing like that whatsoever. And stop helping the enemy."

"Sorry, I got excited," said Spencer sheepishly as he lowered his head in shame. "This is my favorite game of all time."

Death continued to draw his self-portrait and added a scythe to his pseudo-likeness.

"The Grim Reaper," shouted Amber.

Death stopped drawing and looked at Amber. "Really?"

"Cheater!" yelled God. "You're not supposed to talk."

"The Angel of Dark and Light," said Ashley.

"The Grim Reaper," echoed Cam.

"I heard you the first time," said Death.

"Stop cheating!" protested God.

"The Pale Reaper," said Greg.

"The Grim Reaper," said Warren. Offering up the suggestion for the third time.

"Steve," said Ashley.

"Time's up," said Spencer as the last of the sand fell through the timer.

Death slammed down his marker. "Death, it was death. I was drawing me," he moaned.

"I said The Grim Reaper," said Cam.

"Isn't that the same thing?" asked Warren.

"No! It is not the same thing. My name is Death. The card said death. Death. I am not the Grim Reaper." Death slammed the marker down on the desk and stormed over to his seat. He flopped onto the chair and crossed his arms. "I despise all of you. Every single one of you. I'm not playing anymore."

"You're certainly the grumpy, sore loser Reaper," said Warren. "It's just a game."

"It's not my fault you're terrible at it," said Death.

"It's not my fault you can't draw," countered Warren. "It looked like a rabbit."

Death pointed at his artwork. "That is a perfectly good skeleton. How can you not see that?"

"Is it my turn?" asked Spencer as he picked up the dice and ignored Death's protests.

Cindy nodded and passed him the pen.

Spencer rolled the dice. "Three!" he yelled at the same time as Cindy and with equal enthusiasm. "Pinch, poke, buy me a coke," they both said in unison.

"Are you guys done?" asked Warren as he picked up the timer. "You're stalling."

Spencer looked down at his card and nodded. "I'm ready."

Warren flipped over the time. "And go."

Spencer drew one lone vertical line.

"The Eiffel Tower," yelled Cindy triumphantly.

Spencer pointed a finger at Cindy in victory. "Bingo!"

"Oh, come on," protested Death. "You're cheating."

God stood from his chair as the room erupted into chaos. "I'm going to head upstairs to my office if anyone needs me," he said as he excused himself from the group.

♦♦♦♦

God glided his hands over the smooth surface of his desk. His fingers, taking in every grain and knot of the dark wood. Only four weeks passed since he last sat in his office, but it felt like an eternity. He sighed and flopped down into his chair. The current situation had escalated out of control, and for the first time in his life, he did not have a solution.

A soft knock echoed from the door and pulled his attention back to the present. Ashley stood at the door holding a mug. "I brought you some tea. Try not to spill it this time, Gary." She hesitated. "Can I call you Gary?"

God smiled at the kind gesture. "That depends on what kind of tea," he said playfully.

"It's a mint medley."

God raised an inquisitive eyebrow. "Then yes, you can call me Gary. Who told you I liked mint?"

"I had a hunch," Ashley said with a smile.

"I've gotta say, I'm impressed."

"Oh, I'm just fucking with you," she said with a cheeky grin. "I could smell it on your jacket."

"I'm still flattered you paid attention. You're one of few who's ever brought me a drink, outside of Nancy."

"Who's Nancy?" asked Ashley, a little taken aback there was a woman in his life.

"Are you jealous?" asked God.

"No," said Ashley indignantly. "Why would I be jealous?"

"You certainly sound jealous," said God as he teased her. "She's my hot secretary."

"Oh," said Ashley.

"She's sixty-seven," said God with a grin. "I'm just fucking with you."

"You're an ass."

"Did you just call me an ass?" asked God.

"I don't think I stuttered," said Ashley. She looked around in a desperate attempt to change the subject. A coffee cup in the middle of the floor surrounded by golf balls provided the perfect distraction. "You play?"

"Excuse me?"

"Golf. I assume the mug is for practice."

"I used to," said God with a sad smile. "Back when things were a bit less chaotic."

"Are you any good?"

"Depends on who you ask," he said. "Almost anyone here would say yes."

"I'm asking you," said Ashley.

"No, I'm fucking awful," he smiled.

"That's a pretty blunt summary," said Ashley.

"You asked. Besides, I figured there is no sense lying to you. If we ever play a game together, you'll figure it out easily enough."

"Are you asking me out on a date?"

"Maybe. Once this has all blown over, of course. If you'd be okay dating a deity."

Ashley smiled. "Maybe. Is that what you're using to putt?" she said as she nodded towards a club propped up next to his desk.

"Yeah."

"It's a driver."

"I know. I broke my putter and never replaced it."

"It might help with your short game."

"I doubt it. My average on eighteen holes is four hundred and sixty-three. And that's when I had a good putter."

"Yeah, that's fucking dreadful," said Ashley with her usual tact. "I would be ashamed of numbers that shit."

"Ouch," said God with mock distress.

"Would you like me to say it's a good score?" asked Ashley. "I can lie to you if that makes you feel better?"

God smiled. "Honesty is good. I like someone who can be honest with me. It's not something I see very often."

"Get the fuck out of here," said Ashley.

"What do you mean?"

"You're God, isn't everyone honest with you? Isn't that one of the key rules of Heaven?"

"I'm surrounded by sycophants and ass-kissers. They don't tell me what I want to hear. They tell me what they think I want to hear. Yes, honesty is a big rule here, but so is don't hurt people's feelings, so they lie to me, so I don't feel bad." He noticed Ashley was still standing and pointed to a couch on the far side of the room. "Where are my manners?" he said. "Would you like a seat?"

"I'd love to," said Ashley as she turned to face the leather sofa.

"Now it's my turn to offer you a drink. Tea?" God said with a smile as he stood from his chair. "I have tons of mint."

"Tea is fucking gross," said Ashley. "Especially when you put mint in it."

God furrowed his brow, unable to get a read on the blunt, yet quite endearing woman before him. "I can't tell if you're serious or not."

"No, I'm serious. Tea is gross. It's like coffee's sad and pathetic second cousin.

"What else would you like? We have—"

"Coffee?" interrupted Ashley with enthusiasm.

"We don't have coffee in Heaven. It's considered contraband."

Ashley looked visibly disappointed at the revelation. "Oh, that sucks. Maybe I don't want to come here when I die after all."

It was God's turn to tease. "We have coffee."

"Ass," said Ashley playfully as she slugged him on the arm.

God smiled at Ashley. "You know what, forget the coffee. Would you like to go to dinner?"

♦♦♦♦

Ashley sat on a bar stool, watching God carefully slice through a delicate piece of off-white albacore.

"You look confused," said God with a grin.

"One. Where did you learn to prepare sushi? And two, how do you have sushi in Heaven?"

"We have everything in Heaven. Sushi, steak, frog's legs, alphabet spaghetti. You name it. Just because we're in the afterlife, it doesn't mean we don't get to eat well. To answer your first question, I'm immortal. I have a lot of time to practice these kinds of things. After I'm done for the day, I go home and practice my hobbies."

"What else do you do?"

"I play guitar. I play World of Warcraft."

"You're a gamer?" asked Ashley. "That surprises me."

"Of course. We're not savages."

"What's your gamer tag?" inquired Ashley.

"Fozzie."

"Like the bear?" asked Ashley.

"Yep. Who doesn't love the Muppets? Wocka wocka."

Ashley smiled as her mind cast back to watching the show as a child with Amber. "Is Jim here?"

"No," said God as he placed a Rainbow Roll in front of Ashley.

"What?" asked Ashley with poorly hidden shock. She took a bite of the fresh fish placed in front of her. "How the fuck is Jim Henson not in Heaven?" She pointed at the plate with her chopsticks. "This is amazing, by the way."

God shrugged. "I don't know. He never showed up after he died. I thought he was on my list, but I was mistaken. And thanks, I'm glad you approve."

"You keep serving me food this good, and I may not want to leave when this has all blown over. Next, you'll be telling me that Mr. Rogers isn't up here either."

God bit his lower lip and raised his eyebrows.

"MR. ROGERS ISN'T IN HEAVEN?" shouted Ashley.

"Nope. I thought that was weird too. He must have done something we didn't know about. And you're welcome to stay."

Ashley shook her head. "No way, the man was selfless. What about Lennon?"

"Nope."

"Bob Hope?"

God shook his head.

"Gandhi?"

"Wrong religion."

"Oh yeah. Sean Connery?"

God shook his head again. "None of the Bonds came here."

"You don't think there's something suspicious about that?" she said as she popped another piece of dreamy fish into her mouth

"The thought had crossed my mind. There are quite a few people I can think of that I'd want up here."

Ashley paused. "Are we still talking about celebrities?"

God smiled. "Maybe."

It was Ashley's turn for her cheeks to flush red.

"Are you blushing?"

"No, fuck off," she said as she ate another piece of albacore. "You're a lot different when you're on your own."

"There's a lot of people who irritate me." He paused for a moment. "Raphael was one of the few who didn't."

The mood in the room suddenly changed. Ashley wanted to offer God her sincere condolences, but never felt comfortable talking about death. "I'm sorry for your loss," she said softly. "How long had you known each other?"

God put down his knife and removed his gloves. "About seventeen hundred years. Give or take. He was a good man, and I'm going to miss him. You know, I've been up here for so long I've forgotten what grief feels like."

"Good," said Ashley.

God frowned. "I don't understand. What is good about that?"

"That you forgot what grief felt like. Grief sucks. It's irrational, it's inconsistent and it hurts. I know loss all too well."

"Was it recent?"

Ashley nodded. "Yeah. A few months ago. I lost both of my parents in Oceanview."

"Before the outbreak?" asked God. Hopeful his involvement in the Oceanview massacre did not contribute to her pain.

"No. It was during. Greg killed my dad, but he'd already turned into a zombie-demon, so I guess that was what really killed him. Then he accidentally shot my mom through the bedroom door, but she'd already been bitten, so he just sped up the inevitable—" She paused, noticing an uncomfortable look on God's face.

"I—" started God.

"I don't blame you," she said as she reached over for his hands. "So please don't think that. It's not like you came down personally and killed them. Sometimes bad shit just happens and I'm glad you don't have to experience it too much." She paused again. "Christ, look at me talking to you about loss after what happened to your so—" She caught herself again as she held a hand to her mouth. "Sorry, I didn't mean to say Christ. I curse a lot and sometimes say inappropriate things."

God smiled at her discomfort. "Do you always talk so much when you're nervous?"

Ashley shook her head. "Never like this."

"Should I ask why you're nervous?"

"No."

"Okay," said God. "I—"

Ashley grabbed God by the collar and pulled him towards her. "Shut up and kiss me."

God leaned in and met Ashley's lips, and for the first time in hundreds of years, he kissed someone.

After a moment of locked lips, God pulled away. "Wow," was all he could manage.

"I'm sorry," said Ashley. "That was too forward of me."

God smiled. "Don't be." He gently held her face and leaned in for another kiss.

"Am I interrupting something?" asked Warren from the door with a large grin on his face.

God pulled back from the kiss as Ashley hung her head and sighed in annoyance.

"Yes," said Ashley.

"I'm sorry, Warren," said God. "It just—"

Ashley held up a hand in protest. "No, Gary, don't apologize."

"She's right," said Warren. "Please don't apologize."

Ashley raised an inquisitive eyebrow at his odd manners. "What are you playing at, Warren?"

"Nothing, I promise. This is awesome," said Warren as he pointed to the two lovebirds.

"I don't understand," said God. "How so?"

"She upgraded," said Warren.

"Huh?" God was not following.

"Every time I've ever been dumped, it's been for someone worse than me. The next person to walk through the door, the drunk in the park. No one has ever upgraded before."

"You think I'm an upgrade?" said God. "I didn't think you really liked me?"

"I don't, but my ex is now dating God. That is a huge upgrade. Shit that is like the ultimate upgrade. There is no way I could compete with that." He extended his arms and beckoned the couple over. "Come here you two."

God looked at Ashley in confusion.

Ashley simply rolled her eyes and stepped over to Warren. "Just go with it," she told God.

God joined the pair, and Warren wrapped his arms around them. "I love you guys." He kissed them both on the forehead and held the hug just long enough to make it awkward.

"Okay," said Ashley as she tried to squirm out of his grip. "You can let us go now, you fucking oddball."

Warren continued to hold the pair in arms, forcing Ashley to squirm out of his grasp.

"You can go now," said Ashley.

Warren lowered his arms and stepped back. "This is so fucking cool," he beamed as he turned and walked towards the door, a slight skip to his step. "Hey Greg," shouted out the door. "Ashley dumped me for Gary."

"Damn, she upgraded," yelled Greg from down the hallway.

"I know, right?" agreed Warren as he left God and Ashley alone in the kitchen.

Ashley turned back to face God. "Where were we?"

CHAPTER 24

Ashley and God were not the only two enjoying a blossoming relationship. As the afternoon progressed, Cam and Lucifer slowly moved closer to each other, and by the time Warren returned, they were comfortably snuggling on the couch.

"Hey guys," said Warren as he nonchalantly walked into the room and flopped down onto the couch next to Greg. "I think Ash has a thing for Gary."

"Why do you say that?" asked Greg.

"I walked in on them kissing." Warren sighed as he mentally reviewed the experience. "I tried to be supportive, but man, that hits me right here," he said as he tapped his heart.

"I'm surprised it took you this long to figure out," said Greg.

"Really?" asked Warren.

"Yeah, dude," said Cam. "It's written all over her face. It's pretty damned obvious."

"Man, how am I supposed to compete with God?" whined Warren. "He's like the ultimate boyfriend upgrade."

"It does raise the bar considerably," said Greg. "I thought you were okay with it?"

"No, not really. There's no way in hell she'll get back with me now. Maybe if I bought her chocolates or flowers?"

"I don't think that is going to cut it. For starters, you cheated on her with her best friend. Chocolates can't counter that."

"She died in Oceanview. Does it count if she died?"

"Of course it does," said Greg. "Face it, dude, she has moved on in a really big way."

Warren turned to Cam. "Do you agree with him? Do you think she upgraded?"

Cam shrugged, "Don't look at me, dude. I'm falling for Lucifer. This is the best man I've ever met."

"I wish I had a deity that I could crush on," said Warren. "Then I could say I upgraded too."

Greg laughed at the thought. "Warren, let's be real. You'd probably cheat on her too. You don't exactly know how to control yourself sometimes."

"Probably," agreed Warren.

"Weren't you supposed to be getting me snacks?" asked Greg.

"Oh, yeah. Sorry. I forgot about those. The damn machine swallowed my Chuck E. Cheese token."

"You were gone over an hour, and I still don't have food."

"Have you seen the size of Heaven? It's huge."

"I'm so glad your sight-seeing adventures were more important than taking care of your starving brother."

Sensing an opportunity for some alone time with Lucifer, Cam stood up. "We'll go."

"Great idea," said Lucifer as he joined Cam in standing. "I'm sure we can find something."

Greg rolled his eyes as he watched the two of them leave the room. "Well, that's great," he muttered under his breath as the realization set in that he was most likely not going to get any food.

"What's wrong?" asked Amber.

"I guess I'm either not getting any snacks, or I'm getting them myself."

"What are you talking about? Cam and Lucifer just went out to forage for you," said Amber.

"Do you honestly think they are focusing on food?"

Amber smiled. "Yeah, you're probably right. Would you like me to go find us something?"

Greg shook his head. "Give me half an hour, and I should be feeling up to moving around a bit more."

"I think you should rest," said Amber.

"Are you kidding?" said Greg. "I'm in Heaven. I want to explore. I may not get the chance again."

"I don't think that's wise. The Horsemen are still down there. I don't think we should be splitting up."

♦♦♦♦

Lucifer exhaled a nervous breath as the elevator doors closed.

"Are you feeling okay?" asked Cam.

"Yeah," said Lucifer as he rocked back and forth on his heels. "Just a little nervous."

"About what?"

"About what I'm about to ask you."

Cam raised an eyebrow. "And what are you about to ask me?"

"May I kiss you?" asked Lucifer politely.

Cam was unable to suppress a laugh, and Lucifer's face dropped at the somewhat harsh response. "Oh, you're serious?" said Cam.

"Of course I am. You don't have to laugh at me."

"Does the Devil normally ask for permission?"

"When he likes someone, it's only proper that he does," said Lucifer.

"Oh, so you do like me?" asked Cam with a smile, genuinely taken back by the polite gesture. "I'm sure you say that to every woman you meet."

"Would you believe me if I told you I've been single for sixteen-hundred years?"

"Bullshit," said Cam. "Are you fucking with me?"

"Not at all. I am a lot of things, but I'm certainly not a liar." He bit his lip.

"You lied to Go."

"That doesn't count. He and I go way back. It's part of our relationship. I would never lie to a human. Besides, I wouldn't have been snuggling up with you if I was in another relationship. That's not my style."

"I've gotta say I'm a bit surprised at all this. The famous Prince of Darkness, who is hot as all fuck, I might add, is single."

"I just haven't met the right woman. Well, I hadn't until recently."

"So, with all of the orgies and drugs and parties going on down there, you're telling me you haven't been involved with a single woman."

"Or man."

"Well, in that case." Cam grabbed Lucifer by the collar and pulled him in for a deep, passionate kiss.

They continued their intense make-out session for another thirty seconds before Cam remembered the quest they originally volunteered for. "Shouldn't we be looking for food?" she asked as she pulled away from the kiss.

"Probably," said Lucifer with a smile. He pressed a button on the elevator floor selection panel, and the car rose for a few seconds. The door *dinged* and slowly slid open. Lucifer politely gestured for Cam to exit first.

"Thank you, kind sir," said Cam with a grin. "How gentlemanly of you."

"I can't be called the Prince of Darkness unless I have princely manners."

"What's Hell like?" asked Cam as she grabbed Lucifer's hand.

"It depends on how open-minded you are, I guess," said Lucifer. "Hell is a lot of things to a lot of people."

"What's that supposed to mean?" asked Cam.

"Well, there is the Hell that everyone expects it to be, and then there is the Hell that actually is. You know how Heaven hasn't exactly lived up to your expectations?"

Cam smiled. "Yeah."

"And how meeting Gary was a crushing disappointment?"

"Oh, he wasn't that bad. He was just a bit more human than I expected him to be."

Lucifer smiled. "There's nothing wrong with humans. I can think of one I really like."

Cam smiled and playfully tugged on Lucifer's arm. "Cheeseball. Continue."

"Yes, ma'am," said Lucifer with a grin. "When you think of Hell, what comes to mind?"

"I—"

"And you won't offend me, I promise. I honestly doubt you could say anything I haven't heard before."

"I suppose I think what everyone else thinks. Well, at least I used to until very recently. Fire, brimstone, torture, misery, and suffering. You know, the usual clichés we're taught in school. Heaven is the place you go when you're good, and Hell is the place you go when you're bad."

"That's fair enough. Like I said, it's nothing I haven't heard a million times before."

"I'm sorry," said Cam. "I don't mean—"

Lucifer stopped and looked at Cam. "No, no, no. It's not a bad thing. How are you supposed to know what Hell's really like when all you've been told your entire life is that it's a place for sinners. It's not like you've been able to go there and check it out for yourself. It's not exactly a place people have easy access to. I'm not upset."

Cam smiled at Lucifer and waited for him to continue. "All right, I'm listening."

"What would you say if I told you it's a place where people can be themselves?"

"I'd say I think that sounds delightful."

"It's a place where people don't have to lie or deceive or manipulate. We have this bad reputation that it's the worst place in the Universe to be. But it's not lakes of fire and people being burned alive. There's no death or torment, or suffering. Think of it as Heaven without boundaries."

"What about criminals and stuff? We've always been told that's where you go when you do evil things."

"Just because we have no judgment, it doesn't mean we don't have standards. I'm not talking murderers or rapists, or pedophiles. We don't have or condone any of that shit. They have no place in Heaven or Hell. I'm talking day-to-day stuff that some people aren't always open to sharing. If you want to be gay, be gay. If you want to play chess naked all day, play chess naked. If you want to wear nothing but magnolia-colored hats and tell bad puns, wear magnolia-colored hats and own that punnage. My number one rule is, be yourself. Just don't be a shit person. Because when you can truly be yourself, you are at your happiest. And when you are at your happiest, you are by default at your kindest. I am surrounded by happy people who love each other unconditionally. I don't condone racism, sexism, homophobia, none of that shit. I think the most important thing we offer is truth. What is better than that?" He looked at Cam beaming before him. "Why are you smiling?"

"I'm happy to hear that. I was already changing my opinions after I met you," said Cam. "This just cements the deal."

"Really? So, what changed your mind so early then?"

"Well, you're not like the Devil we're taught to believe exists. You're funny, sweet, and extremely caring."

"Really? I'm all those things?"

Cam nodded. "You are."

"I'm not sure how you've come to that conclusion so quickly. You haven't known me that for that long."

"It's simple, really. You came up from Hell for no other reason than to find out what happened to Heaven. But after getting here, you find a human infected with a poison arrow, took a road trip with two people you can barely tolerate to find another person you can barely tolerate. You found God, led him back to Heaven while being chased by undead horsemen, and saved that human from becoming a demon. Either you're one of the most committed con men I've ever met, or you are genuinely a decent person. There's no beneficial endgame to any of your actions if you're a con man. So, my money is on the latter."

Lucifer smiled at the compliment. It was not something he was used to hearing. "What if this is all just an act, and I'm secretly fooling you?"

"Well, then your commitment is inspiring," Cam said as she gently nudged Lucifer. "I admire a man who sticks to something. But I think you'd be lying to me."

"I'm glad you approve," said Lucifer. "And I'd say you have me figured out."

"I do, and I know." Cam smiled at him. "As I've figured out the general overview of who you are, I want to know the minutia. Tell me something no one would ever guess about you," asked Cam, cutting to the chase.

"I have eighty-seven cats," said Lucifer without hesitating. "And I can name every one of them."

"Cats? I'd have put you as more of a Doberman kinda guy."

"Nah, I'm a cat person. Well, more like kittens, really."

"Kittens?"

"Yeah, I keep them for a year, raise them and feed them by hand, then I donate them to our pet therapy department."

"Hell has pet therapy?"

"Of course we do. Mental health is important. Even the happiest people need a little help sometimes, and who doesn't love kittens?"

"That is the single most adorable thing I have ever heard. Are you sure you're not taken?" asked Cam.

"I'm positive."

"What about all of the sin and orgies I've read about?"

"Oh, we have plenty of those. Sexual experimentation is not a sin. Raping is a sin. Pedophilia is a sin. Non-consensual sex is a sin. Getting naked and fucking every willing partner in the room isn't a sin. It's fun."

"So, you did lie to me about seeing other people."

"I never said I participated. But I have no issue with my guests getting their freak on."

"Are there safe words?"

"Just one."

"And what's that?"

"No."

"Really?"

"Really. If people consent, who cares what two or more adults do?"

Cam smiled as she watched Lucifer spilling Hell's deepest and most surprising secrets.

"What are you smiling at?"

"I'm getting a sexual morality lesson from Lucifer."

Lucifer laughed. "I bet that wasn't on your bucket list, was it?"

Cam shook her head. "No, no it wasn't."

"Can I show you something?" asked Lucifer.

"Sure," said Cam. "What?"

"Give me your hand, and I'll show you. But you've got to promise you won't freak out."

"That's a loaded statement," said Cam.

"I won't hurt you, I promise," said Lucifer as Cam offered her hand and he placed it gently between his own.

"What are you doing?" asked Cam playfully.

"I can tell you the greatest day of your life," said Lucifer.

"Just from touching my hand?"

Lucifer nodded. "Yep. Cool, huh?"

"Okay, Mr. Palm Reader, tell me my favorite memory."

"Oh, this is so much cooler than palm reading. You're going to love this. He closed his eyes and focused on Cam. "Your happiest memory is from a few days ago when you met me." He paused a moment. "Wow, really?" He smiled as he slowly opened an eye to see Cam staring at him.

"How could you have possibly known?" Cam laughed at the cheesiness of his pick-up line. "Is that how you hit on women?"

"Did it work?"

Cam smiled. "No. Try again."

Lucifer closed his eye and returned his focus to Cam's hand. "You were five years old. You were laying on the grass with your father staring at the stars. He was pointing out the various constellations and you decided to rename them."

Cam's eyes stayed closed as she frowned in a mixture of awe and discomfort.

"The four stars in Orion's bow are now called Cam star, Daddy star, Mommy star, and silly star."

Cam ripped her hand away. "Shut the fuck up," she said as she eyed Lucifer with suspicion. "How did you do that?"

"I have a gift," said Lucifer, his eyes now open.

"This is my last memory of my dad before he died," said Cam. "I don't understand, I've never told anyone this. How could you know?"

"As I've said, Hell has a bad reputation, but most of it is false. I don't want people to lose their good memories after they die. I can't imagine anything crueler. If I know what your favorite memory is, I can make sure you have a happy afterlife."

"I've never thought of it like that." Cam paused. "I haven't thought of that memory in a long time." She pulled Lucifer in for a hug and kissed him tenderly on the cheek. "Thank you."

♦♦♦♦

Within the hour, the group reconvened in the lounge. Lucifer and Cam returned, and Greg was enjoying his snacks. Warren watched as the group slowly drift into pair and he smiled sadly as he realized he was the odd man out. Spencer and Cindy sat on one couch, their hands inching towards each other like a pair of awkward teenagers on a first date. Lucifer laid across another couch with his head on Cam's lap, pondering how Hell was doing in his absence, and Ashley was querying God about more of Heaven's A-list residents or lack thereof. Greg and Amber were just content being in each other's company and sat silently in front of the electric fireplace. Luna sat on her own at a coffee table and focused on cleaning her pistol. Even Death and David partnered up as they discussed the ramifications and issues of an atheist in Heaven.

Warren quietly stood and walked to the elevators unnoticed by the rest of the group. He pressed the down button and returned to the waiting room to check on their undead visitors. As he pushed the door open leading into the room full of seats, he could see all four Horsemen standing outside the glass doors. They were motionless, and had Warren not known who they were, they could easily have been confused with macabre statues.

His phone buzzed in his pocket, and he fished it out to see a text from Ashley on the screen.

ruok? She asked in her usual lowercase font.

Warren smiled at her lazy abbreviations and typed in his response. *yeah, I just needed some fresh air.*

ru sure?

Yeah. I'm sure. I'm just clearing my head.

whr did u go?

The waiting room, he responded.

r they stll thr?

Yep.

b careful. n' warren ?

Yeah ?

Don't do anythin stupid

Me? Never

Warren smiled again as he placed his phone back in his pockets and walked towards the glass door.

♦♦♦♦

While Spencer was enjoying his light finger touches with Cindy, he craved a cup of coffee. Not the good stuff Amber was previously making in the industrial-strength machine, the cheap bitter garbage made with instant coffee granules that would cause most self-respecting coffee drinker to fall on their sword before consuming it. He briefly excused himself from Cindy's company and walked over to the small kitchenette at the side of the room.

The counters were their usual uncluttered purity as Spencer crouched down and rummaged through the cabinets below. While the surfaces were clean, the cabinets below disguised a different reality. None of the appliances were returned to the correct place, and the cables were an anarchic jumble of knots and kinks and random plugs. Spencer tugged on a cable as he tried to sort out toasters from blenders. "Would it kill people to put things back where they found them," he muttered to himself in frustration. "This type of chaos would not be tolerated in the Baptist's division." He finally retrieved the coffee maker, and after unthreading a couple of knots and yanking on the cable, it broke free. He straightened up to see Lucifer grinning at him like a fool. "Can I help you with something?" he asked as he closed the cabinet door and stood up.

"I heard that," said Lucifer as he entered the kitchen area.

"What?" asked Spencer.

"Your little dig at the Jehovah's Witnesses. I heard it."

"I said no such thing," protested Spencer.

"So, you're judgmental and a liar?" said Lucifer as he mock-scolded Spencer. "I'd say there's a place in Hell for you, but we don't tolerate that type of discrimination down there."

"I do not discriminate!" objected Spencer.

"I must say, I'm rather appalled."

"I love everyone," said Spencer.

"Except for Jehovah's Witnesses, apparently," said Lucifer.

"I was not discriminating. I was merely objecting to their lack of organization skills."

"Hey, I'm not judging your judgment," said Lucifer as he held up his hands. "You can hate them all you want. It's no skin off my back."

"I do not hate anyone," said Spencer as he pulled the coffee maker to his chest as if holding a stuffed bear for comfort. "I'm going to go and make my coffee now. Please leave me be."

Pestilence slowly climbed down from his horse, never taking his eyes off Warren. He removed his sword from its sheath and walked over to the energy field that protected the front door to the waiting room.

Warren smiled and raised a polite hand. "Hello!" he said cheerfully. "Sorry, but Heaven's closed. Please try visiting again at a later date."

Pestilence brushed his sword against the energy wall, and it crackled with a loud electrical pop.

Warren pouted in mock distress. "Aw, you can't get in, can you?"

"Grant me passage, mortal, and I promise to kill you quickly," sneered Pestilence.

"I could do that," said Warren. "Or I could sit here and mock you for not being able to get past a magic wall."

Pestilence bared his rotten yellow teeth and uttered a low growl. "Keep talking. I will enjoy ripping your flesh from your bones and watching you die in unimaginable pain."

Warren remained surprisingly unfazed. "Save the torture lecture, princess. You can't get in here. I know it, and you know it. If all you've got is a few testy words, you might as well go home and find something else to do."

The undead visitor raised his sword and stabbed it into the force field. The impact emitted another loud electrical crack, and sparks momentarily danced around the tip of the sword before racing down the blade, and up his arm. The monster's limb twitched ever-so-slightly. Pestilence pulled his arm back and shook out the sharp pain gripping the right side of his body.

"Ooh," said Warren. "That looked like that hurt. It hurt, didn't it?"

"Keep speaking. Your time will come," hissed Pestilence as he started to pace back and forth. "When we get in, and we will, we'll kill every last one of you. I know everything about you, Warren."

Warren shifted uncomfortably at the surprising mention of his name. How did one of the Four horsemen of the Apocalypse know who he was? "Bring it," he said as he tried to maintain his composure.

"I know you, Warren William Edgar Hart. I will prey on every weakness, every vulnerability you have ever had, until you plead for the release of death. I will slaughter your brother. I will kill the ex-girlfriend that you refuse to get over, and I will rip the unborn child from your future sister-in-law's womb and squeeze anything that resembles life from its fragile body."

"Fuck you!" shouted Warren as he stared Pestilence in the face and raised a middle finger. "We've got a magic wall, motherfucker! You can't get in. All your disease, your death, and you can't get past a magical God wall. You're pathetic."

Pestilence pointed his sword at Warren. "I will kill you last, and I will take my time doing it."

Warren sat on the nearest waiting room chair and spread his feet out. "Yeah, whatever, you useless undead fuck."

A loud electrical crack echoed around the room, and the static glow of the force field disappeared.

Pestilence sneered. "My offer of mercy is rescinded."

Spencer jerked his hand back from the electrical outlet. A wisp of black smoke wafted up from the fried circuit. "Oops." He blew on the plug to dissipate the smoke and turned to the group.

"What just happened?" shouted God from the couch. "What was that noise?"

"Nothing," said Spencer as he looked down at his feet in a lame attempt to avoid eye contact with any of the group.

His overt behavior was not lost on God, and he stared at the awkward man. "That didn't sound like nothing," said God. "Spencer?"

Spencer continued to look away and act distracted.

"Spencer?" asked God for a second time.

The blonde man forced a fake smile as he looked at God. "Yes?" he asked innocently.

"What did you do?"

"I plugged in the coffee maker."

"Where?"

Spencer pointed to the direction of the break room.

"The one that has the sticker next to it that says do not use?"

Spencer slowly nodded his head. "I think so."

God's eyes widened as the gravity of Spencer's stupidity became clear. "Oh, you fucking moron. You just killed the breaker running the force field."

♦♦♦♦

Warren blinked as the force field flickered out. Nothing stood between him and Pestilence.

"Well, that's an unfortunate turn of events," said Pestilence as he cocked his head in amused curiosity. "I guess you don't have a magic God wall now, do you?"

"Shit," said Warren as he scrambled up from his seat.

Pestilence yanked on his horse's reigns. His mount lowered its head and pushed the glass door open.

Warren sprinted across the sterile meeting room as Pestilence aimed his crossbow. He hurtled towards the rear exit and plowed through as a crossbow bolt slammed into the wall beside his head.

As Warren made his way to the elevators, Spencer was valiantly trying to defend his actions to the rest of the group. "I didn't know!" he said. "It's not my fault the power system is so dodgy."

God was not accepting any of Spencer's projections. "What part of don't do anything to mess with the power as it could give us issues with the force field, was unclear to you?"

"Shit," said Ashley as she picked up her phone.

"What's wrong?" asked Greg.

"Warren is down in the waiting room." She quickly dialed her ex-boyfriend's number.

"Why?" asked Greg. "What the hell was he doing down there?"

"He was keeping an eye on the Horsemen. He ducked out a little while ago."

"*Ash*?" answered Warren, slightly out of breath.

"Warren," started Ashley. We've got a probl—"

"*The fucking force field is down*," shouted Warren from the phone. "*We've got a really big fucking problem*."

♦♦♦♦

Warren closed the waiting room door behind him and looked around for something to block it. Spying a nearby trash can, he scooped it up and jammed it under the handle.

"*Did they get in*?" Ashley's voice echoed from his phone.

"Of course they fucking got in," said Warren as he pushed against the chair to test its ability to hold.

Pestilence crashed against the doors, but the trash can held. Warren's ability to wedge a door closed improved since his days of using a La-Z-Boy to block Greg's front door from the horde of zombie-demons. While the door would hold for a few moments, he doubted it would take many blows before it splintered. He turned and took off down the corridor.

"*Where are you heading*?" asked Ashley as Warren panted heavily into his phone.

"To the elevators. They're right up my ass," said Warren as he sprinted to the end of the corridor towards the cars.

"*You're not coming to us, are you*? " asked Ashley, her voice laced with concern.

"I was kinda planning on it, yeah."

"*Don't lead them to us!*" Ashley protested.

"Where would like me to go then, Ash? I feel like we just had this discussion. I could use a little assistance on what to do next."

"*I don't know. Let me talk with the group*."

As the elevator doors slid open, a loud crash of cracking wood echoed behind him. "Too late," he shouted. "They're already in. I'm heading up. Get everyone ready to move, we won't have much time."

♦♦♦♦

The group was already standing when Warren sprinted from the elevator and rushed into the room.

"Where are they?" shouted Greg.

Before Warren could answer, the elevator doors opened, and War and Pestilence exited on their horses.

"Where are the stairs," yelled Warren.

"This way," pointed David. "Follow me."

"Go!" shouted Warren as he ran past the group towards the nearest stairwell and pushed the door open. "Come on," he yelled as he ushered the group through.

"Why the stairs?" asked Cam as she passed by and started up the first flight of steps.

"Because horses can't climb stairs," said Warren as he took a mental count of the group leaving the room.

"Who told you that?" asked Greg.

"Everyone knows that," said Warren. "Hank told me."

"Of course horses can climb stairs," said Greg. "You're being ridiculous."

God led the group up the first three flights of stairs as Warren followed from the rear. As the group made their way up the fourth group of steps, the door below them kicked open, and Pestilence made his way into the stairwell. His horse stopped and sniffed the bottom step, but it declined to move any further.

"See," said Warren. "It can't climb the stairs. I told you."

Pestilence jerked on his reins, and his steed placed its hooves on the first step. It paused as it tested its footing. Pestilence looked up at the group and sneered as he started to make his way up the stairs.

Greg looked up at Warren and pointed at the horse. "Does that answer your question?"

"Shit," shouted Warren as the group continued its mad dash upwards. "Fucking Hank."

"Where are we going?" asked Cam to no one in particular.

"Let's head to my office," said God. "I have a fully stocked panic room we can use."

Warren's ears pricked up at the suggestion. "Did you say panic room?"

"I did."

"In Heaven?" Warren clarified.

"Yes," said God.

"Why on earth would you need a panic room in Heaven?" asked Warren. "Isn't this supposed to be one of the safest places in the Universe?"

"Have you not met Jehovah's Witnesses, Mormons, or Baptists? Holy shit, they are relentless. Of course I need somewhere to hide when it gets too much."

"Where is it?" shouted Greg.

"Ninety-seventh floor."

"What?" griped Cam. "Are you serious?"

"That's a lot of stairs," said Greg.

God agreed with Greg's assessment. "We need to get to the elevators."

At the third-floor exit, Warren leaned over the railing to see Pestilence moving up behind them. "Shit," he muttered again as he took off with Spencer and Cindy a few steps behind.

As they approached the next set of stairs, the fourth-floor exit door flung open and Britney, the Horseman formerly known as Death, stepped into the stairwell, splitting the group in half.

"Shit," shouted Warren for a second time. He leaned over the railing and looked up to see Cam staring down from two flights above. "We're cut off. Keep going up."

"What about you?" Cam yelled back.

"We'll find you." Warren ushered his small group back down to the third-floor door and exited the stairwell. "Spencer, get the door." Warren pointed at the exit ten steps below.

"Ashley?" yelled God as he appeared next to Cam.

Warren stopped and looked back up towards the group above them. "She'll be safe with me," he said. "I'll get her back to you. I promise."

"Okay." God nodded and hesitated for the briefest of moments before slapping the railing. He turned and continued up the stairs with Death, Lucifer, and Cam.

Britney pulled on his reigns and directed his undead horse to follow God's group.

Warren turned back to his group and followed them through the exit.

"Where's the rest of us?" asked Ashley as Warren shut the door behind them.

"God's taking them upstairs. He has Cam, Lucifer, and Death with him. We'll catch up with them later."

"How?" asked Ashley.

Warren pointed to her wrist. "You still have your wrist-com." He looked around the group to determine who had followed him. "Is everyone else here?"

The group turned to face each other as they each took a mental tally of the count.

"There should be eight of us," added Warren.

Spencer raised his hand and indicated his and Cindy's presence. Greg and Amber followed suit, and Warren noted Ashley, Luna, and David's presence. He exhaled as he tried to collect his thoughts.

"What are we going to do?" asked Cindy as she looked around frantically.

"We need to barricade the door," said Spencer.

"With what?" asked Warren as he gestured to the empty hallway. "There's nothing here."

Spencer shrugged. "I don't know. I've always wanted to block a door, and it felt like the right thing to say."

"Where are we exactly, David?" asked Warren.

"We came on the third floor," said David.

Warren nodded.

"Then I think we're on the—"

"Well, then we're obviously still in the Jehovah's Witness division then, aren't we?" interrupted Spencer.

"Obviously," said Warren, having no idea where he was. "Do you know if they have anywhere we can hide out? They're going to be watching the stairs and elevators."

"If I remember correctly, I believe internal construction and zoning just approved the permits for upgrading this floor's primary Kingdom Hall," said Spencer. "We could go there."

"You have Kingdom Halls in Heaven?" asked Warren.

"Of course we do, silly," said Spencer as if being asked the easiest question in the history of easy questions. "Every version of Christianity has houses of worship in Heaven. Why wouldn't we? This is worship central."

"Why would you? Can't you just walk up to his office and say hi? It's not like anyone here has sins to confess. It should be a quick visit."

"He doesn't like people loitering around his office. He says it distracts him from getting his work done."

"That seems a little ridiculous to me," shrugged Warren.

"Well, I think that's a wonderful idea, Pookie Bear," said Cindy as she squeezed his left hand tenderly. "Can I call you Pookie Bear?"

"Of course," said Spencer as he blushed ever so slightly.

"This group is lucky to have you as its leader."

Spencer looked down at his hand and smiled. His bravery increased by about seventeen percent, and he stood a little bit taller than he had a few moments before.

Warren frowned in confusion. "He's not our leade—"

"Shh," said Cindy as she placed a finger on Warren's lips. "Let him have his moment." She removed her hand to allow Warren to ponder his choices.

"But—"

"Green is a color best reserved for grass. It does not look well on your skin." She turned her attention back to the newly promoted Spencer. "If you say we should go to Kingdom Hall, then I will follow you."

"I don't think praying is our best course of action," said Warren, getting things back on topic.

"Not to pray, silly," said Spencer. "The doors to Kingdom Hall are heavy and massive. I doubt anything could break through them."

Warren considered the suggestion and having little to offer in the way of a better idea, he nodded his agreement. "Okay, any objections, ladies?" he asked as he turned to face Ashley and Luna.

The two women shook their heads. "Sounds good to me," said Ashley. "It beats standing around here waiting for them to kick the door in and murder us all. Unless you have something better David."

David shrugged. "I've got nothing."

"All right then," said Warren. "Lead the way, Captain Spencer."

The door to the stairwell erupted open as Pestilence's horse kicked it off the frame. The wooden panel sailed through the air and smashed into the opposite wall with a loud crash.

"RUN!" screamed Warren.

Luna carefully looked around the edge of the door frame. Pestilence's horse stepped out into the hallway behind Pestilence. It sniffed the air, but failed to pick up their scent. Luna quietly unsnapped the safety strap from her holster and removed her gun.

"What are you doing?" whispered Warren as he watched her raise her weapon and aim it at Pestilence.

"My job," said Luna as she closed one eye and targeted the enemy's head.

"Trust me, it won't work," said Warren.

"Nothing can withstand a bullet to the head. Not even one of these undead fucks."

Bang.

The bullet penetrated Pestilence's skull and disappeared. There was no entry wound and there was no exit wound. It just vanished.

"I don't understand," said Luna, her brow furrowed in confusion. "I hit it right between the eyes. I saw the bullet go in." She fired a second bullet and experienced the same outcome. "What the hell?"

"Human weapons don't work on these types of things," said Warren. "Trust me, I've tried."

"How do we kill it?" asked Luna. "How do we kill something that won't die?"

"I don't know. It's a question I've asked myself more than once over the past six months," said Warren. "We need to keep moving."

Pestilence raised his bow and aimed it at the group. He reached over his shoulder and gracefully pulled an arrow from his quiver. A second later, the deadly shaft was cutting through the air towards Luna. The arrow slammed into the back of her shoulder, and she dropped to the ground with a yelp of pain.

Warren stopped and turned around. "Luna!" he shouted as he watched her fall.

Luna reached down to her holster and removed her pistol. A second arrow pierced her forearm, and she dropped her weapon. She screamed in agony as a third arrow embedded itself into her right thigh.

Warren tried to step towards her, but another arrow landed at his feet as a warning.

Luna fumbled for her fallen pistol with her left hand, but instead of aiming it at Pestilence, she tossed it towards Warren. "Go!" she commanded. "Save yourselves."

"Luna!" protested Warren.

"GO!" One final arrow hit her square between the eyes, and she slumped back onto the floor.

As Pestilence reached for another arrow, Warren scooped up the pistol and took off after the rest of the group.

Greg was holding a door open as Warren sprinted around the corner towards him. "Hurry!" he shouted.

Warren charged into the room, and Greg carefully closed the door behind him. The overpowering fumes of fresh paint, drifted into his nostrils as he looked around.

Barely ten seconds passed before the silhouette of Pestilence's horse passed by the frosted glass of the door window. The steed paused and sniffed the air. Warren reached for the pistol, although aware it was useless against their hunter. He looked over at Greg, hoping to find an answer, his eyes full of panic and defeat. Greg shrugged in an equal lack of plan.

Both brothers knew if the Horsemen decided to charge into the room, there was nowhere to run, and no weapons to fight with. Amber squeezed Greg's hand as another agonizing second ticked by. Pestilence yanked on his reins, and his horse moved on down the hall. War followed a few feet behind.

Warren exhaled heavily as though he had not breathed in an hour. "They've gone," she said softly.

"That was close," said Greg. "I thought that was it."

"Why didn't it smell us?" asked Spencer.

"It must have been the paint fumes," said Greg. "I think it masked our scent."

Warren nodded in agreement. "We're not safe until we get to Kingdom Hall. How much further?"

"It's still a bit of a walk," said Spencer. "Maybe fifteen minutes."

"We should get moving," said Greg as he rose and took a step towards the door.

"Uh uh, not you," said Warren. "You and Amber need to sit this one out, it's too dangerous."

Greg shook his head. "What? No way, man. I sat out the last time. I'm fighting with you."

"You didn't sit anything out," said Warren. "You helped get everyone safely up to Heaven. We did exactly what we needed to do. Then you turned into a demon. You didn't have much choice after that."

"I'm not sitting this out, Warren," said Greg as Amber walked over to him and grabbed his hand.

Warren placed a hand on his brother's shoulder. "Greg, you have a child coming. Get back down to the lobby, head to the funnel, and sneak out of here. We'll take care of this."

"If I go, who's going to take care of you?" asked Greg.

"You have to let me grow up at some point, big brother." Warren turned to face Amber. "You know I'm right. I know this isn't what you want to hear, but you know I'm right. Can you convince this fool he is better off getting out of here?"

Amber smiled sadly. "This is our fight, too, Warren. Oceanview was our home."

"Then help preserve the memory by letting that baby of yours grow up and not die here. We've lost too many of us already"

"Warren—" started Greg.

"Don't argue with me," said Warren.

Amber looked over at Ashley to see her sister nodding her head.

"He's right," said Ashley. "You need to go." She pulled Amber in for a hug. "We'll see you soon."

"You can buy me a beer when this is all over," said Warren.

Greg nodded at the deal.

"I mean good shit. Not that watered down crap you used to get at Jacob's."

"You used to drink the same crap," countered Greg.

"Yeah, but you're buying the next round," said Warren, the smile on his face hiding the fear churning inside of him. "I want the expensive import stuff."

Amber watched the brothers saying their awkward goodbyes. "We'll need David to get us through the funnel," she said.

"I know," said Warren.

"How will you find your way through Heaven?" asked Amber. "You don't know where you're going."

Warren turned his left. "I have Spencer," he said as he grabbed the man by his shoulders. "He knows everything about Heaven. He'll get us where we need to go, won't you, Spencer?"

Spencer frowned with an obvious lack of confidence. "Um, yeah. I think so."

Warren turned to David. "Can you help them? Please."

David nodded. "Yeah. I know an access corridor to the elevators. We can stay out of sight."

Warren extended a hand to David. "Thank you."

David shook Warren's hand, and the years of arguments and disagreements between the two men drifted away.

As Greg opened the door and gestured for Amber and David to leave, he looked back at his brother and nodded. Warren returned the gesture as he watched David leading them away. Unsure if it was the last time he would see his brother.

"That was a beautiful thing you just did," said Ashley as she stepped up beside Warren.

"I don't want killing a baby on my conscience," said Warren.

"And then you ruin it," said Ashley with a smile and playful nudge to his ribs.

"That's enough flirting," said Warren as he left the room. "Spencer, can you lead us to Gary's elevator?"

"Follow me," said Spencer.

"I wasn't flirting," protested Ashley.

Warren grinned as he ignored Ashley's defense and turned to follow Spencer.

"I wasn't flirting," she said again as she groaned in resigned irritation. "You are an impossible man to deal with, you know that?"

CHAPTER 25

With Britney's horse struggling to move up the stairs at a decent speed, God seized on the opportunity to quickly increase the distance between them. However, by the twentieth floor, the group was tired and whining about their tired legs and shortness of breath.

"I need to rest," said Cam, as she inhaled deeply. "I can't keep running like this. No one told me there would be so many stairs in Heaven."

"I don't see him behind us," said Death as he leaned over the railing and looked down at the stairs below. "I think now is a good time to get out of here."

"We need to get to the elevators," said Lucifer as he pushed the exit door open. "Follow me."

"Do you know where you're going?" asked Death as the group left the stairwell.

Lucifer paused. He had no idea. His intent was to lead the group to safety, but he held little direction after that. "I—"

"I think we have someone a bit more experienced with the place who can get us somewhere safe," said Death.

God stood by the door as he realized the trio was looking at him. "What?" he asked.

"Do you feel like leading us to somewhere safe?" asked Lucifer. "I don't know where the elevators are."

"Yeah, sorry. My mind was elsewhere."

Cam stepped over and grabbed God's hand. "Ashley will be okay. Warren will take care of her. He'd never let her come to any harm."

Lucifer stepped forward to also offer his words of assurance. "He may be a bit of a screw-up, but he hasn't gotten anyone killed yet."

Cam turned to give Lucifer a frustrated look. "Really? That's not helping."

Lucifer shrugged his shoulders. "I wasn't trying to be insensitive. I just meant we don't need to worry."

"It's fine," said God. "We need to get to my panic room before they catch up with us."

"You think they know their way around well enough to find us?" asked Cam.

"If they have any sense, they'd keep heading up," said Death.

"Why?" asked Cam.

"I would," said Death.

Twelve minutes later, Warren's group arrived at the Kingdom Hall to see the heavy fifteen-foot-tall doors removed from the frame and leaning against a nearby wall.

"Spencer?" asked Warren. "Why are the doors already off?"

"It looks a lot like construction has started," said Ashley.

Spencer held a hand to his mouth. "Well, poop on a wheat cracker," he said. "This is unexpected."

Warren's patience with Spencer's G-rated dialog was starting to grate on his nerves. "Jesus, man, just fucking curse already. This pansy-ass skirting around saying something you deem to be offensive is jarring."

"Well boo to you, Mr. Potty Mouth Pants," said Spencer.

"See, that doesn't even make fucking sense."

"Unlike you, I know how to choose pleasant words to express myself. Every other phrase out of your mouth is Francis this, and Fork that."

"It's still cursing," said Warren. "Swearing is as much about the intent as it is the words being used. Just because you're not saying fuck, it doesn't imply you don't mean it."

Spencer shrugged off Warren's criticism and poked his head into the cavernous room to see it sitting in various stages of construction. He stepped back out into the hallway and rubbed his chin. "Those sneaks. They were only approved for development the day before everything went down. They started construction before they received official approval. I'm going to have to file a complaint with management about this."

"This isn't the time to be stressing about protocols," said Warren.

"Then when is?" protested Spencer. "Without order we have chaos."

"I tell you what. If we get out of this with dying, we can file a complaint together."

Spencer's opportunity to reply was cut short as the nearby stairwell door opened and War stepped out into the hallway.

Warren grabbed Ashley and pulled her into the giant room as he pointed to Spencer and Cindy to follow.

"Did it see us?" asked Cindy.

"No," said Warren.

"Try shooting it again," said Spencer.

"It's already dead," said Warren. "You can't shoot it."

"What about fire?" asked Spencer.

"What about it?" replied Ashley.

"You can always burn dead things," said Spencer. "Leaves, wood, bodies."

"That's brilliant," said Warren. "This could actually work."

"Really?" asked Spencer, as his posture slightly improved at the compliment.

"Do you have any fireplaces on this floor?" asked Warren.

"No," said Spencer.

"Do you have any fire at all?"

"Fire is not allowed in Heaven. It's a fire risk."

"You don't have any firemen here?" asked Warren.

"Of course we do, silly," said Spencer.

"Can't they put out fires?"

"No, they mostly get cats down from places we can't reach."

"So how are we supposed to set things on fire if we're not allowed to use fire?"

Spencer dug into his pocket and fished out a lighter. "I have this."

"You smoke?" asked Warren.

"Absolutely not," said Spencer. "It's part of my Eagle Scouts' survival kit in case we lose power."

"So how come you're allowed to have fire?" asked Ashley.

"Oh, I'm not allowed to use it. In fact, I don't know how to turn it on," said Spencer.

Ashley reached out her hand. "Give it to me," she said as Spencer passed the lighter over and she easily flicked it on. "Seems okay to me."

"How on earth did you do that?"

"Uh, safety lock was on," said Ashley as she pointed it out to him.

Warren's eyes lit up as an idea started to form in his head. "Spencer, do you have more alcohol around here?"

"I hardly think this is a suitable time for drinking."

"It's not for drinking. I want to make Molotovs. Do you have any on this floor?"

Spencer pondered the thought a moment. "I think I know where we may have some. Follow me," he said as he headed to a nearby door and pushed through.

He led Warren through the maze of hallways and doors until they reached a room with a sign beside the door advertising the Entertainment Room.

"This one," said Spencer. "It's the room where we meet with new high-profile residents. There should be a fully stocked cabinet in the corner."

Warren ran over to the cabinet and opened the doors. It was full of wine, wine coolers, and other low-alcohol-volume bottles.

"No," said Warren. "I meant ethanol. Something I can ignite."

"Oh, we don't have anything like that," said Spencer.

"How about whiskey?" asked Warren as his mind moved to alternative options. While not ideal, it may have a sufficient proof to maintain a flame.

"The forbidden items are locked in the cabinet beside it. But you can't look in there."

"Why not?" asked Warren.

"Because it's forbidden," said Spencer.

"I think this is extenuating circumstances," said Warren as he pulled the door open. "It's not locked."

"God told me it was," said Spencer.

"He probably didn't want you getting drunk," said Warren as he looked at a full bottle of whiskey sitting on the shelf. "This will do nicely. Hand me that towel," he ordered Spencer as he pointed to a white rag on a nearby table.

Warren opened the bottle and grabbed the rag from Spencer. He poured whiskey on the cloth and stuffed half of it into the bottle.

A loud crash echoed from outside the door, and Spencer jumped back.

"Hide behind something," said Warren. "I'm going to light up the door."

He pulled his lighter from his pocket, flicked it on, and held the flame against the rag. He shuffled impatiently as he waited for the material to ignite. "Come on. Light you piece of crap." He waited another couple of seconds, but the cloth would not take the flame.

"What's wrong?" asked Spencer.

"The damn fuse isn't lighting," said Warren.

"I don't understand how fruit cocktails work."

Warrant sighed. "It's called a Molotov cocktail. You take a bottle of alcohol, soak a rag, stick the rag in the bottle, light it, and then you throw it at the person or object you want to set on fire."

"So why won't the rag light?"

"It probably doesn't have enough whiskey soaked in yet. It needs more alcohol on it."

"Oh, it doesn't have alcohol in it at all," said Spencer.

"What do you mean?"

"It's alcohol-free whiskey."

Warren frowned and lowered the bottle. "Huh?"

"The whiskey, there's no alcohol in it."

"How is that even possible?" asked Warren. "No one drinks whiskey just for the taste. We want the burn, the alcohol."

"We're not allowed hard alcohol in Heaven. It's forbidden. For those who want to drink whiskey and other hard liquor, Heaven has a range of non-alcohol hard alcohol spirits. The strongest we have is point one five percent volume wine and even that gets me tipsy after one glass."

"Fuck," muttered Warren as he threw the bottle at the closed door. The glass shattered, and the faux whiskey dribbled down the door.

"Why did you throw it if you knew it wasn't going to explode? It didn't do anything."

"Because some poor bastard may have accidentally drunk it. I'm doing them a favor. Do you have anything I can use as a weapon?"

"I have an electric pencil sharpener," offered Spencer.

"What?"

"It's quite sharp. The plastic protector has broken, and I've cut myself on it numerous times."

"You are utterly useless," said Warren. "Is there a back door out of here?"

Spencer shook his head.

"How does this pass fire safety?" asked Warren.

"I told you, we don't have fires in Heaven."

♦♦♦♦

God, Lucifer, Death, and Cam were not faring much better than the other group. Despite numerous twists, turns, and hiding under desks, Britney never faltered in his quest to pursue them.

"My knees hurt," griped Death as they ducked into yet another pair of symmetrical cubicles and crawled under the desks.

Lucifer reached for Cam's hand and gently squeezed it in a gesture of comfort and concern. No words were spoken, no words were necessary, but both were terrified. The shadow of Britney's horse fell across the floor as it approached their hiding space. The bony equine paused outside the neighboring cubicle and sniffed the floor, eager to find its prey and sate its hunger. Cam stared at the entrance with panicked eyes, anticipating the undead creature discovering them at any moment.

On the opposite side of the cubicle entrance, Death and God were hiding in a similar manner to Lucifer and Cam. Death looked over at God as the scared deity pushed into the wall to avoid detection.

"What are we going to do?" God whispered nervously.

In all his years of reaping, Death saw many reactions in the last moments of life. He was no stranger to panic, resignation, and acceptance, but he had never seen the look of fear as apparent as it was on his colleague's faces. He reached into his robe and pulled out a Blood Card. "Let me handle this."

God's eyes widened at the ridiculous idea. "Steve, what are you doing?" asked God quietly.

Death shrugged. "Something?" he mouthed.

"I hardly think that a Blood Card is going to work. They're not on your lists. It won't work."

Death shrugged. "Do you have any other ideas?"

God shook his head frantically.

"Then we're all out of other options. I've never tried it on the dead before. I don't know what will happen."

Lucifer looked at his associate. "Steve, I love you, man, but Gary's right. This is a bad idea."

Death held the card out in front of him as Britney's horse peeked into the cubicle. A putrid smell emitted from the creature's mouth as it sniffed the air. "Who wants to live forever?" said Death as he reached up and placed the card on the tip of the gaunt creature's nose.

The undead horse stuttered and stepped back. It shook its head violently from side to side as it screeched and rose up on its hind legs. Britney pulled hard on the reins to steady his mount. Death jumped back to avoid the horse's thrashing legs. The creature wailed again and toppled onto its side, pinning Britney beneath the heavy beast.

God turned to Death. "Holy shit, it worked."

Death looked just as surprised at the sudden turn of events. "I guess everything dies eventually." He stood as he pulled a second Blood Card from beneath his robe.

"What are you doing?" asked God as he rose next to Death.

"Taking out the rider," said Death with his newfound confidence. "I'm putting an end to this now."

As the horse stopped moving, it was Britney's turn to spasm and convulse. However, his erratic motions revolved less around the Blood Card that took out his horse, and more to do with pure unadulterated rage. "I'm going to annihilate you, Reaper."

Death stepped over and crouched down next to Britney's head. "No, you're not." He tapped the rider on the cheek twice and placed the second card on his forehead. The shrouded rider emitted a loud shriek, convulsed, and fell still. Death held his breath as he waited for the creature to stir.

Lucifer stood up. "Damn," he said as he stared at the two bodies. "Should you double-tap?"

"Double-tap? What's that?"

"It's putting in a second bullet to make sure that whatever creature you've just killed is indeed dead. I don't want this to be like some bullshit horror movie where the heroes think the villain is dead when it really isn't."

"That's not how Blood Cards work. You can't stack them. They are absolute. You either go up or down. There's no back-peddling or reinforcements."

"What happens after you use the card?" asked God.

"Their soul separates, and they go to you or Lucifer at my discretion."

"I assume you sent this one to me?" asked God even though he already knew the answer.

Death smiled. "Of course I did."

"Ass," said God.

"Be nice, Steve," said Lucifer with a grin. "You didn't send it anywhere. These things don't have souls. It should just drop dead and decay."

God rolled his eyes in annoyance. "We need to find the others. Do you have enough Blood Cards to finish the job?"

Death reached back into his robe and pulled out a small stack of cards. He quickly counted the pile. "Five."

"That's not enough," said God. "There's still three more of them out there."

"We could just take out the last rider and leave the horse. I doubt they can do much without a rider. I can come back next week when I get more cards."

"Why do you only have seven? I thought you were sitting on a few thousand?" asked Lucifer.

"After Oceanview, I donated my leftovers back to the Council. I've started using the cards I've been given by the end of the month."

"You picked a great time to start following the rules," said Lucifer with a grin.

Death smiled. "I tried to use one on Miley when she showed up at my office."

A large smile crept across God's face. He disliked Miley as much as anyone. "No! You did not!" he asked with excited glee.

"Oh, I certainly did," said Death with a sly grin.

"Did it work?"

"No. But I sent her to hell for five minutes."

A mental image of Miley surrounded by flames popped into God's mind. "Man, she must have been pis—"

A loud, wet crack erupted from the dead horse, and it twitched.

God turned to face Death. "What the fuck was that?"

Death shrugged. "I don't know. I've never done this before." He looked at the dead horse as something inside it started to move.

The entertainment room was quiet as Warren, Ashley, Spencer, and Cindy sat in a small circle, their eyes never leaving the front door. The verbal silence deafening as all parties refused to speak. The only sound was the occasional scraping of Pestilence's horse clawing at the door, but eventually, even that fell silent.

Aware of the sudden silence, Warren looked up at Ashley and smiled sadly. He knew the end was coming. "I'm sorry," he said softly. "I never meant for any of this to happen."

Before Ashley could respond, a loud screech emitted from behind the door.

"What the fuck was that?" asked Ashley as her head whipped around in surprise.

Warren shrugged. "I don't know, but it didn't sound good." He stood and jogged over to the door and carefully leaned an ear against the wood.

"What's wrong?" asked Ashley softly.

"Shh," said Warren as he held up a finger to silence her. "I can't hear anything."

"Don't shh me," said Ashley as she scowled.

Warren frowned and held a finger to his lips. He stared at the ground as his focus remained on listening to the door. A moment passed before he stepped back and grabbed the door handle.

"What are you doing!" shouted Ashley, Spencer, and Cindy as one as Warren turned the handle.

"Get away from the door," screamed Ashley.

Warren pulled it open to see Pestilence, and his horse collapsed on the floor. Neither of the vile creatures moved.

"What happened?" asked Spencer as he tried to process the scene before him.

"Is it dead?" asked Cindy.

Warren shrugged. "It looks like it."

"Shut the front door," said Spencer.

"There, you just cursed," said Warren as he turned to his blonde associate.

"No, I didn't," argued Spencer.

"Yeah, you did. You said shut the front door."

"That's not cursing."

"No, but you really meant s*hut the fuck up*. Sure, the words are different, but the intent is there. And that is actually worse than cursing, because it makes you a hypocrite. If you're going all in, just go all in. Ash, you agree with me, right?"

"I'm staying out of it," said Ashley. "There's more important issues at hand."

"What happened to it?" asked Cindy, ignoring Warren's argument. "How could it have died? We didn't do anything."

"I don't know," said Warren. "But it's not moving. We need to move before it changes its mind. I've seen enough movies to know it's probably just resting or something."

"Good idea," said Ashley.

Warren crossed over to Pestilence's body and crouched down next to it.

"Warren, leave it be," said Ashley. "We need to get back to Greg and

Amber."

"Don't you want to know what killed it?"

Ashley shook her head. "No, not really. Let's make the most of this and go."

"I just want to take a look. Maybe it has a weapon or something we can use to defend ourselves." Warren crouched down in front of the rider. "Man, this thing is fucking ugly."

Ashley was getting uncomfortable with Warren's casual attitude towards the creature. "Please, Warren. Let's go."

Warren nodded as he stood up. He started to turn as a wet ripping sound emitted from the carcass and a long tear appeared on the horse's abdomen. Warren raised his hands and leaped back.

"What did you do?" accused Ashley as she stared at the rapidly expanding wound.

"I didn't do anything."

The horse writhed and twisted as something bulged beneath the skin.

"What's happening?" asked Spencer, mesmerized by the horse.

"I don't know, but I don't think we should hang around to find out," said Warren.

Ashley started to walk away. She turned to see Warren still staring at the horse. "Warren? Are you listening to me?"

Warren looked over at Ashley. "Yeah?"

"We need to go." Ashley's eyes suddenly doubled in size. "WARREN!"

Warren turned to face the horse. A second horse was emerging from the hole in its torso. "What the fuck?"

A similar sound echoed from Pestilence's body as a long and jagged seam erupted down the middle of his torso.

Warren stepped back as the new horse climbed to its feet. A moment later, Pestilence's body performed an identical action as a second creature split from its host shell.

"What the fuck?" echoed Ashley.

Warren looked at Ashley, unable to find the right words to explain the situation. "We need to go," he said as he took another step back. Before he could reach Ashley, the first horse twitched, and the split in its skin started to heal. A moment later, Pestilence's wound also sealed shut and both he and his mount rose to their feet, doubling the threat and making the situation so much worse.

"WHAT THE FUCK?" screamed Ashley.

"There's two them?" said Warren.

"Yeah, I can fucking see that, Warren," screamed Ashley as she grabbed Warren's arm. "Move it."

"Spencer, get us out of here!" shouted Warren.

"Follow me," said Spencer as he started running.

The group did not need further encouragement as they sprinted after Spencer, leaving Pestilence to his cloning madness.

CHAPTER 26

Warren glanced over his shoulder as the group sprinted past the staircase. "Spencer, you missed the stairs," he shouted.

Spencer shook his head. "Change of plan. We're not going to the stairs."

"Why not?" yelled Warren.

"They don't go to God's office. He was worried someone would use them to sneak up to his office and had the doorway sealed shut."

"Well, we can't take the elevators," said Warren. "They're too risky. The other Horsemen are probably waiting for us."

"We're not taking the elevators either," said Spencer as he led the group down another corridor and took a hard left.

"Then where the fuck are we going?" asked Warren as he followed Spencer around the corner.

"Over there," said Spencer as he pointed to a nondescript door labeled maintenance in front of them.

"What this?" asked Ashley.

Spencer pulled a set of keys from his pocket and unlocked the door.

"Hurry," pleaded Cindy. "It'll be here soon."

The lock clicked, and Spencer pushed the door open to reveal a small six-by-six room with an elevator door on the far wall. He beckoned for Cindy and Ashley to enter.

Warren stepped into the room last and carefully closed the door behind him. "Where are we?" he asked.

"It's God's private elevator," said Spencer in a hushed tone. "This will take us up to his office."

"No fucking shit!" said Warren. "Well done."

"Keep your voice down," said Ashley. "We're not out of this yet."

Spencer smiled at Warren's crude compliment as he stepped over and pressed the button to call the car.

"Why is it in a closet?" asked Warren.

"Because he doesn't want us to know where it is," said Spencer.

"So how do you know where it is?" asked Ashley.

"We all know where it is. We've seen him disappear into one of the closets and doesn't come out. It's not a difficult puzzle to put together."

A moment later, a polite ping rang out, and the doors opened.

"Son of a bitch," said Warren as the group quickly rushed in.

The door to the room flew off its hinges as Pestilence's horse kicked its way in. "Humans!" he screamed as the elevator doors closed before him.

A loud crash echoed violently against the elevator door as it slid to a close. The group rushed to the back wall to avoid any blades or pointy weapons that may slice their way into the carriage.

"That was too close," said Ashley as she looked at the list of floor buttons.

"Top one," said Spencer, out of breath and still in shock at the close call.

Ashley cautiously stepped forward, pressed the button, and jumped back to the wall, eager to stay as far away from the door as possible.

The elevator lurched as the car ascended and quickly picked up speed.

"Cam, can you hear me?" asked Ashley into her wrist-com.

"*Yep,*" replied Cam. "*Are you okay?*"

"We're in the elevator and heading your way. Get the door ready."

The elevator hurtled through the various levels of Heaven and slowed down as it reached the top floor. The doors opened to reveal Nancy's office, and God, Lucifer, Death, and Cam were standing facing a door on the opposite wall.

"What are you doing?" asked Warren.

The other group spun around in surprise, fully expecting them to approach from the main door.

"How did you get up here?" asked God.

"We used your private elevator," said Warren.

"How did you know I had a private ele—" he saw Ashley step around Warren and ran over to her. "You're okay?" he said as he wrapped his arms around her.

"Spencer showed us," said Warren.

God frowned as he stepped back from his hug and looked at Spencer. "How did you—"

"Where's everyone else?" asked Cam as she looked at the small group. "Where's David?"

"He took Greg and Amber to the portal and back to Oceanview," said Warren.

"Why did he do that?" asked Cam, visibly concerned at the change of plan. "We could have used their help."

"I told him to," said Warren. "It's the safest place for them. We can't have a pregnant woman running around fighting demons, and Greg was in no condition to fight. We'd just get them killed."

"Horsemen," corrected Spencer. "Not demons."

"Whatever," said Warren.

"What about Luna? Did she go with them too?" asked Cam.

Warren shook his head and exhaled sadly. "She didn't make it. Pestilence killed her."

"I'm so sorry," said Cam softly. No matter how much death she had seen over the years, it never got easier.

"We'll have to grieve for her later," said Warren. "We've got a bit of a problem."

"Oh, you mean the extra Horseman that just showed up?" asked Lucifer, hoping he was wrong.

"Yeah, how did you know?" said Warren.

"Because it happened to us too," said Cam.

"So, there's eight of them now?" asked Warren.

"Yep," said Lucifer. "Sixteen if you count the horses."

"This doesn't make sense," said Warren. "It's supposed to be the Four Horsemen, not eight."

"Tell that to Death," said Lucifer as he pointed towards his friend. "This is his doing. He used a Blood Card on them."

"What's that?" asked Ashley.

"It's a card he can use for reaping when a person is dying, but it hasn't been determined where they are heading," said Lucifer. "He used them in Oceanview."

"It worked on the zombie-demons, didn't it?" asked Warren.

"Yes," said Death. "But they were once human. The Horsemen were never human. So, in this case, it caused them to split in two and duplicate."

Warren held his hands to his head in frustration. "We couldn't kill one of them. How are we supposed to be able to handle eight?"

Death shrugged his shoulders. "I don't know, but this is way out of hand."

"Well, we'd better think of a way fast," said Cam, equally concerned.

Warren pointed towards the outer door to the receptionist's office the group was previously staring at. "That won't keep them out."

"I know," said God as he pointed towards his office. "I have something in there that will." He led the group into his office.

"Oh, this is nice," said Warren as he looked around the room, taking in the various nuances of his Lord's office.

"Thanks," said God.

"Is that Bocote?" asked Warren as he gently ran a finger over God's desk.

God raised a quizzical eyebrow at Warren's accurate identification of his prized desk. "It is. You know your wood."

"I carve and build furniture in my free time," said Warren as he noticed God's reaction. "Well, at least I used to until all this end of the world crap happened. I found an importer and was planning on making myself a new desk. Any chance this door is made of Australian Buloke?"

God shook his head as he reached for a button beneath his desk. "Nah, I've got something better." He pressed the button, and the wooden wall panel behind his desk slid aside to reveal a large metal door. "Seventeen-inch-thick titanium alloy. Nothing is getting through that, demon or otherwise, but I doubt they'll come back soon."

"What do you mean?" asked Ashley.

"They've already been here," said God as he pointed to a scuff mark on the carpet. "There are hoof marks on the floor. I'd bet this was the first place they came looking for us when they split up."

"Is this your panic room?" asked Warren as he walked towards the large metal door.

"It is," said God. "Do you like it?"

Warren stepped inside to find a twenty-by-twenty room with a couch, a wine rack, and a large fridge. 'This is awesome."

"I have enough food to last me a decade if needed," said God.

Warren was slightly more interested in the security monitor bank on the opposite wall than the food situation. "You like cameras, don't you," he said as he glanced over the various video feeds. "Is this how they found you in Phoenix?"

"No," said Ashley. "They have a basement called Invocation. There are tens of thousands of monitors they have set up."

"You mean like The Dark Knight?" asked Warren.

"Exactly!" said God. "You saw The Dark Knight?"

"Everyone saw The Dark Knight," said Warren. "It's not exactly an obscure movie. So, what did you see?"

"Well, we saw you shoot Ceraphim in Oceanview during the zombie-demon breakout," said God.

"Who?"

"Ceraphim. He was one of my angels. He was standing in the middle of the road, and you shot him."

"I shot a lot of zombie-demons," confessed Warren.

"You were standing in the middle of the road, and you took a selfie with a dead zombie you'd shot."

"I took selfies with a lot of dead zombie-demons."

"It's true," said Ashley. "He has a Facebook album full of them.

"It was your first selfie. I heard you say so."

"Oh, that guy! Yeah, I do remember that. You never forget your first headshot."

Ashley threw him a 'what the fuck?' look.

"You knew him?" Warren said as he tried to look remorseful and compose himself. "I'm so sorry."

"Don't worry about it. It wasn't a huge loss," said God. "I didn't really like him anyway."

"Oh," said Warren, not expecting that blasé of a response.

"I thought God liked everyone," said Cam. "That seems a little harsh given that he died."

"Not even close," said God. "Do you have any idea how many assholes there are in Heaven?"

Spencer gasped at the revelation. "That is most inappropriate, sir," he protested.

"Not everyone can see the good in people like you do, Spencer," said God. "There are some folks who are just simply fucking assholes, and they grate on my nerves. Maybe if you weren't so impossibly optimistic, you'd see it more."

"I will take your insult and wear it like a badge of honor." He plucked the invisible insult from the air and pinned it to his chest. He turned to face Cam. "Is this on straight?"

Cam smiled at Spencer's miming. "I like you," she said as she playfully ruffled Spencer's hair. "I see why Gary keeps you around."

Spencer blushed ever so slightly as he turned his attention back to God. "Maybe once this has blown over, you can finally join us for that picnic," said Spencer.

God paused and looked at the mildly irritating man. "Excuse me?"

"I know it's not something you enjoy doing, but maybe you could come down and join us for our next division picnic."

God sighed as he looked at Spencer. "I don't understand why you're so kind to me. Let's be honest, I'm a total dick to you."

"You are too hard on yourself," said Spencer.

"Come on, Spencer. I ignore you. I belittle you in front of your subordinates. I tell you I'll come to picnics, and I don't show. I've never hidden my contempt for you, but yet you still look up to me, and treat me with kindness. Why would you even want me at one of your picnics? Why would you want someone there who treats you so poorly? I am not a good person to you. You deserve better treatment."

Spencer smiled warmly. "It's simple really. Your son was a good man, a kind man. People loved him. People still love him. Half of the Bible is dedicated to his teachings of love and acceptance. I've always believed that children are a reflection of their parents. They are their best parts combined into one person."

"I didn't raise him," countered God. "He had foster parents."

"But he is of your blood. He is you, and you are him. You may seem a bit gruff on the surface, but I believe deep inside, you are your son. You are a good person, despite what you may think otherwise."

God opened his mouth to speak but failed to find any words worthy of the compliment.

"I think they are on to you," said Ashley with a smile. "He's right. I love what I've seen of you so far."

God continued to stay silent as he blushed at the second compliment in as many minutes.

Warren turned to face Lucifer. "You're awfully quiet. Any ideas?"

"Why do you think I'd have something to do with this?" said Lucifer, mildly frustrated at once again someone assuming he was the root of all evil.

"I just thought as they were evil, they came from Hell," said Warren.

"Well, maybe you should stop assuming. I've never dealt with these guys before. I've no clue how to kill them."

Cam tired of the intermittent bickering and wanted to focus on finding a solution. "What weapons do you have up here? Surely there's something here we can use."

God shook his head. "This is Heaven, we don't have any weapons here. That's Lucifer's area."

"Piss off," said Lucifer. "We have a strict no-weapons policy. We don't need them to have a good time. That's what drugs and lube are for."

"Doesn't the Bible talk about ancient weapons?" asked Ashley.

"Yeah," agreed Cam. "They are all over the Bible."

Warren's mind raced with the possibilities. "Holy shit. Do we need to find the Ark of the Covenant?"

"That's in Area 51," said God.

"Oh. How about the Holy Grail?" asked Warren, still hopeful of a religious artifact quest.

"Joseph of Arimathea lost it somewhere in Glastonbury, England, the last time I checked."

"How about The Staff of Ra?"

"That's Egyptian, and I'm pretty sure the owners of Hobby Lobby stole it anyway."

Cindy coughed softly from behind the group. Although, it was more of a squeak than a cough, and the group would be forgiven for not hearing her.

She coughed a little louder.

Lucifer turned to see her standing behind him. "Watcha got, Cindy?"

"What about the Seven Swords?"

"What's that?" asked Cam.

Spencer's eyes lit up. "The Seven Sacred Swords of Scripture. Cindy, you minx, I could kiss you."

Cindy blushed and looked down at her feet. "Maybe you should."

It was Spencer's turn to blush as he took a nervous step forward and stopped. "But I won't, until you consent."

Cindy blushed again and focused her eyes elsewhere. "I consent," she said timidly as she leaned her left cheek out.

Spencer's nose smashed against Cindy's cheek as he planted a clumsy kiss on her.

"That was the most awkward thing I've ever seen," said Lucifer. "I love the fuck out of you guys."

"It's like two llamas on a first date," said Ashley.

Spencer stepped back and lowered his eyes with a schoolboy's embarrassment.

"I remember those swords in the Bible," asked Warren as he turned his attention to God. "Where are they?"

"I gave them away," said God nonchalantly.

"What?" asked Ashley.

"You gave them away?" repeated Warren, surprised at the casual attitude to such powerful weapons. "Are you kidding?"

"Yeah, possibly," said God.

"You gave away the Seven Sacred Swords of Scripture?" reiterated Warren.

"Yeah."

"What the fuck, dude?"

God frowned in frustration. "Give me a break. Do you know how many ancient relics I have in my office? Every damn item I touch becomes an instant collectible. I pick up a stone, and it becomes a holy tablet. A branch? A sacred staff. That newspaper on my desk," he pointed towards his desk. "Scripture. It's like the paparazzi are digging through my trash and half of it ends up on eBay. At some point, I had to say enough is enough, and I had to start getting rid of a few things. Forgive me if I didn't keep a journal."

"Where did they go?" asked Warren.

"I don't know. I may have given them away in lieu of Christmas bonuses a couple of years ago."

"Who to?" asked Warren, trying to pry anything remotely useful from God.

"How would I know? I don't remember these things."

"Think," said Lucifer. "We need to find them."

Warren's eyes widened in excitement. "Holy shit. This is a quest for a biblical treasure. This is going to be awesome. I feel like Indiana Jones."

"No," said Lucifer. "We can't leave this office. It's too dangerous out there."

"Is this it?" shouted Cam from the reception area.

God stepped outside to see a large sword hanging on the wall above Nancy's desk with a woman's suit jacket hanging off the tip of the blade. "Huh. Yeah, that's one of them."

Lucifer stared at God, then at the sword, and then back at God. "Really?"

God shrugged. "I guess I never really paid attention to it."

"You gave it to your secretary?" said Lucifer. "And it's being used as a coat rack. Quaint."

"I gave some relics to the office admins and secretaries. It's important to appreciate the support staff."

"Our quest is already over?" said Warren, with a hint of disappointment in his voice.

"Looks like it," said Ashley.

Warren sighed at the disappointment. His career goal of searching for ancient relics was going to have to wait. "Are you lot going to keep staring at it, or is someone going to pick it up?"

"That table doesn't look very sturdy to me," said Spencer. "You should do it."

Warren scowled as he looked at Spencer. "You know, if I didn't want a shot at getting in here after I die, I would punch you in the throat."

Spencer instinctively reached for his neck. "I'm sorry. I'm a hemophiliac. The desk is too high up."

"You're thinking of vertigo," said Warren as he climbed onto the desk and looked at the mounted weapon.

"Careful," said Spencer. "It looks really sharp."

"I damn well hope so," said Warren. "We need to stab someone with it. It won't do us much good otherwise." He grabbed the handle and tried to lift it from the hooks. "Jesus Christ, this thing is heavy," he said as he huffed and puffed and tried to lift it, exerting substantial effort. He realized his faux pas and looked over at God. "Sorry."

"All good," said God with a brush of his hand.

"It's moving," said Ashley.

"Stand back," said Warren as the blade cleared the far hook and the sword crashed onto the desk with a heavy clang. A moment later, the table split with a loud crack and dumped both Warren and the sword onto the floor with a loud clang. "What the fuck?" yelled Warren as he leaped back to spare his toes from being severed from his feet.

He stood up and reached down for the sword, wrapping his fingers around the handle. He pulled his arm away to lift the blade, but it failed to move. He tugged at the sword again to no success. "What the hell is this, Thor's hammer?"

"What's wrong?" asked Cam.

"It won't move," said Warren. "It's like it's glued to the floor."

"Stop fucking around, Warren. This is serious," said Ashley.

"I am serious. You try." Warren stepped back as Cam reached down for the sword.

As before, the weapon refused to budge. "Well, shit," she said as she moved away and raised her hands. "How the fuck are we supposed to pick it up?"

"Let me try," said Lucifer. He walked over to the sword with a confident swagger and wrapped his fingers around the handle. He smiled at Cam as he posed with the sword and took a barbarian stance. "How do I look?" he asked Cam.

"Ridiculous. Maybe if you lost the suit and traded it for a loincloth and chest plate."

"Now that would be ridiculous," said Lucifer with a smile. "I think I'll stick with the suit."

"Yeah, that's probably for the best." Cam watched as Lucifer struggled to move the sword. "It's a bit big, isn't it?"

"I think Gary is overcompensating," said Lucifer with a grin. "It wouldn't be the first time."

"I heard that," said God.

"I didn't mumble," said Lucifer.

Cam leaned in for a closer look at the sword. "There's an inscription on the hilt," she said. "He of the purest of heart and hands may raise high and draw first blood." She frowned as she processed the statement. "That's a bit sexist, isn't it?"

"I didn't write it," said God. "Don't look at me."

Lucifer looked at the rest of the group. "So, who here is pure of heart and hands? It certainly cuts me out."

"Me too," said Cam.

"I'm obviously not pure enough," said Warren.

"You got that right," said Ashley.

"What's that supposed to mean?" asked Warren.

"You know exactly what that means," said Ashley.

The group eyed each other as they judged each other for purity.

"Gary?" asked Warren. "Aren't you even going to try? I mean, you are God after all."

"I think we can all agree it's pointless for me to try. I'm not the pure one in my family," said God.

"At least try it," said Ashley.

"Are you sure you aren't Thor?" asked Warren.

"Why would I be Thor?" asked God.

"This whole situation is very Thorish." He held a mock sword above his head. "In the name of majoniliar— majonlin— How the hell do you say that word?" asked Warren as he struggled to pronounce Mjölnir. "I am the mighty Thor."

"Put down the imaginary sword, Warren. You look stupid," said Ashley.

Warren ignored Ashley's jab at him. "Spencer, you should come and try. You're pious enough."

Spencer pointed at his chest. "Me? Oh, I don't think that is a very good idea. I'm not exactly the fighting kind. I prefer peace over war."

"We didn't make the rules," said Lucifer. "You need to try. The sword picks the owner, not the other way around. Go pick up the damn thing and try."

"Swords are evil. I won't touch them," said Spencer.

"Don't be ridiculous," said Lucifer. "A sword is an inanimate object. In its own state, it is neither good nor evil. It only becomes good or evil by the intent of the person's hand it resides in."

"What's the difference?" asked Spencer. "How can it determine if the person holding it is good or bad? I mean, at the end of the day, both intend to kill with it, so doesn't that ultimately make both people bad? It's not like you can use a sword for good."

"Of course you can," said Lucifer. "If you are using it to defend your home or land against invaders, you're using it for good. If you're using it to decapitate children, well, chances are you're not a good person. A weapon takes the form of the person using it. A person doesn't become evil because of a weapon. They become evil and carry a weapon."

"Ooh, that was deep," said Cam with a playful nudge.

"You think so?" asked Lucifer with a smile. "I was going for sagacious, but I'll take deep."

"Well, it doesn't matter," said Spencer as he interrupted Lucifer and Cam's moment. "I won't touch it. I believe in peace and negotiating."

Warren points at Spencer's shoes. "No, you don't. You're wearing leather shoes."

"What do my shoes have to do with anything?"

"An animal died for those. That's blood on your hands."

"You are ridiculous," said Spencer as he reached over and wrapped his fingers around the handle. "Fine. I will pick up your tool of violence. When this sword moves, I will expect a full and sincere apology." Despite his desire to prove his worthiness, he was terrified he would need to be the one to hold it and be forced to lead the team into battle. He tugged hard, but the sword would not budge. "I don't understand," he said as his fear of war was quickly overshadowed by the horror of not being considered pure. "I've never so much as paid less than eighteen percent on a tip. How am I not considered pure?"

"Death, do you want to take a sh—" Lucifer started to say.

"How am I not pure?" asked Spencer again as his voice raised an octave.

Lucifer shrugged. "I—"

"HOW AM I NOT PURE?" Spencer screamed. "I am the very model of purity."

"Well, obviously, the sword thinks otherwise," said Lucifer. Personally, he did not care either way, but he was enjoying watching Spencer's out-of-character meltdown.

Spencer looked at the floor as his mind sped through anything that he could have done to deem him impure. "Oh no," he said. "It was that one time when I was changing the TV channel and paused on a scene of Chris Hemsworth taking off his shirt."

"Being gay isn't a crime, you idiot," said Lucifer. "Shoplifting, however, is."

"I've never shoplifted in my life," argued Spencer.

"No? You don't remember that time you stole water so you could perform an exorcism on me?"

"That doesn't count," said Spencer indignantly. "I was doing the Lord's work."

"Don't drag me into this," said God. "A crime is a crime. I don't make the rules."

"Well, it looks like you are being judged for that," said Warren. "Sorry, dude, you are not worthy of holding the sword."

"One mistake. ONE MISTAKE," protested Spencer. "How could I be judged on one mistake? I have lived my entire life pure. I should be the one to wield the sword." Fueled by anger and ignoring his desire for peace, he grabbed the sword and pulled as hard as he could. "Move, you mother shitter,"

"Whoa!" said Warren as he held up his hands in defense. "Those are some foul words, young man. And it's motherfucker, not—"

Spencer turned and stabbed a finger towards Warren. "Stop talking, you piss face." He squeezed his hand around the sword and pulled it a third time. "I am pure enough," he huffed and puffed. "Do not fight me, sword. I. Am. Pure. Enough. Do you cocking hear me?"

"Fuck me, it's moving," said Warren.

"Really?" asked Spencer as his eyes lit up.

"No," said Warren. "Give someone else a turn, potty mouth." Warren turned to face God. "Any thoughts?"

"Not really."

"So, you're telling me there is no one here righteous enough to pick it up?" asked Warren.

"Seems like it," said God.

"This whole chosen one shit seems kinda ridiculous, and it's really fucking with us right now," said Warren.

"How so?" asked God.

"Well, for starters, if these swords could be picked up by anyone, we wouldn't be in our current predicament. The criteria for purity is absurd. Especially given no one in Heaven seems to be able to move it."

"We're all flawed in one way or another. That's what makes all my creations so unique. Heaven was never a place for purity," said God.

"That's a cop-out," said Warren. "How the fuck is someone as bland as Spencer not pure enough to pick it up? He makes vanilla look like habanero sauce."

The elevator from the outside hallway emitted a soft ping. The group all turned to face each other.

"They're here," said God as he pointed to the heavy round door. "Everyone, in the panic room now."

The group moved towards the room and pulled the door closed. The electronics clicked and whirred as it locked itself tight. God walked over to the monitor bank to survey the internal cameras. He watched as the elevator door opened and a dark figure on a horse stepped out. He exhaled a nervous breath, unsure how the next move would play out.

"Which one is it?" asked Warren.

"One of our new friends," said God as he watched the elevator door slide open on the monitor and one of the cloned Horsemen stepped out into the hallway. They climbed down from their horse and looked around.

"How can you tell?" asked Ashley.

"They aren't as decayed as the first Horsemen," said God. "Something's different about them."

"We're trapped, aren't we?" asked Ashley as she squeezed God's hand.

God pointed at the security monitors, exasperated at their lack of options. "They're everywhere. They're guarding the elevators and they're guarding the portal. "This is all my fault. I shouldn't have brought us here. I've fucked everything up."

Ashley squeezed his hand. "We had nowhere else to go. We did everything we could. All of us."

"It looks like this is our last stand," said Cam.

"It's not exactly a stand, is it," said Warren."

"What do you mean?" asked Cam.

"Well, a last stand typically means going down in a blaze of glory with guns blasting and bullets flying. All we have is a sword we can't pick up and some blood cards that appear to clone things. And we're all hiding in what is little more than a well-stocked closet."

"When you put it like that, it sounds bleak," said Cam.

"It is bleak," said Warren.

"Are there any other exits?" asked Cam.

God shook his head. "Heaven was designed to be a one-way system. No one has ever needed to or, in fact, wanted to leave before. It's safe here. There's no reason for an exit."

"So then how did everyone end up in Hell?" asked Cam. "They found a way out."

Lucifer raised his hand. "That was article four. Temporary replacement transit. The Council initiated it when they shut Heaven down."

"And how did Cindy and I not go?" asked Spencer. "Why did we get left here when everyone else left?"

"You're probably the purest of everyone here. Maybe you're simply too good for Hell," said Lucifer. "Where is Cindy?"

"Oh no," said Spencer as he stared at another monitor providing a feed of God's outer reception area. "She's still out there!" he yelled as he pointed to an image of her cowering beneath Nancy's desk.

"Fuck," said God.

"What happened?" asked Lucifer. "She was right behind us."

"We have to go get her," said Spencer.

"We can't," said God. "It's too dangerous."

The monitor showed the main door shake as the Horseman slammed against it.

"OPEN THE DOOR!" screamed Spencer in despair.

"WE CAN'T!" countered God. "We won't stand a chance out there," he added with a softer tone.

"Open this door, or I'm going to kick you in your asshole," threatened Spencer.

"Spencer, calm down," said God. "You can't go out there."

"I'm warning you," said Spencer.

"Spencer, we ca—"

Slap!

God frowned at the gentle tap on his face and looked at Spencer with mild amusement.

"And there is more where that came from if you continue to stand in my way."

God continued to smirk at Spencer's lame attempt at combat. "Really, Spen—"

Slap!

"Would you stop hitt—"

Slap!

"LET. ME. OUT!" screamed Spencer.

"You won't last ten seconds out there," countered God.

Death placed a hand on Spencer's shoulder. "I'll go," he said.

God opened his mouth to argue, but seeing the look of sincerity on Death's face, he decided to stay quiet.

"Gary, open the door," said Death.

"Fine," said God as he pushed a button on the console. "Be quick."

As the door slid open, Death stepped outside and headed towards God's office door. He pushed the door open and cautiously poked his head outside to see the receptionist area clear. "Cindy?" he whispered. He waited for a response, but after a moment of silence, he continued through the door and looked around Nancy's desk. "Cindy?" he whispered again.

"Who is it?" replied the timid voice.

"It's Death."

"Which one?"

Death sighed at his loss of identity. "The one not trying to kill you."

"I'm under here," said Cindy.

Death crouched down to see Cindy cowering under the desk. "Come on," he said as he extended his hand.

As Cindy took Death's hand and crawled out from under the desk, the outer door quietly swung open.

"Death!" shouted Cindy as she saw the threat bearing down on them.

Death looked behind him as the clone entered the room. It was clothed in similar attire to the Four Horsemen and carried two swords crossed on its back.

"Go!" shouted Death as he ushered Cindy towards God's office. He slammed the office door shut and leaned against it.

"Hurry," shouted Spencer as Cindy dashed towards the open panic room door. He pulled her into the room and turned to face God. "Close the door. She's safe," he said.

"Spencer!" protested Ashley. "Death's still out there."

"It was his choice to go, not mine."

"You should be more grateful and stop being an asshole," said Ashley. Before Spencer could reply, she turned to face God. "Will the office door hold?"

"I don't know," said God as he strained to think. "It was designed to keep out Mormons and Baptists, not demons and monsters."

"Then we need to help him," she said as she ran out to help Death hold the door.

"Ashley!" shouted God as he watched her run past him.

Ashley slammed into the door next to Death as it shook under another heavy blow.

"What are you doing?" asked Death. "Get back into the panic room. There's nothing you can do out here."

"We're not leaving you," said Ashley. "We fight this together."

"With what?" countered Death as he pushed back against another slam. "We have no weapons. Get into the panic room."

"What about you?" shouted Ashley.

"I'll hold them off. Move it!" Death noticed the fear on Ashley's face. "It's okay. I can't die. It's a perk of the job." He was unsure if his words were factual. The Four Horsemen were a threat unlike any other in his long life.

The next impact shoved Death back and away from the door. The cloned Horseman pushed its way into the room. The rider climbed down from its horse and strode over to the group, its sword raised high. It raised a leg and kicked Death hard in the chest. The air quickly departed his lungs as he staggered back and fell to the floor. Being immortal hurt more than he recalled.

Death scrambled back until he collided with the desk behind him. He watched helplessly as the rider removed its second sword from its sheath. This was it. Death's time had come. He raised his hands in front of his face and closed his eyes, waiting for the final blow. A second turned to five. Five turned to ten, but the attack never came.

"Steve?" asked a female voice. "Is that you?"

Death slowly opened his left eye and looked up. "Huh?"

The rider took off its helmet to reveal a pretty woman in her mid-fifties. Her long blonde hair cascaded down her shoulders as she pulled the helmet away. A pink balloon of bubblegum extended from her mouth and after a moment of expansion, popped. She slurped the sticky mess back into her mouth and smiled.

Death opened his other eye and stared at the woman. "Ivy?" he said, his voice tinged with disbelief.

The woman smiled and extended her hand to Death. He grasped it tightly, and she pulled him up and into a hug. "Oh my god, it is you," she said. "I can't believe it." She squeezed him hard and closed her eyes. "It really is you."

The two continued to lose themselves in their embrace as the rest of the group stared at the unexpected reunion in surprise and confusion.

"Holy shit," said Ivy as she broke away from the hug. "I was totally going to stab you in the face. What are you doing here?"

"It's a long story." said Death and a smile. "You probably wouldn't believe me if I told you."

Ivy looked at the rest of the group and upon recognizing God and Lucifer, raised an inquisitive eyebrow. "That's quite apparent. So, you're hanging out in Heaven with deities now?" she said as she blew another large pink bubble that popped across her chin. "You've certainly moved up in the world."

"And mortals," said Death as he pointed to the Oceanview survivors. He turned to see the rest of the group looking expectantly at him. Each one with a look of genuine confusion.

"They can see you?"

"Yep," said Death. "Different chapter of the same long story."

"Who the fuck is this?" asked Warren with his usual tact.

"Oh, sorry," said Death. "Where are my manners? Team, this is Ivy. Ivy, this is the team."

"Great," said Warren. "That explains absolutely nothing."

"She's my ex-wi—"

"Wife, actually, sweetheart," Ivy interrupted. "You never signed the divorce paperwork."

"Wait," said Warren ignoring the legal wrangling of their nuptials. "You're married?"

"Why is that so surprising?" asked Death.

"I just never expected the Grim, er Death to be married."

"I do have a life outside of reaping," said Death. "We were happily married for decades."

Ivy smiled as she stared at her husband. Taking in his pale complexion and dark eyes. "So, you went full time with the reaping thing, huh?"

"Yeah," nodded Death. "It became an all-day job. I didn't have time to do everything, and I had to make a choice."

"And you gave up baking?" asked Ivy with a strong hint of both surprise and mild disappointment.

Death nodded a second time. "Not enough hours in the day."

"You were a baker?" asked Cam.

"I was."

"Wow, I never would have guessed that in a million lifetimes," said Cam. "You are full of surprises."

"Why do you think I carry a scythe?" asked Death. "For show?"

"Because you're the Grim Reaper," said Cam.

Ivy cringed. "Ooh, I wouldn't call him that if I were you. He gets all kinds of grumpy."

Death smiled and suddenly the nickname did not grate on him as much as it used to.

"He was the best baker in the county," said Ivy. "His blueberry muffins were to die for. Where is your scythe, by the way? You never left home without it."

"I keep it at the office these days."

"You have an office? Man, you have changed. What are you doing with these folk?"

Death smiled again. "It's a story for another time. Right now, I don't understand what you're doing here."

"I don't honestly know. I was out collecting a bounty, and the next second, I'm here covered in some black goop next to a twitching horse."

"You're a bounty hunter?" exclaimed Warren. "That is so cool."

"We all were."

"There's more of you?" asked Warren, excited at the opportunity of potential reinforcements.

"There's four of us," said Ivy. "Well, at least there used to be. I don't know where the others are."

"Do you work with the Horsemen?" Asked Cam.

Ivy shook her head, settling their worst fears. "No, fuck those guys. Same parent company, but way different goals."

"Are you here to help us fight?" asked Warren.

"Fight?"

Warren nodded. "Yeah, the Four Horsemen. They're trying to kill us."

"Ah, so that's why they're prancing around downstairs looking like they own the place. I wondered what was going on. What the hell did you do to piss them off?"

"We saw God and lived," said Warren.

"That's serious," said Ivy. "But it doesn't explain why they're here."

"Warren killed the Caretaker," said Death.

"Ooh," cringed Ivy as she popped another pink bubble. "Yeah, that'll do it. That's a big no-no."

"Yeah, we've had a rough few days," said Death. "Well, months really, if you want to go back to the beginning."

"And you haven't been able to kill any of them yet?" asked Ivy.

Warren shook his head. "Nope. We've tried, but we're just not strong enough."

Ivy furrowed her brow as she mulled over the situation. "Weird. I'm trying to figure out how we got dragged into this. I assumed it was because you killed one of them."

"Oh, that was me," said Death. "I tried using one of my Blood Cards on them."

Ivy snickered. "Are you serious?"

Death shrugged in resignation. "We were low on ideas. I figured it was worth a try."

"How did that go?" asked Ivy.

"Not well," said Death.

"I'm not surprised. This isn't exactly what Blood Cards were made for."

"You're here with me now," said Death. "I guess I did something right."

Ivy smiled at her husband and grabbed his hand. "You were always so sweet to me," she said with a smile. "What can I do to help with your four Horsemen predicament?"

"We need help killing them," said Warren.

"I can help you with that. I have some tricks up my sleeve. What have you tried so far, excluding the Blood Card debacle?"

"We've mostly been running and hiding," said Ashley.

"And how's that been working out for you?" asked Ivy with a slight playful grin.

"Not well," said Ashley.

"What weapons do you have?" asked Ivy. "It's hard to fight if you don't have the right tools."

"We have a sacred sword," said Warren.

"Why aren't you using it?"

"Because no one can pick it up," said Warren.

"Too heavy?" asked Ivy.

"Too blessed," said Lucifer. "And no one in Heaven is blessed enough to pick it up."

"Is that right?" said Ivy with a smile. "This one?" she said as she pointed to the sword lying on the floor next to Nancy's broken desk.

"Yeah," said Lucifer.

"May I?"

"Be my guest," said Lucifer. "Don't feel embarrassed if you can't move it. None of us can."

Ivy reached down for the sword's handle and with minimal effort, hoisted the sword above her head and swished it around a few times. "It seems I'm worthy enough."

"Holy shit," said Warren. "This is awesome. Someone can finally hold the sword. So, wanna go kill some Horsemen?"

"Sure," said Ivy. "Anything for Steve."

"Shouldn't we wait for your friends to show up?" asked Cam. "Safety in numbers and all that."

"Nah," said Ivy. "I kill demons for a living. I've got this." She looked over her shoulder at the two swords crossed on her back that she no longer needed. "Anyone want these?"

"I do," said Warren as his eyes widened in excitement at potentially holding an ancient weapon. "I can use one.

"Anyone who isn't a mortal?" asked Ivy as she dismissed Warren's excitement.

"Hey, we can fight too," protested Warren in frustration. "We're not completely useless."

"Fair enough," said Ivy as she reached over her shoulder and unsheathed one of the two swords. "Catch," she said as she tossed the blade over to Warren.

Warren fumbled to catch the sword, and after a couple of awkward flips and almost dropping it on his foot, he held it out in front of him in a fighter's pose. "Ready."

Ivy lifted the Sacred Sword and, in one rapid flick, disarmed Warren and sent his weapon flying towards the nearest wall. It slammed into the surface with a dull thud. "No, you're not," said Ivy. "Would anyone else like to have a weapon?"

Warren frowned as he walked over to retrieve the blade from the wall. "I wasn't ready," he whined as he pulled on the sword. "I want to go again."

"Okay," agreed Ivy.

In the time it took Warren to retrieve the sword, Ivy walked over to him and stopped. As he turned around, she was already facing him and disarmed him for a second time.

"Oh, come on. I still wasn't ready."

Ivy reached down for the sword and scooped it up from the floor. "Perhaps you shouldn't have anything pointy." She turned to Lucifer and tossed the blade towards him. "How about you, solider? If the legends are true, you should be able to hold your own okay."

Cam's eyes widened as Lucifer caught the sword and deftly spun it around.

"Both of you should," said Ivy as she passed God the second sword strapped on her back. "Have you kept up on your combat skills? I could use the help."

Lucifer looked at God as he shifted the sword between his hands. "I'm a pacifist these days."

"No, you're not," said Spencer.

"Have you ever bothered to ask me?" queried Lucifer. "You might be surprised if you did."

"I—" Spencer paused. He indeed neglected to ask. "I just assumed with you being Satan—"

"See, that's what you get for assuming," said Lucifer. "For someone so pious, you're very judgmental."

"But, she said you were a soldier. Soldiers are supposed to fight. You're Lucifer, God of War."

"I think you're confusing me with Ares. I do my best to stay out of combat whenever I can."

"What about all of those paintings of you in combat?" asked Spencer. "I've seen them everywhere."

"Photoshopped," said Lucifer. "And they were all published without my permission. Although I do like the ones where I have a six-pack, so I have less problem with those. But there has been a lot of creative licensing in my history, so don't believe everything you read."

As God noticed Spencer's awkward stance, he decided it was time to interject and save the poor man from an anxiety attack. "Stop messing with him, Luc. This is serious."

Lucifer smiled. "Fine. Yes, I know how to use a sword. I'm a little rusty, but it's probably like riding a bike, right?"

God shrugged as he held his own blade before him. "I've never ridden a bike before."

Spencer retreated to the panic room to monitor the screens. "They're here," he shouted as he stared at the digital image of Pestilence exiting the elevators.

Ivy inhaled as she prepared to take control of the situation. "I want the mortals to stay in the panic room and keep the door locked, no matter what you hear."

"What about us?" asked Spencer as he gestured to himself and Cindy. "What should we do?"

"You seem a little dainty," said Ivy as she eyeballed Spencer. "You should wait here too."

"Good idea," agreed Spencer, thankful he was not being called into combat.

Lucifer turned to Cam as he prepared to close the panic room door. "I'll be back for you, I promise."

"Let me help," pleaded Cam.

"I can't risk losing you," said Lucifer. "This is too dangerous."

"And I can't risk losing you," countered Cam. "This is our fight too."

Lucifer paused and reached for Cam's hand. "Trust me, sweetheart, we've got this, I promise. Gary and I have had some experience in combat over the centuries."

"I used to be pretty good with a sword back in the day," added God from the door.

"He's being modest. Gary was one of the best soldiers in the galaxy."

God looked at Lucifer and smiled. "You weren't half bad yourself. You could hold your own on a battlefield."

It was one of the few times God offered a compliment to Lucifer, and the Prince of Darkness smiled to himself. However, it was not the time to gloat.

The glowing review did little to ease Cam's nerves. Even with her narrow escapes during the Oceanview massacre, she was concerned that Lucifer and God would be insufficient against the Horsemen and that their luck would eventually expire.

"We'll be fine, I promise." Lucifer smiled as he let go of Cam's hand and followed God out of the door.

Warren, Ashley, and Cam stared at the heavy door as it closed and left the group in silence.

"I don't like being cooped up in here," said Warren. "It makes me feel useless."

"I don't either," said Cam. "But what can we do?"

"We can fight," said Warren.

"Come on, Warren. You know we don't stand a chance against them. We don't have any extra weapons, and the one we do have, we aren't blessed enough to wield. If we do go out there, we are not going to last ten seconds."

Warren sighed. He knew Cam was spot on with her summary, but he still yearned to be facing their threat head-on.

"Well, if you want my opinion—" started Spencer.

"We don't," said Warren, cutting him off. "You are welcome to sit here in silence."

"I think we are much safer in here," said Spencer as he ignored Warren's objection. "I am much more relaxed now."

Warren's patience with Spencer was at an end. "Have you fought for anything in your life?" he asked. "Or have you just hidden behind others and let them do the fighting for you?"

"Of course I have," said Spencer "When I was twenty-two years, I got a speeding ticket, and I did traffic school."

"That's not fighting."

"I could have taken the points, but I fought back by sitting in a classroom for eight hours. I even got a certificate at the end of it." Spencer crossed his arms and grunted as if admitting victory.

Warren attempted to respond, but felt silence was wiser. Arguing with an idiot would do little to pass the time.

CHAPTER 27

Outside the panic room, Ivy stood by the door leading to Nancy's reception desk. "Let me go out first. I'll signal you when I need you."

God and Lucifer nodded as Ivy stepped towards the door.

A horseless Pestilence was already waiting for the group as the outer receptionist door slowly opened. Ivy looked down the hallway, searching for the other three Horsemen, but they were not present.

Pestilence sneered as he stood before Ivy. "So, you're the champion of the mortals? How utterly pathetic they put their last hopes on the shoulders of a mercenary. I assure you, your efforts will be quite futile. You will fall, and I will squash those insignificant ants you are protecting."

Ivy shrugged at the insult but remained silent. She refused to allow him to get inside her head before the battle. She tightened her grip on her blade and held her stance.

"You would be best to get out of my way, clone," said Pestilence with a sneer. "You have no business protecting these fools. If you impede my mission, you will die by my hand. I will not show you mercy."

Ivy remained focused as she raised her sword.

Pestilence smirked again, mildly amused at his opponent's position. "You can choose to stay silent, but I will break you." He paced back and forth before Ivy, never removing his stare from her eyes. "Do you want to perish for these insignificant worms?"

Ivy continued to hold her composure, never taking her eyes off Pestilence.

Her opponent tilted his head in admiration for her persistence. "Perhaps

I can persuade you to feel otherwise," said Pestilence as he raised his right hand and flicked his wrist.

Three elevator doors slid open and from each one stepped the other Horsemen, their undead steeds gone.

"I've brought you something that may help with your decision."

Ivy clenched her jaw as she waited for Pestilence's next psychological tactic.

The three horsemen each tossed a severed head towards Ivy. Her eyes dropped for the slightest of moments to see the faces of her team staring back at her. If she felt pain, she did not let it show. She returned her stare to her opponent.

As the heads stopped rolling, Pestilence smiled, revealing his mouth of rotting teeth. "I believe these belong to you," he said. "They fell so easily. I expected clones of such skillful warriors to at least put up something that resembled a fight. If these are an indication of your abilities, then this fight will be brief. If you desire mercy, step aside."

"You talk too much," said Ivy as she flexed her fingers around her sword.

"And you die too easily," said Pestilence as he removed his bow.

"You'll have to go through me," said Ivy as she raised her sword and prepared herself for the inevitable first blow.

"Good. I was rather hoping you would say that," said Pestilence. "Surrender is always so boring." He aimed his bow at Ivy and let off the first volley.

Ivy moved faster than any of the Horsemen expected and sliced the incoming arrow out of the air. As her hands completed the swing, she plucked a dagger from her belt and launched it launched towards War. The blade cut through the air and slammed into his forearm.

War groaned in pain as he pulled the arrow from his arm and threw it on the floor. "Your pet is annoying me, brother."

Pestilence held up his hand and gestured towards Ivy. "She's all yours. Finish her."

War grinned and advanced on his opponent. He removed his sword and threw it at Ivy. She twisted her head as the blade slammed into the wall beside her. War jerked his wrist, and the sword flew back into his hand as he continued advancing.

Ivy moved with grace, poise, and intent. She parried and ducked and somersaulted. She attacked, and she defended. War would advance, and she would push him back. She advanced, and War would press the assault.

For three minutes, Pestilence watched with intrigue as the pair of combatants danced. "You're a slight improvement over your fallen comrades, but your efforts are worthless."

Ivy spared Pestilence the briefest of glances. "We'll see about that," she said. "Your first champion has been weak."

"War, I tire of this. Finish her."

War looked towards Pestilence, and in his moment of distraction, Ivy ran her blade across his thigh, and he dropped to his knee in a roar of pain. His sword clattered onto the tile, and in an instinctive motion, Ivy kicked it away from his reach.

"As I said," added Ivy. "Weak."

Pestilence flicked his wrist again. "Famine," he ordered. "Assist your brother."

Famine reached over his shoulder for his ax and advanced on Ivy. As he passed War's sword, he kicked it towards him, and the injured Horseman climbed to his feet. Famine raised his weapon and swung at Ivy.

From the corner of her eye, Ivy saw War launch his sword a second time. In between parrying Famine's attack, she deftly swatted the blade out of the air. It crashed to the floor with a loud clang. War reached out his hand to summon the weapon back to his grasp, but Ivy reacted faster and stomped her right foot onto the sword, preventing it from moving. As Famine increased his assault, Ivy kept her foot on the ground. While it stopped War from continuing his attack, it limited her movement. But despite her disadvantage, she managed to fend off Famine, without rearming War. The blade trembled beneath her feet as it threatened to return to its owner.

Seeing she was gaining ground, Pestilence signaled for Britney to join the assault. "Death, bring an end to this insolence."

Britney raised his spear and advanced on Ivy. She blocked his first blow and was forced to leap back as Famine pushed his own assault. Ivy's step freed up War's sword and he summoned it back to his hand. He climbed to his feet and pushed towards Ivy, joining his brothers. The three Horsemen started to flank her and pushed her back towards the receptionist area.

As he closed in, War swung his sword across Ivy's torso, and she jumped back, narrowly avoiding the tip of his blade. Swooping in on her imbalance, Britney lunged forward and stabbed his spear. Ivy twisted, and as she turned, she brought her foot down on the wooden staff, snapping it in two. Britney picked up the pieces and held them together. A green glow emitted from the break, and the two halves fused back into one piece.

"Are you kidding me?" Ivy muttered under her breath. Her dismay was short-lived as she made the most of Britney's distraction and flicked her sword across his right arm, opening a dark pus-filled wound.

Britney threw his spear to the floor and in a moment of unfiltered rage, charged at Ivy and slammed her into the wall. Ivy gasped for breath as her back made impact. While the air returned to her lungs, she brought the handle of her sword down onto Britney's head to no avail. War and Famine charged forward, and each grabbed an arm, pinning Ivy to the wall.

Pestilence chuckled as he slowly walked towards the group. "Your insurrection is brief." He shook his head in mock pity. "As I expected it would be."

"Oh, I'm just getting started," said Ivy.

"Your predicament looks far less positive from my position, and your optimism is misplaced," said Pestilence as he closed the distance between them.

"Bring it," said Ivy.

Pestilence slung his bow over his shoulder and pulled a knife from his belt. "I'm uncertain if I'm going to show you mercy and gift you a quick death or make you suffer."

"Whichever is more convenient for you," said Ivy. Her tough exterior masked the fear creeping over her as the reality of the situation set in.

"While I'd get nothing but joy from tormenting you, you are not the only person I've been tasked with eradicating." He moved towards Ivy and raised his knife. The uprising was coming to an end.

Ivy looked towards the outer office door. "Okay, whenever you're feeling like helping, I could use some assistance," she yelled.

On the other side of the door, God, Lucifer, and Death looked at each other on hearing the verbal cue.

"Ready?" asked God.

Lucifer nodded. "Are you kidding? I was born ready."

Death shrugged. "It would have been nice if someone had given me a weapon," he griped. "I'm not sure how much use I'm going to be."

"Just pull one of them away," said Lucifer. "And I'll bring the stabbing. We should make quick work of this. Besides, you're the only one of us who's still immortal. You'll be fine."

"About that," started Death. "I'm not certain that's entirely accurate at the moment."

"Guys! Now would be a really good time," shouted Ivy from behind the doors.

Lucifer pushed the door open, and with two swords raised, the three men charged towards the Horsemen.

God's noble assault was short-lived. As he sprinted at Britney, his opponent spun to face him. Britney raised his arm and backhanded God hard across the face. He sailed through the air and slammed onto the floor with a loud thud. His sword slipped from his grasp and clattered on the floor beside him. "Shit," he muttered under his breath as he painfully climbed back to his feet and picked up his weapon.

Lucifer sidestepped Britney and aimed for War. He crashed into the Horsemen and knocked him away from Ivy.

"Thanks," yelled Ivy as she regained control over Famine.

"Anytime," said Lucifer as he knocked War to the ground. Lucifer leaped back to his feet and assumed his defensive stance.

Death took aim at Pestilence and, in a moment of either selfless bravery or utter stupidity, sprinted at his target armed with nothing more than grim determination. His attempt lasted approximately seventeen feet as Pestilence turned and ran an arrow through Death's torso.

Death looked down at the shaft protruding from his stomach and frowned. Not only did the wound hurt like hell, but he was also bleeding. Pestilence yanked the arrow out and returned his attention to Ivy, leaving Death in confused pain.

"Steve?" asked Lucifer with concern, knowing Death was supposed to be immune to the effects of blades. "Are you okay?"

"I think I need to sit this one out," said Death as he stumbled back and collapsed. "I need a rest." Blood started to seep through his robes.

"Nothing can stop the inevitable," said Pestilence. "I am a killer of gods, and you will all fall to my blade."

"Fuck," said Lucifer as he realized the tide of the battle was turning against them. "How are you holding up, Gary?" shouted Lucifer as he watched War stand up.

Before God could launch a counterattack, Britney pinned him to the wall with the handle of his spear under his chin. God kicked and struggled to break free. "Not well," he replied as he huffed and puffed to push the weapon away from his throat.

War sneered as he squared up against Lucifer and held his sword out before him. "That will cost you, deity."

Lucifer flexed his fingers around the handle of his own weapon and stared the Horseman down. "Hey, Gary," he said. "Did you hear that? He called me a deity."

"He probably misspoke," said God as he continued to struggle against the spear.

"Well, I appreciate the gesture," said Lucifer as he continued to spar with War.

Ivy looked over to see God trying to get the upper hand. "Need help?" she shouted.

"Please!" he gasped.

She reached down and pulled a second knife from her belt and threw it at Britney. The blade sailed through the air and buried deep into the side of his head. Britney roared as he fell away from God and released his grip on his spear.

God dropped to the ground grasping at his throat, desperately trying to get a modicum of air back into his lungs. "Thanks," he said between short breaths.

Lucifer glanced over at God, and in the moment of distraction, War reached down and grabbed him by the collar.

He lifted God six inches off the floor and turned towards the nearest elevator. "Brother Pestilence, open the door."

Pestilence backed away from Ivy and crossed over to the elevator. He jammed his fingers between into the center seam and forced them apart.

"No, no, no," said Lucifer as he struggled to look behind him at the black void beyond the open doors. "You're going to mess up my suit."

"Silence, gnat," said War. He plucked a dagger from his belt and jabbed it in Lucifer's ribs.

Lucifer groaned as the blade was removed from, his chest, and in a smooth motion, War tossed him down the elevator shaft.

With his opponent disposed of, War turned his attention back to Ivy. "You're next, Clone."

"No, brother," said Pestilence. "I want you to get into that room and wipe out the survivors. Famine and I will take care of this one."

"What about the other worms?" asked War, referring to God and Death. "We're not supposed to kill the none living."

"Kill them all," said Pestilence. "Heaven should not have gotten involved in this. This was not their fight." Pestilence sneered. "Every deity dies eventually. Today is their day."

In the panic room, Cindy watched the monitors with concern. "Spencer, do you think we should be out there helping? It looks like they are struggling"

"Nope," said Spencer. "They told us to wait here, so I'm waiting here."

"But they never said what we should do if they needed help." She pointed to the image on the monitor. "And it really looks like they could use some help."

"I'm only doing what they told me to do."

"Quit being an ass, Spencer," said Warren. "She's got a point."

"I'm not a soldier," argued Spencer.

"And neither am I," said Warren. "None of us are." He gestured to the rest of the Oceanview survivors. "But I am not going to sit in here and wait for the inevitable."

"And what is the inevitable?" asked Spencer.

"They're going to get in here, and they're going to kill us," said Cindy. "He's right. We have to do something to help."

"Don't be ridiculous," said Spencer. "God would not have told us to hide in here if he thought it wasn't dangerous. We're safe from anything out there. I promise."

"I think the situation dictates otherwise," said Warren as he pointed to the monitor. The display showed War entering God's office and walking towards the panic room door. "We need to make a stand now."

The color drained from Spencer's face as he turned to face Cindy. It was time to accept that Warren was right. The moment to fight was upon them. He inhaled sharply as he tried to summon even an ounce of courage, desperate to stay strong in front of his crush. He reached out for her hands. "If this is the end for us, I want you to know that there is no one in the entire Baptist division I'd rather spend my last breath with. This has been a wonderful adventure."

Cindy smiled at Spencer. "What on earth are you saying? We're not going to die, silly. This is Heaven."

The situation exploded as the door was ripped off its hinges and tossed aside.

"People can't die in Heaven," continued Cindy, oblivious to the chaos erupting around her. "It's against the rul—"

Cindy stopped mid-sentence and spasmed violently as the tip of a sword bolt erupted from her throat. A fountain of blood sprayed out of her mouth and splashed across Spencer's face. Cindy looked down at her wound and then up at Spencer, tears welling in her eyes. Her jaw trembled as blood dripped down from her chin. She held a hand up to the tip of the arrow protruding from her neck. "I'm, I'm so—, sor—"

"No, no, no," cried Spencer as her grip on his hands loosened. He wrapped an arm around her back as she started to collapse. Cindy's body became heavy and limp as he cradled her and lowered her to the floor. "Not Cindy. Not Cindy. Don't take my Cindy away from me," he wailed in agony. He turned to face Warren. "Do something."

Warren shook his head. "There's nothing I can, I can't—"

"DO SOMETHING!" screamed Spencer as he sprayed saliva and Cindy's blood into the air.

Warren looked up to see War pointing his sword at them. "Fuck," he muttered under his breath. Without employing sufficient time to think through anything that could even remotely resemble a sane plan, he sprinted towards War. He launched himself at his neck. "No, you don't, you son of a bitch," said Warren as he wrapped one arm around War's face and grabbed his sword arm with the other.

"Warren?" shrieked Ashley. "What the fuck are you doing?"

"Something," he said as he struggled to maintain his grip. He increased his grip on War's neck as he tried to wrestle his sword away. "I could use a little help here. Grab his arms. GRAB HIS FUCKING ARMS!"

Ashley and Cam charged at War, and each grabbed an arm.

"Get off me, mortals," hissed War as he tried to shake Warren from his back.

"Spencer" yelled Cam as she struggled to maintain her grip. "We need your help."

War jerked his arm forward, and Cam lost her grip. He raised his arm and slapped her hard on the cheek, knocking her to the ground. Cam gingerly touched her face and felt blood beneath her fingers. With his free hand, War pulled Ashley off his other arm and threw her at the nearest wall. Ashley landed hard and fell to the ground next to Cam. War reached up over his head and grabbed Warren by the shoulders. It was time to remove the pesky little gnat.

"Spencer!" pleaded Warren. "I need your fucking help."

Spencer stared at Cindy's lifeless body, and for the first time in his life, he felt something new. Something that tore at his insides. It started in the pit of his stomach and churned and twisted as it coursed through his system. He felt rage. Pure unadulterated rage. And someone was about to pay dearly.

"Mother shitter," Spencer seethed between his clenched teeth and looked up at War. "I'm going to pissing kill you." He let out a scream and charged at War. He lowered his head and planted it directly into the center of War's chest.

The sudden impact temporarily stunned the Horseman. War lost his grip on his weapon, and it fell to the floor with a loud clang. He reached out to summon his blade.

"Spencer, grab the sword!" screamed Warren.

There was no need to ask Spencer a second time. He stomped on the blade, preventing it from returning to War. His eyes locked with the monster as he reached down for the weapon, and without a moment of hesitation, drove it into War's heart, killing him instantly. "Take that, you piece of fuck!"

Warren released his grip as the body fell to the floor. "Holy shit," he said. "You killed it." He looked over at Spencer, who was huffing and puffing and staring at War's corpse. "Are you okay?" he asked.

"I— I— I don't know what came over me," Spencer stammered. "I've never done anything like that before." He looked at the sword still in his hand. He loosened his grip and let the weapon crash to the ground.

Cam stepped over and wrapped her arms around Spencer. "Holy shit, you were incredible," she said as she planted a heavy kiss on kiss cheek.

Spencer stepped back from Cam and turned to face Cindy. "I'm so sorry," he whispered softly he dropped to his knees and held his fallen crush's hand. The first of many tears started to roll down his cheek.

♦ ♦ ♦ ♦

Outside in the hallway, the other three Horsemen froze as they felt their comrade fall.

"Brother," said Famine softly as a pang of intense loss ripped through his system and caused his attention to drift away from the battle for the briefest of moments. His pain quickly gave way to rage. But before he could act on it, Ivy seized upon the second of confusion.

She spun and drew her blade across Famine's neck, severing his head from his shoulders. His body buckled as the detached cranium fell to the floor. A second later, his body collapsed. Ivy exhaled as she turned to face the other Horsemen, her strength and resolve invigorated at the sudden change in fortune. And then there were two.

With the deep psychological connection between the Horsemen, Famine was not the only one to suffer the distraction. Matters continued to escalate for the enemy as God used his own window of opportunity to gain the upper hand on Britney. He grabbed onto his foe's wrist and tried to wrestle the spear away from him. With a final tug, the Horseman's grip loosed, and God yanked the weapon away.

As God readied himself to take the death blow, Britney regained his focus and blocked the attack with his forearm, swatting the spear aside. The defense was not convincing, but was enough to interrupt God's concentration and shake his confidence. Britney pulled the spear away and pushed God to the floor. God frantically crawled away as Britney spun his staff around over his head and aimed it at God, ready to strike. "Any last words, deity?" asked the Horseman with a sneer as he prepared the final blow.

"Catch," yelled Lucifer from behind God

God looked up to see Lucifer climbing out of the elevator shaft.

"Finish this bitch," yelled the Prince of Darkness as he tossed his sword towards God.

God reached up and caught the shiny weapon. A second later, he drove it under Britney's chin and deep into his skull. He stepped back and brushed his hands together as he looked at Pestilence. "Well, that wasn't too difficult. What else do you have?"

Without eyeballing Britney's killer, Pestilence kept his attention on Ivy. He removed his crossbow, aimed it at God, and fired. The arrow slammed into God's shoulder. He yelped in agony and fell to the down, clutching at his wound.

"Enough of this insolence," screamed Pestilence as he pointed at God. "I will deal with you next, fool." He turned back to Ivy. "This ends now."

Pestilence swung his sword with renewed aggression. Ivy ducked as the blade carved through the air and narrowly missed her neck. Defying physics, he immediately swung his sword back, and Ivy held her own weapon high to deflect the attack. The intense assault pushed Ivy back into the receptionist area. Blow after aggressive blow caused Ivy to remain on defense. Each impact moved her closer to God's office and the last of the survivors.

As Pestilence continued his relentless offensive, Ivy looked around the room at her injured comrades. She knew that she was all that was standing between them and death. If she fell, they would meet the same fate. There were no more chances. There were no more reinforcements. She was the last line. Whatever action she took next would decide their fate.

Ivy glanced at Death, who sat in a similar pained position as the others, clutching the wound on his chest. The time had come to end the battle. She lowered her sword and stepped back, putting some distance between her and Pestilence. Ivy smiled at Death one last time. "I love you, Steve. Until the next life, my sweet."

Death's eyes widened as the finality of the comment sank in. "No, Ivy, don't!" he shouted as he held up his hands.

Ivy sprinted towards Pestilence and wrapped her arms around him. She charged towards the French doors looking out into space. They flung open with the impact, and Pestilence slammed into the railing. The continued force of Ivy's attack shifted his center of gravity, and both flipped over the railing.

Death staggered over to the edge and stopped. He looked down into the dark abyss to see Ivy and Pestilence tumbling to the Earth below. As they reached the outer layers of the atmosphere, both bodies started to glow, and in a flash, vaporized. They were gone.

Death stumbled back and collapsed onto the floor next to Lucifer and God, all three in varying positions of pain and discomfort. Death opened his mouth to speak, but the aches in his body changed his mind.

Lucifer painfully turned his head towards God. He inhaled as he prepared to speak. "Well, that was fun," he said through clenched teeth. "Want to do this again sometime?"

"No," said God. "It was awful."

Lucifer nodded in agreement. "Yeah, that was not the most enjoyable thing I've ever done."

"I didn't realize altruism could hurt too much," said God.

"You think what we did was altruistic?" asked Lucifer as he pondered the possibility.

"Maybe," said God. "We did help out others without the promise of a reward."

Lucifer shrugged. God did have a point. A stretched point, but a point, nonetheless. "Are you okay, Steve?"

"No," grumbled Death.

"Aren't we supposed to be immortal again?" mused Lucifer. "Because if we are, this hurts way more than I remember."

"Not yet," said God. "We won't be immortal until I throw the switch and reopen Heaven, but that means getting up, and I really don't feel like doing that at the moment."

"Where's the switch?" asked Lucifer.

God raised a hand and pointed towards his office door. "In the panic room."

Lucifer carefully lifted his head to follow God's finger. "That feels like a long way from here."

"Yeah," agreed God.

"Well, when do you feel like doing that?" asked Lucifer. "I'd offer to help you, but I'm in a lot of pain."

"Not yet. I think I'm just going to lay here for a moment," said God as he stared at the ceiling.

"Yeah," said Lucifer in agreement as he lowered his head. "I'm okay with that."

The two men remained on their backs, focusing on the tiles above them. After a minute of pained silence, Lucifer started to smile. "Remember that time when you were saved by the angel you cast out of Heaven?" he said with a broad grin.

"You're not going to let this go, are you?" said God.

"Not until my last breath," said Lucifer. "And seeing as how I am about to become immortal again, this is not going to get old for a while."

"I could stop you from becoming immortal," said God. "I could leave things just as they are and go back to being a tow truck driver."

"Yeah, but you won't. You want everything back to normal as much as I do."

God sighed in resignation. Lucifer was right. "What's it going to cost to make you forget this?"

"Do you want to let me back into Heaven?"

God sputtered. He never expected Lucifer to ask such a pointed question. "Uh," he stammered, desperately trying to find a suitable response.

Death leaned in close to Lucifer. "Is that what you really want?" he asked softly.

"Oh, fuck no. I just wanted to see how serious he really is about making amends."

"How about we meet for coffee every other week?" suggested God.

"And caviar?" asked Lucifer.

"How about a danish?" countered God.

"Dutch apple?"

"Cherry."

"Fine, I'm good with that," said Lucifer. "Put it on my calendar."

God waved a hand in agreement, but continued to lay on the floor in pain, still unable to find the motivation to reopen Heaven.

The outer office door opened, and Warren and Cam stumbled into the room, supporting each other. Ashley followed them out and beelined towards God. "You're okay," she said, her voiced tinged with relief.

"Mostly," said God as he carefully stood. He reached down and offered a hand to Lucifer, pulling him to his feet.

"I'm fucking tired of Heaven," said Warren. "I want to go home. It's way more peaceful down there."

"Is everyone else okay?" asked Lucifer as he noticed the smaller size of the group.

Warren shook his head as he passed Cam over to Lucifer. "We lost Cindy."

God closed his eyes and sighed. "How's Spencer holding up?"

"He's hurting. He's in your panic room waiting for you to come and reopen Heaven. I think he needs a distraction."

God nodded. It was time to get up and get Heaven back in order. He looked over at Lucifer. "Ready to get things back to normal?"

The private elevator in God's office pinged, and the doors slid open. God rolled over as panic clawed its way back into his heart. "Now what?" he sighed.

"Hey guys," said David as he poked his head out and looked at the wounded group. "You lot look like shit. What did I miss?"

"Everything," said Lucifer. "It was a blast. You really missed out."

"Are you kidding me?" said Warren. "Now you decide to show up? Great timing, dude. Don't worry, we did all the hard work. You can put your feet up and relax."

"Did we win?" asked David.

"What's this we shit? Yeah, we won. Always bet on Oceanview."

EPILOGUE

Two days passed as God and Lucifer worked on the re-population of Heaven. It promised to be a painfully slow process for all involved. The two men worked closely together to make sure that everyone who was forced to relocate to Hell came home, and to speed up the seemingly endless flow of arrivals, God turned the floor above Invocation into a mass teleportation room. He hired a technician to come in and repair the machine and signed the purchase order as soon as it crossed his desk. He even opted to upgrade the machine to operate as a walkthrough portal which rapidly improved the procedure. Things ran efficiently for the first time in many years. Although as he watched the database synch up with the previous residence logs, he was certain there were a few people short.

From beside the elevator, David halfheartedly watched the endless stream of people shuffle their way back into Heaven.

"There you are," said a voice from behind as the elevator door opened.

David turned to see Cam heading towards him. "Sorry, this is taking a while," he said. "Is it time to go?"

"Yeah," said Cam as she stared down at her feet, uncertain of what to say. "They're getting ready to close the funnel." She paused again. "I really suck at goodbyes," she said as she continued to analyze the floor.

"Look on the bright side. We actually get to say goodbye this time," said David, trying to lighten the mood. "I'm not going to be diving across the floor in front of anyone and sacrificing myself."

Cam smiled and looked up at David. "Yeah, you did kinda run out on me last time. It was very dramatic, though, so you do get plenty of points for that."

"I like to make an impact," said David with a grin.

"Sorry I can't stay."

"I mean, you could, but I'd have to kill you, and that's a lot of paperwork. Besides, I think Luc is looking forward to seeing you. He'd be sad if you were stuck here"

Cam's cheeks blushed in embarrassment. "Yeah, he makes me happy. I'm not trying to get ahead of myself, but this feels different. It feels right."

David opened his arms and pulled Cam into an embrace. "Good. You've earned it and you've paid your dues. Let it become what it's meant to be."

"Thank you," she said as she rested her head on David's chest. "Are you going to be okay up here?"

"Absolutely. I think the place needs me to liven things up a bit." David pulled away from the embrace. "I want to show you something before you leave."

"More surprises?" said Cam. "I think I'm spent."

"You're going to like this one, I promise."

♦♦♦♦

Five minutes later, David escorted Cam to a large lounge with a massive fifty-foot-wide and twenty-foot-tall window running along the far wall. The glass looked out into the blackness of space. An endless blanket of stars stretched out before her.

"It's beautiful," said Cam as her mind cast back to sitting with her father renaming Orion's Belt.

David smiled. "It is. But this isn't the surprise."

Cam raised an eyebrow and wondered what could be more breathtaking than a front row view of the galaxy.

David walked over to a small control panel on the wall beside the window and pressed a button. The view outside the glass started to move and as the room picked up speed, the stars blurred.

Cam watched the images streak by, and the blackness slowly gave way to a brighter image, but she was unable to determine what she was looking at. "Where are we?" asked Cam.

"The observation deck. It's a moving floor that can carry us around Heaven to check on its residents. Now we have so many people here we seldom use it." The room slowed down, and a large lounge moved into focus. David gestured to the glass. "Be my guest."

Cam frowned as she walked over. On the other side of the window, Donald from Oceanview sat on a couch reading a book. Beside him, a woman slept with her head rested on his shoulder. He looked happy and at peace.

Cam's face lit up. "Holy fuck."

David smiled at her reaction. "You're welcome."

"Can he see me?"

David shook his head. "He can't. Now that Heaven is working again, residents can't see the living. It's another of their ridiculous rules."

"I can see you."

"I'm an anomaly. You know, the whole atheist in Heaven deal. It's broken a lot of things."

"So, I can't say goodbye to Spencer?"

David shook his head again. "No. Only Gary, Luc, and Death can see you now. You're invisible to everyone else."

Cam turned her attention back to Donald. "Is that Laura?" asked Cam, referring to Donald's previously deceased fiancée.

David nodded. "It is."

"How did he find her?"

"They were reunited minutes after he passed on. We have an express lane for people to meet their loved ones. When our database is actually working, it's quite efficient. It's really cool to watch people getting back together. It feels like an airport terminal. People come in, glance around for a moment, they spot a loved one, a spouse, a child, a friend, and they bolt into their arms."

"It sounds nice."

"It is. It's my favorite place to be."

Cam placed her hand on the glass. "Donald?" she said softly.

Donald looked up in Cam's direction and their eyes locked. Cam's eyes widened as Donald smiled as if recalling a distant memory.

Cam turned towards David to see him frowning in confusion. She looked back at Donald, who still smiled at her.

"Are you sure he can't see me?" asked Cam.

"Yeah. It's impossible," said David.

Donald continued to look at Cam. "Thank you," he silently mouthed and waved at her. He looked down at Laura's head on his shoulder and planted a gentle kiss on her forehead. He smiled again and returned to his book.

A tear slowly crawled down Cam's cheek. "Holy fuck. He saw me," she said with a smile.

David furrowed his brow in genuine confusion. "He couldn't have. It's impossible."

"But he looked up at me. He waved. You saw that, didn't you?"

"I— yeah— I did—"

Cam reached down and squeezed David's hand. "This was wonderful. Thank you"

David pressed the button again and the room started to pick up speed. He nodded and pulled Cam in for another hug. "Take care of yourself," he said.

"You too," said Cam with a smile as they finished their embrace.

David nodded towards Lucifer, waiting at the door. The Prince of Darkness patiently rocked back and forth on his heels as he waited for his turn with Cam. "I think you'll be in good hands."

Cam smiled. "I have no doubt," She hugged David one last time. "It's been good seeing you again."

"Ready?" asked Lucifer.

Cam nodded and squeezed David's hand one last time.

David beckoned Lucifer to join them. "Cam is one of my closest friends. You treat her right," said David.

"You have my word," said Lucifer as he bowed in respect. "She'll see you again. I'll make sure of it."

"I'll hold you to that," said David.

"I am nothing if not a man of my word."

David watched the elevator door slide closed and turned his attention back to the observation window.

"David?" a female asked from behind.

The voice sounded familiar. "Yes," he said as he turned to see a woman in her mid-thirties standing before him. His eyes widened. "Karen?"

"David! It is you. I can't believe it." She launched herself at him and wrapped her arms around his neck.

David stepped back in dismay and stared at his former girlfriend, certain he was dreaming.

"Oh, my ***." The last word silently passed his lips.

Karen stepped back from the hug and reached out for David's hands. "Are you okay? Your voice disappeared."

"Yeah. I'm not allowed to use his name in vain while in my probationary period."

"Your probationary period?"

"It's part of my internship."

"I can't believe it. You're actually in Heaven. I heard about the car accident."

"Car accident?" said David, his confusion obvious.

"Yeah. I received a letter in the mail about six months ago. It said you had a life insurance policy, and I was listed as the beneficiary."

David frowned. "Really? A car accident, huh? That's interesting."

"The check is still on my nightstand. I couldn't find the strength to deposit it. I've never been able to say goodbye to you. Cashing it felt like I was finally letting you go." She reached for David's hands. "I wasn't ready." She eyed David quizzically. "Why are you here?"

"I died."

"I get that, but I didn't think you believed in all of this religious stuff?"

"I didn't. I still don't," said David.

"But you're here. In Heaven."

A broad smile swept across David's face. The one that first made Karen fall in love with him. "It's a really long story."

"I have all the time in the world."

David frowned. "Wait, if you're here, that means—" He let the sentence hang as the realization slammed into him like a truck.

Karen grabbed his hand and smiled tenderly. "Breast cancer," she said sadly.

The color drained from David's face. "I am so sorry."

"So was I." She reached out and grabbed David's hands. "Until now."

David smiled and looked down at their hands. A decade of shelved emotions washed over him. "But you're still so young."

"It was aggressive and fast."

David tried to find the words, but none came.

"It's okay," said Karen with a smile. "That just means I get to be here in my prime. So, what about you? Did you ever meet anyone?"

"Does gin count?"

Karen smiled again and shook her head. "Not in the slightest."

"Then no."

"You still haven't told me why you're in Heaven."

David sighed and frowned. "God unleashed an army of zombie-demons on Oceanview, killed all but eight of us. I sacrificed myself to save one of the other survivors." No matter how many times he explained it, the whole thing sounded absurd.

Karen smiled. "I always loved your sense of humor." She frowned as she tried to get a read on David's face. "You're not joking, are you?"

David shook his head. "Do you honestly think I could make this up? I'm not that creative."

"Then it wasn't a car accident?"

"No. I died at the hand of God. Apparently, altruistic sacrifice earns you a place here whether you want to come up or not. I didn't get any say in the matter."

"Who is Gary O'Donnell?"

"Why?" asked David, surprised at the mention of God's real name.

"His name was on the insurance check."

David smiled as things started to make sense. "You might know him by his other name."

Karen's eyes widened. "Wait. Do you mean God?"

David nodded.

"Really?" said Karen with a confused frown. "His name's Gary?"

"Yeah," said David.

"That's a bit anticlimactic."

"I thought the exact same thing when I first heard it."

"You know him?"

David smiled. "I do."

"And he knows you?" asked Karen.

"Of course he does. I'm the first atheist that has ever gone to Heaven. I'm kind of a big deal around here. Hence the trial period. Would you like to meet him?"

"I'd love to." She paused. Her mind cast back to Gracie and their discussion waiting in line to get into Heaven. "But, I know someone who would appreciate it more."

"Are they here?"

Karen nodded. "Yeah. I was standing behind her line when we were waiting to get into what ended up being Hell. Her name was Gracie."

David skimmed through his list. "I have a few thousand Gracie's here. Do you have a last name?"

Karen let out a breath and looked down, trying to remember their introduction. "I think it started with M."

"I'm going to need a little more than that," said David with a smile.

"Mitchell?"

David shook his head.

"Maddocks?"

"Twenty-seven years old?"

Karen shook her head. "No, older. How about Mason? You know how I am with people's names." Karen paused. "Oh, she said like the president."

"Monroe?"

Karen snapped her fingers. "That's her. Gracie Monroe. She would love to meet God."

David scanned the list for the new information. "Her names here, but she never checked in."

"Is there another door?"

"No, this is it."

Karen frowned at the news. "Is there any chance she slipped in unnoticed? There's a lot of people coming through."

"Nope," said David. "We've been thorough."

"Then where is she if she isn't here?"

"If I were to guess, I'd say she opted to stay in Hell."

"You're kidding?"

David shook his head. "It's a big party down there. We've had more than a few who were supposed to come back, but didn't." David looked around at the bland hallways. "Can't say I blame them. It's a little boring around here."

Karen smiled as realization set in. "That dirty old cow."

"Can I buy you a drink?" asked David. "It's watered-down crap and barely passes as alcohol, but the offer is sincere."

"I would love it."

David's wrist-com chirped to life as Lucifer's voice piped out. "*David, are you busy?*"

"A little, yeah. What's up?"

"*Death can't get through the funnel anymore. Can you escort them down to Oceanview?*"

"Can it wait? I'm kinda busy at the moment."

"*Not really. We need to shut it down.*"

Karen smiled. "Go help your friends. We have all the time in the world now."

♦♦♦♦

Upstairs in God's office, Ashley and God were saying their own temporary goodbyes. Although most of their farewell communication was performed lip to lip.

"You promise you'll come to me when everything is settled?" asked Ashley as she pulled away for a moment. "That this isn't really a final goodbye."

God continued to kiss her before responding. "I'm God. I'm not allowed to lie."

"Bullshit," said Ashley with a grin and pulled him in to continue their kissing.

Barely ten seconds back into their lip combat, a slight cough echoed from the door. God looked sideways to see Nancy standing at the door. His eyes widened at the sight of his secretary, and he pulled away from the kiss as though he was a teen being caught making out by his parents. "Nancy!" he exclaimed excitedly. "Hi. You came back!"

Nancy examined the two budding lovers with suspicious eyes. "Of course I came back. It's against the rules to quit a job in Heaven. Who's this?" she asked.

"This is Ashley," he said, pointing at her. "Ashley, this is Nancy, my secretary."

"Personal assistant," corrected Nancy as she looked Ashley up and down to determine if she was suitable to date God.

"Right," said God. "What she said."

"It's a pleasure to finally meet you," said Ashley with a smile. "He speaks so highly of you."

"He'd better," said Nancy as she crossed over to her broken desk. "He'd fall apart without me. I've kept him in line and focused for years."

"She's right," said God.

"What happened to my desk?" she asked as she stared at the two halves.

"I'll get you a new desk," said God.

"And where's my sword?"

"We have a lot of catch up on."

Nancy pulled out her chair and sat down. "So, what's your story?" she asked Ashley.

"We're uh, just fr—" started Ashley.

"Dating," added God. "We're dating." He looked at Ashley. "Aren't we?"

Ashley smiled. "Are we?"

"I hope so," said God.

"You're blushing," said Nancy.

Both Ashley and God reached for their cheeks in embarrassment, unsure as to who she was referring to.

Nancy smiled at the sight before her, having never seen God with a girlfriend. She loved seeing him so happy. It was long overdue. "You'll have to tell me all about her later. I think Death is looking for you both. Shall I mark you out of the office?"

"Please," said God.

"Shall I say you're playing golf?"

"No, you can say I'm helping a friend."

Nancy's eyebrows raised in surprise. God was right, they certainly had a lot of catch up on.

Warren was already sitting by the exit doors as Cam and Lucifer entered the waiting room from the private entrance beside the customer service window. Their fingers entwined as they walked over to him.

"Eager to leave?" asked Lucifer with a smile.

"About time," said Warren. "I thought you'd forgotten about me. I want to go home, grab a beer, and take a long hot bath."

"That makes one of us then," said Cam as she glanced at Lucifer.

"You're not staying with Lucifer?" asked Warren with an air of surprise in his voice.

Cam shook her head. "Nope." She nodded towards Lucifer. "He won't let me."

"She can't," said Lucifer. "It's against the rules. She has to go back to Earth."

"What about Ashley?"

"The same," said God as he and Ashley entered the room. "The living aren't allowed to be in Heaven or Hell."

"Can't you bend the rules a little bit?" asked Warren. "I mean you're both in charge."

Lucifer shook his head. "No, that's what got us into this mess to begin with. The Council is going to be watching us very closely from now on."

"Weren't they the ones who shut Heaven down to begin with?" asked Warren. "I mean, they sent both the Caretaker and Horsemen after us. Their hands aren't exactly clean in all this."

"Gary and I had a conference call from the Council about an hour ago."

"And how did that go?"

"They claim no knowledge of any of it. They allowed Gary to come back while they investigate. Lots of apologies."

Warren frowned at the update. "So, if the Council didn't send them, then who did?"

"Oh, trust me," said Lucifer. "Gary and I fully intend to get to the bottom of this. We're not letting this drop. Somebody knows what happened. But for now, we're just focusing on getting things back to normal."

"Are you breaking up?" asked Warren.

"Of course not. We just have some logistics to figure out. That's all," said Lucifer.

"Neither one of you thought about this when you fell in love?" asked Warren.

God shrugged. "I don't think neither of us expected to fall in love."

"Can't you both visit Earth on like a day pass or something?" suggested Warren. "I can't believe this is the first time this has happened. Love is kind of a universal thing."

The front doors to the waiting room swung open and David walked in. "Are we ready to go?" he asked. "We need to get moving and shut the funnel down."

"I am," said Warren as he stood up and walked towards David. "Lead the way Angel-man."

Cam turned to face Lucifer. "I'll see you soon, right?"

Lucifer nodded and pulled her in for a hug. "I promise. We'll figure this out." He leaned down and kissed her tenderly.

"The same goes for you," said Ashley as she embraced God. "Figure this out. I'll be waiting for you."

"You have our word," said God.

"Guys?" said David as he tapped his wrist indicating the clock was ticking. "We need to get moving.

As the embraces ended, Cam and Ashley walked over to David.

"Let's go," said Cam.

David held the door open and gestured for the trio to head into the hallway. "This way, if you please."

Lucifer and God followed the group outside the waiting room front door and watched the group disappear around the corner. The funnel flashed brightly as the survivors and David made their way back to Oceanview.

"I love you," Lucifer said softly under his breath. He exhaled as the funnel light disappeared. He turned to look at God. "This isn't the ending I would have ever expected."

"You are not kidding," said God. "Look at us. We're glowing like hormonal teenagers."

"It's a good feeling," said Lucifer. He felt something push against his lower legs, and he looked down to see Nipples the kitten staring up at him.

Lucifer smiled and bent over to pick up the kitten. "Nipples!" he said with excitement. "I was wondering where you'd gone to." He nuzzled into the ball of fur. "What do you think? Do you want a new mom?"

The kitten purred contentedly as it rubbed against Lucifer's chest and snuggled into his arms.

"That sounds like a yes to me," said God.

"Shall we head back?" asked Lucifer.

"Probably. Not much to watch here, and we still have plenty of work to do."

Lucifer opened the waiting room door and politely gestured for God to enter first. "It's good to have you back, Gary."

"Thanks," said God.

"Just one thing?" asked Lucifer.

"What's that?"

"Please don't get fired again."

"I'll do my best," said God with a smile as the two men crossed the waiting room.

"Are you doing okay?" asked Death with genuine concern from one of the nearby chairs.

Lucifer stopped and sat down next to Death. "I'm not sure," said Lucifer honestly. While he was excited for Cam to join him in the afterlife, and the decision was consensual on both sides, a part of him felt guilty about cutting her life short. "This is a whole bunch of new emotions I haven't felt before."

"You know Blood Cards don't hurt, right?" said Death, trying to offer a mild attempt at comfort. "She won't feel anything if I bring her down to you."

"It's not that. It feels unnatural."

Death raised an eyebrow. "In what way?"

"I'm used to people coming down before what they consider to be before their time, but it's always been the natural order of things. You live, you die, you go somewhere else, depending on your belief system.

But this—" Lucifer paused. "But this is different. This isn't the Universe at work. This is me pulling strings to make things go in my favor. It feels like I'm manipulating the status quo."

"It's one person," said Death. "Two if we do Ashley. I've used plenty of Blood Cards over the years."

"Yes, but you're using them to ease the pain of the victim, not to spend eternity with them. This is different." Although no stranger to bending the rules from time to time, Lucifer struggled with his reasoning to bring Cam to Hell with him.

"I don't see it as anything different at all," said Death.

"How so?" asked Lucifer.

"No one is going to care. She wants to go with you. So why shouldn't you be happy? You've put in the years, and you've put in the work. Maybe it's time for you to reap some of the rewards of your labor. You've earned it."

Lucifer was genuinely grateful for the kind words. "Thanks, that's nice to hear."

"After what we've all been through recently, we deserve a little happiness. Let's finish getting everything back to normal, then we can work on getting you two reunited."

A bright light flickered from down the hallway outside of the waiting room as the portal between Heaven and Earth began the process of shutting down.

As Death and Lucifer crossed the waiting room, the door besides the customer service window started to open.

"I swear I'm destined to never get out of this hell hole," said Warren as he looked around the empty Oceanview church. He carefully climbed over the large pile of trash at the base of the funnel. He leaned down and picked up the janitor's mangled cart and tossed it aside. Beside him, Ashley appeared and walked out of the funnel. A moment later, David and Cam stepped out and joined them. The bright tube flickered in the same way it had done in Heaven.

"It's getting harder and harder to come back," agreed Cam, knowing the future that awaited her with Lucifer. "Even more so knowing what I'm leaving."

"Do you think he'll come back for you?" asked Warren.

"Don't be a dick, Warren," said Ashley. "Of course he'll come back. They both will."

Warren opened his mouth to reply before a familiar voice spoke up. "Took you long enough."

Warren smiled to himself. "Well, someone had to pick up your slack," he said as he turned to see Greg and Amber standing at the door to the backroom. "Come here, you useless bastard," he said as he pulled Greg in for a hug.

"Glad you all made it," said Greg. "We felt awful leaving."

"Yeah, it was a shitty thing to do, leaving right before an intergalactic battle. But we made do."

"You're an ass," said Greg with a grin as he pushed his younger brother away.

The funnel flickered a second time.

"I think that's your cue," said Cam as she smiled at David. "You can't bear to say goodbye, can you?"

David stared at Cam, with a vacant look on his face, but he remained silent.

Warren turned to see Amber and Ashley in a similar embrace. "You still haven't popped that baby out yet?" he asked his future sister-in-law. "What have you been doing?"

"Warren, it's been forty-eight hours," said Amber with a grin. "Give me a break."

"It felt like months. What are you guys doing here anyway?" asked Warren. "I thought I told you to get somewhere safe?"

"Do you honestly think we'd completely abandon you?" asked Greg. "Give us more credit than that."

"Yep, I actually did," said Warren.

"Ass," echoed Amber with a similar smirk.

Warren grinned at his future sister-in-law's insult. "Have you been waiting this entire time?"

"No," said Greg. "We'd been staying in Flagstaff hoping to hear from you. We came over as soon as you called us."

"I didn't call you."

♦♦♦♦

"What are you doing back there?" asked Death as David stepped into the waiting room.

"What do you mean?" asked David. "I needed the bathroom before I came down."

Death pointed to the front waiting room door. "You just left. How did you get back there."

David frowned. "I was in the bathroom taking a leak. I haven't left yet."

"What are you talking about? I saw you go," said Death. "We all did." He pointed to Lucifer and God. "Right?"

"Are you fucking with us, David?" asked Lucifer. "We watched you leave."

"About peeing?"

"No, not about peeing, about getting back here so fast," said Lucifer.

"Guys, I haven't left yet. I needed to go pee, then I was going to take them back to Oceanview. The funnel plays havoc on my bladder. I've done enough undignified things in my life. However, peeing myself has not been one of them."

"We saw you go," said Death.

"I promise you, I didn't."

"Then who the fuck just went down with them?" asked Lucifer as panic washed over him.

♦♦♦♦

The funnel in the church flicked a third and final time and a moment later pulsed and disappeared with a loud electrical crack, leaving the room in a punctuated silence.

"David!" said Cam with alarm. "The funnel just closed."

David ignored her announcement and continued to stare at them.

"David, the funnel closed," repeated Cam. "You can't get back,"

"The time has come," said David as he turned to face the group. "I am closure."

"Huh?" said Cam.

"I am closure. I am the Bringer of Ends."

A look of concern swept across Cam's face. "David, what are you saying? What are you closing?"

The rest of the group turned to face David, all equally concerned at his sudden change in demeanor.

David snapped his fingers, and the door to the church hall violently slammed closed. "You humans are pitiful. You scream, and you fight, and you kill. You are supposed to be born of my image, but I find you insolent and petty."

"Greg?" asked Amber as she squeezed his hand. "I don't like this. I want to go home."

David was not finished with his tirade. "You are a mistake. A blemish on the Universe, and as with all mistakes, it can be rectified" David extended his left arm, and a sword materialized in his hand. "I am here to purge the mistakes of the mighty."

"Who are you?" asked Ashley.

Warren stepped in front of the group and held out his hands to protect them. "Back the fuck down, bitch" he said as he clenched his fists. "I've had a really long day."

David walked towards Warren. "Silence, fool. You will know me by my name."

"Yeah?" said Warren indignantly. "And what's that, because it sure as shit ain't David."

"And my name is Nigel."

"Fucking Nigel?" laughed Warren. "What is this nonsense? Are you shitting—"

Nigel, or rather the man formally known as impostor David, lashed out his hand. In a single motion, his blade separated Warren's head from his shoulders. A spray of blood splashed across Ashley's face as Warren's gaze froze as every nerve, bone and blood vessel in his neck was cleanly severed.

"Warren!" screamed Greg in shock. "WHAT THE FUCK? What did you fucking do?"

Ashley's eyes widened in pure, unadulterated terror, and before any of the group still in possession of their heads could scream, or cry, or mourn, Nigel's hand swung a second time and his sword cut each of the survivors in half at the waist.

Before the bodies hit the floor, Nigel snapped his finger again and disappeared.

The number seven holds significance for a variety of reasons. Warren's severed head rolled seven times before it came to a stop and stared accusingly at the ceiling. His jaw twitched seven times as his muscles contracted and froze. It took seven seconds before Greg, Amber, Ashley, and Cam's decimated bodies fell to the floor in a bloody pile of limbs and torsos. And seven rolls of Heavenly toilet paper had spilled from the janitor's cart onto the floor.

And it took nine days for the Oceanview Seven to be eradicated.

♦ ♦ ♦ ♦

To Be Concluded
in

Death Just Wanted to Eat Waffles

♦ ♦ ♦ ♦

www.ingramcontent.com/pod-product-compliance
Lightning Source LLC
LaVergne TN
LVHW010631110826
845149LV00014B/2827
9780990901037